A DISAFFECTION

by the same author:

An old pub near the Angel, and other stories
Three Glasgow Writers (with Tom Leonard & Alex. Hamilton)
Short Tales from the Nightshift
Not not while the giro, and other stories
The Busconductor Hines
Lean Tales (with Agnes Owens & Alasdair Gray)
A Chancer
Greyhound for Breakfast

A DISAFFECTION

JAMES KELMAN

SECKER & WARBURG
LONDON

First published in Great Britain 1989
by Martin Secker & Warburg Limited,
Michelin House, 81 Fulham Road,
London SW3 6RB

British Library Cataloguing in Publication Data

Kelman, James, *1946–*
A disaffection.
I. Title
823'914[F]

ISBN 0 436 23284 7

Photoset in Garamond by
Rowland Phototypesetting Limited
Bury St Edmunds, Suffolk
Printed in Great Britain by
Redwood Burn Ltd, Trowbridge, Wiltshire
and bound by Hunter & Foulis Ltd, Edinburgh

sections of the novel were first published
in *Edinburgh Review*, *Emergency* and *Magazing*

The poem by Okot p'Bitek (1931–1982)
is taken from *Song of Lawino*
(Heinemann African Writers, 1984).

Patrick Doyle was a teacher. Gradually he had become sickened by it. Then a very odd thing happened or was made to happen. He had been visiting the local arts centre and having a couple of drinks, found himself round the back of the premises for a pish, and discovered a pair of old pipes. They were longish and reminded him of english saxophones from a bygone era, the kind that reach to the floor and are normally performed on by seated musicians. Now by no means whatsoever would Patrick have considered himself a musician – if anything his secret hankering was to be a painter, doing fairly large murals. He could imagine covering the gable ends of tenement buildings, or even better, the interior walls of tenement closes, inserting various nooks and crannies and twists and corners; evil shapes and sinister figures – different things: but always inclining toward Goya's work of the black period.

The pipes were strange kind of objects in the response Patrick had for them. It was immediate to begin with. As soon as he saw them it was, christ! And he shook his head, still just standing there, staring at the two of them. He picked the thinner one up and glanced about but nobody was watching. It was still winter yet. It was dark and it was cold. People seldom wandered round to here. Patrick scratched his head; then, without smiling, proceeded to blast out a long deep sound. He stopped. And now the glimmer of a smile did appear on his face. Again he glanced about: still nobody. He took a very long deep breath and once more he blasted out this long, very deep sound. It was really beautiful. Of a crazy sort of nostalgia that would aye be impossible to describe in words, and not in oils either. He noticed the other pipe but already the decision was made and it would make no difference one way or the other how it sounded, he was taking them both, the pair of them.

They were not heavy, nor particularly bulky. He carried one under each elbow, back via the fire-escape door and along the corridor into the main lounge. He was of the company of a group of teachers which was discussing the Christmas Pantomime they had produced at school a couple of months ago. This year Patrick had opted out of it and was aware of being slightly excluded from things. One of the women chuckled. She was recounting an incident that had occurred between herself and a boy pupil during rehearsals. Patrick watched her. She was called Alison and he thought her something special. If she had not been married he would have asked her out ages ago. And that something as well in the way she communicated with people, the way she addressed them, a quick flick of the head which seemed to indicate she was noticing everything, every single thing that was going on.

He turned to see if the bar was still open for business and a pipe clattered to the floor. The company peered at it then at the one he was holding. He nodded downwards. Aye, he said, I found them round the back, they'll come in handy.

He reached to collect the fallen one, he balanced it and the other one against the side of his chair. He smiled and stood up, walked across to the bar and ordered a tomato juice. It was one of those things: he would be driving home and already he had taken far too much. He was meaning to cut out this drinking and driving carry on altogether. Alison occasionally commented on it. Tonight she had made a joke about it to him but obviously she wanted the point taken seriously. He would take it seriously. She was dead right. Maybe the tomato juice would meet her approval! He sipped at it while the barmaid was getting his change from the till. It was really fucking virulent tasting stuff and he grued. This was part of the problem of nonalcoholic drinks, how they were so untasty. Without vodka tomato juice was almost not to be spoken of.

Back at the table a nosy bastard by the name of Desmond was examining the pipes. He nodded at Patrick as he sat down, pursing his lips in an ironic manner, as if to say: Quite a nice pair of pipes.

Patrick shrugged. They'll come in handy.

Somebody else in the company was yawning and muttering about having to get up early in the morning for the swimming beginners so it was time to hit the road home. And soon chairs were being shifted and folk were swallowing the last of their drinks; now rising and buttoning or zipping their coats and jackets. Patrick walked ahead of Alison, managing to hold the door open for her with his left foot, the pipes being held beneath either elbow as before. Want a lift? he asked.

Are you up to it?

Aye, he grinned.

She nodded. A couple of the others were looking across and he called, Anybody else wanting a lift?

Where you going? asked a man who had recently taken up a temporary post at the school.

Home – but I'm dropping off Alison first.

Nah it's alright, thanks all the same.

Suit yourself . . . Patrick smiled, he turned to say something to Alison but Alison was some yards off now, chatting to Mrs Bryson.

On the journey to her street he drove in relaxed fashion and he spoke fine, keeping her quite interested and amused by wee events in the classroom. And he felt as happy in himself as he had done for what seemed like ages. Maybe since the day he had graduated nearly six years ago – although fuck sake it seemed like yesterday morning. Yet in other ways a hundred years; all those failed plans and principles and ideas for the future, all those ways ahead. And now here he was, a teacher – still a teacher! What was to be done. Nothing. Then here was this pair of pipes. What about them. What was to be done about them. It was really strange. Also that feeling, as if it was his last chance to make good or something. Daft. Crazy. A cliché. He glanced into the rearview mirror. He smiled at Alison.

You're very cheery the night Mister Doyle.

Uch, I'm always cheery.

You are not. You're about the most depressed character in the entire school.

Does that include Old Milne?

Old Milne's not depressed, not with his salary.

You're right! He looked sideways at her, frowned a moment then added, How's the husband these days?

Pardon?

[3]

Your husband, how's he doing?

Alison made no comment.

Eventually Patrick said. Is he okay?

Yes.

Good . . . He turned the steering wheel now at the junction of the main road and her street; the car entering; and parking outside her close. A very brief silence and then she was moving to unlock the passenger door. She paused, glancing at him. And he winked and grinned. Take care and sleep well, sleep well.

You're in a funny mood . . . Alison frowned.

Am I!

Yes, ye are. She smiled before manoeuvering her way outside onto the pavement where she waved, and crashed the thing shut. Patrick groaned. Other people had a habit of doing that as well and the door was no longer hanging properly on its hinges. That horrible grating noise when somebody pushed it too far ajar. High time he had a new motor altogether. This was probably why folk crashed the thing shut so hard, their assumption it couldnt be working right because it looked so ancient. Fucking hopeless.

Alison was attracting his attention from the closemouth. She maybe thought he was going to fucking fall asleep and stay there all night. He grinned and waved back at her, flashed the headlights a couple of times: and she vanished. Not even a puff of smoke. He continued to stare at the closemouth.

When he parked the car in his own street he was aware of the pipes as a new problem in his life – even in such minor events as exiting from the car e.g. did one for instance take them in one's arms before rising from the seat? or get out first and then fucking drag them after you? or else prop them against the side of the car while you're still sitting down! It was almost like having a pet. Oddly enough the sister-in-law tried to dump a six-week-old puppy onto him quite recently, but he had declined. It would have been no good with him being out all day at the teaching. The wee beast would not have been happy. Plus holidays. Other difficulties too. And if he had wanted to stay out all night what then.

The pipes could be looked upon as a surrogate pet. Even better! a surrogate child! Or wife for god sake! In fact, these very pipes represented the whole wide world. With these pipes in tow anything was possible. Nay! Probable!

Pat was laughing aloud while walking up the stairs. And there certainly was a lot of irony involved in it. But what could not be ignored was the existence of happiness: he felt genuinely happy. This was the point at issue. He had not felt genuinely happy for years.

Could that be true. Years? Aye, it was true, years.

Inside the lobby he propped the pipes against the wall beneath the coathooks but changed his mind and took them ben the parlour; if he left them in the lobby the temperature might affect them, being far too cold and draughty and then if he left them in the kitchen it would be too hot sometimes and too damp othertimes; either one of which might not be good for them. But this front room he used rarely, so the temperature though not warm was not cold and, more importantly, would remain constant.

In the kitchen he switched on the electric fire, crouching down to heat his hands at the two bars, with the jacket about his shoulders, keeping it there till he got warm — that was one of the problems of being alone, always coming into nothing, coming home to this coldness, a permanent dearth of warmth, of the warmth brought into being via the presence of another party, a fucking person in other words. He prepared a pot of tea, sat down on his chair, hands in his trouser pockets and his shoulders hunched. He was beginning to feel very tired indeed. That coupled with the cold he was probably better off going to bed. Fuck the tea. He unplugged the kettle and undressed, switched off the fire, having to visit the lavatory out in the lobby, before climbing swiftly into bed and under the blankets, huddling into as small an object as possible. And if he had drunk a big mugful of tea he would have had to get back up during the night. There again but, if he was better organised in regard to his pishing habits he would never have found the pipes! For a moment he considered rising to have a go on them but it would not have been right; it would have been wrong; it would have been the wrong thing entirely. If he was going to blow on them at all he wanted to do so in earnest and that meant being in the proper condition, the correct frame of mind and the correct frame of body. Give up the drink for a start! He would get fit. And that was another point: he doubted, quite fucking seriously, if ever he had felt truly healthy for years. Ages! How come he was not married to someone like Alison for instance? She was actually physically beautiful and without any doubt was obtainable – attainable. Or had been when she first arrived last summer. Maybe even now, if he was to really try, just depending on how he went about it; if he asked her out, just to see what transpired. It really was time. He had to do something. He really had to do something because it was driving him crazy, it was fucking driving him crazy. He could ask her out, just to see what transpired. Take her for a meal and a drink maybe, nothing startling, just a quiet kind of unobtrusive carry on. Something not to put her off. Not to be too forcible otherwise, otherwise it really would put her off. Simply to get her on her ownsome while the two of them were alone and by themselves, and without any of that fucking school mob watching what you were doing, wanting to know your business, the way they were aye wanting to keep tabs on everything you did, every last thing you got involved in or did not get fucking involved in! Like the stupid bloody pantomime. And the pipes of course. They would be gossiping about them as well. Desmond and Mrs Bryson and all the rest. Hubbubs in the bloody staffroom. Complete silence when he enters and then fucking hubbubs once he goes fucking back out again. O aye, did you see them! Even the way he acquired them did you notice! No kidding ye he just fucking lifted them from behind the fucking arts centre! How fucking bloody damn appropriate right enough!

At school the next couple of days he was in better spirit throughout with all the different classes. It was good and it was cheery. During the past while he had been becoming close to overwhelmed by the darkest of feelings over the influence he could have with pupils. Each and every single relationship he had with each and every pupil seemed totally unhealthy, each and every one of them, girls and boys, they were all the same.

The Teacher!!

The Great Man!!

How they regarded him as the perfect being. This great man of the universe. Statesman, philanthropist and diplomat. The final arbiter. He whose pronouncements on all subjects – including of course physics, politics and mathematical logic, the arts and philosophy; in short the entire history of the world – were to be listened to and paid the utmost attention. Their parents and/or guardians did not come into it. In comparison to his their values and opinions were absolutely worthless, absolutely worthless. Fucking obscene really, when you pondered the issue. Occasionally he could bore them stupid about it in the staffroom. Very occasionally. In fact, not very often. Far better remaining silent in the midst of such crassness, in the midst of such utter cant and hypocrisy, in the midst of such

christ! quite often he had to jump up and walk out of the bloody place! Even during conversations he was a part of. And he knew fine well this made him seem a queer sort of oddball of a character; maybe even queer in the sense of gayness, of his being homosexual, because he was not married and never had been married and the way things were going never would be married.

He hadnt even really lived with anybody. Nor had he ever been engaged or anything like that, although once it could be said he had come near. That was at uni. But they hadnt slept together! At the time he was so naive he considered that a strongpoint. Sheila Monaghan was her name and she was now teaching in a school somewhere in Aberdeen. If she had honestly liked him they would have slept together. There was no doubt about that. She used to let him feel her breasts and take her bra off but nothing more than that. Plus there was that occasion she let her hand rest on his bollocks and it drove him daft although she seemed to be unmoved unless of course it was a pretence. It wasnt easy to know what was what with Sheila. But fair enough, as far as he knew she never ever slept with anybody else either. And he did, eventually, whenever he could get the chance which was not often and usually standing up in the shadowy bits in the admin section of the students' union. Also on four separate occasions at parties when space was made by pushing the coats and jackets to one side. Quite funny carry ons. The type of thing that never happened nowadays. That had never happened at all except at uni and twice while at the teachers' trainers. It was all very fucking pathetic. A situation full of pathos. To hell with it! He just wanted something different. To not be a teacher perhaps!

What a temptation!

There were these amazing paintings done by Goya when he was quite old, late middle age or thereabouts – no, much older than that, he was really elderly at the time. Could that be true! They were actually astonishing. Incredible pieces of art. And gruesome. And yet! Plus that hollowness of tone. Was that it? A hollowness of tone? Or was he just thinking of the pipes.

He had not been thinking of the pipes at all. But neither had they gone from his head; rather the opposite, a kind of luxuriation, they were so much a part of him. But maybe they had gone right enough. The imagination works in its own way. It was easy to assume the whole backdrop of his perception had altered whereas it might not have; there was no reason to think it had, rather the opposite, if reason had anything to do with it. But there was little to trust in reason. Fuck that for a racket. A method of approaching the thing, perhaps, was to say he had been subconsciously avoiding all thought on the subject because of a growing awareness that it could prove momentous, all too fucking momentous.

He bought tins of enamel paint on his road home from school next afternoon; one each of the colours silver, red and black. He wondered whether a better depth of sound might be obtained by blocking the ends. When using them before he held the top section with his right hand while his left was covering the bottom in such a way that only a tiny fraction of air escaped. It worked fine but with something affixed permanently and made adjustable, a variety of notes would become available. That is, if a variety of notes was what was required. Even the term itself, 'variety', could scarcely be deemed satisfying. In an odd sense it almost cheapened the pipes as instruments, as though there must be an 'object of the exercise' and this object was to play a fucking tune. And it was not that. It was not that at all. Was it something better than that? Something better than playing a tune? Or was it just something different? Something different, not better? What could it be? This great feat he was setting out to do. This amazing thing that was not connected with playing a tune, a plain ordinary tune. This astonishing accomplishment he would achieve on a pair of discarded pipes, found dumped behind the rear fire-escape of the local arts centre.

And yet it probably connected to notes and to intervals, those spaces between them. If he got the right tone or pitch then that would be it and the distinctions between them, and the gaps in time, all such elements would be part of what was important. There was nothing mystical about it, although, fair enough, it did occur to him that reading more deeply into the Pythagoreans and how they used sound and number or rather, what they thought about sound and number, their uses, and their universal reference; and yet.

and yet, this conceptualising. Creating a distance already. Only a couple of days since the first sounds and now here he was attempting to get away from it, from the actual physicality of them. That was hopeless. That was the kind of thing he always seemed to be doing nowadays. The totality of it: the totality of it; the way the sounds had been the other night, or was it last night, the way the actual sounds had been, that was it – that was that! How come he had even felt the necessity of painting them in these bright enamels? What was wrong with their own colour? Their selfcolour? What was wrong with that, their self colour, the colour of their selves? Had that also been done to create a distance? And even the time it took for the paint to fucking dry! Was that also an excuse, a way out, an escape route, so he wouldni be obliged to actually blow them? But no, it wasnt that either, there was no self-deceit going on there, he knew himself well enough for that. If there was cheating going on he would know about it. Probably it was just a straightforward thing, that he wanted it to be right. He wanted the pipes to be 'as finished' as possible. He wanted them to appear as instruments, to actually look like musical instruments to the ordinary wo/man-in-the-street. He wasnt in any rush either. It was not as if he had to get it all over and done with in a certified period of time. Everything was to be proper, that was all; regulated, thought to the fore.

There was that temptation

It could even relate to field-theory, the whole thing, the sound and the number, insofar as such a theory ever managed to appear in relation to the lives of ordinary individuals, the manner in which each person, each organism, related to things as a totality, that old business of harmony, linked in the universal chain. And how in the name of fuck did the two guys with cudgels relate to that! Stuck fast in the mud, the miring quicksand – like the wee dog. Belabouring each other with those stout sticks. That magnetic force – an enactment? between the men just? or did Goya himself have a physical part in it? And what the hell did it matter anyway. This was him off with the concepts once again. Theoretical webs, dirty webs, fusty webs; old and shrivelling away into nothingness, a fine dust. Who needs that kind of stuff. Far far better getting out into the open air and doing it, actually doing it, something solid and concrete and unconceptualisable.

And now there existed a great temptation: to stop being a teacher. To stop being a teacher. To concentrate solely upon things of genuine value, things of a genuine authenticity, of a genuine physicality. Teaching by performance instead of pointing the finger.

But could all that be achieved on the pipes? What was it about them?

The actual idea of finding a pair of discarded pipes and turning them into musical instruments!

And yet the idea only appeared daft because they were ordinary pipes like the sort used by plumbers and electricians. If they had been called something else perhaps. And maybe this is why he had bought the enamels and painted them. If for instance he was performing on them in public and the audience saw them as ordinary pipes the reaction would be predictable, if not a silly kind of laughter then a degree of skepticism that would be better avoided if possible. Laughter would be okay if it came towards the end, but not at the beginning, before he could even be said to have started. The problem was fairly old hat, functionalism and nominalism, the naming process and imperialism, transforming commercially produced products into aesthetic weapons. The whole affair had been kicking about for years, probably several centuries! Even Goethe but, had he not been involved in something akin? To hell with it anyway. It was not something he found especially worrying. What he sought was the doing, the act.

And absolutely no attempts to conceal the artefact. Any person could recognise the pipes for what they were and good luck to them. That they had been painted would simply be seen as a sort of public affirmation, that the pipes could now be regarded in such and such a way, and without irony. Unless that irony was seen to be wholly enmeshed in the essence of the actual performance. The best way of looking at it might be in terms of jazz, particularly those great old bluesmen who used to manufacture washboard waistcoats. In fact that was precisely it; that was *the* analogy. Everything about it. And then that incredible moment of nostalgia or whatever, that amazing beauty, a crazy kind of incredible beauty which appeared to sum up all those failed ideals, the plans and the principles right from boyhood all the way up and now dead, deadened, rubbed out by the low-lying roof, that weight pressing down on you, like that medieval torture where they lay enormous stones on top of you, crushing out your breath, that kind of weight, society, that you hated and detested more than anything else in the world, that was forcing you on and on and on and on and fucking bloody on and on and on, and all the time grafting away on its own behalf, on account of its own propagation.

It was all so bloody sentimental, that was the problem.

But so what. So what if it was fucking sentimental. Was there not a place for sentimentality. Were you not allowed to start bloody greeting nowadays, was that it! Was that the way things were. Because if so Patrick would not be all that bloody bothered about hanging around, quite frankly. He would as soon be off; away. He would simply get away, be away, away from it all, all the fucking terribleness. He heard them in the staffroom. He was sitting there in his usual wooden chair and on and on they were talking about things that were totally unconnected with anything that could make sense of the world. They were saying things that were just such absolute shite, keech and tollie, such unbelievable rubbish. He had a magazine on his lap; he gripped its pages. He stared at the magazine. It concerned computers. Computers were not sentimental. Aye they were. They were just as sentimental as anything else. It was all a question of hanging on. There were certain concepts. Recursiveness for example. Hang onto that ya fucking idiot. The poor old temporary English teacher; this poor old temporary English teacher who had lately come aboard, was making some kind of remark to the effect of its being a pity that Wilson's TALES OF THE BORDERS remained out of print. And Desmond had nearly fallen off his fucking chair. What do you mean? he cried, half smiling and half glowering i.e. a sneer, he was actually sneering at this poor guy who had lately been press-ganged into this so-called establishment of learning. What do you mean? he said.

But the temporary English teacher was standing his ground. He just replied as though he was taking Desmond's question as of serious intent. Well, he said and he glanced round at the rest of the company, I just mean I think it's a bit of a pity it's out of print and looks like staying that way. Quite a lot of good stuff in it.

Ho! Desmond swivelled about on his arse, giving a mock gape in the direction of Joe Cairns who just shrugged. And then he said: As far as I'm concerned it's a load of dross, a load of downright dross.

The temporary English teacher raised his eyebrows but did not speak. He started rolling a cigarette. Desmond and the others watched him for a moment. He wasnt the first to have rolled a cigarette in the staffroom but it was uncommon all the same. Possibly the guy was just using the action as a method of not speaking and eventually, when it seemed as though the conversation would veer off in some other direction altogether, Desmond cleared his throat and said directly to Alison: Have you read Wilson's TALES OF THE BORDERS?

One or two.

Mrs Bryson smiled: They're not great!

Desmond chuckled. No need to be polite about it. Overwritten unwieldy clutter. And worst of all: an unspeakable sentimentality!

A very short silence, was breached by Patrick calling, Pardon?

Desmond paused. He turned slightly and looked at Patrick. After a moment he continued, I was just saying to Norman that I thought Wilson's TALES OF THE BORDERS was a load of dross.

Mm.

Mrs Bryson smiled at Patrick. Do you know them Patrick? she said.

Aye eh, yes, I do . . . He glanced away from her. She liked Patrick and it embarrassed him. How come she liked him the way she did? Probably if she had been twenty years younger she wouldni have granted him the time of day. That was it about so many women, this kind of contradictory behaviour all the time so you didnt know if you were fucking coming or going, it was hopeless.

Mrs Bryson was smiling yet again. What was she smiling at now. Maybe just trying to keep the peace. And to the side of her Alison was saying something to Joe Cairns – science teacher and exprofessional footballer, man of the Twenty-First century, who didnt often come to the staffroom but here he was today. Patrick jerked his thumb in the direction of Desmond and he said, The trouble with this yin is he thinks there's no room for sentimentality.

That's correct, replied Desmond.

It's your problem.

It's not my problem it's yours.

Patrick shook his head and he gazed down at the magazine and muttered, I canni be bothered talking about this.

Neither can I, particularly . . . Desmond sniffed and added, I just think there are great dangers in it.

What in TALES OF THE BORDERS?

Yeh, if ye like.

Mrs Bryson leaned forwards on her chair and she inhaled deeply on the cigarette she was smoking; she tapped ash into the ashtray on the coffee table beside her. I wouldnt have thought there were dangers in it, she said, glancing at Alison.

Okay then fine, replied Desmond. Admittedly there are a few snippets worth browsing over but I certainly wouldnt advocate it for the classroom.

But how no? asked the temporary English teacher.

Dross! Desmond shook his head and gave a brief sarcastic laugh. Dross!

Dross! Exactly!! Bloody dross! called Patrick. That's why it's so bloody ideal for the classroom. Because everything that goes on in the bloody place is a load of bloody dross in the first place! That's how I'm bloody leaving!

WHAT!!!!

Everybody seemed astonished by this. They were all gawking at him. Even those teachers who rarely allowed themselves to get involved in staffroom conversations, they too were gawking at him.

I'm just bloody fed up with it, said Patrick. He shook his head

[13]

and he lifted the magazine and footered with it. He then raised his head and addressed them collectively: Okay, as far as I'm concerned there's something very very fishy about being a teacher. I mean we're all secondbest for a kick-off, that's what I canni go. Plus none of us wanted to be a teacher in the first bloody place but here we all are, bloody teaching, it's bloody terrible so it is. I'm really bloody browned off with it all, I'm no kidding ye.

Desmond smiled, nodding his head. That is the most sentimental drivel you've spoken for months, he said.

O come on Des . . . murmured Alison.

Patrick stared at her. Above her head was a window. There was the wind and there was the rain. Above her head and beyond. It was all there. The temporary English teacher was speaking. He was saying, Becoming an English teacher was always first best to me.

Was it?

Yeh.

Patrick smiled.

Me too, said Mrs Bryson, and she glanced at Joe Cairns once again.

Patrick nodded. He gazed at the magazine on his lap. There was the face of a computer gazing back at him. Pat smiled. Desmond had begun talking as if in an aside, a genuine sort of an aside, and yet it was not genuine at all. He really was a fairly bad bastard and in reality he was addressing every individual within hearing range, and he was saying: He's the bloke who can show Gödel's Theorem to the average first-year class in a sentence remember!

That's correct, said Patrick, I've just got to find the right sentence!

Some of the teachers laughed.

And Desmond replied, Okay but you actually believe it.

Course I actually fucking believe it! If I didni actually fucking believe it I wouldni actually be fucking teaching! He laughed for a moment and shook his head, and smiled slightly at Mrs Bryson who was giving him an admonitory look. So too was Alison. She had the right but Mrs Bryson didni. What did she do it for? How come she could take it upon herself to admonish a mature male adult of the species in this fashion? He had a mother of his own and several aunties including two great-aunts, living somewhere in the middle of Dumfries. He also had a sister-in-law and a mother and a wee niece by the name of Elizabeth whom he loved dearly. What he didnt have was a lover. That was what he needed. That was what he needed. He didni need any of this, this sort of shite, fucking Desmond and Mrs Fucking Bryson and that idiot of a temporary fucking English teacher.

Pat . . . Alison was whispering to him. In fact she was not whispering at all she was just speaking normally. He had been gripping onto the edges of the seat with both hands and maybe set to leap across and start punching in at Desmond. It was possible. He was a fucking bastard and Patrick hated him. He was the kind of bloke who devalued everything, who devalued every last thing in the world and he was the last kind of person who should ever have been let loose in a classroom. Or outside in the real world. It was an utter obscenity, an utter obscenity. What was it about them, about that kind of person, that got them there, that made them so successful. Just exactly that, their cynicism; the way they could sneer and scoff at every last thing that might be of value. Even Alison seemed impressed by it. Her husband was probably the same type. A millionaire seller of double-glazed windows. They could fucking stuff the schools full of them as far as Patrick was concerned. He was finished with it, finished with it; he was just finished with it.

Dinnertime crept up on him. The bell went and he was sitting on his stool having a laugh with something one of the boys was saying. This was very unusual these days. He had definitely been enjoying the class, a bunch of stupit fourth-yearers, they were all stupit; fourth-yearers. What was it about fourth-yearers. A couple of them were smiling at him as they headed for the door, instead of the usual, avoiding the eyes. It was like how things used to be. They really did, they did use to be like that, things – back when the spark still existed. Before it had been extinguished. But it hadnt been extinguished; it still existed, it was just fucking dormant.

The door shut and a rustle of the paper on his desk. What a peace. He could just sit here until the afternoon began. Awaiting the afternoon! Pat grinned. What was that quotation. There was a good quotation about it.

Most things have got good quotations. Patrick was smiling; he was shaking his head, and getting down from the stool. He dawdled on the walk along the corridor and down to the playground. He was not wanting to meet the colleagues. He paused at the doors and he crossed slowly to the schoolgates, but the place was deserted, but for the two polis standing sentry duty. They nodded to him and he nodded back to them.

He peered along the street but Alison and the others had walked on ahead. They were going to the local boozer. So was Patrick. Friday dinnertimes were now as institutionalised as everything else. But this was fine; just a few teachers making a point of going out together for a couple of jars and a nice lunch. Pat had no objections. For some reason it was always good and relaxing, the atmosphere more congenial, more companionable, than at any other time during the week. He enjoyed these fifty or so minutes a lot, but perhaps he was beginning to look forwards to them far too much: a symptom of his lifestyle, viz. the lonely man.

And today was no different though maybe he was just too sad a bit and he kept having to avoid cuddling Alison. It was almost asexual. Or maybe it was sexual. Maybe it was just that his brand of sexuality had become somewhat different from the norm. Maybe he was now thinking in terms of cuddles rather than penetration. For fuck sake. It was probably a direct effect of the total lack of practice. He would just have to do it more often. Maybe even if it meant something like paying. Maybe he could just pay and get things cleared up. The preliminaries. He could get all them out the road and over and done with and then that would be that and he could just carry on until the ordinary daily routine of communion with the female sex picked up, until he was able to conduct a normal physical relationship with a young woman, rather than the big sister/mother/auntie routine which seemed the case at present if cuddles were to be the end of it all. Alison's physicality was very delectable indeed and she had certain ways of standing and taking part in general conversations, as if she was

[16]

watching every solitary, individual action performed by any one person. And if so she would have to be completely aware of Patrick for the fundamental reason that he was so completely aware of her. Plus she was a vegetarian – a central factor in how come they always wound up here every Friday, the vast selection of fresh salads and stuff. Becoming a vegetarian was something he had considered doing himself except it appeared extremely difficult to think of what you were supposed to eat. Tomatoes and toast and boiled eggs, vegetable stews and cheese omelettes of course. Perhaps he was just being lazy. He never used to be lazy. Here again was one further symptom, a further manifestation of something.

Desmond was being friendly to him. It was evident. Not so much talking to him directly as not especially not talking to him. Or was that true? Maybe he wasni really being friendly at all, he was just wanting it to appear as though he was. If anything he seemed to be his usual sneering self. But perhaps that in itself was a sign of friendliness. It was obvious he was not a happy man. Plus too his marriage not being of the best; and that general habit he had of sighing whenever the chat drifted backwards to university days and the good times had by all. It was distinctly possible that he envied Patrick. His own life was awful and his future seemed more awful. He had passed forty years of age whereas Pat had yet to hit the thirty mark. He used to loan Patrick an occasional record, but not for a long long while. Not that Patrick wanted to borrow anything from the likes of Desmond. Poor bastard that he was, stuck in a job he hated, forced into the role of classroom cynic. Patrick almost felt like buying him a drink but he was not going to buy him a drink because he was a fucking bad bastard and there was no sense in falling into any of these sentimental type traps to do with pity. People dont thank you for pity. Look at Pat, if you were to pity him he would punch you on the fucking gub. The job was secondrate and that was that. Who wanted to be a teacher. Nobody. And no fucking wonder. You could hardly blame Desmond when it comes down to it. A lot of teachers were like him, or tried to cultivate the appearance of being so. Not the women right enough. They didnt seem to regard the job as settling for secondbest in life. They regarded it as something different. They thought of it as a plum. No they didnt, that was the temporary English teacher he was thinking of. Wait till he was made permanent! Then he would fucking know all about it. Him and his fucking TALES OF THE BORDERS. What a fucking idiot. At present he probably thought of teaching as a fairly comfortable method of earning a better-than-average salary. And it wasnt a better-than-average salary. Well it was, but only in relation to the average hourly-paid wage of working-class people and teachers were not interested in the average hourly-paid wage of working-class people, they were interested in the average weekly wage of a full-blooded member of the professional classes, and if you compared it with theirs then the teachers' was fairly damn bloody abysmal. The women didnt seem to worry too much about that either. Some did of course. Some felt exactly the same as the men. And yet some of them were not all that perturbed. Patrick was one. He didnt really worry about the wage. He used to, but not nowadays. There were more important things. Maybe the women were right. Which women? Not Mirs Houston; she thought teachers were pretty hard done by. Maybe her and Desmond were having an affair. That would be the kind of thing that happened. Obviously she hated him and that was often a spur for women like her and for men like him. He would try to bend her to his will while she, totally detesting him, would appear to succumb by having sex with him, even though she wasni really succumbing at all but was remaining firmly in control viz. she would be in control, he would be in her power. And in one sense at least she would have won a battle over cynicism. Patrick could understand such reasoning. For some women cynicism is supposed to be anathema. And Alison was also the sort of woman who would regard moral battles as worthwhile, very worthwhile. This was part of her attraction for Pat. Or was it? She had the knack of making him feel confident. And yet she could also make him feel less than confident; she could undermine him quite easily. But that is because he was a transparent fellow. There wasnt much going on below the surface. Most of it was going on right at the surface. That was aye the problem with his way of living, his way of seeing existence, that he couldni allow things to remain unsaid, he had to bash on and go and fucking yelp; that was why he was now in the present fix, that was why he was now on the road to the Department of Health and Social Security, that was why

What was the DHSS? Apart from a shadowy form of nightmare. There was a guy lived down the stair from Pat and it was terrible meeting him in the close or out in the street because of these fucking horrendous yarns. And these yarns were absolutely fucking genuine. But his big brother was the worst. Because of what he didn't say. Gavin didni say things. He went about not saying things. That was how he survived, he went about and didni say things, especially to his young brother; that was to whom he did not speak most of all, and most particularly about the things that mattered, the things of essential consequence in the world – these were the things Gavin never spoke about with his young brother. So how in the name of god were folk to find things out, if those who knew kept it all fucking to themselves! Hopeless. But never mind, here was Patrick about to be finding out at first hand. Was he though. How come? Nobody was actually forcing him to resign. Even now it was as though the friendliness was there as a purpose, to make him feel like staying in the job. Maybe Alison had buttonholed them all. Maybe she had told Desmond to lay off. That was the sort of thing she would take on herself. That was how she was in the world, with people, that was the way she was. Why was she married to a bastard that didni appreciate her, that made her stay out at all these boring after-hour drinking sessions. Christmas Pantomimes. Who really gave a fuck about such shenanigans. Especially ten weeks after the event. Christ almighty it was shameful. Imagine finding yourself in such a position. It was beyond talking about. Just actually being in such a pub, in such a group of people, at such a time of day, week or fucking year. This was it. This was fucking it. Patrick smiled. He smiled and he shook his head. It was really just so fucking bad. There was nothing that ever could be worse. How could anything ever be worse. There wasnt anything. Alison was looking at him. He smiled. No, he said, thanks Alison, but to be honest with ye I'm just sick of the whole carry on, teaching and the rest of it. I mean for fuck sake I might end up like him! Patrick grinned, gesturing across at Desmond who was sitting on the other side of the table.

Desmond waited. He sighed, then answered, I always admire your use of sarcasm; it's so eh blatant.

Some of the others chuckled. Joe Cairns looked a bit apprehensive. He was quite pally with both Desmond and Pat and didnt like taking sides.

Alison moved. She was leaning to nudge ash off the tip of her cigarette into the ashtray. The action stopped Patrick from saying whatever he was about to say. He had been about to say something and now no longer. He had no idea what it had been. Could it have been something good. No, it would have been something bad, something silly, something to have made him appear an idiot. Alison was safeguarding him. It was good the way she could do that, make him stop dead, to not do it, whatever it was, to not do whatever it was, that he was doing, to make him not do whatever it was he was doing, in the middle of doing, or just about to: this was it, her ability to safeguard the susceptibilities of folk, different folk; all sorts of folk from all sorts of walks of life, all having the one thing in common, the one thing in common, all these other people, they had in common that they were not Mister Patrick Doyle – Master Patrick Doyle, a wee boy, not yet a man, not yet a husband and/or father, a bachelor, a single chap. What a life. What a fucking life. When even bastards like the cynical Desmond

the cynical Desmond. What the hell right did he have to call the bloke cynical! And was he not just the cliché of it all. The Staffroom Cynic. He probably wasnt cynical at all; he was probably just embittered, like everybody else, having had to settle for secondbest. Ah well. There was no point talking any longer. The time for that had passed. If it had ever existed. The temporary English teacher was looking at him. He had asked Patrick if he wanted a pint.

Naw, thanks.

Ye sure?

Patrick frowned. The temporary English teacher was smiling in a very amicable manner. Patrick smiled back at him, he was actually quite a nice guy. Patrick quite liked him. No, he said, thanks all the same.

Well what about a wee whisky?

A wee whisky.

Eh?

Eh aye, okay – ta . . . He grinned at Alison and added: It's Friday Mirs Houston, surely I'm entitled to one wee whisky? Then he turned immediately from her, not wanting to witness her response, he was not wanting to witness her response. Because what would happen if he broke down! What would happen if he laid his head in her lap! If he laid his head onto her lap. Into her lap. Snugly. The warmth on his cheeks; and his tears wetting her thighs through the dress, her patting his head, a poor wee boy, much given to asexual caresses of a maternal fix.

As soon as he stepped outside he was hungry; he hadnt bothered to eat while the others were doing so and now here he was paying the penalty. He returned to the bar at once. He bought a bridie, a hot bridie. But the pastry was too crisp. It covered the front of his shirt in burnt flakings. It was desperate. But what else could he do except eat, he was fucking starving, so he gulped the rest of it down almost before reaching the exit.

Along the road the group walked slowly, Alison tagging along at the rear, gazing into a shop-window. Pat gazed in alongside her. And she said, Are you okay?

Yes.

She nodded.

I'm totally fine.

You could go home sick you know.

Aye.

Old Milne wouldnt mind.

I know he wouldni; but I'm fine . . . he smiled although he didnt feel like it. And he had to walk on ahead of her. He passed Diana and Mrs Bryson. Desmond and Joe Cairns were walking with the temporary English teacher and he stayed with the trio as they approached the schoolgates. They were talking about going for a pint on the way home from school. Patrick would go as well, just as long as it wasnt to the arts centre for the entire night. Their all being teachers during the daytime and wiring into the pints at the arts centre during the evening. No point in discussing such glaring symbolism. Just too fucking depressing to be true.

Patrick burped quietly. He felt the beer into his belly, tasted the nauseousness. He allowed the other three to continue on and he turned to see Alison and Mrs Bryson, but instead came face to face with one of the janitors, Mister Peters, a right crabbit bastard who aye seemed to seek out Patrick to make his complaints. And he muttered, Your boss . . .

Patrick nodded. What's he done now?

What's he done now! It's what he's no done. That upgrading we were supposed to be in for, well we areni, cause he's no even bloody bothered his backside.

What? That's out of order.

You're telling me it's out of order. The janitor lowered his voice; a wee group of latecoming weans hared into the building. I'll tell ye something else, he said, that boss of yours, he's in for a rude awakening – and I'm no joking.

He's your boss as well as mine.

Aw is he!

Aye. Patrick smiled a very false smile.

I see, said the janitor. His mouth set, his gaze shifted away from Patrick and became a scowl; immediately he walked off in the direction of the lower ground.

Someone had appeared behind Pat. It was MI6, the second headmaster.

Hello, said Pat.

Hello Mister Doyle. Friday eh! The weekend looms the weekend looms.

Patrick nodded, glanced at his wristwatch. The lobby was deserted now. Patrick was late. He nodded again and strode towards the staircase. He had just been given a reminder on timekeeping. The janitor had been given his on timewasting. This was one of the central functions of the post of second headmaster, to remind staff of any shortcomings they may have. Patrick went up the steps quickly, and along the corridor but broke stride before reaching his own classroom, to enter Alison's. She stared at him. So did about thirty third-year pupils. Excuse me Mirs Houston . . . he waved to her and she followed him outside. Sorry, he said, just confirming you're going for a pint later on.

Yes.

Great. Where is it we're going again? Patrick almost touched her on the elbow as he spoke; her perfume too.

The arts centre I think.

Aw.

We can stop off somewhere else first . . . Alison whispered.

Aye, fancy? Miller's?

She nodded. Then she had clicked the door of her classroom open and was now shutting it behind herself. And had she been irritated by him? Who knows. And he walked rapidly along to his own room. It was as if maybe there had been a slight sarcasm in her voice but so what so what. He opened the classroom door and the hubbub ceased. Peace reigns, he said, great stuff. He shut the door and without glancing at the pupils he strolled to his desk, sighing and saying, Ho hum . . . He clasped his hands and looked at them all: a first-year class.

Now weans, he said, today is Friday and tomorrow is Saturday. I am demanding a bit of order, a bit of order, otherwise I'm closing the pub early. Okay! Right: open your fucking jotters and get scribbling.

He moved behind his desk, letting his gaze drop slowly to where a book lay with its pages open. The desk-top slanted and none of the kids could see the book without walking to the front of the room. Not that it would have mattered anyway. Plus as well they would have seen it when they came in. It was a good book though. It was by a German thinker who was enmeshed in the pre-Socratics, more especially the Pythagoreans, who were an odd bunch of folk although there again, not so odd as this present-day society which was extremely odd indeed, extremely odd, altogether. He chuckled briefly, shut the book and proceeded to address the class:

Weans! I have to advise yous all that I shall be having a couple of weeks on the panel. I am unwell. I wish to perform upon musical pipes.

The pupils were grinning. They were used to him and not at all nonplussed by such information. He was the kind of teacher who likes to spend an entire period on essential side issues. Pat nodded at them and he grinned. I wish to discuss an important topic. I wish to discuss leges de indigentibus factae. Now who can give us an immediate translation? Catriona! Come on, you're always good and I've got no time to waste!

Is it to do with the poor-laws?

Ah Catriona, a girl destined for great things. A wee bit like the famous Mirs Houston, her self-assuredness. Aye, that's exactly what it is fucking to do with, the poor-laws. Now then, I want you all to repeat after me: The present government, in suppressing the poor, is suppressing our parents.

The smiling faces.

The present government, in suppressing the poor, is suppressing our parents.

Fine, smashing, good. Right then, one more: Animi egestas! Immediate translation! Ian!

Is it to do with poverty of the mind sir?

Yes sir, precisely. Now class, the lot of ye, repeat after me: Our parents, who are the poor, are suffering from an acute poverty of the mind.

The smiling faces. When Goya embarked on his black period what must he have been thinking on? There he was, fifty years aulder than Pat Doyle and stuck fast in quicksand.

The smiling faces. Pat smiled back at them. Children, there is little to say and I'm not the man who can say that little. I'm a man who is fucking sorely bemused, sorely bemused. And I'm standing here in front of you, right out in the bloody damn open.

Yes, the faces all smiling. The wee first-yearers are good. Maybe they are Patrick's favourite group. Just at the age they are approaching teenagehood. He seems to have an okay relationship with them. I'm chucking this job in because I want to play the pipes. But these pipes have got fuck all to do with Scotland. Does anybody know the term 'fugisticism'? And dont answer too fast because I dont think the term has existed before this last five minutes. So there you are, that's the way things are, how ye can just fucking walk in here and invent your own terms. I've got my own terms and so have you. You've just got to make sure they're no your

The door was opening. Mirs Houston, it was Alison . . . Patrick smiled a moment then frowned. She remained by the door. He walked across. She turned side on to the class, so they wouldni be able to read her lips. She had very expressive lips, her whole mouth in fact. She tapped him on the arm! and she said very quietly indeed, Are you going to the staffroom at the interval?

Naw.

She paused.

I prefer no to.

But you're definitely going for a pint later on?

Eh aye.

I'll see you at the gates then.

Aye.

Then she was out and away, the door clicking itself shut. He stared at it, the door, then about-faced to stare at the weans a moment, then he strolled to the desk, gazing to his other side as though examining the large blackboard which occupied most of that wall. He stood by his desk and called: Saepire circumdare?

Silence.

He nodded. He glanced at Catriona.

Is it to do with fencing in?

It is precisely to do with that. Now, all of yous, all you wee first-yearers, cause that's what you are, wee first-yearers. You are here being fenced in by us the teachers at the behest of the government in explicit simulation of your parents viz. the suppressed poor. Repeat after me: We are being fenced in by the teachers

We are being fenced in by the teachers

at the behest of a dictatorship government

at the behest of a dictatorship government

in explicit simulation of our fucking parents the silly bastards

in explicit simulation of our fucking parents the silly bastards

Laughter.

Good, good, but cut out that laughing. You're here to be treated as young would-be adults under terms that are constant to us all; constant to us all. Okay then that last bit: viz. the suppressed poor!

viz. the suppressed poor!

Cheering.

But that was okay. Patrick nodded. What time is it somebody? And he checked the time given with that of his watch, and he gazed at the book on his desk. He reached to close its pages. There wasnt long to go now. And the weans were watching the weans were watching.

I'm reading about the Pythagoreans, he said, I've had the book open on my desk. They were great believers in harmony. Does anybody know what harmony is? And dont answer because it's fucking impossible. By the time you've reached third year you'll just burst out laughing when somebody asks that kind of thing. Okay. What time is it now? Patrick looked at his watch. He wanted to get out and away. He needed to think things out. He opened the pages of the book and closed them at once. He smiled at the class: they were that fucking wee! I'm so much bigger than you, he said, these are my terms. My terms are the ones that enclose yous. Yous are all enclosed. But yous all know that already! I can tell it just by looking at your faces, your faces, telling these things to me. It's quite straightforward when you come to think about it. Here you have me. Here you have you. Two sentences. One sentence is needed for you and one sentence is needed for me and you can wrap them all up together if you want to so that what you have in this one sentence is both you and me, us being in it the gether.

Please sir!

Yes sir?

Do you think that we shouldnt be here?

Aye and naw. Sometimes I do and sometimes I dont. I think your question's fine. I think for example in Pythagoras you'll find ways of looking at things, at flitting from one thing to the other. And oddly enough it really does have to do with transmigration and maybe even with certain taboos. It makes things fucking really interesting.

Patrick glanced at his watch. The weans didnt notice him doing it thank god. But he had taken great care for just that reason.

When the bell rang he was sitting on his stool with his elbows on the edge of the desk. He didnt look at the kids as they headed toward the door. He didnt feel like a terrible hypocrite. But nor did his stomach feel in as great a condition as it could be. A couple of the kids looked as if they considered lingering. Sometimes they did that in order to ask a question. There was nothing wrong with this in first-year classes. Patrick inclined his head in the direction opposite them and they soon departed.

When Patrick's parents forced him into going to university because let us face it they hadnt done that at all although having said this of course he had in no sense desired to attend that institution, especially because he had or had not wanted to go in the first fucking place.

[26]

So that's that then.

Out in the corridor he walked to the banister and leant his elbows there. All the weans marching about below. He continued along towards the staircase in a slow manner, his hands in his trouser pockets, jacket buttoned. His shoulders were hunched in an effort to retain body heat, this being a situation wherein attempting just that seemed necessary to the following second's survival. The following second's survival. An insulation. When Patrick's parents had forced him into going to uni

ah shut up; who the fuck cares, who the fuck cares. Patrick swung his shoulders from side to side, it was all so fucking stupid, daft, plain daft, just fucking crazy, crazily diabolic, crazy in diabolic fashion, in the style of Goya's black period. He stopped his shoulders from swinging.

He could have become involved with prostitutes, or at least have obtained sex on that basis. What basis? Nothing. What basis? Nothing, just that sort of basis. But what sort of basis are you talking about? I'm not talking about any basis. The children filing past him here at the head of the stairs, filing past him o so respectfully filing past him, so respectfully. Patrick nodded, smiling at the one or two he recognised more than others. Insulation. That insulation. Protecting oneself against the encroachments, the encroachments. There was Old Milne below, stalking the ground floor in his MA gown. What a man! What a chap! He was a curious fellow. A Congregationalist Protestant Christian. A believer in the teachings of the Congregationalist Protestant Christian teachers. In his absent-minded quandary

he was aye in this absent-minded quandary. Prowling the corridors lost in thought. A contradiction, to absent-mindedly prowl – no doubt he was just wandering the place in a kind of limbo. Pat could see the man as a fellow sufferer, the sort of headmaster he himself

he himself!! What was he talking about he himself; he himself? what did that mean he himself. He himself! In the name of fuck.

Mister Doyle . . .

Mister Doyle . . .

Yes aye . . .

It was Isabel and Shenaz. What were they up to. Plus another couple hovering to their rear, all with these cheeky wee looks on their faces. Ach no really cheeky, just fucking happy, in some unfathomable way.

Your shoelaces are undone sir.

Lassies dont call men sir!

Your shoelaces are undone Mister Doyle.

O christ. Such an old fucking carry on, these merry pranks of the innocent they were so fucking horrendous. Aye eh . . . he smiled, glancing at the kids to the rear and it included Catriona. He didnt bother checking his shoelaces; he did know this particular pair of shoes and shoelaces however and strange as it may seem the laces did have a habit of working their way undone, it was as if they had faulty fucking eyes or tongues or insteps or something. It was himself to blame for buying the cheaper efforts; why did he not buy dearer goods. There were shops selling shoes right at this very moment. He could just rush out and buy a pair. Why didnt he. Because he had to go and be with another class of weans for christ sake why else. He would make a point of this tomorrow morning, Saturday. Saturday is the day to go shopping. The lassies were still there. What were they still there for. He winked and grinned and walked on quickly. The main purpose was often just to make such contact with a teacher beyond the classroom, to let him see they thought funny things about him. Funny things. Unclear things. Could it be sexual? Of course. And they were well aware of his marital status. What age were they at all? Wee first-yearers! Twelve or thirteen. The stirrings. No doubt about it. Isabel had probably been dared to speak and only agreed if Shenaz would stand by her, plus Catriona in the near vicinity, her being thought to be the teacher's pet. But she wasnt the teacher's pet. He occasionally used her because she had a good memory and he would have to stop it because just it was not fucking fair, poor wee lassie christ it was just not fair. In fact she reminded him of Louise McGilvaray. That was a name from the past! Louise McGilvaray, god. She was a nice looking lassie. Probably married with a couple of kids by this time. If he hadni've gone to fucking uni that would've been him, married to Louise and living the life of Reilly. But if he really meant it he wouldni be so fucking flippant.

[28]

Eh ah . . .

it was Old Milne. Pardon?

Eh ah . . .

And the weans had vanished. Old Milne, with his hands clasped behind his back, tucked beneath the gown.

I had been wanting to have a word with you Mister Doyle.

Well I was actually in a hurry the now.

Old Milne's baffled look!!! That somebody could be in a hurry when he was wanting to talk!

I was supposed to be meeting somebody . . . Patrick stopped; he glanced at his wristwatch. He was gibbering. If he had been supposed to be meeting somebody it would mean he was either going to be late or else miss the next period altogether. The headmaster was gazing at him. Pat smiled. He pointed at his watch. In fact I thought it was later than this. I was actually thinking of the interval.

Mm . . . Old Milne relaxed, the roles being re-redefined.

And the two continued to stand there. It was a crucial factor about the headmaster, this failure he had of clinching matters; these conversational pauses he seemed to introduce so that the other person became dutybound to blurt something out. Patrick was not fucking falling for it. It was incredible the arrogance the old dickie had. He was almost lounging there, slightly rocking on the balls of his fucking feet! How inferior he must have regarded Pat. Christ almighty. And now that nice actor's speaking voice which had come into existence courtesy of a few thousand ounces of thick black pipe tobacco or so he liked to confide to folk at the annual licensed functions. At ten minutes to four then Mister Doyle . . . in my eh ah . . .

And he continued to fucking stand there as if he was muttering internally! What the fuck could he be muttering about internally in the name of god what on earth was up!

He was being carpeted. Doyle was on the carpet! Ten to four in the heidie's office he was going to get a punishment exercise. Auld fucking fart. Well if Pat was about to get carpeted then he wouldni find out till Monday morning because one thing was definite, fuck him and his office.

And leaving such an event cloaked in mystery was only good sense. How foolish he would be to attend and discover. Definitely much better to postpone matters. Even going on sick-leave for a fortnight, and playing the pipes. Playing the pipes for fuck sake! And maybe Alison's thighs!

Ten to four in his office but what a joke. What an actual joke. Poor auld Old Milne; his absolute certainty that everybody will stick to the rules of the game. He was probably an edwardian aristocrat in disguise. And still standing there! Maybe Pat was supposed to end the interview! Gazing straight at him. Maybe he was trying to form some kind of tacit relationship – convert him into a Congregationalist Protestant Christian! In the name of the holies! Patrick gestured in the direction of the corridor. He said: I've got to go to the toilet Mister Milne.

O I see. Old Milne was gaping but moving aside with a swirl of the gown, to allow him by.

At ten minutes to four Patrick was back in the corridor but outside the door to Alison's classroom. Some fourth-years were in with her. All boys of course; trying to get her to bow her head so they could see down her blouse. His entrance allowed her escape; she smiled, waiting for the boys to leave before she did. Pat held the door for her and they walked down the stairs together. He left her at the foot, she to go to the staffroom while he strode out and into the carpark. He went swiftly. Old Milne had many spies; and from his secretary's office window it was possible to see the driveway to the main schoolgates.

The engine started first time. As he approached the gates a couple of youths from the sixth year were chatting to the two polis, about career prospects no doubt – it was either that or the fucking army. More pupils loitered outside. Then Alison was coming. He leaned to open the passenger side for her, but the temporary English teacher was also there, he appeared suddenly from behind her, walking a standard pace; and he frowned at Patrick. What the hell was he wanting? And how come he was frowning. Patrick wound down the window and called: Okay?

Eh yeh eh I was just wondering if you were going along the road?

Going along the road?

The guy stared at Patrick.

Patrick nodded.

Alison said, Pat . . .

Aye, said Pat, we're going along the road. We're actually going for a quick pint. D'you want a lift?

The temporary English teacher grinned: I wouldni say no.

On the pavement across the street the pupils were all spectating. It was amazing how they could find the likes of this interchange so fascinating – especially it being a Friday and tomorrow the weekend. When he was a boy he would have shot off home and would have got there before the bell had stopped ringing. Changed days right enough. Unless of course they were spying for the heidie! In fact it was a good thing this bloke was accompanying the pair of them: it would offset any gossip. And weans were notorious gossips. Another batch of them stood along by the Commodore Cafe and they also appeared to be totally intrigued by the encounter at the gates. The temporary English teacher made a sort of joke to do with being celebrities. Alison had had to get back out her seat and raise it for the bloke to climb in but then she seemed to hesitate and she got into the rear seat and allowed the fucking male to take up the responsible domain in the front. Unless she was just being polite. Patrick stared at her via the rearview mirror, then he said to the temporary English teacher: Dont slam the door, the hinges are rusty.

The bloke nodded, adjusting the seatbelt round his waist and shoulder, and pulling the door shut gently. Thanks for the lift, he said.

Aw no bother. Patrick glanced over his right side, eased his foot off the accelerator pedal, edging the motor out into the street. And there were the wee lassies from his first year of that afternoon – no doubt hating Alison because she was sitting near Sir Doyle. There again mind you they might well have hated him because he was with another woman. The Commodore Cafe was down by the corner into the main road. Patrick braked there to await the change at the traffic lights. He said to the temporary English teacher: What's your name by the way?

Norman.

Norman?

Yeh.

Cause I just realised there I dont think I've heard it before.

Norman's an English teacher, said Alison.

Yeh but I'm only temporary.

You'll be permanent soon enough, Patrick replied.

I dont know if it's desirable!

Ah you'll be okay.

Yeh, I was being facetious.

Norman specialises in the Renascence, said Alison.

The Renascence?

Yeh. He had taken his cigarette papers and a small tobacco packet from his overcoat pocket and he gestured with it: Alright if I smoke?

Whatever you like. Alison smokes as well.

Far too much, said Alison who had brought out a magazine and was leafing through it.

They crossed the Kingston Bridge, taking the first exit down onto the road west and he drove on as far as Yoker to the pub called Miller's. The temporary English teacher made a display of puzzlement which Patrick ignored until having parked the car. You were probably expecting to go to the lounge bar in the arts centre, he said, smiling at Alison over his shoulder; and here we are well off the beaten track.

Yeh . . .

We come here once or twice.

It keeps us out of sight of the pupils, grinned Alison. And it isnt only us two that come!

Patrick glanced at her; there was no need to have said that, why had she said that.

And she continued: We may find Diana and Joe here already, and Desmond.

It's just sometimes nice to get a bit of peace and quiet, said Patrick, before everybody meets up together.

Good idea, the temporary English teacher was muttering while assisting Alison out of the motor car.

[32]

Patrick waited then pulled shut the door for her. He wondered whether to go home. It would not be difficult to just drive off, to just leave the two of them standing there on the pavement, in a cloud of dirty exhaust fumes. Maybe that was what they were seeking. It didnt require an enormous leap of imagination to make something of the guy's sudden emergence at the schoolgates. This type of thing happened with Alison. Exactly the same in pubs and places where you could spot the eyes all following her when she strolled to the Ladies – like a pack of wee dogs. Patrick was also a wee dog, a lap dog. He wanted onto her lap. Maybe this is where he would sit in the pub.

The temporary English teacher was at the bar ordering. Patrick walked with Alison to one of the many empty tables. The place was usually quiet at this time. When they sat down he quickly told her of the headmaster's invitation, and here he was instead.

Alison was exasperated. She lighted a cigarette. She said, You should've gone; that's just being silly.

It's not being silly.

Yes it is.

It isni.

It is because it'll just irritate him. He's a petty man and he doesnt like being irritated by people. He bears grudges, you know that.

Pat grinned. It wont matter.

It will matter.

No it wont. He smiled, he closed his eyes. He was right and she was wrong. It would not matter. It would all be forgotten about once he had gone on sick-leave. He would phone for an appointment tomorrow morning. And when Old Milne heard he would simply make allowances. Nothing was more certain: sick folk always get the benefit of the doubt.

The temporary English teacher arrived with the drinks on a tray. The Renascence! He was obviously fired with spirit. The Spirit of the Great Teachers and Educators. Yet he looked too old for that. He looked in his early thirties. Patrick had been fired by the Spirit of the Great Teachers as well but that was fucking years ago. That is not true. It is only at the moment he required a bit of a rest. He needed peace. That was it. He needed peace. Some peace – nothing startling, just a wee rest, a bit of time away from the onslaught. He *also* believed in teaching, he *also* believed in being a teacher, the spirit of that, of what it was — what was it? A wee rest but, that was the thing, definitely. Even stopping these thoughts of Alison all the time. Because they were unhealthy, it was becoming unhealthy, the whole thing. He was just doing too much of it, the thinking, her being on his brain all the time, seeing her or something, the image or sensation maybe it was a feeling of her. And really unhealthy. Too pervasive. It was too pervasive, too forcible or something. The temporary English teacher was looking at him. Patrick nodded. And he smiled at Alison who was also looking at him and he said to the temporary English teacher: Usually a couple of us come to the likes of this place and then later on . . . He shrugged. That's what us two would've been doing, if you hadni come along, if it had just been the two of us — eh Alison?

Yes, we'd have gone on to the arts centre a bit later.

So I mean . . . Patrick shrugged. If you want to tag along you're welcome.

Aw ta, ta, if you dont mind.

Of course Norman dont be silly, Alison replied.

Norman. He was a quite good bloke by the looks of it. No sense in denying such clear-cut realities. He was just being friendly, glad to be part of the company of a bunch of teachers with whom he wished to spend the rest of his working life. Fair enough. Plus he had bought Pat a nice whisky at dinnertime and here he had bought him a nice big pint of heavy beer which would have to be his last since he was driving. And it had been Patrick's round of course. It was he who should have bought it. And he had forgotten. His memory was definitely not as it was. This had become noticeable on other occasions. Maybe it ran in the family. His maw was inclined to be absent-minded too, she forgot the most stupit kind of things. The last time he was up visiting she had forgotten where she'd put the fucking teapot. Now that was really stupit and daft and really in fact quite worrying. And they had discovered the thing sitting on top of the cistern in the bathroom. And so bloody fucking embarrassing — excrutiating for christ sake. And then he had forgotten her birthday of a week past. He could just have dropped her a card and she would have been pleased. And his sister-in-law had phoned him to remind him. Nicola, his beautiful sister-in-law whom he regarded more as a sister than sister-in-law, he just liked her so much. But enough of that enough of that. And of course his da, there was the fucking da to worry about as well for fuck sake what a life. Existence could have been much better, much better indeed. But that's the way existence is, you canni fucking ask for this that and the next thing, you've just got to take whatever they fucking throw at you. Aye but you dont have to take it. You dont have to accept it. It's this age. This age. This age was getting on his nerves. No it wasnt. Even that wasnt true. He didni really care. People said twenty-nine was a landmark but he didni really care one way or the other. Gavin was fucking three-and-a-half years older than him. And you never heard him grumbling – at least no about his fucking age, he grumbled about everything else! He was smiling and Alison was smiling as a reply. She thought he was smiling at what the temporary English teacher was saying, old Norman there, who was in rare animation about something that had happened to him at the teachers' trainers. It was obviously funny because Alison was genuinely smiling. And she could put on the false yins when she wanted to but this smile was definitely genuine. Patrick inclined his head as though to listen all the better. Something seemed to be wrong with his ears though. He couldni fucking hear a damn thing the guy was saying and yet Alison seemed so damn pleased with it and now taking a puff at her fag, her pale lips.

. . . with these two pipes you found?

Pardon.

I was just wondering if you'd made use of them yet, I meant to ask ye . . . said the bloke.

Patrick lifted his pint of beer and sipped at it. Naw, he said, no really. Sometimes I just pick things up and take them home with me and then I keep them for a wee while. Usually but I just end up dumping them.

Aw I see.

He would have been a gold prospector in the old days, chuckled Alison.

Pat grinned. Actually my favourite job amongst all else would be . . . He raised his right forefinger and wagged it at her: Guess!

O god Pat I'm always hopeless at this kind of thing.

No you're no.

[35]

I am! Maybe Norman.

Norman?

Eh . . . Norman was grinning; he tilted his head to one side, his eyelids shutting momentarily; his face became all screwed up, and then he said: Is it to do with motor cars?

Motor cars?

Alison was smiling.

You fucking kidding! said Pat.

Well you did ask him to guess, said Alison.

Patrick gazed at the floor.

What job was it? the temporary English teacher asked.

After a moment Patrick smiled; he was still gazing in the direction of the floor. Beachcomber, he said, as a matter of interest.

Beachcomber.

God yes, said Alison. Yes, I could see you doing that. And you'd be content for the rest of your life.

Of course. It'd be wonderful.

No me, said the other bloke.

Patrick replied, You're only saying that because you're new to the teaching racket. You're still keen to get involved in the whole carry on, all its different aspects, the whole fucking kit and caboodle.

Alison chuckled.

Kit and caboodle! muttered Patrick. What in the name of christ does that actually mean!

Alison was saying to the temporary English teacher: He's the staffroom cynic Norman pay no attention.

Norman grinned.

Patrick frowned. Thanks Alison, thanks a lot . . . He reached for his beer and swallowed a large mouthful. Then without further comment he went to the lavatory. The way things were going he would have had a better time of it in with Old Milne. Whose name alongside that of Norman ended in 'n' sounds. As did Alison's. Maybe if you wanted to be content in this world you needed that. Look at poor auld Desmond: a fucking sad case with a 'd'. And Patrick with a 'k'. A 'k' was terrible. Both it and 'd' had a similar sort of feel to it.

In some ways initials and letters were as interesting as numbers, but not quite. The Pythagoreans called numbers 'figures'. The whole of matter could be reduced to them. Numbers or figures were the elemental parts, the constituents. And of course you have bodies still being called figures. Plus 'soh' 'lah' 'te' 'doh' etcetera being scales, numbers. Everything went together and could be reduced to numbers, even names of course. The initials P: D for instance, they could be reduced to 16: 4 based on the twenty-six-letter roman alphabet; 4^2: 2^2, or even 2^4: 2^2. Numbers are great. You can do anything you like with them. Plus it gets you away from objects and entities, always allowing for the fact that neither objects nor entities exist to which these numbers correspond, because some folk believe there must be a '1' and a '2' somewhere out there, if only they or it can be found, discovered or come upon.

Back at the table Norman and Alison were yapping away together and when Patrick sat down Norman said to him, Alison was saying ye wouldni mind if I asked ye something. When you were at the toilet there I was eh saying to Alison if ye would mind if eh I asked you something.

What?

It was just something I was wanting to ask ye. About in the staffroom this morning, it was something . . .

Patrick frowned, then he rubbed his eyes with the fingers of his left hand.

What it was, it was just eh . . .

Patrick glanced at Alison, he smiled slightly.

I was just wondering.

Patrick looked at him. What did ye say?

It was something in the staffroom this morning.

Aw.

Patrick for god sake, said Alison.

Naw it doesni matter if he doesni want to say. Norman said, It doesni matter.

Patrick nodded.

It was just it was interesting.

That's good.

Pat! Alison glared at him.

Well for christ sake have I got to bloody fucking . . . he shook his head and exhaled breath studying the ceiling.

You're so damn aggressive.

Patrick looked at her.

If you have to blame somebody then blame me. Norman just wanted to ask you something that's all, because he thought it was an interesting point, and I told him it'd be alright, I told him ye wouldnt mind.

Thanks.

Alison glanced at her wristwatch. And Patrick lifted his beer and swallowed most of what was left. He laid the glass on the table and said, Come on we'll go to the arts centre and talk about Christmas Pantomimes.

Alison stared at him.

Sorry, would ye prefer to stay here? Or have ye got to go home or what?

After a few moments she answered: I wish you would calm down.

And he nodded at once. She was dead right. There was no question about that. It would have been better said when they were alone but. When it was just the two of them. Not like this, with this other bloke. It wasni the sort of statement you liked hearing about yourself in front of strangers. And Norman wasnt exactly a close friend although having said that, it should be admitted that Patrick had met a lot worse guys. His openness for a start; that was good – not being afraid to ask the awkward question. Usually only Desmond could be relied upon for that. Patrick nodded. Aye. He said, Do yous fancy another before we hit the road? Eh Norman I mean you've bought the last couple so it's definitely me on the bell!

Him on the bell, said Alison. In his reckoning women dont count . . . And rising from her seat she had opened her handbag and she walked to the bar without another word.

Norman smiled. I like her, she's nice.

Patrick didnt answer. Not only was Alison nice she was beautiful. She was beautiful and she was honest and gentle and truthful and she was sympathetic as well, she could listen to folk when they were down and out and didni fucking . . . Christ. He shook his head and shut his eyes. Then he shrugged, glanced at Norman: The guy she's married to, he's a bit of a dickie, to be honest; I mean I'm no being eh . . .

[38]

Norman nodded.

Patrick sniffed. He shouldnt have said what he had. He shouldnt have said it it was daft, totally daft. It was the kind of thing

He just shouldnt have said it.

Norman was smiling now. And he leaned his elbows on the edge of the table, glancing swiftly towards the bar, and whispering, Hey Patrick, you dont mind me asking and aw that, about Alison, I'm no being cheeky or anything

Patrick had his eyelids shut fast and there was this roaring noise like a fucking crescendo in the eardrums, an eruption or something, a cacophonic roar of the blood in the head.

He smiled. He was going to answer but Alison had returned. He smiled. He was going to say something to the guy but she had returned. She beckoned to him, at his empty pint glass: Is it beer or lager Pat or what is it?

Tomato juice.

Honestly?

Yeh, thanks. He laughed. What had he laughed at. He laughed again. Alison had returned to the bar. It was a girl serving and Alison and she were talking together. They were probably talking about – what? what would they be talking about?

He glanced at the temporary English teacher who smiled but looked away immediately. He was not at his ease with Patrick. That was for definite. It was as if he was just – as if he was maybe thinking he was not really able to say what might happen in the next couple of minutes. As if maybe he was worried Patrick might break down or something maybe and end up

not well perhaps. As if Patrick would end up not well.

Fucking not well! He was fucking not well right now. Right fucking now. He was christ almighty in fucking bad trouble. Bad trouble. What did it take! What did it fucking take! Here he was about to resign from school in order to play the pipes. Play the fucking pipes! In the name of christ. Fucking predicament and a half that was. For somebody who was supposed to be not off his head, somebody who was supposed to be not cracking up.

Alison.

My god. She was holding a circular tray with the drinks standing aboard. A smile on her face: yet downcast, in her gaze – not to be looking at one if not at the other. Being equal to the pair of them in other words, the two men.

That was typical. That was what like she was. But this type of equality, it was surely a way of sounding the death-knell. Patrick stood to his feet and saluted as she sat down; he then bowed.

Such a gentleman, she said.

Just apologising for the last faux pas.

She nodded.

Total sexism, you were dead right to pull me up for it.

I know I was.

Of course I earn more money than you.

What?

I earn more than you do.

Dont be stupid.

'I'm no being stupid Alison; I earn more than ye; it's to do with responsibility payments and these exam study group reports.

What?

Patrick shrugged. We're no supposed to tell anybody.

You're being stupid.

I'm no.

That's unpaid work.

That's what you think.

Alison made no response for a moment, then she said to Norman, See how rumours can start!

Norman looked from her to Patrick and back to her again, smiling.

And she said, God Pat sometimes you can be a real pain.

He grinned and raised his glass of tomato juice: Slàinte! He tasted it and grimaced.

Serve ye right, she muttered.

The temporary English teacher chuckled but became serious at once. He said, I applaud you for it. I used to drive a motor myself but I found it nearly impossible to keep off the bevy. I mean properly. At the wind-up I more or less had to chuck it all the gether, the driving I'm talking about. It was a case of either/or, the drink or the car.

Patrick gaped at him. Is that the truth?

[40]

Yeh.

For fuck sake.

It would be impossible for him! said Alison.

Ah well it isni easy, replied Norman, the temporary English teacher. He grinned and raised his tumbler. All the best, he said to the two of them before taking a drink.

Patrick watched him follow it up with a sip of his half-pint of beer. It was the action of the strong drinker, the comfortable drinker. Something Patrick was not. He wasnt a comfortable drinker; and nor was he a strong drinker – not particularly, not in comparison to others. You only had to see others to appreciate the point. Although maybe if he didni have a motor he would drink a bit more. You married? he asked Norman.

Yeh.

Patrick nodded.

And Norman frowned, then smiled.

Dont pay him any attention Norman! Where marriage is concerned Mister Doyle is inclined to get things into his head!

Aw thanks Alison thanks a lot.

Well so ye are.

Am I.

Yes! Alison chuckled and flicked her lighter at a new cigarette.

Thanks.

For god sake dont take things so seriously Pat.

Alright but I just wish you wouldni go around making explanations on my behalf I mean fuck sake it's terrible.

Sometimes you need explanations.

Okay but you still dont need to bloody christ you know what I'm talking about! Patrick shook his head; eventually he glanced at her; she was staring at him. He muttered, Sorry.

If you would just calm down.

I know.

Alison was looking at her wristwatch. I think we better go soon, otherwise they'll be wondering whether we're going to turn up at all.

Patrick said nothing. There wasnt anything he wanted to say. He footered with his drink. He lifted it to his lips, returned it to the table. Norman had started talking. That was good, it was good that he was talking. And in a friendly manner he was acting as if he was including Pat in the conversation although obviously he wasnt thank christ because it was really boring – it was to do with being a teacher. And suddenly there was that awful feeling, that awful feeling; it was a feeling

what was it like it was like as if, as if, just as if things werent going aright, not going aright. It would be great being whisked straight home on a magic carpet. One of Goya's things. But it was definitely the sort of situation, the kind that it was burdensome to remove from, to just carry on within, it was even just carrying on in the company for fuck sake that was difficult and to be able to reach freedom, to be able to get out from under this and away, away, gone, freedom, liberation, flying high in the fucking sky, away way up so high, out of reach. He raised the tomato juice to his mouth, right in front of his nose, and attempted to taste it with relish, an act of great heroerism. He grinned and said to Norman: This stuff is only palatable with vodka.

Norman nodded, breaking off from what he had been speaking about.

Alison smiled. She said: I think it's good you showing this new-found resolution Mister Doyle.

Patrick did not look in her direction for several seconds. When he did he chuckled.

Alison had her bag in hand and was arising from her seat. Maybe she would float straight up with a pair of angel wings flapping. He shook his head, grinning; returned his empty glass to the table although there again the glass could hardly be described as empty with all the dregs of tomato it contained. He stood up alongside Norman. They followed her to the car, Patrick waiting until both were inside; he shut the passenger door, strolled round to the driver's side.

When he eased off the handbrake he was not going to the arts centre. He turned to inform Alison but she was listening to Norman who was telling her something Mister Mills had said. Mister Mills was the second headmaster, otherwise known as MI6. Once more it was pretty boring stuff but probably he should have taken note of what was being said if only for the sake of future reference to do with social obligations in a freemarket economy, but he had the road to watch, being the driver and all that ergo having to take care not to crash the fucking machine. And it appeared as though Norman, the soon-to-be-erstwhile, was no longer even pretending to seek his attention. He was now swivelled sideways on the seat, actually straining to see into her eyes it looked like. And him being married as well, was his marital state satisfactory? did he have children? sitting here chatting away with Mirs Houston in this fashion. It was strange how married folk aye seemed to rush headlong at each other. Here you had millions of single people all crowding out the gravitational waves and all anybody was interested in was another married person. It was actually unfair. Daft as it may sound, it was unfair. I'm not going to bother going, he said, glancing sideways as the car approached a junction. He glanced to the other side then to the first side once again.

Neither of the pair answered until the vehicle's path had been manoeuvered safely onto the main road. You're not going to bother going? said Alison.

The arts centre I mean, I'm no going.

O Pat.

Nah it's just all the faces christ you know what I'm talking about, ye see them all week and then at the weekend you're supposed to meet them all again during the leisure time. Sometimes I find it hard. Desmond and them, Mrs Bryson.

Mrs Bryson just goes home on Friday evenings.

Ah but Desmond'll be there and so will Diana and Joe Cairns.

Alison didn't respond. Patrick glanced into the rearview mirror: she was peering out the window.

Joe Cairns, said Norman eventually, that's the science teacher?

He's *a* science teacher no *the* science teacher, there's thousands of the bastards.

Yeh but is he no the one that played football?

That's correct.

Stirling Albion?

Mmhh.

God sake! said Norman.

At one time there was talk of him moving to Manchester United.

What!!

Was there? asked Alison. Honestly?

Well right enough maybe it was Scunthorpe United. Patrick laughed for a moment. Naw, he said, it was Carlisle United. But they were up in the Second Division at the time.

Norman made a whistling noise. Wait till I tell my boys!

Ach he was good, said Patrick, I actually mind reading his name in the English papers a couple of times. You'll see for yourself when the pupils v. staff comes round. It makes ye sick so it does – *we* all try to kick his ankles never mind the fucking opposition!

The drive continued in silence for some time. Alison said, Why are you not going Pat? You did say you were.

I know. I'm sorry. But look, I just dont want to eh get too tempted with the booze – because what it ends up doing, it ends up making me spend too much time doing things that're totally ludicrous, things that're totally stupid and absurd. Plus my brain's dying.

Patrick could see Norman frowning at that – then he nodded and looked like he was wanting to add something he considered very pertinent but was holding himself back in case it could be construed as presumptuous. And then he glanced over his shoulder at Alison as if in the hope she would say it for him. But she didni. She had been listening to Patrick but she made no comment. When Patrick looked at her in the rearview mirror she smiled at him and he acted as though he took her smiling for granted, continuing on to say: I mean here I go as usual, meeting people in the arts centre for a pint and christ almighty I hate the place, the whole atmosphere of it. And let's face it, some of the folk! Okay I absolve Joe but you've still got Diana, she goes on and on and on about her own subject. That's all she ever talks about, her own subject. Who the fuck's interested! Christ sake we could all go on about our own subjects.

What is it she teaches? Norman asked.

History, replied Alison.

That's the lassie with the blonde hair?

Yes, said Alison.

Any special period?

I think the First World War.

No kidding ye, said Patrick, sometimes I used to go staggering home moroculous drunk from such nights. Can you imagine it!

Unbelievable. Getting drunk and bored like that at the same time for god sake it's almost like a logical contradiction I mean ye wouldni think it was possible.

He swung the wheel too abruptly and apologised once the corner had been turned. That's me gabbing too much instead of trying to concentrate on the road. Yous two talk.

But neither did.

Okay? said Pat.

Alison said, Is that it definite then, you're not going?

Nah. Yous two go. I'll still drive yous but.

Another silence. It was obviously difficult for them; perhaps especially so for Norman because he didnt really know Pat, so this sort of carry on must have been a mystery. He was probably thinking along the lines of:

Is this the true state of affairs? Or is it all a ploy to get rid of me so's he can be alone with Alison?

And the guy couldni be blamed for thinking that. It was partly true anyway. In fact Patrick had gone in a huff, from that moment he eased off the handbrake back when leaving the pub. Its cause could be traced directly to Norman who should have had the gumption to appreciate Patrick was wanting to be on his tod with Alison. He was a brother man. Brother men should appreciate such things.

They do appreciate such things. They just sometimes are obliged to shove a spoke into your wheel. Sour grapes or something. And there was also a certain look on Norman's face occasionally, as of a person secretly enjoying the havoc s/he is wreaking. It was a bit reminiscent of Wringhim in old Hogg's novel. Norman would have to watch himself: one of the dangers inherent to the teaching racket is starting to act out the character parts of the topics you get paid to encounter.

The silence had been breached. Alison asked Norman a question concerning families. He replied. Gradually Norman attempted to involve Patrick by glancing at him and smiling. Patrick smiled back at him. In the rearview mirror he saw that Alison was also smiling at him. So perhaps a question had been asked him. A traffic light on the amber; he accelerated to get across. No polis motors. This was a bad corner. The bastards had a habit of hiding in the vicinity. One time they had stopped him under the pretext of examining a faulty tail-light but obviously they had wanted a look inside the vehicle and to see whether they should bring out the breathalyser. Wee John and Elizabeth – his nephew and niece – had been in the back. He had been taking them to the pictures as part of a babysitting night, a Walt Disney film.

Gavin and Nicola didnt ask him to babysit these days. He would quite like it if they did.

At the next corner.

Pardon?

Just if you drop me at the next corner, Norman said, gesturing at the window.

Patrick stopped the car. After an exchange of goodbyes the bloke got out onto the kerb, banging the door shut. Alison didnt have a chance to move in to the front seat but appeared quite content to remain where she was, gazing out the side window, nibbling at the corners of her fingernails. She looked tired. Some of the classes she had to contend with were not the most easy. It was Old Milne's policy to mete out the more difficult ones to the newer staff. She did look tired. She should probably have gone straight home. But the idea of being able to just sit down for a couple of hours would be very tempting. That was how it was for the rest of them as well; they were just glad to sit down – it was the reason these sessions seemed to drag on so interminably; it was a shame. Patrick waited a moment. Then he said, I think I'll just snatch a very quick pint, before hitting the road.

She didnt say anything.

Naw, he said, eh . . .

Alison sighed. She shook her head and sighed again. Norman went away because he thought you were wanting rid of him. He was right.

Uch come on Alison.

She didnt reply. Patrick blushed. The drive continued in silence.

It was after 6.30 when they arrived at the arts centre and okay to park on the single yellow line. A small crowd had gathered on the pavement near to the entrance, as if they were waiting to greet a visiting celebrity.

Alison continued on into the lobby of the arts centre and Patrick went quickly after her once he had locked the car door. He followed her along and into the lounge bar where the group would be.

And there they all were in the usual corner. Patrick waved and called: See yous on Monday! He gave a smile to Alison and about-turned. Off he went back along the corridor and out through the small crowd, getting into the car immediately and banging shut the door. He felt too bad to be true. Not good. It was not good. He felt not good. But he couldni stay there where he was at the pavement so he shoved the stick into first gear and switched on the ignition, but the engine did not work, the starter not turning or whatever. He switched it off and then on again. But it still was not working, it still

what it was it was the choke; he had pulled out the choke, by habit, in error. He turned the ignition key and first time now easily.

A happiness based on selfishness. If he was genuinely happy it was based on selfishness and was therefore false. The falsity with both Alison and the guy Norman. Norman had been consistently friendly, consistently so. And Patrick had done nothing but punch him on the mouth. It didnt bear thinking about. There were people crossing the road. It didnt bear thinking about. And Alison of course, she was

it didnt actually bear thinking about.

And that temptation! O god. That fucking temptation, that fucking o god and jesus and everything else and everything else; slow down, slow down; just stop and grab up the handbrake nice and snugly and gaze at the pedestrians walking at the CROSS NOW. Nice ordinary beings whose existential awareness comprises an exact perception of all that there is and can conceivably be; that's the nature of it, that's the fucking way of it; and inside the close Goya's unblinkingness, that steady hand and honest vision, a crazy sort of nostalgia. That's the most sentimental drivel in a long time. Have ye seen his face? The face. Have ye seen it? Patrick squinted into the rearview mirror, seeing the devilish cunning to the set of the eyebrows. The lights gone green. So this was the way ahead. He grinned, letting his foot rise from the clutch pedal. But wait a minute. The temporary English teacher whose name is Norman has a wife and three weans plus there's the mother-in-law living with them, and then too his wife has missed her period. This is what the guy was blabbing to Alison about, his wife and three weans and that period. So what does that mean, missed a period, is that a pregnancy? Does it mean they're going to have another kid? Or do mistakes still occur beyond such a point? If not the situation is dire right enough, him being temporary and soon to be back on the broo. That's the way it goes poor bastard, a Bob Cratchit if ever this was one.

Then that story of Dostoievski's! Imagine it! Going up and chapping the bloke's door to see if he'll come out for a pint. And then getting invited in and finding there's a wee crowd of relatives and well-wishers gathered inside, all involved in a sort of party to celebrate the forthcoming happy event as implicit in the missed period. And Patrick blundering around trying to apologise for his conduct. Heaping congratulations and thanks onto his wife, praising the other three children and the proud mother-in-law who was probably quite elderly and large, or maybe even thin and frail. Then the ceilidh dancing would begin and he would be invited to remain and enjoy the proceedings; and he would invite the mother-in-law onto the floor and she would wind up fucking collapsing with a stroke because of the way he's throwing her about during a Dashing White Sergeant for example. Then battling with folk – uncles and brothers and cousins – who've taken offence at the bad jokes he's been cracking; horrible ill-conceived and ill-considered remarks and comments which amount to no more nor less than a very bad insult to Norman's wife, or his wife's mother. That kind of blundering stupidity. Just the actual idea of it! Christ. But it really was what you call going to the brink. Right to the very edge. Bending slightly to see over and into it; the precipice; over into the crater – just bending slightly, perched at the very edge, to see over it, into the very depths, right down and into the very depths. Ho. Jesus christ almighty, it was enough to make
something or other.

A fish-and-chip shop at the end of his street and he went there for a bit of grub; he got a fish supper and two buttered rolls. The people behind the counter were an Italian family by the name of Rossi. Four generations of them took turns working the place although the elderly patriarch hadnt been around for several days now. He was maybe ill. The shop stayed open till past midnight most of the week and the old boy was there the same as anybody else. He should probably have retired at least a decade back but kept on because he liked the company; the district itself – he probably liked that as well, having had to move out to a posh place on the south side to please the family but where he never really settled. So he continued putting in the long hours, much to the dismay of the younger folk who secretly must have wanted to see the back of him because when all was said and done he probably was a bit of a tyrant, maybe butting in too often on affairs that were private, telling the young yins whom they were to marry and so on and were they the correct religion and of the right family tree etcetera and if they werent then hard luck and buona sera ya bastard. You couldni blame the auld yin entirely though because it was him built the business up from scratch; slaving over a hot fucking fryer for seventy years only to see all these young whippersnappers and rascals throwing it to the dogs, the fish suppers and so on, all the rest of it! Patrick was chuckling quite loudly while fiddling with the key in the lock of his front door.

And if the truth be told it was these wee yarns he told himself that kept him fucking sane. Without them where would he be? Up a fucking gumpole.

The house was freezing. He kept on his outside clothes till the two bars of the fire glowed orange. He shoved a kettle of water on to boil, flipped the fish and chips onto a plate, used his fingers to eat it all up with. There was hardly a lick of butter on the rolls. One thing about the Rossi family: their total lack of sentimentality; he had been a regular for fucking donkeys but still there was nothing for nothing. The actual fish was not exceptionally white either although fair enough it was at least boneless. But this grey colour meant it had been frozen far too long. It was not unfresh, just not wholly white and new tasting, i.e. in a place like Montrose or fucking Pittenweem they'd have thrown it back in your face.

There was nothing quite like a good piece of bone-free haddock. And that was something else about being a vegetarian; did Mirs Houston actually give up fish as well as all the rest. You would be better off fucking who knows what, no point even considering alternatives. And yet it was one further instance of control, of gaining control over yourself, over your body, your physical well-being. Doctors had shown that vegetarians would generally be in finer health than meat-eaters. There again which doctors are we talking about are we talking about doctors who are vegetarians and therefore biased? Nothing worse than a biased doctor. And how could eating the flesh of dead animals be better than the other thing? The other thing? What other thing? What is this in reference to? Animals fed for the slaughter and those that are trapped in their own environment ergo fish? The distinction between being a cannibal and the straightforward eater of other human beings where these other human beings are bona fide victims of battle as in bygone eras when flesh of the dead brave was consumed by the victors in the belief that a portion of that courage would become part of themselves. In some countries they would kill fierce beasts for the same reason – lions and tigers, and bits of brave fighting bulls in Spain. Nothing wrong with that insofar as reason is regarded as the be-all and end-all. The Pythagoreans had a few wild theories, never touch a white cock for example which is obviously the same as do or dont touch a black cat. Whole lists of superstitious nonsense although it is wrong to describe them as nonsense, simply the common sense of an earlier stage in consciousness, and no more nonsensical than some of our present-day theories. It is always a matter of sifting the good from the bad, the theorems of reality from the shapes of absurdity. Seek and ye shall find. Old Milne's face when the hands of the clock crept ever on and still the fellow hadnt arrived. Studying the door with that quizzical expression on the fizzog. Confound the fellow, where can he be! How on earth can he have forgotten!!

The very idea he could have forgotten deliberately.

The kettle of water was boiling. His hands were greasy from the fried food and he washed and dried them before sitting back down with a cup of tea. 7.40 p.m. In two hours time he would play the pipes. It wasnt because he had wanted to talk to her about them, it was because he'd had some fanciful notion of playing them with her there as audience, that was it, that was why he had been attempting to manoeuvre things so they would have got away from the idea of the arts centre, to get the temporary English teacher out the road, and then he could have invited her up for a coffee in his place.

And it wouldnt have been difficult for him to play with her there, something very different from playing 'for' her. The distinction was keen, and once discovered self-evidently true. And it probably shed a fair amount of light on the whole subject of the performing player. Or rather, the player who also performs in public. That Dostoievski story again: taking the pipes round to that bloke's house and playing them for all the relatives and well-wishers. It actually made you feel like hiding your face to even think about it it was so bloody horrendous. That brink yet again. He would be as well trying it inside the gas oven. That was what you called a brink. No nonsense about it. Just stick in the head and good-night folks, sorry about the mess on the kitchen floor, putting my big clumsy foot in your basin of fucking jelly. O god and the chest is going going going, the pulse pumping in the temple and the ticking wrists the ticking wrists. That's the recognition of it. That's the recognition, the existential flash; revelation; being and not being; fucking oblivion. Stick in the head and turn on the tap. Just play them in public, play them in public. Like unveiling a new painting. Here is my latest masterpiece. I shall be at such and such a place at such and such a time, just pay your admission fee and I'll be turning up to perform. I shall be blowing the notes; the thing of such timbre, you will not recover, you cannot recover, it shall not be possible to recover. Then there's the set of the eyebrows.

Patrick had his mug of tea and he sat close to the fire, sipping steadily, with a fair degree of contentment. And it might well have been one of these moments of luxurious absorption; so total that reflection was not the thing at all, not at all.

He was tired, a sudden event. It was as if he spent whole days doing natural chores and the build-up from it was so unobtrusively exhausting that eventually there had to come the collapse. Perhaps if he closed his eyes for a wee while he would awaken refreshed. Also, having had the couple of drinks during the day, this helped engender the lurch into dreamland. One further motive for the resignation from booze, the amount of time he gave over to sleep. So much so the term 'sleep' had to be examined, was there something more apposite, what about opiate. Opiation. The brain lulled into opiation through the ravages of alcohol and deep-fried food. That build up of grease and alcohol hardening all the outlets roundabout the heart which has to result in a blockage, the blood not pumping as well up to the brain as it should, thus brain damage, the death of the brain. If the truth be told and looked at unsentimentally then it has to be said that the fish and the chips were not of the best. The Rossis were an okay family but they really should have been throwing the fish overboard far sooner than they did. And here; this is odd; Patrick had a very strange dream about fish some night or other very recently for fuck sake, catching one and trying to dash out its brains on the bottom of the rowing boat because he didni know the ordinary scientific method of death-dealing. He had the poor old fish by the tail but it kept on fighting and slip-sliding its way out his hand and him trying to grip it and then dashing its head on the bottom of the boat until that dirty stuff came oozing out and it was sickening and in that shudder he sent it overboard.

Masturbatory. The 'ordinary scientific' must be the ordinary act of sexual intercourse and so on. Although it hadnt been a wet dream. Nowhere near it in fact. More like a dry nightmare if anything. Best not to analyse such things – especially since it sounded a bit sado-masochistic.

There was a letter to be written to Eric right enough. That was something to be done, if he was really desperate. It was good to keep in touch with folk and apart from Eric he didni really have anyone to keep in touch with. Maybe he should get a pen-pal, a pen-chum, a pen-mate, a friend of the pen, one whose existence

Eric was the only person he remained in contact with from university and probably that was because they had gone on to teachers' trainers together. He was okay, in some ways quite a good guy in other ways a bit of a pest. He taught in a further education college down in East Anglia and was very involved in a club for sailing boats. He was born an Englishman. His maw and da were Scottish. And he had married an English lassie a couple of years back whom Pat had yet to meet. Eric had sent three invitations to go down and visit. Maybe it was now time to accept – if Eric sent a fourth. But Pat owed two letters. He just couldni get down to writing to him. What would he actually talk about! But if he did go down and visit they could maybe sail a boat across to France. That would be good and exciting. Patrick had never sailed on a boat before but it looked great from what you saw at the pictures. And Eric's missis probably had pals she could bring to make up a foursome.

Another mug of tea.

Two or three days, that's all he would have been able to take of Eric. No more. Then they'd be at each other's throat. At least Pat would. Eric would just be slightly taken aback then conciliatory. They were all like that, these middle-class bastards, lying fuckers, so absolutely hypocritical it was a way of being, they never even bothered reflecting on it, all these lecturers and students, so smugly satisfied and content to let you say what you wanted to say and do what you wanted to do, just so long as it didnt threaten what they possessed, and what did they possess why fucking everything, the best of health and the best of fucking everything else. It was a joke, just a joke. But it was pointless being bitter. It was pointless being bitter. Being bitter was fucking silly. Patrick had stopped being bitter. What it did was just fucking stopped you from doing things. At uni it stopped him from doing things. If he had stopped being bitter he might have done things. What might he have done? He might have done things. Obviously he canni be expected to say what exactly these things are. But there are things he would definitely have done and that means he would not right at this fucking moment be a fucking damn bloody bastarn schoolteacher, one who does fuck all in the world bar christ almighty nothing at all. It was them wanted him to go to uni and no him, his parents and his fucking big brother. It was all so stupit. Really, so stupid. He had not wanted to go. And even once he was there it was something else he was after. Something else altogether. But how do you explain that to your family. What – explain what? Explain what you had wanted to do. Patrick had wanted to do something. That was fucking definite. But what had it been? What actually had that thing been, the thing he wanted to do. Something massive, that's all, something massive.

There was no tea left in the mug. He needed another mug, mugful. Or did he? Did he need more? No. What did he need? Nothing.

8 o'clock on a Friday evening. Surely he needed something! No,

he didnt need a thing, he did not need an anything, the thing that he did not need was an anything, there was not that anything that he needed in this world, that anything was not there, it was not here.

Alison and the others would still be chatting the night away at the arts centre. Let them.

He could go and get Gavin out for a pint. They had been going through a less than friendly stage this past while but so what. Go and get Gavin out for a pint. But Nicola isni too keen on Gavin going out for pints. Then go and offer to babysit so *they* can go out for a pint. Or to the pictures or something. Too late. But maybe he could get a couple of cans and a bottle of wine and just go and visit, have a yap — maybe even have a quiet word with Nicola about the certain Mirs Houston because if you canni speak to your sister-in-law who in the name of the holies etcetera.

Or just go down to the pub for a quiet pint on his own, put the initials on the board for a game of pool. Patrick quite enjoyed a game of pool, as long as it didnt last too long because it got hell of a fucking boring seeing that fucking ball go zigzagging about the table all night.

Coffee.

It was pointless spending so much time and effort over Alison. Either he went the whole hog and asked her out or else he fucking let go altogether. She wasnt his last chance. He only acted as if she was.

But that last time he went to a disco was pathetic. He wandered into this place along Sauchiehall Street and it was all kids from the fifth year. O look, there's auld Doyle in to spoil the fun. A slight exaggeration. But most of them did look around the eighteen-years-of-age mark. The only place to go was a pub. But when he went to pubs he drank and he was sick of bloody dranking because you end up doing things that are most odd indeed and also your brains become deceased.

What about a woman of the streets? Was that something to consider? No.

He could renew his membership for the hostels and go tramping across the highlands once more. That was quite a happy time. That was the thing that made uni a less than hopeless place to be. But what about outdoor clubs, maybe there were outdoor clubs, for adult males and adult females. Where you just went for walks and to be meeting each other. And now that spring approached walks up Goat Fell or The Cobbler or Ben Lomond, just to get back in action again. He and Eric used to do a bit of climbing. It was good. Why not start doing that. Why not indeed, but not just fucking now, 8 o'clock on a Friday fucking night.

What he could do was play the pipes. No! He didnt want to play the pipes! Not just now. Not just now.

He had marked the time out for it already. 9.40. Twenty minutes to ten p.m.

There were also clubs where people went. They existed for single parties, divorced folk and widowed folk but not necessarily older folk. And the beauty of it was that those who went to such clubs went to meet others in a similar situation to themselves which meant the initial hurdle had been jumped, and the woman would be there to give the man every encouragement. She would be well aware of the difficulties men can have in establishing that first contact, that fucking leap you always had to make to begin things. Christ, sometimes it could really fuck you the way that worked. But with the woman there to help you along. It was definitely something to consider seriously. He was sick of wanking. It just made him aware of his age all the time. He did not wish to dwell continually on the passing years. Here he was turning thirty years of age. Thirty years of age is regarded as a landmark, a watershed, a stage of departure. At that age Jesus Christ entered the teaching profession and Joseph K worked out his guilt. So here you have Patrick. But to be honest about it the idea of age doesnt worry him greatly. His brother is thirty-three. His sister-in-law is thirty-one. Desmond is fucking ninety-nine! No he's not he's forty or forty-one or something, poor bastard. And the da's fifty-seven and the maw fifty-six.

And then there's Goya!

And Hölderlin, poor auld fucking Hölderlin.

But why wait until twenty minutes to ten to play the pipes? Why not whenever he likes? Why not right bloody now? At this exact moment. Because he was not wanting to do it on a full stomach, his lips covered in grease and his belly full of fish and buttered rolls and chips and oceans of tea. He put two hours as the period of proper gestation. The fish would have drowned by then, and the chips would have merged into his very parts, his very being; it would all have become part of his very flesh, forcing its way into his very character, his very psychology and personal traits being heightened by this solid mass of fish and fried potato. And his very breath.

Not to be charged of fried food when the blowing took place, this was the object. He was after a form of purity in the act itself. A clear wind and a freshened breath – unclouded by the fats of dead animals.

He would have to stop thinking like this. This business of the body. Was he becoming fetishistic? That could be Alison's fault. Before you knew it he would be signing on as a religious convert. It was really unhealthy. This again was bound in with why he wanted out. But did he want out? Really? Did he really want out? It was a jump. It really was. A fucking jump and a half. And one a person had to be sure about christ you really had to be sure about something like that and Patrick was not yet absolutely there on the brink of it, not yet – the pathway perhaps but not the actual brink. Not really. Not at this juncture. He had things to live for.

Things to live for.

These many things.

Alison could of course save him by simply having left the arts centre. She could simply have made her excuses and marched out, head held high and not giving a fuck about the scandalmongers, she just had to see Patrick and didnt care who knew it. Even Desmond.

Could Desmond be described as a scandalmonger? Probably no. The cynical little smile if somebody drew his attention to an article of gossip but he wouldni mind when all was said and done. He would maybe even appreciate it. Maybe he was a guy who wished folk well – even fellow males. Maybe he just had trouble showing his true nature. Poor bastard. It is even possible he wanted to be friends with Patrick. When had Patrick ever asked the bloke if he fancied a pint? Never. Not once. And yet Desmond had twice invited Patrick. So it was definitely his turn. So why didnt he? Because he couldnt fucking be bothered, it was too boring; there was an incompatibility between them. They could never be bosom buddies. And that was a fact. And part of growing up is the ability to admit facts. A fact is a fact. A fact is indeed a fact. A fact, this is what a fact is, a fact. Facts have to be admitted. So let us admit them.

But the truth is it was even doubtful if Desmond was truly interested in Alison. Maybe she would just add to his problems, another woman. Yet it was guys like him usually ended up with the women. Funny that. What could it be about cynical bastards? Was that it their fucking cynicism! Surely not. That would be bad. Maybe he could ask and find out. He could ask Gavin, maybe even Joe Cairns who was also married yet scarcely to be described as cynical, whereas Gavin might well be. Joe Cairns! the tall and silent type but when he lets drop that one word or phrase everybody is supposed to faint with fucking gratitude, just so the pearl of wisdom can be heard the more clearly. A good footballer; that cannot be denied. So what! Nothing except Pat is fond of football, both playing and watching; his preference are the Juniors and he might in fact go and see a game tomorrow afternoon if he fucking feels like it. Joe is probably just silent because he is resigned to his lot, he has settled for secondbest but without confessing it. But is a confession necessary? Maybe a confession leads to suicide. Maybe guys like Joe Cairns are only alive by virtue of their absolute refusal to give in and confess. Why the fuck should he confess. In the whole school he is one of the few persons with an actual belief in his/herself as teacher, and this a silent belief, an assumed thing, not to be spoken of, a faith. And maybe there was a total absence of smugness in this silence. It could simply be a form of good well-wishing. One who has seen the light, hoping that others may too, but not via their direct intervention, i.e. one who leads by example and not by fucking command, by dictum, e.g. the fucking teacher who is a bad influence, who is going about in this unhealthy manner, these unhealthy relationships being entered into between himself and all the pupils, the great magician and all his disciples. Time to play the pipes, time to play the pipes. And Patrick was up onto his feet then bending, crouching, down onto his hunkers, his hands vertically to the bars of the fire, staring in at them, the bars, their orangeness now bordering on whiteness, occasionally crackling at the ends as though about to explode. These dangers of electricity. An inherent danger. Danger inhering in the article, the magnet, being caught between the poles, being caught between the poles. It would be nice to be left that way forever.

Caught between the poles? Not exactly. But yet

Caught between the poles. Would that be death automatically? Or is there a halfway house? a state of total

nothingness for fuck sake. Old stuff. Not worth the bothering.

The healthy; the doing. A well-being; a good-to-be-alive-ness. All such terms for general states of spiritual nourishment. In other words get out the house and stop fucking worrying about oblivion. I mean how unhealthy can you get! How fucking un-of-this-world-ness! Time to cut out all forms of sentimental drivel. And nostalgia. Nostalgia is

Desmond was quite correct. In his usual blunt fashion he hit the nail on the head. The trouble with Patrick Doyle: an inclination towards the sentimental. He would get up off these fucking hunkers immediately and march straight ben that fucking parlour and grab a hold of the pipes! He chuckled and rubbed his hands together, still crouching by the fire.

And the chap at the door!

Loudly as well. Now followed by a flap of the letter-box. Who the hell could it be could it really be actually Alison? no. No. Could it really be? Could it really be Alison. Flap of the letter-box again. And one of these

di di di di di
di di

Who the fuck? Gavin maybe? His father had had another stroke and been rushed to hospital. Poor maw, poor old fucking maw and that was him because his fucking smoking and drinking but mainly that stupid fucking smoking after all the fucking warnings.

Patrick waited a moment by the outside door, his right hand a fraction away from the handle. Then a bustling movement from without and he opened the door at once. A polis. A big guy about 6' 6", rain dripping off the great waterproof coat he was wearing. He stared at Patrick. He said: Is that your car at the foot of the close? After a moment he sniffed and wiped at his nostrils with the back of his hand.

Pardon?

I'm talking about the blue yin. Guy down the stair said it was yours. The polis squinted at Patrick. It's just you've left your headlights on.

Aw aye, god!

The polis was already moving back now, his hand on the railing; he paused at the stairhead. Your battery'll be knackered, he said.

Aye, thanks.

The polis nodded. A wee word about your tax . . .

My tax!

It's alright, you've still got two or three days.

I forgot all about it christ I meant to get it.

The polis was gazing in his direction in such a way that their gazes could never meet; and he swung himself around by the banister to begin the descent.

Thanks, called Pat.

The sound of the footsteps clumping down the stairs and then the man's whistling in a kind of loud breathless style so that the whistle itself could not be heard, just this loud harsh breathing, a song from the current pop charts.

Patrick closed the door, returned to the kitchen and sat down immediately but then jumping to his feet immediately afterwards and lifting his keys from the mantelpiece and going back out into the lobby. He frowned at the outside door, then lifted his anorak from its peg. Into the kitchen, he switched off the electric fire and checked the other electrical points, the gas cooker and oven. He rubbed his chin, to feel the stubble but it would do until the morning. He couldnt be bothered with shaving. He was getting sick of such things. What else? He glanced about the room; he needed his money of course and that kind of stuff.

There were no worries about the battery at this stage, it would be fine, it would start first time. Maybe if the lights had been left on all night but not just the hour's worth. It was where to go he was thinking about. He didnt want to go to the arts centre he was not going to the arts centre; but where else? a pub up the town and look for a bit of company. Drive out to Cadder and visit Gavin. Or the maw and da. He hadni seen them for three weeks. He had forgotten the maw's birthday. She didnt like presents anyway but still and all, a wee box of chocolates or something. That tune the polis was whistling, quite a catchy sort of thing; the weans were all playing it on their walki-talkies. A dancing song. Maybe an omen. Head for the disco young man! Find yourself a healthy young lass who is single and in search of a healthy young lad with a reasonably bright stance in this economic land.

There was pastry down his shirt. Where had it come from. The soon-to-be-elderly bachelor. Drops of decayed food down the shirt-front. Next thing he would be drooling at the desk, becoming senile under the steady gaze of the kids.

But where to go where to go. He was driving along Dumbarton Road in the direction away from the city centre. At this rate he would end up in Dumbarton and that wasnt a place to go. Maybe it was right enough. Dumbarton was the kind of town you passed through without paying any heed and no doubt it would prove to be the brightest spot in West Central Scotland. Plenty of whisky of course. That was one thing about it, the capital of whisky. He could go and get blootered in a strange hostelry and then try and wing his way home, just get into the motor and point the bonnet on a southerly course. And if steering clear of accidents he would arrive in England. Go and see Eric and have a sail in his fucking boat. Anything was possible. He had plenty of petrol and oil and so on – enough to last. Enough to last!! If it ran out all he had to fucking do was buy some more! He was rich. He was a fucking schoolteacher with bankers cards and limitless credit and a fair fucking tidy wee fucking sum in hard paper currency. He was nobody's fool the fucking Doyle fellow. What do you think he went to fucking uni for! That was the thing about settling for twelfth-best, the capitalists paid you a fortune, they fucking showered you with gold. Shite. Luxuriating shite. Absolute fucking shite. Keech and tollie. Keech and absolute fucking tollie! Wooaa there. Wooaaa. The needle on the speedo hitting the forty-five to fifty m.p.h. mark and very heavy rain a-falling. Plus these polis. Thank christ the car was blue and no red.

And Yoker he was now passing through and on, on to Clydebank wherein his first post had arisen upon leaving the teachers' trainers. Happy memories right enough. But reasonable yins; no need for sarcasm. Clydebank is an okay place. Patrick could walk into a couple of pubs and find folk to talk to, expupils and their parents and maybe even a couple of excolleagues.

If this had been the summer it would have been grand indeed. To have been heading nowhere in this set of circumstances, a blue blue sky and a nice mellow sun, still a couple of hours till nightfall, and perhaps heading all the way north with a weekend to spare – that kind of freedom, and maybe a tee-shirt-clad female hitchhiker. No: these fantasies are not good. Cut them out. They border on a very, a very dubious perception of the world. P. Doyle has no need of them. And to see him in the mirror you would probably not take him for more than a young chap of some twenty-three or -four summers. He had nothing to worry about when it comes down to it. See these eyebrows, their devilish set once the corners rise. Imagine looking into the mirror and seeing Goya's self-portrait, that one from the black period, and you had painted it of yourself. You were Goya in other words. You could see into your own soul with total honesty of vision and find the wherewithal to get it down, that steady hand. At fucking eighty damn bloody years of age! That is it! That is surely it. What more is there to be said. Just pull the ladder up behind yous and pause, let us just pause, and consider what such a thing amounts to.

And the swimming baths here at the foot of Kilbowie Road. This was where he used to go for a swim when he was in the middle of a strong get-healthy period. It was next door to the library. Leave that world of books! Grab your trunks and get out into the real mccoy, the genuine elements. Be a fucking amphibian. Away and swim ya bastard. That's the way to do it! Night driving is at its worst when the rain falls like this; all the lights on the windscreen, the altered perception, those blobs blob blob blobbing blob and the swish swish, swish swish, lulling you into something or other, that constant yellow all the time having to stare – to gape; gaping while you drive, attempting to see in a normal manner but having to gape to achieve it. He was being forced into the side of the road!

A massive car on the outside cutting his nose off, forcing him to the side so that he had to slow right down to avoid hitting a parked fucking vehicle. Like a big yankee cadillac or something, here in the centre of Clydebank, the bastards are bloody everywhere. Pat thrust the gearstick into neutral, his foot on the brake pedal, and now turning the wheel – the big car now gone – and returning out and continuing as calmly as possible for this type of event is not something to get all het up about. Totally abysmal driving of course, whoever the fuck was responsible. A colonel from the U.S. Navy or something, away down to check out their neutron bombs at the Holy Loch. A high-powered sales executive travelling north to a selling jamboree. But definitely no need to worry over it; no need to let it prey on one's imaginative faculties. If anything a little sympathy should be extended. That's the kind of bloke who winds up with a coronary at forty. The car as penis etcetera. I've got a bigger one than you. Did such a relationship exist though? In the way people said it did. What sorts of inference were to be drawn on individual cars owned by individual male parties. The bigger the engine the smaller the dick? Perhaps. Perhaps that truly was the way of it. Especially in Glasgow and surrounding environs where maleness was a function of

of what? A function of what for fuck sake! Patrick was slowing again and moving back into the nearside lane, pausing to allow three cars to pass on the offside, then indicating to go right, and moving into a U-turn.

Back to the city. There was no point heading in a northwesterly direction, not at this time of night anyway. And the weather too christ it was just fucking too bad. So the arts centre. But how come? Why go there? Particularly now. There again but, it could appear quite natural, turning up at this moment. They would all stare at him of course and pretend to be interested in a puzzled manner but really they wouldni give a fuck one way or the other. They would just assume he had said cheerio earlier on because his body was demanding food and plus he wanted a quick wash and a shave and so quite naturally he had returned home for just that purpose. And because let's face it yous fucking married bastirts, unlike yourselves he was only gonni be using this arts centre as a stepping stone. He was going on to someplace else afterwards. When yous were away home to watch the fucking telly he was gonni be going nightclubbing. Nightclubbing. Plus of course he did not want to drink too much and get too damn intoxicated, his being a driver and so on ad infinitum forever. Tomato juice was the new direction. This is where the road lay.

He was supposed to have been playing the pipes at 9.40. At 9.40 p.m.

The whole world was going crazy.

Patrick Doyle was not able to make a decision and stick by it.

Stick by it. He was not able to even remember what it was fucking about. As soon as it was done he forgot all about it. That was him and his decisions, as soon as he fucking made one he forgot all about it. Until some terrible inappropriate time such as this second, the thing turning up to remind you how in extremis pathetic you were, incapable of doing what you had decided to do – facta non verba. Actions speak louder than words. One of those sentimental wee sayings that contain a quotum of truth of huge enormity. Actions speak louder than words. It was the kind of ditty you wanted put on a poster and stuck onto your rear window. From now on no decisions, just go and do it. And aye, fucking stick it on a poster and fasten it to the rear fucking window, and let all these mad drivers get a look at it and maybe derive a wee bit of common sense, a wee bit of understanding, make them maybe stop careering about the streets knocking innocent bystanders for six. Calm down. Patrick's chest is heaving. The chest is heaving Pat calm down. Letting things get to you. Red light ahead. Wooaa there. Nice and peacefully. Good. And also allowing the shoulders to not be so rigid. Good. That sort of doioioioinggggg up about the bottom of the neck, doioioinnggg. Shudder. A fucking shiver. Death my fine fellow, its recognition intuitive. Now then: if Patrick were to make a left turn at this corner it would lead him to a pub across the bridge of the Forth and Clyde canal into which he used to go with numerous frequency. Into what? The Forth and Clyde canal or the bloody damn fucking pub! Just shut up and drive. Just shut up and drive to there. Indicate and make to shift the wheel. Although right enough to be honest there isni that much point going to this especial boozer. He hasnt been in the place for years. He probably wont know anybody to talk to. And even if he does know that anybody to talk to, what the fuck does he talk about? He is not able to talk. If he could talk he wouldnt be here. Where

would he be? He would be someplace else. That's fucking straightforward. Plus as well it would make him late for the arts centre and he
had to get there before they all went home. Being too late would be
just too bad to be true. Tonight was a night for company, the
company of those to whom Patrick could relate even when, to whom
Patrick could relate even in, when

O god. Pause. Stop the car. No; drive, just drive, carry on, carry
on, and carry on, carry on and carry on – does Alison have a lap? Does
Alison have a lap!! Does Mrs Bryson? What? Have a lap? does Mrs
Bryson have a lap? Who the fuck cares if she has a lap for christ sake
who wants to nestle in there! Not him anyway. Not fucking Pat Doyle
and that's for fucking definite. And from now on it's definate. It is
definately the case that Patrick Doyle MA (HONS) has definately no
plans for nestling in the lap of the married person Mirs Bryson who
occasionally seems to be giving him the eye which is absolutely not
true the woman just likes him in a maternal sort of big sisterish aunti
routine that is hopeless nowadays, hopeless. That rain lashing down.
But also a nip in the air this evening; if the rain stops you could
imagine it frosting up. It would be very fine to talk Alison into going
away with him to somewhere like England, tonight; to walk into the
arts centre and get her into a corner and ask if she fancies a drive down
to East Anglia, they could spend the night at Eric's place until come
morning with the blue skies they could travel south to Dover. And
thence Calais; and on to the Mediterranean for some sun and warm
seawater and maybe across to Spain, pausing among the Basques,
maybe to Aragon to see where auld Goya was born. But no, it was
time to return home, time to return home. The rain is falling and the
windscreen wipers swish swish, swish swish, and occasionally, quite
occasionally, the sensation that evil entities are abroad, that this very
evening is an evening when malevolent creatures stalk the highways.
It is a night for the warm fireside and the music playing in a friendly
fashion, a nice well-known symphony or a nice homely play on radio.
Maybe Alison is in trouble. Maybe she is walking home right at this
moment, the bus left her off at the wrong street accidentally and she is
having to hasten along, not wanting to go too quickly lest she draws
attention to herself but hold; and she isni sure – is that the sound of
soft, soft footfalls, the soft foot falling, the lurking evildoer, a sinister

shape at the closemouth, in the yellowing glare of the old gaslamp, waiting there, waiting there, and then the echoing clip clip clip of her highheels as she turns the corner. Alison! For fuck sake watch yourself! There's danger up there for christ sake danger ahead, Alison! And the screeching tyres of the highspeed motor car swerving corners and hitting pavements at ninety-nine miles per hour in his lastditch attempt to get there and fucking rescue the heroine, the hero, Master Patrick Doyle. And yet a lassie like Alison who regards herself as more than a match for anybody, male or female, this can be the kind of lassie who ends up in trouble – challenging herself to walk down the darkest alleys at as slow a pace as possible in order to prove the point, just to show she's got her head screwed on the right way and is well up to taking care of herself which is how come

It was high time he had a new motor car altogether. With a new motor car things would be better. Because if Alison had, by some weird stretch of the imagination, agreed to a drive to East Anglia it was fucking all too probable the engine would explode before reaching the damn border. It wasni only the doors that were going bad, so too were these other things, they were going bad as well. Different noises were becoming audible, getting made to become audible, the kind of noises that made you shut your eyes in immediate reaction. You heard them when turning a corner too fast or when sometimes he coasted to a stop with the engine switched off, that distant gentle thudding. Sometimes he wakened in the middle of the night with this really horrible feeling, a cold dankness smothering him, then gradually piecing it all together he would become aware of the motor car, it was that that was causing it, the motor car. Hopeless. A hopeless fucking vehicle. A no-longer-good vehicle. If it ever had been good. He had bought it privately through the newspaper car-sales pages. And if certain facts are indeed admitted, he probably only did it that way to impress the da and big brother. He usually

who cares.

The rain looked to have become a slush. An ice-rain, piling up on the lower parts of the windscreen, getting packed by the wipers. He was sitting forwards on the edge of the seat, head craned near to the windscreen, gaping into the glare. This ice-rain – sleet. It was sleet. Sleet a-falling. Not a night for driving. Definitely. Especially down that deathtrap of an A74 with all these bends and roadworks and these big picketmurdering artic lorries right up your arse. One time Patrick helped Gavin out as co-driver doing a fair-sized flitting for one of his neighbours and they hired an oldish three-ton van from a guy Gavin knew. It was a terrible drive. The van was overloaded and you felt the thing swaying as if about to topple over when the camber was out. And nobody gave you any fucking quarter either. These drivers, some of them are crazy. And then when they're sitting behind you! having to hit up to eighty just to keep your nose in front. Terrible. And in bad weather even worse.

The sleet storm could mean that the arts centre mob would remain where they were until late, having poked their heads out and seen the state of it.

We'll give it another half hour, says Desmond, and just see if it goes off.

Good idea, says Alison and back they all trudge, not especially wanting to return but better that than braving the wintry elementals. They will have had enough of each other by this time, stifled yawns and so forth, the occasional surreptitious glance to see if any acquaintances from other walks of life are in the vicinity.

With the new car he would certainly opt for a stereo hi-fi radio and cassette; whizzing along there listening to music or talks or taped radio drama, relaxing, tapping the fingers on the wheel the way you see other folk do when they're stopped at traffic lights, and that pleasant look of soporicity, soporificity, a Latin root; sopor – sleep. Those drivers whose gazes are aye vacant. Pamp pamp, pamp pamp. Toot tooooooot! O pardon me Charlie I was listening to the fucking in-car entertainment. Taking your mind away from itself, allowing the being to relax; thus driving becomes a pleasurable activity, something akin to smoking dope, the pipe of peace, slowly but surely the company lulled into slumber, the eyelids drooping, drooping, them trying o so hard to stay awake but no, they drift, drifting off into sleep, a pleasant soporicity, soporificity. The type of thing he never achieves. His fucking mind is always going this way or that way and he just never is able to get down and relax somewhere. Or even just becoming so totally exhausted that you collapse, that would suit him, just to collapse, after a momentous mental or spiritual task. Such as playing the pipes. Through that sort of act, attaining that sort of peace. But it all sounds so hopeless. It makes you turn from the actual thought; something you do not want to admit of – but it has to be faced, and with a smile! A brave smile. But get rid of the distancing. Stop trying to widen the gulf between yourself and the playing. You must approach it as arranged. Twenty minutes before the hour of ten. That remains the time. For sitting down and playing the pipes. I know, yes, but these things must be faced, the very notion itself being that wee bit, just that toty wee bit somehow well foolish, foolish, aye, that's it out now, okay:

One grabs a pair of pipes from the rear of an arts centre and proceeds to blow sounds, and these sounds seem so perfectly stated that the pipes themselves are henceforth transformed, they are become transcendental objects, instruments of music! instruments of something greater than anything previously experienced, anything acted upon with you. With you.

What was it about that sound? as a matter of interest just. Was it something in the hollowness of tone? Was it something

What was it?

Such questions but, they cannot be formed in an authentic sense when the actual objects are divorced from the context. In order to realize their nature they have to be blown, the sounds are to be blown, the pipes must be blown. The pipes being the sounds of course. Hold onto that. And so what if you do have to resign. P for Patrick Doyle Esquire, a single man, a bachelor; a chap with little or no responsibilities. A teacher who has become totally sickened, absolutely scunnered. A guy who is all too aware of the malevolent nature of his influence. He is the tool of a dictatorship government. A fellow who receives a greater than average wage for the business of fencing in the children of the suppressed poor.

That's the way of it, really.

And then you look at fucking auld Goya. Look at Goya for fuck sake, a man and a half. Ten men and a half! Still going strong there at seventy-five years of age, and that twist of the eyebrows. Ah for christ sake good night messrs one and all for this is indeed the way of it, the very essence of it.

The Clyde Expressway.

The sliproad up from Anderson Cross.

He was on the road to England.

Okay, settle down now; stop chortling, although:

Patrick, having opted for the M8, and now being on the road to England but it could be the road to Edinburgh or even Stirling – or even fucking Easterhouse and Barlanark – being not yet beyond the boundary of the city itself; and also

he was going to England.

No he wasnt he was going home, he was returning home. Maybe by way of a local pub, just for the one pint before heading upstairs to bed. He was drained, in a state of exhaustion. Such a long long day. When had this day started. 7 o'clock in the morning? Who could believe in such a devilishly hard thing to believe. It was positively disbelievable. $\sqrt{4} : \sqrt{2}$ always found such

How to get home. He should immediately snatch at the Fruit-market turn-off, head back down the Castle Street route, along Cathedral Street. That is the escape for someone in his predicament. Then why has he not fucking done it? Because the mental bastard is still on the road to England, and not stopping. How come he's doing this? Whom is he trying to impress? Alison canni see him. She has no idea. Nor will she ever find out about it, about this great feat of derring-do. Not unless he fucking tells her!

But what is he doing it for?

And there now yes, the road to Stirling on the sweet sinister and there now yes, full steam ahead on the right, he has fucked off, he is making a bid for freedom. He is feart to face Old Milne on Monday morning. And there you have it. The heroic Doyle. Feart to face the fucking headmaster. In case he gets a row!

The Garthamlock turn-off. Are you not taking that either? No. Well, why bother even talking. The road to Edinburgh is soon and he will not be taking that yin too. He has decided to drive south on the road to England. So there you have it. Okay. It can be on his own head. Let it be on your own head. Okay then. Nobody in his right mind would know what to do with him. Let the damn fool stew in his own bloody fucking goose. Draw a veil over it. And so he continued thus, avoiding the road to Edinburgh, and onwards, straight ahead for England – maybe just to see how far this fucking rag tag and bobtail of a motor would take him because maybe it wouldni even get him as far as Ecclefuckingfechan, maybe no even Lesmafuckinghagow! Ha ha ha. So goodnight, buona sera ya fucking donkey.

And so he continued on.

Okay.

But his teeth were chattering. Mind you, the sleet had long ago stopped falling and the windscreen was good and clear, the wetness having given it a great clean. And the fucking engine believe it or not although this is definitely disbelievable if anything is, the engine sounded beautiful, of a crazy nostalgia of a sound. And why the fuck shouldnt it be healthy I mean for christ sake he had it fucking serviced less than three months back so's it would get him through the winter. Regular servicing is one of his better habits. He even used to play squash! Nowadays the occasional game of table tennis. Perhaps after all it really would take him across the border. His teeth chattering once more. A distinct manifestation of the existential leap. Here he goes, into the vast unknown. Hang onto your hat! He will not do it. He'll never get beyond the outer reaches of greater Glasgow. Such a thing is scarcely possible. He has always lacked a certain bon vivre, a certain affirmatio, a certain

Patrick Doyle, drove right out of Glasgow, late that Friday evening. He had decided to visit his old pal Eric who teaches in a technical college somewhere in the East Neuk of Anglia, not too far from the sea, where he has a boat. And upon awakening tomorrow morning Patrick would knock the fucking boat and bid adieu, continuing ever onwards, south to Dover thence Calais, Paris, Marseilles, Aragon, Barcelona, Pamplona and a quick stop off at Guernica just to see what's what.

Ah christ Pat, call it a day. Away you go home. But look, just eh

And slow down slow down; the car moves too fast, far too fast. He has been driving as if to keep abreast of the high-and-dry fast movers on the outer lane. That is always pointless, especially in an elderly vehicle.

There were no lights now. It was sudden and it was dark. And the peace! It was so bloody quiet! He was beyond the boundaries, beyond the outermost motorway route to Stirling and Perth. He was on the M74 and heading south, south, south to the English border, home of the Auld Enemy, now curtailing the speed to a steady fifty-two m.p.h., which gave time to think and reflect, time to become accustomed to the blackness, of using the headlight beams. Eric would be glad to see him. And it was high time he re-established contact. It was bad of him not to reply to the letters the guy had sent. It really was bad. And then never having met his wife. She was probably beautiful. Eric was quite lucky with women. He used to get into 'scrapes' with them, these occasions where he was involved with more than one woman at a time. This lassie called Mary Busby who used to in Patrick's opinion humiliate herself because she knew Eric had the other involvements and she would just more or less wait for him to finish. Patrick used to talk to her until one day he realised that she actually didnt like him. My christ! That was a terrible feeling that. And it was fair enough because she had recognised he was patronising her – Patrick had been patronising her. He hadni realised it until that very minute when he could see she hated him. Fair enough. The trouble is of course it's not nice having people hate ye. It's actually horrible. Once or twice it happens with schoolweans. Not too often thank christ because it is not good.

So little traffic around. The weather was pretty bad of course. Plus it was that quiet time between 8.30 and 10.30 in the evening. Just wait until the pubs closed and all the fucking idiots emerged from here there and everywhere, zooming, zooming – the headlights way miles behind then suddenly at your back and passing, passed, away now in front, the red dots, over the brow of the next hill.

The humming of another big articulated lorry. They all seemed to be enjoying this lull as well; a real peace and quiet; and when they passed and indicated Patrick flashed the headlights in reply, enjoying their double blink of acknowledgment, the drivers settling back into their own daydreams, putting forward their plans for the future and reflections on the past, where they had gone wrong and how come here they were where they were, at this moment in eternity, driving down the M to A74, towards the latter end of what had been a fairly depressing winter.

But it hadnt been too depressing. There had been a nice couple of things. And Fiona Grindlay of course who was in sixth year and given birth to that wee baby then had stayed on at school and without divulging the name of the father. That was good. And a couple of nice arguments with the fourth year that no matter how sentimental gave him a wee glow – a bit like your first sip of whisky when that whisky is a fine single malt, a nice thick one from the Inner Hebrides, and you've just come in from a slog across the hills, maybe even a climb. Which is what Patrick would wish for himself just now, right at this moment, he would wish himself into a small friendly hotel whose bar stayed open till the last customer left, and Patrick wouldni leave, he would remain forever. But it would be something very special being in such a place with a woman you really fancied. The thick peats burning in the fireplace, having to avert the face slightly from the fire because it is so hot. And a nice pint of draught beer on tap and maybe a nice sort of late meal to come, with a bottle of cool wine, then upstairs to bed, but even lingering say, if it was with Alison for instance, being relaxed and cheery the way sometimes he could be with her, maybe looking out and seeing the bluishblack of the sea, the solitary lighthouse beam flaring away to the southwesternmost point, a couple of seconds interval, making its own pause, allowing the two folk to settle into it, that kind of tranquillity, that rhythm. She did have the knack of getting him calm, making him calm himself, getting him to calm himself, and become towards his best. And his best could be fairly amusing in not too loud a fashion – quiet asides. They could be sitting up in bed doing it. Doing what? Pat chuckled. He shook his head. He had been sitting back in the normal driving position but he sat forwards now, the rain having begun again, and quickly came streams of it down the windscreen and he had to shove the wipers onto motorway-action, awaiting the next turn-off. There was only one thing worth bothering about and that was the truth of the matter what was the truth of the matter was the truth of the matter 'love'; love, was that it? Love? Love. That was it out in the open now. He was in love with Alison Houston. And he wanted to grab a hold of her. If he didnt grab a hold of her bad things would happen.

So, what was to do? What was he to do? He laughed – a sniggering kind of guffaw. But no wonder! So, what to do? One of those romantic carry ons? stealing her away from under the nose of everybody – her and her husband sitting there watching the telly and the door goes and when it gets answered, in bursts Patrick and he shouts, Okay Alison. Coats on! That's us, we're leaving.

Leaving?

Aye, right now.

What about my husband.

Fuck him.

And she gives Pat a huge smile, but very somehow underplayed at the same time because she is saving the main bulk of it for when they are alone. She rushes out the room to pack her stuff.

Dont waste time, says Patrick, we can hit the department stores first thing in the morning. The department stores. It sounds like something out of a Hollywood picture. Patrick shook his head but he was grinning. He had to remember and concentrate though because the road conditions were abysmal, really abysmal. And sitting hunched forwards like this aye made you stiff and cramped, stiffened shoulders and cramped back muscles, down at the small of it, the back, at the foot of the spine. He felt exhausted. An actual physical sensation of acute tiredness, as if even just shutting the eyelids for ten seconds would genuinely help matters christ just ten seconds. Being able to stretch right out! The legs and the arms and wrists, the fingers – instead of this having to drive nearly pressed right into the windscreen with your face in the glare and getting that cold blast from the demisters somehow hitting the crown of your head, never a good sensation although it can keep you awake and alert when you are driving and you shouldnt be driving because you are too tired to be good at it, too exhausted to actually

Alison's husband always said nothing. He stood in the background. It was possible he had a deeply rooted inferiority complex. In the company of teachers a great many folk suffer the same problem. Teachers intimidate people. He was a funny sort of bloke in some ways and didnt remind you of a high powered salesman at all; he was more like something else, an undercover detective perhaps, working for the Economic League or Special Branch, or MI5 and the CIA. It was possible. Everybody knew they had all infiltrated the educational establishments of the entire country, and that includes primary schools and nurseries. If Alison

Ah christ.

He dropped the gear from top to third to second, slowing at the roundabout up from the Motherwell sliproad, returning back onto the M74, heading home to Glasgow.

How to progress through the rest of the night. He tried reading, different volumes, and then listening to foreign stations on his shortwave radio. It was all useless. His mind was just too totally crazy. At one stage he thought he was going to burst out greeting. He had been sitting with his toes toasting at the fire and had managed to read nearly two pages of a book, the memoirs of an old politician, and then he had to stop and start and stop and start and at last shut his eyelids so tightly, so tightly, to halt the tears. Now, that was something about Kierkegaard. Patrick had never quite managed to trust him for it; and it was that, it was to do with that; but just leave it there, just leave it; and dont even get it out, what you are thinking, close to thinking, dont even try it.

He shut the book and was fiddling about beneath his chair. What was he doing he was looking for his shoes he was going to go out again. Where was he going, to the boozer probably, he felt like a pint, a last pint, or maybe two, the two pints, if he swallowed that down he'd sleep alright, the sleep of the just. The just fucking knackered. Where's the shoes. The shoes have walked. The shoes are over next to the bed. But he was fucking knackered. And why shouldnt he be, out fucking teaching all day. It was something that annoyed him, the way a lot of bastards scoffed at the work teachers performed in return for their time off, as if they didni deserve it. Bastards. Fucking bastards. He closed his eyelids and strode the three paces to the sideboard so that when he stopped and opened them and look straight ahead he would be looking into the wall mirror and seeing the two little fuckers there in front of him, his eyes: look into my eyes, especially when they're fucking your own, look into them, see the sharp lines of light, the way they mock you, the little bastards, your eyes, what the fuck do they look at all the time, what do they see, do they perceive, when they are not honest and not steady, when they are fucking dishonest and always fucking not being steady.

The pipes. In all their majesty of colour. The bright silver and red and black. Shiny and fine. The painting had been a good idea. It was a freshness. Perhaps as well as if he blocked up the ends so that the sound would be more correct, without any too much

There existed very long saxophones from years ago. The player sat on the chair like a cellist; that same sort of feeling to it as well – unlike for example the way a harpist would be: the whole act differing in a very fundamental sense. Although harpists are fine. There is nothing to be said against harpists by any means whatsoever.

Patrick lifted the thinner of the two and he returned it to the floor and he lifted the other and carried it, in leisurely fashion, across to the bow windows, there being a pair of them in this room, the front room, what the old folk referred to as the parlour, what his grandparents had referred to as the parlour, the room wherein nothing occurred but the dusting of irrelevant objects twice weekly or monthly as the case may be, in that of Doyle P., never. Would his grandparents ever have had sexual activity in the parlour? Did this type of query take the form a family would acknowledge as valid or would it be recognised at once as unsound, an inauthentic entity that already proved beyond the shadow of a doubt the massive gulf between on the one hand this university-trained younger son of the household

And yet, he does precisely the same. This room has no function. It is an appendage. There are large numbers of homeless people and Master Patrick Doyle has this room wherein nothing takes place.

Sentimental drivel.

No it isni.

Sleet again, pelting the windows. He liked to stand here staring out but aye took care to have the curtains partly drawn so not to be witnessed from below. A lassie used to stand at one of the windows across the street. It's not that he was a peeping tom, but if she happened to be standing there then Pat enjoyed seeing her, but kept back so not to be seen; it would be awful to be seen. Imagine the headlines. Singleman found peeping out window. Patrick Doyle, schoolteacher and bachelor was today found guilty of being a peeping tom. Such improper conduct cannot and will not be tolerated, said Mr Milne, headmaster of the school in question. No excuse for it either. But it was just one of these aspects of the single, the solitary — probably if he had been a married man he would have spent half his life jumping up and down in broad daylight, naked.

He replaced the pipe next to its mate. He went out into the lobby and picked up the telephone receiver and dialled seven digits and after a short delay his brother had lifted the other receiver and said: Hullo?

Gavin?

Aye.

Pat.

Aw hullo. How's things?

Fine. How's things yourself?

Okay. No bad . . . Want to speak to Nicola?

Okay.

Hang on and I'll get her.

Alright. Patrick took the receiver away from his ear but was still listening carefully, gazing at the coat and jackets on the pegs facing the front door. Then movement and Nicola:

Hullo. Pat?

Aye hullo eh I was just . . .

Everything alright?

Fine, aye. Naw it was just, I was trying to phone the parents earlier on but I kept getting an engaged tone.

Did you?

Aye and I was just wondering if you'd heard anything yourself.

Is that recently?

Well it's about an hour ago.

You should try again.

Aye, I was just thinking it was a wee bit late.

It'll be alright Pat, it's no even eleven yet.

True.

And they're usually up till midnight.

True.

. . .

. . .

So how's school?

Aw fine, fine. How's the wee yins?

Elizabeth had the cold.

Christ.

It was just a cold.

Is she okay now?

It was just a cold Pat, aye, she's fine.

Is she back at her playgroup?

She was only off for one day! You know what like she is.

Yeh . . .! Patrick smiled. And how's wee John?

Aw! Need ye ask!

Okay?

Yeh.

Good.

. . .

. . .

So when you coming round for your tea!

When am I coming round for my tea, I'm coming round for my tea any time ye like!

You always say that and you never do, you make excuses.

I do not.

Yes you do.

Patrick laughed.

Listen, we're having some friends up a week tomorrow. Nothing fancy. Bring your own bottle.

Sounds good.

So you'll come?

Aye.

You can bring somebody as well of course I dont have to tell ye.

Great; good.

So you're definitely coming?

Yeh.

I'll hold you to it then.

Fine.

Tch, Pat, you're a pest.

Pardon?

A pest.

What do you mean?

I mean you'll no come, that's what I mean.

I will.

No you wont.

. . .

It's a week tomorrow. Any time after eight o'clock. But you could come at teatime and get something to eat.

Great.

You'll let me down if ye dont come.

I will come.

Well you'll let me down if ye dont.

But I will.

After a moment Nicola said, Gavin's telling me to tell you when's the next game of table tennis?

Aw! Aye – christ.

He says there's no to be any excuses this time for getting beat.

Ha ha ha.

You've just to give him a phone and arrange it. Alright?

Aye.

Any time's fine for him.

Great, I'll remember.

. . .

Okay then cheerio Nicola . . . and he shoved the receiver down, away from his ear. And there had been no chance of her saying anything further. There was nothing she could say anyway. Yet another impasse. Getting beyond it might have meant a total breakdown! An emotional collapse! Patrick smiled. But he did find it very difficult being honest with Nicola at times. This is because he found it so easy. And stick Gavin and the weans in alongside her and he found it impossible, the whole thing, sitting there with them all as a family group.

And them feeling sorry for him! Terrible – absolutely pathetic in fact. Imagine being pathetic. Imagine being regarded with pathos by your family! For fuck sake, wee brothers should not be pathetic they

[77]

should be solid bastards, rocksteady; the backbone of the community, filling all these minor posts in the church and armed forces.

The Teaching Profession.

Yes, fuck it, the teaching profession fits that fucking bill nicely, exactly and very ably, a tight fit. Heraclitus would be proud of him. High time he entered politics in fact, the New Member for Glasgow Central, setting society to rights; jus dicere on behalf of The Royal Majestics. Or else fuck Heraclitus he could take to the streets and become an urban terrorist, an urban fighter for freedom. Who was stopping him. No bastard.

He was in the kitchen filling a kettle for coffee although coffees too late at night often stopped him from getting to sleep and probably the very last thing required tonight was not to get to sleep. But for christ sake he was knackered. Tonight had been absolutely shattering, everything about it – shattering. It would be no surprise if he wound up sleeping straight through till fucking one o'clock in the afternoon! He did have a can of Ovaltine right enough. Maybe that would send him to sleep. His maw swore by it. Imagine swearing by Ovaltine! Fuck you Ovaltine.

When Patrick was dead.

Woooosh woooosh! Woaa wooaa. Ssshhh for fuck sake ssshhh ya devil, ya fucking devil, ya devilish besom. Is that you Goya ya dark auld bastard, with that twinkle to your eyebrow! Look at them all dancing! Nobody could call it a dance! It's a form of ritualistic stepping which must end in human sacrifice. See the faces! O fuck. O jesus christ you're dead ya bastard.

evil

evil

evil

Patrick likes to run the faucet, the Northamerican tap. He turns the tap and dashes out the water. EEEevilLLL. Evil is as evil does right enough. Look at the auld tollie swallowing his son with such lipsmacking enjoyment! And yet it's a kind of ornery enjoyment. A bit like what you'd expect from a cheery old boy who enjoys getting up to mischief, merry pranks and so on. One of these ancient bleery bastards with big red noses, the type that beautiful young lassies seem to like so much. But if somebody such as Patrick was to act in the same manner they'd all pounce on him and fucking tear him limb from limb, limb from limb.

Get out! Get out!

Tonight *is* a night for suicide but. Anybody would have to admit that I mean just let a psychiatrist appear on the scene with a sharp analysis of the driving. Had the client set out to crash bang wallop the motor? Did he set out to attain death? Was the opposite of self perpetuation the object of the exercise? The opposite of self perp

What about a prostitute? A prostitute was sensible. Surely a prostitute was sensible? If it came right down to it and he did really feel as low as all that and the notion that female company, that

Not all the pubs would be shut. Up the centre of the city they stayed open till later. Half eleven. He could go out the now and snatch a couple of pints no bother, and if he really was as lowly

Plus what he could do for example; a quick wash and shave and fresh clothes and then off up to a latenight disco, to just fucking try one for fuck sake nobody's asking more that. But what about the depression never mind the depression the depressings. And it's no as if people have got these mammoth expectations. Just to see you're making an effort, that can be enough. It would be enough for Gavin and Nicola. So long as they know he isni fucking giving up. So long as they know he isni a fucking pathetic specimen I mean nothing's worse than that, nothing, nothing is worse than that, nothing, nothing at all. Get the coffee made, and made strong to keep you alert, an indication of your intentions, that you intend doing something of an optimistic bent. And obviously a prostitute is nothing to be ashamed of; it is quite common-sensible – fairly rational, as a proposition, as propositions go for christ sake, at least rational ones. There is that aversion of course which is also fairly rational, to do with the imagery, of a succession of pricks. But so what? If she is clean? If they were clean? What possible difference could that be from the same one going in and out all the time? Apart from the obvious A.I.D.S.! Venereal disease for fuck sake anything!!

The temporary English teacher would be at home just now with the wife and the weans and the grannie. They would all be sitting in front of the telly, in the middle of a movie, The Wizard of Oz or The fucking Sound of Music, a tray full of various sandwiches, cakes and chocolate biscuit. Happy Families. The television is good for that sort of carry on, everybody being together without having to communicate conceptually. People have suggested Patrick buys a television. And he has been considering it. Televisions must be good for loneliness. When you are lonely you just go and switch it fucking on. Simple. Nothing to it. And then you just relax with your eyes staring straight at it. But it could put you off reading and listening to music and what Pat likes is playing music and reading books at the same time which is a bad habit maybe but very comforting. And comfort is important. He is not getting any fucking telly unless comfort is guaranteed. Do you guarantee comfort with your tellies? No! Then away and fucking fuck yourself Charlie!

Even discussion programmes on the radio, Patrick can listen to them while reading. Probably just for the company. To avoid the

gaps. It is gaps.

And what about the pipes?

Fuck the pipes. It was a weanish notion from the kick-off. He would simply discard them. A not uncommon occurrence. But is that really true? Well it seems to be, even although it is the sort of trait Patrick approves of and here he is having it himself for christ sake he isnt a total failure, what do you expect, everybody's got at least one thing going for them. He was reading this short story recently and the guy in it tried suicide, hacked away at his throat for ages with some kind of fucking supposedly sharp-edged instrument though obviously it was blunt as fuck; the usual, suicide as a last-gasp action rather than a considered event, something you prepare for. How did young Werther accomplish the deed. It is a couple of years since Pat read the novel. And the parallels! Christ, he hadni even thought of that. Young lover on behalf of beautiful-but-not-to-be-got young lass. Had she been spoken for? Was she actually a married woman? Could that be true! Christ. Right: no suicide till you rush out and re-read the book!

So God is dead is he, well well well.

Where did that come from?

Hölderlin was once alone in the same room with auld Goethe but didni know who the fuck he was because he was only there to meet fucking Schiller and was so excited he wasnt able to concentrate!

Amazing these coincidences in life. You could actually just be walking down the stairs and something totally amazing could happen to you. Such as? Away ye go.

Such as?

Away you go.

Well how come the pipes are finished? They arent finished. Why was it a weanish notion? It wasnt a weanish notion. It was not a weanish notion. There was something about them, at the very outset. It can be recaptured. There was also something else about that night, a kind of oddness about things. Was it an eerieness of atmosphere! Fuck off.

But there was definitely an oddness, a strange kind of dullness – like the senses had been dulled and things were being viewed via that of a perception unable to give colour to things. It had been cold right enough. And draughty, at the back of the arts centre. And yes, Patrick had certainly been shivering – no joke when you're having a pish. And it iced up that night as well because some poor bastards were having trouble with their starter-motors on Wednesday morning. Patrick hadni; that side of affairs is quite good as far as the mechanics of his own motor is concerned. It got him right through the entire winter. Which is more than can be said for so many of these bastards with their big highpowered efforts. Pat's motor is okay – if it wasni for the fucking bodywork it's the bodywork that lets it down.

The coffee was cold. He had a whole mugful of it sitting on the edge of the fireplace and it was cold, the entire contents, the exact 100% of all that there was and could conceivably be, there in his mug, cold, with its regalia of the english monarchy, imperialism's holy of holies, leaving aside the fucking vatican of course, not forgetting the kremlin, plus of course the fucking white house, then again you've got the fucking zionists. Patrick sipped the coffee. It was a good idea to sip the coffee. Healthy. The life force. Plus as well it's aye interesting to watch how the line of skin affects the inside of the mug, as it shifts and makes its way down. No doubt it was such an enterprise that inspired Copernicus, stuck away in his tower and getting upset at folk. His relations had something to do with it. Did he have fucking cousins that didni get on with him or something. At one point he was living near to the Hook of Holland. Is that right or a load of fucking rubbish. The Zuider Zee. That must be a nice place to visit. How far is it from Jena. Plus you could visit that museum-cum-monastery on the northern section of the Germanias wherein you may find there ancient literary treasures of the old Irish-Scot scholars, that would be fucking good fun. I know: let us get up and go ben the parlour once again and we can look at the fuckers and see what there is to see, if there is anything at all, anything remotely of interest.

Pipes Two. Painted in Bright Enamels. Of the colours Three. Silver Red Black.

And the thinner yin:

okay, fine. Pat stretched out his arm, aware of the weight at his wrist, the weight of his hand or just the strain there because he had been sitting with the arm in question at his side for so long and he lifted the thin one up, as an aid to its description just. But it was not easy to describe at all. Once you had said pipe you had named the world. Consider the panpipes: they have been performed on by mankind since way back at the ancient of days. Aeons. At least six thousand years. And men have been playing the pipes. And here you have Patrick Doyle MA (Hons). What about a pair of fucking bagpipes! No, sarcasm doesni work. He laid his hand on the pipe. Maybe it was just another aid to the relief of sexual tension. Anything was possible in this life. And playing music has always been medicinal, psychotherapeutic. Maybe this was the key to the entire meaning of art. Of course. Obviously. Soothing the troubled soul.

But all of that which is necessary. All that is required. That is integral and essential and not able to be hidden, that must be to the fore, that has to come right out and enter the

Enter yourself ya bastard. Play the fucker. Before it is too late. Fine. What is done is just that Patrick raises the pipe to his lips and closes his eyelids; he blows a very long and very deep sound; just one, lips compressed, eyelids shut tightly, and tears springing there at the corners, like a form of ecstasy, something that has sprung from way out of and has relaxed these shoulders and eased that terrible terrible fucking tension, just got out from under that pilloriedness, self-pilloriedness, self-flagellation, that Goya one, something there maybe to do with the flagellants but now away there away there, just there, there, there, getting further and further away, not a great distance but a distance, definitely a distance, just enough now so that he can open the eyelids, the eyes maybe and just blink a bit, and a smile of sorts, looking at the pipe and smiling to it, an old friend and a treasure. It was time to walk to the windows and peer out at the side of the curtain; and he breathed out, a sigh; it was followed by a shiver, a shuddering movement of the shoulders, a wee convulsion. Dear dear. Dear dear. The rain falling steadily. The halo round the streetlamp.

It would be good to report that that night's sleep turned out to be one of these smashing, all-embracing types of sleep where the body and mind both feel relaxed afterwards but it had not been like that, although neither was it the precise opposite, where you feel like a gang of baddies has been booting you about for the whole seven hours.

A breakfast might have been useful. He did have a packet of Weetabix in the cupboard, but not enough milk. There was no point in stocking a lot of milk. He only really drank the stuff at breakfast time – discounting coffee of course, he still preferred milk in coffee. Although in tea it didnt bother him either way. Milk-buying was a habit he never seemed able to develop. Perhaps if the maw did give him her old fridge. But that was an awful waste of resources. Then as well if she did give him the thing he would probably stuff the freezer bit full of raw meat and poultry.

Having a snack bar in the vicinity would be good. Glasgow is very short of snack bars. Why did the Rossis not seize the opportunity and open at the crack of dawn so that the solitaries of the district could arrive for coffee and hot rolls & croissants and salami on rye and maybe a couple of fucking bagels, like they get in all these great wee cafes in New York. Elderly couples meeting for a chat across pots of steaming coffee and hot pancakes with maple syrup! Fucking Mark Twain and Peter Pan territory, Never Never Land, sentimental maudlinity. Uch no, auld Twain was better than that.

Even if resignation was not the answer it could be a good idea to jump on the panel for a fortnight, just to get things into perspective; it would give him time to set forwards a plan of some description, a way ahead – even if he could just map out the next three months, once the summer arrived it would be all over. And yet resignation for christ sake what a temptation.

And it always would be a temptation. How could it be anything but? To resign from anything is good, is exhilarating. Just like, for instance, if he was to resign from Monday morning's interview with fucking Old Milne. It was a while since he had been carpeted. Ach well, no point worrying about such things. Old Milne was a bit of a headbanger but apart from that. Even resigning from a family can be good and exhilarating. One of the better decisions Patrick has ever made centred upon the leaving of the family domicile at the start of his second university year. No matter that he was to stay in a house less than a couple of miles from where his parents lived it wasnt his fault if the university was as close as that. It had been a wise move and necessary to a fuller realization of his male potential i.e. that he could become involved with women properly, or at least come home steamboats.

One straightforward decision concerned Mirs Houston: it was henceforth silly getting hot under the collar about her. She was the wife of another and that was that. A more practical plan might involve these singles' clubs where single people meet. But whatever and no matter, the whole carry on, it was something to treat in a less serious fashion. There was a lot of truth in the old cliché about sex being a comedy; it was best Pat found something to smile about, the way married couples were wont to, seeing the entire palaver as a joke; something to share a laugh over, something to be enjoyed in its differing aspects, and not something to crack up about. So much of life concerned sex and its attendant miseries and mysteries, its laughter and its heartbreak. Why get involved? Obviously he would get involved and indeed wanted to get involved, but

but a problem was one of banality. Once you started in on the subject as a method of easing your mental condition, once you began looking at the situation; aye, it did seem so totally banal. In itself this was encouraging; it meant the problem was not specific, it was run-of-the-mill and not to be taken too seriously. And even aside from the sexual aspect it was better leaving Alison out of the question. What was the point in harbouring feelings as burdensome as he did? It was far better to seek out a proper object for his affections. It was just causing him fucking pain, to be honest about it. If he actually could be said to love her then it was just time to fucking not love her, or else to be doing it in a less pervasive manner.

He went down to the wee dairy at the corner of the street to buy a paper, also something to eat because he was fucking starving. One of these individual breakfast trays. Terrible efforts. A lump of square sausage and a lump of round black pudding. A wee dod of currant dumpling and a round slice of haggis haggi feminine. To be frank about the carry on, this was a breakfast he enjoyed tremendously, never mind about Alison and her fucking vegetarian hostelries. He was a heart-attack man and that was it finished. If she wanted to save him from himself then that was fucking her problem.

Once the frying pan was fairly hot Pat placed the pieces of food inside and waited. He could have counted three hundred and then turned them onto their other sides, a further three hundred and drop in the egg to fry with them. Yet okay, the thought of lettuce and cucumber and tomato, healthy portions of cheddar cheese; that had crossed his mind; he was thinking in these terms, maybe for tomorrow. I mean he wasni really that fucking interested in becoming a genuine vegetarian he just fancied getting fit. Not in a daft way. Pat had never really been that interested in going for the swimming, jogging, bicycling, running, hopping, skipping routine; but just to get reasonably fit and healthy! that would be good. Get a regular game of table tennis going with Gavin once again. That last time they played together he had been easing up and trying to let Gavin win and then suddenly he wasnt having any say on the matter, Gavin was fucking running him ragged. Of course he was an ordinary married man and therefore an active healthy male unlike Patrick who was a flabby eunuch. But big fucking brother also smoked a lot of cigarettes and could drink like a fish so fucking explain that one. Some things are fair and some things are not fair and this is a thing that is not fucking fair, and what more can be said except praise the lord if you're a lucky bastard.

But just to be reasonably fit and healthy. Just to be in a sound condition. To maybe have a wee go on the pipes. To maybe have a big go on the pipes. A genuine go. That was something. To even just think about it was something: for it must be admitted that in the cold light of an early spring morning, the idea of the pipes as musical instruments and so on. Which made it the more crucial to contemplate.

Seeing the young woman in the dairy had something to do with it, when Patrick was down getting the grub. She had been standing chatting to the older woman behind the counter. She had a baby sitting on her hip. She had short blonde hair and lived three closes away. Pat saw her quite a lot, usually in the launderette on Sunday afternoons. The baby was aye with her, as if she didnt have a man about the place, whether deliberately so or not.

In juxtaposition to the pipes.

Being sentimental had nothing to do with it. It was just a matter of taking it all seriously. Because let us be frank about something: this is what it involved. It was *the* issue. He had to take it seriously. If he didni he was finished. And irony could have no part in it. Irony was death. And trying to work things out in advance, that was the last thing to do. He would just be there to do it, to accomplish it, what he was to do. Other folk could discuss the other things. Being a teacher caused people to spend their lives worrying out concepts, postulating this that and the next thing, all manner of hypothesising. The further from activity the better. Please allow us to conceptualise your problem, thus we can attain a sensation of nourishment ergo that your problem, though not yet solved, has been conceptualised, which is tantamount to a solution of course. That kind of shite. Challenges that must always remain academic. Causes you can throw yourself into. The efficacy or otherwise of reprinting the full unexpurgated twenty-four volume edition of Wilson's TALES OF THE BORDERS. Tremendous. Earthshattering. Existencestopping. Lifebeginning. Getting a bunch of wee first yearers to think you're the smartest guy in this here universe then off to the staffroom for a brief but earnest discussion with the peers. Great. And onto the local boozer for a quick bout of mutual backslapping and a vegetarian lunch. And a halfbottle of whisky when nobody's looking. Aye, we've all done it. Smashing, great, fine, yes, and now go and enter the various nooks and crannies, take a look at your ceiling and then take another look at auld fucking Goya and relate that to your fucking life and the way you're quite content to perform the fencing-in job for a society you purport to detest right to the very depth of your being. Sentimental keech, according to Desmond. The kind of comment that always comes from those whose true desire is steadfast inactivity, those whose one lust is for the absolute maintenance of the status quo, and their own wee remunerative numbers within it. They were probably laughing at him last night. He didni give a fuck anyway. But even Alison. When it comes down to it. And this is a fact he must admit of sooner or later, that the delectable Mirs Houston is aye prepared to sit in that company and to not go rushing off when Pat goes rushing off. She doesnt. She is happy to sit on chatting about fucking Xmas Panto-mimes when he is not there, when the company comprises Desmond and Diana and fucking Mrs Bryson and the temporary English teacher. His presence is not at all necessary to her enjoyment of the socialising, amongst her cronies of the teaching racket. It is these types of facts that Patrick wishes to be capable of admitting. It is these types of facts he must be capable of admitting, if ever he is to achieve a genuine vision, a genuine honesty in his method of continuing. And let us further admit – and it is a corollary of last night – Patrick Doyle continues only insofar as he desires that he may continue. If he seeks to fucking die then he dies and that's that. It is the easiest thing in the world to crash the fucking motor at seventy miles per hour. And dont think he doesnt know about that possibility because he does and he has – o christ since way back when he was doing his Christmas Postman as a student and earning the money for that selfsame damn bloody fucking licence. The incidents of last night relate directly to the moment. He was not in a state of befuddlement. He was not of a disorderly brain. A bit neurotic but nothing unusual in that and nothing for fuck sake in the slightest extraordinary about it. Most of yesterday evening could occur at any time of the day or night. And this is important to remember. And last night was a Friday night as well. Thus today being Saturday. Saturday.

Formerly the finest day of the week.

Saturday!

Hurrehh!!

Three cheers for Saturday!!

But not nowadays. Nowadays it is a day for recovery. Nowadays it is a day he could stay in bed and nobody would notice. A day when, if he felt like it,

And what did that Russian poet say about doing things as opposed to having them done to you? But what about Oblomov. Then that auld Cynic who wouldni get out his fucking bath! Quite right. Pat likes having baths as well. But it's not to do with that. But there again, the whole world is obliged to rise from its place of repose. Patrick is no different. Except that he gets paid a better than average wage, et sumptu publico, which can be said to apply to everyone in one way or another. He has become scunnered by the carry on, that is all. The process has been gradual. Or has it? It hasni really. In some ways it seems to have in other ways no, in other ways it has crept up on him and then let fly with a crack on the fucking jaw.

Is there a party at whose door the blame can be lain. Apart from the fucking obvious. The schoolweans dont seem able to comprehend the obvious. Although no doubt they go rushing straight home each day to inform their parents of the day's indoctrination who then pass on the information to the proper authorities, the name Doyle P., being filed under something or other which is not very good in terms of promotion e.g. Subversive Blasphemers: One Who Seeks To Overthrow The Present Government And Do Away With Plutocracy And An Hierarchical System Based Upon Monarchy. Plus other things as well of course, not excluding the daily denial of the deities. Which deities? Any fucking deities. When it comes to deities Doyle isni fussy. For christ sake even blowing the pipes could get him listed; an early-warning sign of senile dementia – coupled with that suspicious state of bachelordom while in charge of the nation's children; a bloke who would probably, if the truth be told, be much more at home sitting in the queue of the local DHSS office. What the fuck was Old Milne wanting to see him about? Whatever it was it would include some paternal advice of course. Old bastards like him seized every possible opportunity for dishing that kind of stuff out. Aye well Patrick has plenty of paternals of his own. That was the last thing he needed, another of the bastards. Plus what he didni need, what he did not need, not at all, was another Alison. In the cold light of day, when sexual gratification has receded into the distant horizon, when he is once more of the disposition

In fact, she is not even what can objectively be described as 'good looking'. Dark hair and dark eyes. She has been described as 'beautiful' but at certain oblique angles at certain times of the day, Patrick has been totally flabbergasted to see

Fuck sake she is just woman and that's that. No paragon there. Nothing to get all het up about. Also her political stance, it is somewhat innocent – naïve is a better word. She believes the future exists! Unbelievable! So why then does he have this urge? Even in the cold and watery light of a late winter's morning, a day such as today, he can imagine her speaking, actually imagine her speaking, listening or looking right at this very moment, and that smile she has, which is sentimental tollie, all adding up to the following:

Alison Houston has been available for some long time now but having become scunnered by the procrastinatory nature of potential lover number 1 (Doyle) she has opted for potential lover number 2 (Desmond). And at this moment, at this very moment, while her husband is out of town on a selling jamboree, the two of them, they are sharing a bed maybe, lying beneath the big quilt, her just absent-minded there and smiling at nothing at all, moving slightly, her

When Patrick was a boy

Get out of the house.

The house is not a place to be. Get out of it. There is the great temptation. It is not to be spoken of. Because once stated it has become part of something or other – reality. Patrick stood to his feet, of course, smiling. He turned to face the kitchen door and he began to walk to it, to place his hand on the handle, opening this door, this door that can lead into the parlour wherein lie the pipes, or else the front door if he wishes to don an outer garment and he is continuing beyond it and into the parlour, this room wherein the pipes, in their constant temperature of let it be known roundabout the fifty-six to sixty-two degree mark Fahrenheit and this thinner of the two which he has lifted and seems to be examining is in fact the one his fancy aye leads him to but this morning it is the other, the thicker and the heavier, that is demanding the playing, that is requiring a form of attention. This thicker pipe was more enjoyable to paint, its space being vaster. Patrick now sitting on a dining chair, the pipe propped onto the left toe of his shoe. Once balanced correctly he covered the top opening with both hands, his mouth compressed into the right one, and the barest fraction of a gap only, and if he could stop that up too he was looking to do it, but it

and he had begun the sound high in his mouth, back near the gullet and up at the roof, and it was a kind of soh; and he lowered it, the sound now nearer the gums, a deeper note which he continued till his breath was giving out but he broke it off calmly before arriving at the gasp and he breathed in deeply but regularly, eyelids shut, no frown etched into the forehead and no smile. No nothing. Just getting on with making this sound he was making as if it was definitely everything in itself just to accomplish.

It took a wee while to reach beyond the moment because reflection not being possible and it being something he had to take absolutely for granted, no smiles even; not to take any risks because there was not anything at this stage worse than not getting it properly, not getting the thing done in its proper fashion, the nature of it not being sustainable, not sustainable, and then he was standing, now across to the window, no rain but looking set for it later, summing up how this winter had been, everything about it, even solid snow would have been better than continual rain, sleet, slush, soaking into everything and keeping folks huddled into coats and anoraks, hats and umbrellas so that they even found difficulty in seeing each other let alone engaging them in conversation. Maybe that was a basic explanation for Patrick's state of mind. It would be good practice just to slow things down, just to take it more easily, be less aggressive with ordinary everyday details, petty items that cannot be helped. He shivered. The room was quite cold for people if not for pipes. He smiled, returning ben the kitchen. A coffee. Heat the toes at the fire.

A coffee, yes. It was not a bad kitchen. It was quite not unhomely. People wouldnt call it unhomely. Would a woman call it unhomely? Maybe a woman would call it unhomely. The last time his maw was here she shivered. What was wrong with that, everybody shivers now and again. In the middle of a fucking heatwave! Nah it was actually November, on her way back from visiting the da in the death ward at the Western which he had fortunately given the go-bye and got well and so on and left his cares behind, including death, ha ha.

Escape from the head, that was the best policy. The weekend had begun a while ago. It was almost Saturday afternoon. Okay. A time of the week for enjoyment. Of course it was. A time people anticipate with great pleasure. Certainly not a time for thinking: what the fuck happens now! or roll on next Friday so's I can go for a publunch with a bunch of fucking schoolteachers. He had reached to the mantelpiece. What for? For a notepad and a pen. He was catching himself in the act of writing a letter to Eric. Imagine writing a letter to Eric? on a Saturday morning, only minutes away from Saturday midday, that great time of magic throughout the football-speaking world, when you hit the boozer for a couple of jars just prior to heading off to Ibrox or Parkhead or Firhill or Love Street or old Shawfield if the Clyde ever return. Well well well, and here he is about to write a boring letter. How are you and here is how I am and the school and do you ever do this and that and the next thing because it reminds me of when a few years back and the rest of it when it seems as if life was occurring whereas now for christ sake the very idea of writing to Eric. He was long overdue a reply but so what. Fuck that, a fucking Saturday, and you're writing letters; he'd be as well returning to school and marking a stack of ink exercises. Okay. So

but poor old Eric, two letters and no response, he probably thinks P for Patrick has taken the huff at something because he used to be no a bad correspondent and now here he is, never a peep. So what. Who wants to fucking peep. Pat has never peeped in his fucking life and he doesni fucking intend to start fucking now, if it's alright with you I mean d'you know what I'm fucking talking about I mean you dont have to fucking bloody damn christ you know what I'm fucking talking about – right. So

So: what was he going to do he was going to write out a list of things to do, that he could do, this afternoon:

1) Football match; Clyde versus Raith Rovers. Always a good game between these two so that was a real possibility.

2) Phoning up Gavin to see if he was doing anything. He could

be going to a game – maybe to see the Thistle, but if Clyde were at home the Thistle would be away. So that's that. Gavin doesnt stray too far because it means leaving Nicola with the weans. In fact, these days, Saturday afternoon was becoming a time when they did things together, these two. He could phone up and offer to babysit, then they could make a real day of it.

3) He could do something else. He could go out and maybe go to the Art Gallery or else go up the town and see if he could buy himself a pair of shoes. O dear, why is life so exciting. He could go and sign himself in at a highclass hotel and kid on he was somebody else. People did that. They signed themselves into hotels under assumed names and had a laugh, pretending they were members of BOSS and the CIA and so on. So fucking belaboured with boredom but that was the problem. Pat grinned. He crumpled the notepaper. Life was daft at times. He uncrumpled the notepaper. In fact the football was not a bad idea. He ticked it off.

And Yoker Athletic was playing at home today. The sign had been up when he passed along Dumbarton Road yesterday evening. He could go and see them. He had a soft spot for the Yoker since working in Clydebank and an expupil had played for them, a good midfield player with a tremendous shot. He used to take their penalty kicks and their free kicks. It was a couple of years since he had left the team for pastures unknown. Patrick never saw his name in any team lists, so probably the boy had just not made the grade. But Yoker was a good wee team at present and they were playing the Perthshire; a tough match was in prospect. Okay. Or else he could fix the car! That was an outstanding chore. Chores. What the hell job did he tackle first? The rust or the fucking hinges of the door. He could maybe start by giving under the bonnet a good cleaning and oiling, then sand down some of the panel rust and consider using the Cataloy. He would have to buy the Cataloy. Okay then. Also there were some wee jobs needing done about the house. That terrible draught coming in the kitchen window so a putty round the frame wouldni go amiss. Dirty washing to the launderette of course but that was a Sunday job. He could go up the Barrows and have a look through the secondhand books and records, and also their antiques. He knew fuck all about antiques but this maths teacher by the name of Bill Todd went regularly and was supposed to be making a small fortune, finding stuff which he then resold to dealers apparently. It was a good hobby and with luck he hoped to finish with teaching forever. Good luck to him for christ sake you had to wish him well. But on a Saturday afternoon! Browsing among antiques! The guy deserved to succeed with that kind of tenacity.

Have a bath and listen to the sport on the radio. Take in a couple of books, maybe blast out some music.

No. And the one omission from that list of course suicide! Imagine failing to mention suicide. Plus he could maybe buy a wee something for his maw's birthday. He should at least have sent her a card. The da would go in a huff about it – very subtly of course, it would take Pat the rest of the week to appreciate it had actually happened. Ah well, it was his own fault. If people wanted to go in the huff then they could go and fucking fuck themselves.

Maybe there was an artshow on somewhere. But what if he had been an artist himself! Being an actual painter! Or sculptor! What age was Meurier when he kicked the bucket? What a fucking stupit expression! And why worry about folk's ages. That is the problem with being lonely, dwelling on the advantages and disadvantages of living on into a ripe old age. And most of these painters lived forfuckingever – never mind Goya, look at auld Pablo and Renoir. There again but, it is perfectly laudable that such as the elder Rossi should retain his overriding interest in the affairs of the family business, that, okay, such as Goya should remain so interested in the fate of humanity, Picasso spending all his latter years on sex and female beauty in general, and the old Eubie Blake still tickling the ivories at a fucking hundred odd years and telling everybody if he knew he was gonni live so long he'd have taken better fucking care of himself.

They were all dead now right enough – apart from auld Rossi. Maybe Pat could murder him and get in the good books of the rest of the family.

He picked a book down from the shelves to the side of the mantelpiece. When he opened it at his mark he was aware of the cold in his fingers and he saw himself as Ebenezer Scrooge with death impending, the icicles spreading up the joints of his old bones. Christ that was a horrible way of seeing at yourself at the relatively young age of twenty-nine. Twenty-nine! Christ almightly he's a boy, a boy – what's this talk of death all the time! Just turn up the fire full blast and if you really are cold then switch on the oven and leave the door open. The place'll be hot in seconds. There isnt any point in being economical in these matters. Hypothermia isnt the property of the elderly. Other people can have it too. Normally he wasnt a skinflint by any means but lately, lately it could seem to be the case if other folk had chanced to witness his actions in particular monetary situations. Take for example the manner whereby he allowed the temporary English teacher to buy him drink after drink and then be content to have Alison buy him the next yin, without getting a further round in on his own behalf. But there again mind you, he never ever charged petrol money for all these trips in the motor. It was aye him having to drive everybody else about, a chauffeur without the uniform. On ye go James and dont spare the fucking horses. And nobody thinking to say O here ye are Paddy my boy, a couple of bob towards the price of a gallon or three – plus the wear and tear on the engine and bodywork for christ sake because all that running about costs dough. And then the time involved.

A bang on the landing outside. The neighbours' door.

Patrick was in the lobby and listening at the keyhole. With a wee spyhole affixed things would be even more interesting. He could have witnessed the actual intruder! All so fucking fascinating! Was it a murderer out there? less than four yards from where your man was now crouching . . . sshhh . . . hear that muffled breathing . . . ssshhh . . . a beautiful and enigmatic woman . . . a door-to-door seller of evangelical merchandise.

That creak on the lobby floor! It was another oddjob he might undertake; two or three nails in the floorboards and that would be that. But this kind of task was doomed to be ever beyond him. Especially after these past few days. In fact, when it comes down to it, last week was a bastard, and worse was to come – the future!

And yet the temperature had to be rising surely. March for fuck sake I mean things like sleet are a joke, a joke. March is the basic spring according to many, the month wherein that season begins, that month which blows away the last of wintry chills and coughs and sneezes. There was of course something he could do right at this moment in time, he could turn the fire on fullblast like he said he would and also the oven fullblast with the door open and in general be turning this place into a fucking hothouse cum sauna, a really cosy place to be. He did have it in his power to make of this kitchen a warm and very pleasantly habitable abode. Not even bothering to go out the entire weekend but just remaining here at home, nice and comfortable, going about in the semmits and the swimming trunks, the summer sandals, beating nature at its own game. What was it Schiller said in reference to that? Or was it Heine? To do with defeating it, nature, overcoming it, developing your own aesthetic. And the irony of it was of course

He aye seemed to be thinking in terms of irony nowadays. Was this ironic or was that ironic or was he fucking ironic, in relation to himself, or what.

In fact, if he did transform the house into something really warm and snug he could don the summer casuals and start playing the pipes properly. He was about getting beyond the self-conscious stage and there was no question that a genuine well-being resulted from it. No question, that it calmed him down; a bit like how masturbation could be, at its best, as a retrospective appreciation. Yes. Just sitting there and playing the pipes, with the room at its most comfortable i.e. nice and warm; it would be good, and conducive to it. What he had fancied doing, back when he found them – and now he could bring it right out into the front of the brain – what he had fancied doing, or even just as a sort of mild consideration, just as a consideration, a way of maybe looking

what he had half, deeply down had, occurring to him, was the notion of doing something on the pipes that warranted performance. There you have it. He had fancied the idea of reaching such a pitch/level that he could put on a sort of performance, just of him and the pipes. A type of arty crafty avant-garde affair but so what, fuck off with your fucking inverted snobbery. What he could do was hire a large room somewhere and send out invitations to folk. It wouldni be too difficult. It sounded mad and vainglorious; as if he thought he had something unique to offer. But he didnt at all – although there again, it might be said quite easily that just being an individual human being was a uniqueness, that individual human beings were as unique as each other; a race of specifics in non-specific terms – in which case

And also another thing

what the fuck was it? the other thing, it was to do with a relation, the expression of a relationship; it was to do with this and it was very important, crucially so, and for that reason best left alone, not spoken about too much.

And now, there, that was it, and getting away, getting right away from that terrible stance, that irony; it was good, it was good. Because that was always the fault, that was always the way of it with him, everyfuckingwhere, with the family and all the rest of it this continually seeing the mirror image, casting doubt upon your motives. It was hopeless. Perhaps; perhaps, it was an idea just to go over a great many things and see what and why, what had happened and why it had happened, and what was to be done. Even on a big issue such as post-university existence I mean for fuck sake surely the parents could not be happy with that? Never mind Gavin! A huffy bastard at the best of times. But had he been expecting something? What would a brother expect? Something especially outstanding? Or just another cop-out, somebody else selling themself to the system. All these sentimental questions. The all-important fucking fundamental ones.

There is no time for sitting about. On the other hand of course it is essential to realise you have all the time it takes. So, then,

And as well something not good even about that, that fucking So, then, like that, really not good, not good at all, best just.

He had to curtail it. He really did have to curtail it. He had to stop himself at all costs. It was that important. Because it was no good thing, it was no good thing. A very very bad habit, a very very bad habit and it was fucking what was it like it was like fucking whatever it was it had to stop it had to stop. He had to stop himself from doing it, it was something that was not good, just not good, and he was up from the chair and into the lobby, where the telephone in repose, nestling away, the telephone, its own tiny existence, awaiting its next though not unenforced, its not unwelcome

He dialled the number of Alison. It was of course unlikely

And the receiver had been lifted. It was Alison, saying: Hullo?

Eh, is that Alison?

Who's speaking?

Eh Pat. Pat Doyle. I was just eh wondering, the thing about last night eh the arts centre, about me going away and that; I was wanting to apologise.

Yeh.

. . .

Pat?

Aye eh just really, that I'm sorry.

Good.

Aye. And what I was thinking, I was wondering, is it alright to speak?

Of course, yes.

What I was wondering then eh about whether I could meet ye, about something. To talk to ye about something.

. . .

Just to talk to you about something.

To meet me ye mean?

Just to talk to you, about something in particular, and eh

When were ye thinking of? Things are quite hectic at the minute.

Fine eh it doesni actually matter.

When were you thinking of though?

Eh well

It's only because I have things on.

Fine.

. . .

Eh.

So it would have to be tomorrow.

Would tomorrow be okay? I mean what it was I was just actually wanting to talk to you, about something.

What time?

Well just to suit you eh maybe what about twelve? Is that too early? A Sunday. If it's no convenient I mean, is it too early?

I'll get used to the idea.

Pat laughed then. It was just good and a relief. Everything. And

[97]

her voice sounding really okay as well, and it was making him have to force his head to go sideways and his eyes closed for fuck sake but he opened them again and he was nodding, he held the receiver nearer to his mouth. So eh just about meeting, I was thinking maybe, the People's Palace?

The People's Palace?

I think it's open on a Sunday. Maybe I mean if we met at the Barrows we could just walk along and see; if it was shut we could just have a coffee or something, in a cafe. What do you think yourself?

I think we should go for a coffee at the start, when we meet.

Of course, aye.

What about say The Commodore?

The Commodore?

We both know it.

Yeh, fine.

Is that alright?

Aye. Fine. What time again?

Twelve o'clock? That's what you said.

Fine. Is it okay I mean?

I'll get used to it.

Pat grinned.

And his receiver was down. He had managed to get in a cheerio, but only just, before the receiver was down. It was stupid, to put it down so abruptly like that except his heart, not being able to cope with it, daft; too much. What was going on for fuck sake he was not

He strode ben the parlour. And to the windows, hands clasped behind his back, surveying the pedestrians below of whose existence Descartes had once required to doubt; quite rightly, the walking coathangers and so on. Descartes used to settle down for the night with his little garret extremely snug, getting everything aright prior to the evening's doubt – and what about the dancing shadows on the wall, cast by the glow from the fire, the guy who's been lying on his back all his days and thinks a person is a shadow on the ceiling; these are a different type of questioning. Shadows on the wall are different. They are distinct, from actual people.

Alison was fine. Much more in control of the world.

Patrick inhaled a lungful of fresh air but did it too quickly and had failed to empty his lungs first so he did a wee exhalation and then a wee inhalation and began again. The idea of not even being able to breathe properly was just a fucking joke really and he smiled, and then chuckled, before exhaling as much breath as he could from his body; and he paused before inhaling, and he inhaled very slowly and calmly, taking in great wads of new air, sending this fresh oxygen flying through his brain. Then he turned away from the windows and strode back to the kitchen, and back out into the lobby, to the bathroom, because he was now having to empty the bladder at once, if not sooner had he been an elderly chap with prostate problems, not something to joke about touch wood touch wood.

And a football match a football match! Holm Park and see the good old fucking Yoker! Who were their opponents for christ sake! Did it matter! Not a whit, not a bloody damn whit! Okay. Fine, that'll do, and let it go, let it go, easy, easy, easy oasy, a nice easy oasiness, scarcely moving at all, like a hibernation, one bit of oxygen lasting ye god knows how long, and just being able to move with as few movements, acting with as few exertions, just biding, biding

It was a good day, and that was a surprise; and it exemplified much of what was going on. It went side by side with things. There were two things always and just now one of them was this being a good day. Ideally Patrick could have had the two things out in the open so that he could compare them – even just to have seen them side by side, that he could have known he had seen them so that in the future there would be these two things that had happened and he had known and borne witness to them. Perthshire was the opposing team. They came from around the High Possil district and if Patrick minded correctly their own football park had one touchline about six feet higher than the other which was great if your team was hitting in corners but rubbish if it was the other mob. Anyway, Holm Park was not like that. The pitch was really muddy today. It was great. The full-backs came sliding in with mammoth upenders of tackles, leaving deep scoops out the ground and one occasion nearby the touchline a big guy came crunching in on this poor other guy and he goes crashing to the deck, a big shower of mud came flying through the air and the spectators had to fucking all duck in case they got spattered. It was fucking marvellous and made everybody laugh. There too was the sound of the guy peching when he finally got himself onto his feet and trotted back down the field. You could see the gash down his shin, the blood and the muddy streaks, that especial whiteness at the bit where the studs had erased the outer skin. He was a lanky big guy and he reminded Patrick of an inside-forward who used to play for Partick Thistle years ago, back when the family lived in Maryhill and the da used to take him and Gavin to some of the home games. It was a teacher he reminded Patrick of. Not any teacher in particular. It was just something about the way he looked when he got himself back onto his feet and trotted back into the fray. And the way he played the game, an attitude to it, as if the playing was just some strange sort of obligation he had, and that absent determination. Patrick felt the kinship. He had felt an awful pity for him at the same time and dreaded the moment the ball was passed to him. He couldnt watch the game because of it, not being able to look away from this man. And he couldni have been more than ten years of age at the time and yet recognising that something. It was something important.

But was it something good? Probably it was fucking something bad – a stupit fucking self-consciousness. He was probably just a big self-conscious fellow who felt he was just too skinny and lanky to be playing professional football, he was all knees and fucking elbows. And Patrick felt like greeting. My god. Imagine a ten-year-old boy wanting to greet about something like that! How in the name of fuck had he managed to survive the next fucking twenty years. Christ. He was a poor big guy but. And he was out there doing his best. The sort of player who hears every last shout from the crowd:

Ya big fucking flagpole ya cunt ye! Gone ya big fucking flagpole! Ya big drainpipe! Heh look at the state of that cunt man he's a fucking drainpipe, look!

And the poor guy blushing as he attempts to hit the ball round the full-back and ends up tripping over his own two feet.

Look at the fucking poof! Heh you Hen Broon, ya fucking dickie ye! Your maw's a fucking shagbag, she's a darkie ya cunt! Beautiful cries from the heart. Gone ya fucking dumpling ye ya cunt ye couldni score in a barrel of fannies! A what? A barrel of fannies. A barrel of fannies? What in the name of christ!

It had taken him another couple of years to work that yin out and he would have been best left in ignorance. A barrel of fannies. It was enough to put ye off sex for the rest of your life. A case of the shudders everytime he thought about it. What was it like at all? a barrel of fannies – was it actually a nightmare, a form of male nightmare?

A man with a hat and a mournful face was standing a couple of yards from Pat. He looked like the stereotype of a hardbitten football journalist. Or a scout. He could have been a scout for one of the senior clubs. But no, definitely more like a journalist. Unless even here you were getting the fucking CIA or the fucking MI5. Dirty bastard. Here he was infiltrating one of the last bastions of ordinary life. Journalists were a lesser breed than teachers. Or were they? maybe they were on a par. They all sold out. What the fuck difference did it make. At least the MI5 were proud of being fascist rightwing bastards.

He had his hands in his coat pockets, the man, gazing at the play, his head turning to follow the flight of the ball, a cigarette wedged in at the corner of his mouth. And his mouth had a meanness about it. A kind of a crimped look there, in the lips.

Shocking!

To say that about somebody. Just because of the physical characteristics of the face you make snap judgments on personality, how the person makes his or her decisions, how they move in the midst of their fellows. Desperate. It is just not fair. It is not good. It is shocking.

Patrick missed the only goal of the game at this juncture. And serve him right. He was shaking his head and looking in the direction of his shoes, and then the blokes roundabout were cheering and applauding and waving. Yoker had scored. And what a goal as well according to everybody: their winger had cut in from the right and chipped the ball over the heads of the defence and back to the eighteen-yard line where the striker caught it on the volley and bump, straight into the corner of the net, a fucking beauty. And you aye remember goals. It is a fact one does not hesitate in admitting. There

[101]

was one Patrick scored when he was playing for the BB and it was a real fucking beauty although painful, a header, but him letting the ball bounce that wee bit instead of actually meeting it on the attack, which is the correct way of using the nut, you have to go and meet it and not let it come and crash against ye. Joe Cairns said that as well, about remembering the goals you scored. He didnt talk about football very much but when he did Pat liked to be in the vicinity. There was that good yarn about when he was with Stirling and they were up for a cup game at Ibrox and holding them to a draw right up till the last couple of minutes and then the jammy bastards got their usual last minute Loyalist handshake of a penalty. So typical. So absolutely typical.

Junior football was much better. Although some of the suppor-ters there were just as bigoted and fascist and some of them were fucking maniacs. Pat was at a game just after Christmas and he was standing down near to the corner flag; up comes a player to take a corner and the entire section of the crowd nearest started clearing their throats at him, dollops of catarrh. They were all men as well, no boys. Frightening. A shower of catarrh. Worse than a storm of hailstones.

There was one goal and I missed it.

That would make some fucking epitaph right enough! Missing the only goal of the game. But who cares. Life just cannot be taken as seriously as that. Otherwise it becomes too much. It becomes a total burden. Pat's life

Pat's life! Who the fuck cares. In the name of all that is and is not holy, that becomes as holy.

The man with the mournful face was looking at Pat. He was actually looking at him. It was funny. No it wasnt. But just as well paranoia was not a problem. No doubt he was an emissary from the education department of Scotland, sent to keep an eye on the chap Doyle who fails to turn up for headmagisterial appointments on top of everything else, these ghastly rumours, the chap's political beliefs, it seems he's agin the government. How awful. How absolutely fucking awful and incendiary. Dont tell us the bounder dislikes being a teacher! Dashed uncivil! And he has the dem cheek to stand up in front of children! Old Milne should maybe not have been ignored though. Patrick has probably shown him disrespect. But he deserves disrespect. That is the thing he deserves, disrespect. Him and his fucking flapping MA gown. Auld Clootie come to haunt the weans. The wee first yearers going to the big school for the first time and meeting up with that sort of reality. Middle-aged warders. Middle-class warders – policemen; professional wanks on behalf of institutionalised terror. Institutionalised terror Patrick you tell them! Aye I'll tell them, dont worry about that. What happens is you want to punch some bastard in the mouth, him with the mournful face for instance. I'll give him something to be fucking mournful about, him and his crimped fucking lips the bastard.

Poor old bastards. What have they done to deserve all this, this opprobrium. Children whose parents never got married for whatever reason. And right beside the mournful-faced bloke was this younger guy who looked about ages with Pat, or even slightly younger. How come he hadni noticed him earlier. He actually resembled a polis who had come to the school recently to give a talk on public initiatives with third-year tearaways, for the benefit of the teaching staff. Pat attended. It was really interesting. And if he hadnt gone it would have been noted. But if people were being sent to keep watch on him then they would not have sent somebody he'd seen previously; they would have sent somebody anonymous. That was obvious. And yet was it? Christ but it was easy to become paranoiac. And rationally: rationally one had to admit of certain facts, that certain tenets one held to be true, certain activities that one hoped would take place, that would not endear him

But surely not in a public place. If they were going to do something to him they would surely choose somewhere private – not an actual football ground. What could be more conspicuous than that! And yet, when you thought about it, this was precisely the type of place an assassin would choose to perform the dirty deed; while the crowd roared on the two teams the poisoned umbrella comes out and is quietly inserted between one's shoulderblades. Maybe a crowd was the last place to be if safety was sought. Perthshire was about to take a shy. Patrick stepped to the side, and back a pace, and was on par with the mournful chap in the hat. He smiled at him and nodded. The man looked at him and nodded in reply. And Patrick said, I missed the goal. What d'you make of it? one goal and I missed it!

We'll get another yin, said he. He touched the brim of his hat, glanced at his watch: There's still time yet.

The younger man was not paying any attention to the interchange. He was straining to follow the play now, the Perthshire forwards moving upfield toward Yoker's goal area. They had a small boy out on the wing who was really good with the ball at his feet but was tending to slow things down, if he had been that bit more direct Yoker might have been in trouble. And then Yoker attacking out of defence. Exciting stuff and not at all square. Not bad at all. Patrick nodded. It was good. Football could be a direct game. He closed his eyes and stepped backwards.

Before the end he was making his way to the exit. He paused at the gate and continued out and along the road to where the car was parked. The same road he had driven last night, the route to Dumbarton. Nothing peculiar in that. Unless! The Fates were trying to tell him something! Could his destiny lie in such a direction! West to the Highlands and to the Islands. A Scotsman of the old school. Maybe he was put here on earth to decide the fate of a nation! And that nation was the one of his birth! Patrick Doyle, son of the great Feinn, descendant of that band of mighty warriors who bestrode the northern wastelands in defiance of central authority.

That fucking bastard Milne, when you thought about it. Here was an arse, a total arse, a total shite, an absolute fucking piece of tollie. Here was a fellow who disbelieved in the great teachers. Here was a congregationalist who was not to be trusted, who would sell out his staff and his pupils and his fucking grannie, who

And yet these fuckers were being set in front of you. They were placed there on the mantelpiece to be looked upon and admired ye mighty. There they were, stopping you from doing it; using everything in their power. Hardly worth talking about except that it was, because for christ sake ye know there was something approaching evil lurking somewhere within.

Even poor old Desmond was better than that. He might be a bit sarcastic but none could describe him as evil. But the headmaster. And the second headmaster. These two males – one hesitates to call them men, if we accept the term as one of merited achievement but is it fuck, it's just a fucking fact. Two men. Things with bollocks and a prick. A pair of rascally fuckers, paid by a sick society, accountable to themselves on behalf of a corrupt government. Well then, what is to be done. Move the motor for a kick-off. Find the gear and fucking etcetera, get it going. Some wee boys and girls are watching. If you give them a wave they'll throw stones. Quite right. Just fucking turn the ignition key properly. Fine. With the in-car entertainment this form of shenanigan would not entail. One would simply drive along carelessly, the hand tapping the wheel in accompaniment to the tune being heard on the airwaves.

Uch indeed, life life life.

Fuck off.

He was returning home he was returning home, but decided against it and drove to his parents, rejecting the notion of a pint along the way although Partick and Finnieston were chokablok with good pubs, or at least not bad yins. He stopped at a newsagent to buy a big box of mixed plain and milk chocolates, for the maw's birthday. He liked her. He did. There was something good about her. His da as well. He could be grumpy and he could be huffy but at the base of it all he was okay and Patrick liked him. He liked them both. They were a pair. They were happy together. They had their ups and downs of course but who didni for christ sake we've all got to go.

Ssshh.

Patrick's relationship with his parents can be described in this way: no irony as the basis of it. And if you cannot be ironic with your parents life is no dawdle.

What did Hölderlin say about parents?

Fuck all. He never said nothing about parents, he fucking knew better with that maw he had. What did he say about brothers? did he say anything about brothers? Sisters-in-law, what did he say about them? Because sisters-in-law are a different breed altogether. Patrick would have married his if his brother hadni got there before him. She was special. She had to be with him for a husband. He definitely had faults. A huffy bastard so he was. Mind you she was no paragon and once told Pat she had slept with other men before getting married to Gavin. But of course so had Gavin slept with other people for christ sake they never got married until their fucking mid-twenties, what do you expect!

[105]

So; that was the two of them.

The maw answered the door. She gave him a beamer of a smile and he stepped in the doorway and kissed her on the cheek. Hiya maw!

Pat . . . she smiled and shook her head.

Bloody chocolates for your birthday! He gave her the packet. Then from the kitchen his da shouted: Who is it Kate?

Pat!

Pat? Aw! And then the da's baldy head poking round the door, a frown of a grin at him from the opposite end of the lobby: Where've ye been hiding yourself young man!

Ah!

Seriously but?

Patrick shrugged. His maw shut the outside door. So that was that and this was him. His da came forwards and placed his hand on Pat's right forearm, holding him there, and he said to Mrs Doyle: I dont have to tell you what he's in time for! His bloody tea!

Mrs Doyle smiled. Leave the boy alone.

I'm actually no that hungry, said Pat.

Aw well that'll be the first time! Mr Doyle relaxed his grip on Pat's forearm, stepped aside, gesturing Pat on ahead.

There is extra fish, said his maw.

Are ye sure?

Mr Doyle laughed briefly: Dont give us it! Are ye sure! You'd eat my head if I laid it on the table!

John! That's bloody disgusting! Mrs Doyle frowned at him.

Ach I'm just kidding Kate for god sake . . . He smiled, tapped Pat on the back: On ye go, we're in the living room.

But Patrick hesitated and he said to his maw, Alright if I ran a bath?

Of course.

Great.

Did you no bring your dirty washing as well! said Mr Doyle, smiling.

I'm no that bad!

Although he had a bath in his own place, at certain times of the day there was something about bathing there that did not appeal. It had to do with the imagination. Then the rituals. He was aye having to perform rituals, such as counting to thirty before getting up out the water, counting another thirty once he had dressed and was about to unsnib the door. The light switch for the bathroom was through the wall, in the lobby. Sometimes he found himself having to step out backwards. Other times he forced himself to stay in the bathroom and reach round to switch it off. And the idea of his wrist being grabbed by an unknown assailant whose intent was murder! And of course the obvious point: how come he snibbed the bathroom door if there was nobody else in the house? Because he was frightened. It was simple. He was just actually frightened. Not badly, but just that wee bit. These old tenement buildings were erected more than a century ago. What had they not seen? What had they not borne witness to? And with him having been locked away in the bathroom for almost an hour all these auld memories were becoming the more palpable. That outlandish image he kept getting of something like a crowd of masked stormtroopers, shadowy dark figures, who rode slowly ben from the kitchen; muffled conversations were in progress; desultory, matter-of-fact; they were just travelling on their way maybe and he was observing from a different dimension, neither able to be seen nor to influence any event that might take place. Daft of course. What's the point in dredging up these mental things. People dont. They keep quiet. Quite right too, it's fucking stupit. Grey figures. And not evil though definitely spectral. There is no question about Patrick's being an atheist but, however, when one

All-powerful deities have got nothing to do with it.

Also, using the bath in his parents' place was a nice and peaceful method of exploiting them and they enjoyed being exploited by him. They would like it if he moved back into the family home, into the spare room. But he wasnt about to do that. It was not a possibility.

Chocolates are a nonsense to give to a grown adult. But she was so hard to give presents to, she just didni like them. You give your maw a present and then you're in playing with the wee boy across the stair and you notice his maw's got the selfsame present, the one you had saved the pennies to buy, your maw's given it away to her. What a psychological slap on the gub that was for a kid! Uch was it fuck it was good experience. It made you feel a wee bit hurt at the time mind you but that's good, good training. And weans need to learn; if they never learn they've never discovered. O dear. Patrick closed his eyes, but opened them again. If he could stop all this internal and external sighing the world would be a more upright place.

The football had been good. Amazing how much he still enjoyed it – the actual game itself, never mind the getting-out-and-about and seeing folk and being part of a crowd. It was a good and interesting game to watch. He had been yapping about that with Joe Cairns the other day and Joe asked him if he wanted to help out with the school teams. It was sincerely meant. But it would entail one more evening per week, plus of course almost the whole of every Saturday.

Ach as well, no use sighing over juvenile dreams. When he went to kick the ball during training it would bounce off his knee, bounce off his cheek when he tried to head it; never mind all his fucking theory. Rotten auld bastards, Zeus and his fucking henchmen; all sitting there on Olympus cutting cards on the individual fates of wo/mankind. If Patrick could only get his big toe wedged in the cold tap a plumber would come and rescue him and if in Russia or Eastern Europe or someplace else where female plumbers

        Alison Alison Alison
        Are you the woman for me
        I've been lying here sinking

A rhyme for ee apart from pee?
The penis floats on the sudsy surface of the water.
Mirs Houston.
Mirs Houston.
She wears an illfitting blouse, having neglected to don the bra, her brassiere, that underbodice women wear to support the breasts.
My god, the pathos.
No but that would be the way of it. It would be. Her breasts. The texture of the skin so different from his own. Her nipples probably that dark reddish brown you see. Dear dear, the pity of it: Patrick has never really actually ever, never really actually ever, been, the way

that the female and the male are with each other, lying side by side in broad daylight during entire stretches of time such as days, days, whole days, body to body, just kissing and lying, lying there. He can imagine for example cupping one of her breasts in his hands the way that maybe an artist would, just testing its weight and substance, its texture; while being watched by her in an amused way, her being kindly and gently amused by him, by how he is so interested, so fascinated – in a sense not even erotically as such but even fuck it's terrible to say, aesthetically. Aesthetically interested in tits. But tits are wonderful. In the name of christ. Poor old Patrick. P for Pat. P rhymes with pee. And p for pipe so fuck off. And p for prick of course what about p for ptarmigan.

His feet moved in the water; he waggled his toes, disturbing the surface, causing ripples. Masturbation could never be a possibility here in the home of his parents. That was one thing about P. Doyle. That was one tried and true thing about him. This is how come he's the man you see today. What the fuck does that mean. It just means that eh etcetera.

Fried fish in eggy breadcrumbs; chips and tomato and sweetcorn. The sweetcorn was an innovation. They had never had such luxurious delicacies when he was a boy! Sweetcorn by christ! Mind you it was tasty. Why did he never buy fucking things like that? sweetcorn. He would have to remember it.

His bloody damn maw had set the table properly, the nice tablecloth and so on, its creases well apparent; fresh linen from the drawer! And the condiments: salt and two flavours of sauce, tomato ketchup and the brown stuff; a clear vinegar and a wee jar of mint dressing for the fish. The cups and the saucers and a plate with biscuits. Cut bread and a dish of actual butter as opposed to margarine, something they insisted upon. Table setting was a dying art. But no grace was spoken nowadays. It had been when Gavin and Pat were boys. It had all stopped. And no analysis. Okay, but a nice kind of general thanksgiving would be no bad thing. Get rid of the silly theological aspect but surely there had to be room in this planet for secular appreciation? Surely there had to be a place for good fucking atheists who wanted to say thank christ I'm no starving to death and I'm able to sit down amongst friends and relations! Or was there? Maybe there wasnt. Maybe the very idea was a load of sentimental drivel.

He had sliced the fish and was isolating the bones. A fact to be admitted: he preferred fish à la chip shop because they always contained far fewer bones. He liked to pretend that this preference had to do with saving time in the course of eating, but it was nothing of the kind. His maw looked at her plate as she ate. She had glanced at him.

Good fish, he said.

Whiting.

Yeh, I thought it was actually haddock.

Too wee for haddock, replied his da.

I wouldni be too sure nowadays, said Mrs Doyle. At one time you might've said that but no now.

Of course ye know if you're buying your fish at the pier it's twice the size of what you get here in Glasgow, Mr Doyle said, I mean dont think because it's whiting it's got to be a wee fish. Some whiting ye get's big. But the best of the catch aye gets sent down south to England. The posh big restaurants, it's them that buys it all up. Mr Doyle glanced at Pat: Yous go on and on about Scotland's oil, well they've been stealing our fish for years.

I dont go on about the oil at all, but okay da I take the point.

Yous dont complain about things, that's what I mean.

We do so.

Aye *you*, but nobody else.

It's no as bad as that da . . . Pat grinned and he forked a chip into the sauce at the side of the plate. I'm no the only one that complains.

O naw, right enough, so does your brother!

Mrs Doyle sighed and gazed briefly at the ceiling.

Mr Doyle glanced at her:

I'm no saying nothing. What am I saying? nothing! Mr Doyle frowned at Patrick: I'm no saying nothing.

Two nos make a yes, said Pat, so you're definitely saying something! He winked at his maw who sighed again:

Dont start him Pat.

He doesni need me to start him!

Mr Doyle stared at Pat then he smiled for a moment. How did ye no give me a phone? If I'd knew you were going to a game I'd have went with ye – I've no been to watch a match for months. Since Charlie died! Mr Doyle glanced at Mrs Doyle and his mouth curved in a manner Patrick couldni remember having noticed before. His da was saying, We went up to see the Jags at the end of last season – a no-hope league game against Queen of the South. They got beat too! Imagine that. Imagine getting beat by Queen of the South. At home? Ho! No way. Bad.

The Thistle have fell by the wayside, said Patrick.

And they'll no come back, said his da. Charlie Murray'll no come back either. He winked at Pat and gestured at Mrs Doyle: Somebody in the company'll be pleased to hear that!

John, that's no nice.

It's no nice but it's true.

The man's dead, we dont want to hear about it.

She didni like him Pat, your maw there, she didni like him. Mr Doyle glanced at her: How come you didni like him?

I just didni, okay?

Mr Doyle winked at Pat. She just didni.

It was spur of the moment, said Pat, about going to the game. If I'd thought about it earlier I'd have phoned you.

Aw aye I know that.

I'll mind the next time.

His da nodded, and he went on to ask about the game; they continued chatting about football generally and it encompassed the football fixed odds coupon Mr Doyle had bet upon. Nottingham Forest had been beaten at home and this had beaten the whole bet. Patrick found this not so much boring as undecidable and his brains were becoming fankled. His maw was still eating; she ate in a very painstaking fashion, unless she was maybe having problems with her dentures; it was almost like she had to break the food all up on the plate before inserting it into her mouth. For a brief period the talk returned to fish and the quality of fresh in comparison to frozen and back to how the best stuff ended up in the high-class kitchens of English eating establishments. A homely sort of prejudice this, hating the posher restaurants of England, the kind of prejudice you can relax into in a sleepy sort of way. Sopor soporifimus. As a boy Pat had the welcome habit of falling asleep at the table – except that his maw used to bang him on the elbow. The mastication process seemed to last eternally. Big long stringy bits of fatty mutton. One end was in your stomach and the other end was still between your teeth and if you gulped suddenly it sprang back out your mouth. Sleep was the only method of coping. It was surprising he never choked to death. His maw of course, banging him.

When you are a wean things do last eternally. Literally. That is a literal truth, about the nature of the eternal. And kids have apprehended it. When Pat was a boy he was a much better individual than he is nowadays, having lost a great deal. And his da was looking tired and drawn, his skin drooped at the jowels and around the eyes and he was looking a lot more than fifty-seven years of age it was terrible to state, but true. The maw was also looking tired and there was something else in her face, a fixed kind of irritated expression. She had come into the conversation now; it had got round to football hooligans and she mentioned something in reference to himself so he would have to become involved. It was not too difficult, a case of clearing the throat and speaking. At a point in the future he would get the conversation round to revolution, its efficacy or otherwise in reference to the vagaries of childrearing, and the single man. She did look tired. That was because she was having to attend to him, Pat's da. But here she was on about that hoary old prejudice, the mollycoddling of today's school-weans in comparison to those sterling youngsters of yesteryear. He laid his knife and fork on the plate and said, Maw, you're prejudiced.

I'm no prejudiced at all, you just stick up for them.

I dont. I just tell the bloody truth, as I see it.

I'm no saying ye dont, but let's face it as well Pat, ye do like to be different.

Naw I dont.

Your maw's right, said Mr Doyle. The same with bringing back the belt, you've got to be different there too.

Tch da.

Nay tch da about it – you've aye been against the belt. But at least the weans'll show some damn respect. And you canni deny it.

Aye I can.

What? Naw you canni. You canni deny it.

Of course I can, I can deny anything I like and I'm denying that.

Och . . . Mr Doyle shook his head and turned from him a moment. Then he said: Aye well it never done anybody any bloody harm.

Da, it never done anybody any bloody good either.

It never done anybody any bloody harm!

Aye but it never done anybody any bloody good!

Wwh!

Less of the argy-bargy, said Mrs Doyle.

It's no argy-bargy maw it's conversation.

Aye well, conversation, it's noisy . . . She looked at Patrick. He had lifted his fork; he pierced a chip and ate it. His da said:

Your maw doesni like noisy conversations. Dont ye no Kate?

That's right.

See! His da gave Pat a false smile.

Mrs Doyle sniffed slightly: Yous'll end up arguing.

Patrick nodded. After a pause he swallowed a mouthful of tea and resumed eating. He took another slice of bread and wiped up the sauce at the rim of his plate. His da was looking at him. Pat glanced at him. They both looked away. It was quite sad because it was hitting old nerves or something and shouldni have been causing such a big kerfuffle. He looked at his da again but there was nothing he could give him. He couldnt. He couldnt give him anything. He didnt deserve to be given anything. So how come he should be given it? People get what they deserve in this life. Even parents. Maws and das. They dont have a special dispensation. Except maybe from the queen or the pope or any other of these multibillionaire capitalist bastards. But no from their equals, they dont get any dispensation from them. So fuck off.

Sauce streaks on the plate. Crockery is a chalk-like substance. Clay, china; china-clay.

Well: at least he was freshly scrubbed and sweet-smelling. And he had minded to buy the fucking box of chocolates. And then too, also, he could leave soon, as soon as he was ready and it was decently acceptable within this stench of a society. Once that was done, once that was completed, finalised.

Bringing things from there to here. Moving from one position to the one that comes next. A sprinkle of magic dust and a boisterous abracadabra, the puff of smoke and Pat materialising back in his own kitchen, in front of the fire. He should have gone straight home after the match. He just shouldni have come here. How come he came? He shouldni have fucking came. It was stupid. Guilt probably. His first visit in three weeks – nearer a month in fact. Who cares. No point in worrying over it.

The fish was a dead animal. It had lain there on the plate open for inspection, eager to impress s/he who is about to partake. Just please devour me. I'm as good as the next thing you'll catch. Whatever you do dont not do it, dont not devour me, I'm a good wee fish. Courageous and heroic. Its body sliced open for examination by the education authority. Give it a tick. A plus. Five out of ten. Fine for a Glasgow table but dont send it south to the posher restaurants of England.

Gibberish. Outpourings. People see facial expressions of silence, not seeing, not

How is it all contained? The heads craned over the plates, the three people eating, this man and woman and man, while within the limits of each an intense caterwaul. We are alone! We are isolate beings! The good Lord alone

Fucking bastards.

And of course Patrick, going in for a bath to avoid being alone with his da.

Pardon?

And of course Patrick, going in for a bath to avoid being alone with his da.

Is that possible?

Fucking right it is ye kidding! The only reason. His maw had to go into the kitchenette to see to the grub and Pat would have been left in the living room with his daddy. And he couldni handle it. The very thought. It is just that he canni quite feel them, the pair of them, his maw and his da, he would like to be able to feel them. He does get urges to cuddle them but that is different, almost the exact opposite.

Mr John Doyle, a man of 5′ 6½″, with a head that is bald at the crown, having hair round the sides, who used to sport a moustache when Pat was a boy. He still works as a machinesetter in a factory. He is not a deep thinker but so what and go and fuck yourself. Patrick reached for the teapot. He half refilled his cup. His maw was gazing at her plate. She had glanced at him. Anybody want a refill? he said.

Mrs Doyle held her cup for him.

Mr Doyle said, Yous pair are too quick. I'll have mine in a minute. I like to take my time. It's no good for your digestion either, if you drink your tea while you're eating.

He glanced at Pat who nodded, even though he had actually finished eating. There again but he had been eating and drinking together during the meal. There were always problems in this life. Even being more like his da could be worthwhile. A man in his mid- to late-fifties, which is young compared to some folk with sons as old as Gavin and Pat. Charlie Chaplin had been fathering weans into his eighties. If Patrick had been his own father not only would he be a grandfather he would be an ordinary run-of-the-mill sex-performing male.

Gavin was the lucky one. He took things nice and easy and didnt get upset over trifles and things of mammoth import. No. What he did

But he did get on with living. He had his wife and his two great wee children, just like his own da; the two of them, the father and the elder son, being involved with the women they're involved with, the wives and the lovers and the mothers and so on, the sentimental sort of shitey stuff. Patrick

It is not his fault. He just cannot get on with things. It is a form of living that so far he is unable to encounter in a personally meaningful manner. He is involved with other affairs. He is involved with a pair of electrician's pipes. He is going to take this pair of electrician's pipes and create harmony – no he isni, that isnt even what he's after, he just wants to fucking make music from them. Not exactly music either. Something else. Not anything greater. It isnt to do with that. Something else. Something good. Just something good and fucking new, newish, different anyway, at least. He smiled. He smiled at his maw. She was holding a plate of biscuits to him. And why not? If plates are to be held why not by mothers and why not with biscuits? Delicatus delicatessen. Otherwise he would just end up in bother. If he was no able to play the pipes. Something would happen. Something bad. He knew it. Maybe he would murder Old Milne! Or else be murdered by him. Old Milne would make a good murderer. So would Patrick right enough. The pair have that in common. If nothing else.

Something was definitely going to happen.

It was this being alone.

There's another biscuit there, said his maw.

No thanks. He smiled. He didnt have any option, smiling and not smiling.

I think I'll open the chocolates . . .

Aw maw, said Pat, they're for you, they're no for me and da.

Aye, said his da.

I just want to open them, she said, if it's alright with yous. She got up from the table. In the time it took for her return Mr Doyle had nipped across to his armchair and got his cigarette packet and matches, and was back at the table seated, smoking his cigarette. It was comical. Not once did he glance in Pat's direction and Pat stared at the milk jug, pretending to be lost in the depths of thought. But if only the two of them had been yapping together when she came back in. Even if it had just been about hospitals. Ach well. It was not something to worry about. It related to the dreadful Doyle fucking huffiness. His da was really bad for it. There again but so was his maw. They could both be huffy. And so too could Patrick, when it comes down to it, though maybe not so huffy as Gavin. Gavin was the world's worst. He still wasni speaking properly to Patrick because of something that happened last summer, nearly nine months ago! Bloody terrible how these unfashionable traits run in families. And you couldnt even blame your parents for it because they were just picking up the habits of the rest of the clan. Probably the whole of

Scotland is huffy. This is why their history is so shitey. The English are not huffy, just fucking imperialist bastards. Which ones? Quite right. And that applies to the Northamericans as well. Imperialists cannot be huffy: it would be a contradiction.

And fuck the tomato juice he was going for a pint. He was going to go home and dump the motor and then come back out. Where was he going to come back out to? Anyfuckingwhere, it doesnt matter. He just required to get out; he just required to get away; if he did not get away he would collapse and die in front of the two of them, right here at the dining table, the nut landing on the sauce-streaked plate. What else could he do? Could he do anything else? He couldni go and have a fucking bath because he'd already had one. I'll do the dishes. He moved his chair back and started collecting plates while rising onto his feet.

You will not do the dishes, said his maw.

I'm doing them, said Mr Doyle. I always do them on Saturday night.

Naw. Honest. I want to do them . . . Pat was saying, I really do. Plus it gives me a chance to think as well. Pat chuckled: Hey, no mind when we were wee how I always had to do the drying. Gavin wouldni let me wash, it was always him had to get doing that because the one that did the drying was aye last. No matter how fast you dried them you were aye last! It just wasnt fair!

Mr and Mrs Doyle chuckled.

His da was standing beside him. A heavy smell of tobacco and sweaty socks. He had just come in and lifted a teacloth, and he started doing the dish drying without a word. Patrick acknowledged him with a brief nod. What else could he do. He stared into the soapy water in the bowl in the sink and stuck his hands back in to find the washing clout. Poor Hölderlin. In his early thirties he finally succumbed to that insanity which seems to have been threatening him for years. Years he spent fighting it, a form of melancholic schizophrenia. He used to be Hegel's best pal as a youth. They were exactly the same age and so on.

Hegel was never near to insanity. He never was. Or so we are given to understand. He had a good cheery lifestyle as a student. He caroused with women and drink. It is best not to talk. What one does is say nothing, one says nothing, especially to parents and to other people. He caroused with women and drink and no doubt that is why Schopenhauer hated him. Kierkegaard didnt fucking like him either.

And Hölderlin had become involved with this woman, the wife of the guy who employed him to tutor his child. Also of course; she died while he was still in control of his faculties. It was only after she was dead that he succumbed. She wrote him smashing letters.

Mr Doyle was whistling – not really whistling, his breath way to the back of his mouth; a noise but not a whistle; a more sort of intimate thing, it signified security. A man who had nothing to worry about, standing here in his own kitchen at his own sink with his younger son. It was best as well. What was best as well? Nothing.

He stands there drying the dishes.

> do de do de do
> whw whw whw whw whw
> di do di do di do

Blues. A Glasgow working man's blues.

> do di do di do
> whw whw whw
> do di do di do

Fred Astaire and Ginger Rogers, Bing Crosby and Doris Day. Do di do di do. Where's my television weekly programme guide, my carpet slippers and hot water bottle!!

It was just the way things were, the way things are. Not having anything to talk about. What was there to talk about? Nothing. Fuck all. Pointless worrying about it either. Fathers and sons and brothers. A load of tollie. Plus education and class warfare, revolution and disease and starvation and torture and murder and rape. There is nothing to crack up about. A polis battered him over the fucking head with a cricket bat the naughty picket; well he must have been bloody misbehaving then that's what I say. And how's yourself, are you okay, nice as nice, what about you? Getting on fine? Seeing your way clear? No! O dear, that's a fucking wee pity. It's really tough. Tough tough tough. And if there's any truth in afterlives I'm sure yous'll fucking

Mr Doyle had his fag balanced on the edge of the worktop to the side of the sink, snatching drags as he went, the quick wee puff, di di di di di di, puff puff puff, a cosy wee smoke and back through to the telly: me and the boy there had this minor fusion while involved with the fucking crockery cleansing.

Perhaps Patrick could wipe his da's pate with a brillo pad. That would

He loves his da, he really does. It's just that fucking hopeless reactionariness. How do ye pierce it? It's a fucking tortoiseshell. You would need a Moby Dick harpoon. Father! Daddy! Dad! How are ye doing! How is your drying hand? Okay? Good, that's good. And have you wiped your gaffer's arse recently? Last week? Fine. Aye. Consistency is a desirable category. Here you are.

Patrick dried his hands. He turned from the sink to do it. The towel was damp. Why had he not put on the radio? he could have put on the radio. He walked from the kitchenette to the bathroom although he was nowhere near to tears, just getting into a bit of an emotional state and was wanting a few moments' peace, in which to calm himself. That was all. And no sooner said than accomplished, the deed, the doing. There was a nice smell in the bathroom and the atmosphere held a warmth, damply so, because of the bath he had had. He stared into the mirror at his fine fizzog. It was true: he did look like a mature twenty-nine-year old chap. With a face like that there was no reason to be as he was. But what about tomorrow! Tomorrow was yet to come! He was fine. Things would yet prove unburdensome.

No they wouldni. He was down and out. He really was down and out. What he needed

What did he need?

Ink exercises! A whole host of them. Why was he not marking ink exercises? a whole host of them. The new rates had just come out and if he got himself down to doing it he would earn good bonuses. And then he could go out and buy a new motor with plenty of in-car entertainment. Christ but the actual work itself would have been okay. He could have purchased himself a couple of flagons of nice red wine, a couple of cans of superlager, a few red biro pens; a blast of music in the background softly. He could have developed new theories on examining the pre-school age-group, just to see if some of them were actually fit to learn because a lot of these wee bastards are so fucking unknowledgeable they shouldni even be allowed in through the primary schoolgates in the first place. Auld Swift had the right idea. Fucking eat them.

He sat down on the throne. His recurring daymare was the idea of seating yourself down on the outer lid by mistake, and crunching the bollocks to a pulp.

In the name of fuck!

And yet, his parents would have been delighted to discover he was meeting a young woman tomorrow. It would really please them. Except of course her being a married woman. That would not please them. It would not upset them, just not please them.

They wanted him settled down. They didnt think he looked after himself properly. As if being involved with a woman would change all that. Maybe it would. There were things he would have to alter if he was so involved. He would have to get a fridge, for example, so that he could store milk and fresh dairy products. Also a hoover vacuum machine for cleaning carpets.

He pulled the plug, gazed at the water flushing the pot. He waited until the cistern refilled. As a boy he used to have to wait for the final click before being able to wash and dry the hands. But now such superstitious nonsense could be shoved to one side.

Time to go for a pint.

But he had yet to finish the dishes. His da would be waiting.

But his da wasnt waiting. His da had finished both the washing and the drying and was now sitting on his armchair and watching the telly. Patrick remained by the door and he called: For another pot of tea anybody?

Now you're talking! said his da while Mrs Doyle raised her head briefly from the newspaper on her lap, and smiled in reply.

He almost crashed into a bloody lamppost on his way home. A big patch of black ice on the ground just beyond the turn into his own street. It was bitter cold. He had stayed on at his parents' home until after midnight, just watching television and yapping about old things from the past.

He was awake at 3.45 a.m. looking at the ceiling. It was a very very bad dream. He was unable to close his eyes and drift back into a good slumber. The things were all continuing to happen. He was in the middle of it. A crowd of evil phantoms had sprung to existence in the room. Each space he looked to contained someone and they had lives of their own, these phantoms, and they were evil and wearing a dishevelled type of waistcoat with these sort of ankle-length cloth boots like sixteenth-century peasants, or maybe fur yins they were and not cloth, with straps of twine tied round the top uppers to keep them from falling off.

They were actually there and had big sort of staves or hoes and they just were hovering and when he shifted onto his side and stared into the recess wall with the blankets firmly at his chin there came a couple moving towards him from the rear and he knew exactly where they were and it gave him this sense of weightlessness. He spoke to himself. A method of eradicating it all. He spoke distinctly. I have had this very bad nightmare, a very bad one, but only a nightmare; there is no reality to it unless one of insanity, unless, since it is not only a nightmare but here and now, something that is occurring at this moment, while I am awake, it is not a nightmare but a living experience, reality; and a reality of which I am the central part, a central part. But what is to become of me now? Is this the end of my sanity? maybe now I am to be like this for all the time and what will happen to me? If I maybe cannot move out of my bed for all eternity and the nurses will have to break my door down.

And it was becoming expedient, to turn round the way and look out from the recess wall, now, expedient, to turn, to confront them, because there would be not a thing there, no phantoms, nothing, and it was worthwhile turning just for that very reason and he moved slowly but surely from the hips firstly and the shoulders and head lastly and true to form there was not anything there but the darkness of course and the gloominess, there was a kind of integral gloominess to this room which appeared to be charged from the middle someplace, all related to it, threads, silken and steadfast, threads.

This sensation of feeling behind the eyelids, an ordinary feeling though in some way, as if he had been scratching there. Maybe it was just a sign of tiredness. But he was not exhausted. Occasionally he did have these terrible mornings when he was exhausted, tired and drained, through lack of sleep – although sometimes it couldnt really be called a lack of sleep.

In the word itself, 'sleep', there was something implying succour: the term required redefining. 'Sleep' simply as a word to denote a concrete state of non-reflective consciousness and just fucking leave out all suggestions of mental or physical relaxation, recuperation, and so forth.

There are times when it is best to play music. And also perform any wee bits of business needing done about the house, the more mechanical the better. One project he did wish to begin at some point was erecting a bedshelf, with a small ladder for climbing up to; a square platform 8' in length would do it.

And the motor car as well of course there were a million and one things needing attention to there. But fortunately you couldni drive the car up the bloody damn stairs and park it in your lobby. So that was that. But the grating noise was definitely worsening. If maybe the hinges were slackened off and the door panel hoisted aloft, and the hinges fixed on firmly while the door is being held. A job for two people. The sound was awful, that grating – close to the anguished cry of a human being, and continual, like a wail. A flattened worker, a carassemblyman, one from Linwood, has been squashed inside the door for the past decade, right since the final asset-stripping occurred. The guy was working cheerily away inside the panel and then came the bell for teabreak and the rest of the gang went off while he was in applying grease and paint to the interior surfaces, him being slightly deafened at the time because of the echoes. And then it was a case of:

Where the fuck's Bertie?

Bertie . . . maybe he went for a shite.

Okay, will we just pour his tea the now or what?

Better no, in case it goes cold, you know how fussy he is about that.

But poor old Bertie never reappeared and gradually everybody forgot about him. He and his missis had been having a series of difficult arguments around this period and when he didni return from work at the usual time she assumed he had gone and left her, and now she and the kids would have to fend for themselves. But poor old Bertie had got stuck, he was wedged tight inside that door, his lower jaw twisted so that he couldnt scream out for help, and when the motor moved on down the line the ends of the panel were sealed fast together by the heavyduty punchguns, totally flattening him. Fucking way to go! Poor auld Bertie. Nice guy as well apart from having that wee bit of a bad temper.

Frost still showed in patches on the street and rooftops, though the sun was shining between clouds. He collected the *Observer* and *Mail* from the newsagent. Often he would have had his dirty washing with him and he would go there and then to the launderette and enjoy the read while the stuff spun round in the machine. But he had other things to think of. Back up the stairs he ate a boiled egg and toast and it was most enjoyable. There was this feeling he had, as though some sort of unstated vow about fried food had been made by him. Was he going to give it up! It was quite exciting to contemplate. What the fuck would he eat in future? No, he had probably just decided to stop eating so much of it. Fried grub was one of the main factors in why

Glasgow suffered the highest incidence of heart disease in the whole of Western Europe.

The whole of Western Europe.

There was a mighty ring about that. Odd to imagine Glasgow being an everyday part of something so grand and majestic. Right at this precise moment in the history of the world Patrick was one of its numerous legions, a fellow of such as the heroic Basque, a spiritual descendant of those great Free French who had declared the new Republic a nice healthy region of unashamed cardcarrying atheism. Two centuries ago! And still you were getting bastards like Old Milne managing to make weans guilty because they open their eyelids during assembly prayers. It was fucking unbelievable, the hypocrisy. And then when you spoke about it in the staffroom. When you actually spoke out about it. Christ. How in the name of fuck could they stand back and look at themself in the mirror!

Maybe this is why he was being carpeted. A blatant failure to conceal his nonbelief in the deities. But it went against the grain. How on earth could the kids ever trust any teacher who persisted in regarding himself as a dead man?

A dead man? Where did that come from?

He should have shaved either last night or early this morning so that his cuts would have had the chance to heal prior to leaving the house. Plus his skin often turned a blotchy and purple hue, as if the blade was dull; he would need to buy a new one soon. Or perhaps it was an effect of a too-cheap soap, inferior perfumes and oils maybe. Horses. What have horses got to do with it? Pat shivered. He was standing in the bathroom staring at his face, having just tapped himself on the chin for some unfathomable reason – the moment when a person sees his or herself in a mirror, seeing a stranger, and peering at this stranger with furrowed brow. Who is this fucker and where is she or he off to? Is he or she off to enjoy her or himself or is it an errand of filial dimensions e.g. away to pay the rent and rates for an Aged P. or guardian?

More! More!

Or is this he or she a being whose outer surface of skin, flesh and hair is simply a shell for the most nefarious of inner essences?

A hideous sight in there. Behind the skin and flesh and hair. This rotten inner core of a soul, hideous to behold in its stuckfast permanence, the kind of sight no ordinary mortal seeks to look upon. Quite fucking right if ye ask me. Who wants to look upon hideous souls? Nobody but a fool, an innocent fool. Fools are naïve. Patrick is no fool ergo he is not naïve. He is an innocent. He quests.

A number of cuts round the adam's apple and beneath the lower jawbone, tender parts of the neck, the portions where the suicide

probably suicides are fascinated by these portions of the neck, leaving aside females. Because they've not got any fucking adam's apples.

The Commodore Cafe had a jukebox. It contained all of the current pop singles and not a few of the golden oldies. They would be blasting them forth. And Alison would sit, smiling quietly, ignoring the winks and stares of the weans. Would Patrick cope but? It is worth considering. Of course he would cope. Yet it is a fact, that many children can see into your mind; it is a faculty they have evolved. They know exactly when you are undergoing hellish torments. They know exactly that very instant the horrible self-consciousness is set to surface, has surfaced, in the act of perception. They would see him sitting there and be trying to restrain the general smirk, but this general smirk would alter, gradually, becoming an expression of great suffering, for nobody can experience empathy like a wean, and nobody can suffer like a wean either, and Patrick would have become a crucified soul in their very midst. His anguish all too apparent. And maybe only Alison would have failed to notice its manifestation. It was best not to go to the Commodore but it had to be gone to now.

The clothes. He was going to don a shirt and tie and generally affect the conventional appearance of an establishment sort of bloke, an ordinary upholder of the Greatbritish way of eking out this existence. He would polish the shoes. Naw he fucking wouldni. He was stopping at that point. No further. Polish the shoes! The very fucking idea! All for the sake of a beautiful woman!! What a fucking hoax! Hoax? What has hoax got to do with it? Hoax. Hoaxish. Hoaxum. And the root? Intocsickation of course. Patrick is fucking drunk. Drunk as a lord. A lord? Drunk as a monkey then. Fine. And he was sticking on the good sports jacket and trousers and a good thick vest under the shirt, and too a quite thick V-neck jersey so the tie could be seen and everything would be correct and presentable more or less, for any occasion, any eventuality, just in case of anything vaguely out of the ordinary occurring, such as going somewhere that a too-casual outfit was frowned upon. In the name of fuck what could that possibly be? especially on a Sunday. Well, church of course. Such things canni be predicted. Poor old Joseph K ended up in a cathedral and what was he wearing was it a suit of black – a black frockcoat and tails? And also, wearing the thick underclothes means he wouldni have to don the overcoat or heavy anorak which is perhaps the central reason as to why he is dressing as he is, so that Alison might esteem him the type of guy who doesnt care what like the weather is, he just wears the same outfit come hell or high water. It was probably quite a machismo carry on. Maybe he would impress better by sporting the overcoat. And a fucking woolly scarf if it comes down to it! And shove a jar of Vick Vapour Rub in the pocket in case of emergencies, a couple of hot water bottles strapped to the upper trunk. Yet the truth of the matter

And take enough cash as well. That was important. For the full range of possibilities. He had a motor car and little or no obligations to any man, woman, wean or pet. Nothing. He could go wherever he wished. His desire was his command, whatever he wanted, he could set to and simply get it accomplished.

It was good. It was good and it was cheery. There wasnt really very much he wanted out of life, not really. But it, or maybe just the knowledge, the knowledge just, of being able to go and do whatever he thought it best to do, at that particular time, without having to worry too much about what other folk thought, not really. Although there again, it has to be said

But fuck off. What in this life was there to be proud of? I mean some fucking good thinkers would affirm truly that just managing to be alive by thirty was worthwhile. Look at Wittgenstein's brothers.

He pulled all the plugs out the electrical points before leaving. He didnt know when he would be back. But he usually pulled them out anyway because of the possibility of electrical fire. Which would be one of the drawbacks to the acquisition of this fridge his maw was threatening to dump on him. Refrigerator plugs had to be kept on at all times otherwise you got flooded by defrosted ice. He would, however, be able to buy fresh food and keep it fresh, including milk, cheese and poultry meats and pig, cow and sheep meats. But the idea was silly. Plus also that deeply held away far away sense of solidarity, wanting to show some sort of solidarity, with those who had fuck all to eat and were probably dying of starvation right at this very moment. Even the thought of doing it, storing vast quantities of food for the sole consumption of one single man. There was something not good about it, something not good about it at all.

At the foot of the staircase he continued on into the rear instead of going out the front. He walked a few paces, gazing at the peeling paintwork on the walls and ceiling. He found it special hereabouts. It had to do with the dullness of light, the position of the rear exit in relation to the front, how the shadows were eternally fixed, even at night. When the only kind of lighting was electrical the exact same shadows – or rather, the lines of those exact same shadows – remained, but had these other shadow-lines superimposed so that different layers of shadows were in existence. It was a good and a clear area of space, even allowing for the peeled paint. Then the constant wet of course; even during the summer months the condensation was horrendous and just out from the rear close was the greatest of stinks it has ever been Patrick's something or other to witness. It emanated from a drain which was the top hatch of a dark dungeon of a sewer, and this sewer, its exploration.

The motor was still where he had left it. Nobody had stolen it. The bonnet and wings and doors as unscratched as usual, the hubcaps all intact.

So then:

it was only half eleven.

Too early really.

The possibility of the motor failing to start, of having a bad accident on route, of a breakdown somewhere difficult, the polis picking him up. He checked the oil level, the level in the battery, looked at his tyres. These things to do with regular car driving that are boring. The mechanical aspects of any regular operation are boring. That includes conversation, having to chat to people from nothing, these things too are boring, no matter the embellishments.

What did you do this morning, inquires Alison.

O eh I went out eh and eh bought the papers and a bit of grub, checked the oil with the dipstick and had a shite and then I shaved and brushed the teeth to perfection in case of having bad breath because sometimes I think I have it and I dont think it's eh very good, bad breath, because it puts people off.

And only the introduction of the bad breath makes it at all interesting as a result of the ambiguity presented: has he an ulcerous set of gums, decaying teeth, dirty plastic ones, a cancerous set of tonsils or bad fucking adenoids or so on, throat cancer. Although, if he could be bothered, if he really did want to make an attempt, he could simply tell the truth, and it would become interesting:

In fact Alison, my dear Mirs Houston, checking the oil isni too straightforward because I have to insert the heid beneath the upraised bonnet and there's always for some fucking reason a lot of oil dripping out of someplace and if you arent fucking careful it lands on your napper. Sometimes I comb the fucking hair and it all comes out greasy black and manky. Plus the soiled patches on the pillow I mean see if you were to be in the same bed as me you would very soon – and so on. Plus of course if you neglect to raise the thing up properly, the bonnet, it falls down and decapitates ye.

Sunday morning peace, the quiet roads. Eventually, when he does get a new motor, he will be insisting on in-car entertainment. To be driving along the road listening to music or a discussion. It was the sort of thing Pat would enjoy. The sort of thing that takes the mind out the body, that allows the physical functioning, the bits in between, the nonambiguities, they take over and can relax the mind and the soul. The soul? Since when has talk of 'soul' become such an intimate part of his states of affairs? Soul. It must stem from a lazy approach to this morning, and also of course this morning in itself viz. Sunday, the day for Greatbritish Christians to get the soul surfacing.

Okay now, fine, when he meets Alison he has a variety of possibilities perhaps the most important of which is not to enter The Commodore Cafe. He should sit and wait for her in the car and when she turns up he should simply whisk her in and off they drive to somewhere else. That is Number 1: and once Number 1 is underway other possibilities will present themselves. And the bloody damn sky was clear of cloud, the sun melting last night's frost. Maybe set off out Arrochar way and on over the Rest-and-be-thankful. Although cold outside the sun would heat the inside of the motor and would make things very pleasant indeed. They could mosey on down to Inverary for a nice cup of genteel tea and stroll out onto the pier, dynamite the resident aristocracy and then home for dinner. Boswell and Johnson once

Alison was already there. It was ten to twelve. She was standing in from the corner of the junction, next door to the cafe, which seemed to be shut, the outside door closed. Alison there, she was looking good; she had on eh clothes. She had spotted him in the car but made no sign. She stared in the direction of the schoolgates which were locked and bolted.

He slowed, winding the window down, and he waved to her and drove on into a U-turn, and parked for her. She walked round to the driver's door. The owner's inside, she said, he must be opening soon. Do you want to wait?

Eh

We could go somewhere else I suppose.

Aye. He smiled and looked away.

Do you think we should?

Eh, I think eh aye maybe it would be best.

She nodded.

Fancy it?

Yeh, she said and returned round to the passenger's side. He leaned to open the door for her. When she was adjusting the seatbelt across her shoulders she spoke; she asked, Have you had a nice weekened then?

Eh okay I suppose, the usual . . . He smiled, letting the handbrake off and manoeuvering the car out into the centre of the road. What about yourself?

Alison sighed. Her perfume was strong and she was looking like she had a lot of make-up on at the eyes, maybe as if it was a mistake. That was funny, unexpected. And her cheek, there was something about her cheek, how it glistened. It's just I've got my parents coming this afternoon, she said, and then she shivered in a kind of spasm.

Okay? asked Patrick.

Yeh.

He grinned. I was up seeing mine last night. Boring boring boring. Are all parents boring!

Cockadoodledoo. Judas Iscariot.

What I mean is, he said, just having to watch so much television. I dont mean that eh they're boring as people.

I was just kidding.

Aw I know, I know. He smiled, he stared at the road ahead, a rawish sort of taste at the back of his throat, a dryness; he licked his lips. It wasni a good thing to say. How come she had said it?

She smiled, clicking open her handbag and giving herself a cigarette. Pat shook his head. And he shook his head again: All I said was they were boring and you come in with that – Judas Iscariot. Christ sake Alison, know what I mean.

It was silly, it just came out, I didnt mean it the way it sounded.

Naw I know, it's just, christ.

I was only kidding Pat. She smiled again, flicked the lighter and inhaled, puffed out the smoke and returned the lighter to her handbag.

He was shaking his head once again but he stopped it quickly and settled his head down rigidly on his neck, feeling the flesh maybe doubling up at the jowels; he relaxed, sighing. A brief glance across at her. There was this wee lump of glitterstuff on her cheek, you could have actually picked it off with your fingernail. She flipped open the ashtray cover, tapped in ash from her fag. What was wrong with her? She was so bloody beautiful as well. But yet there was that

there was something. But he liked her an awful lot. He wanted to shut his eyes and screw up his face; he gripped the steering wheel, his arms inflexible, inflexible. He relaxed. It's too early for the Art Gallery, he said, it doesni open till two on Sundays.

She did not reply. She watched the road ahead.

Where do you want to go? he asked.

O.

After a couple of moments he added: Because otherwise, really I mean . . . he smiled, I dont know where I'm driving.

A cafe?

Aye but it's just I mean which one?

Mm. She then looked at her wristwatch. He felt like jamming the brakes on immediately.

He said, I only mentioned the Art Gallery because they've got quite a good yin, a cafe. I'm no interested in seeing the paintings. I was actually up a couple of weeks ago, seeing an exhibition.

Mm.

Pat nodded. She was frowning at something. She maybe wanted to get out. That was probably it, she wanted to get out, just inside the fucking thing and she wanted out, to get away, because of him, the way he was carrying on, the usual. He was clenching the wheel of course. How come he was doing that? clenching the wheel. He was clenching the wheel because he was thingwi he was fucking bastard, he was thingwi.

At least she looked like she had relaxed. She was gazing out the window and she seemed to be comfortable and quite content. Maybe she wasni. But she seemed to be. What else can we do except infer. That's all. She was gazing out the window, smoking. Did ye think I was going to kidnap you? he chuckled.

You never know.

Christ! Imagine being suspected of dishonourable intentions! It's almost a compliment!

Is it – well it's not meant to be.

Naw; right; I was actually meaning, just thinking, of myself I suppose, the act itself, the forceful sort of way. You're right but it is sexist. Stupid. Sorry. Daft.

It's okay.

Thanks for coming.

Och!

Naw I mean honest, really, thanks.

She nodded, twisting her body slightly to see more fully out of the side window. The car was stopped at a set of traffic lights. A pair of wee boys stood at the corner; one with newspapers under one arm, the other held a bottle of ginger. In the rearview mirror he saw the driver of the van parked behind picking his nose, an alsatian dog was sitting in the passenger sear. People have a different type of awareness in the presence of animals, and maybe even it all depends on the species of animal as well – if it had been a parrot for instance, he might have used a fucking hankie. Alison was still staring out the side window. It was stupid. Idiocy. Everything should have been straightforward. Having a woman beside you in the motor should be no big deal. When she came into the thing in the first place he should just have driven to some secluded niche where they could have conversed in intimate fashion, after which they each would have sought the other's lips with their own lips, each's own lips, his or hers for fuck sake even getting it into language is difficult.

She was definitely not at her ease.

But what had he been hoping for? Just what exactly? How could there be anything? There couldnt really be anything. She has suspected him of kidnapping! A joke of course but even so. If this had been East Anglia that would never have happened. In places like East Anglia there are certain events, a finite list of them, that may or may not occur and this was the event that would never occur. Plus also, if in East Anglia and further, a citizen of that fair shire, then his whole experientiality would differ. I am cracking up. In the presence of Alison Houston née Mirs whose right breast is noticeable, its bulge beneath her coat, I am cracking up. And in the offside wingmirror a driver signalling. These drivers who begin a whole carry on with you for no reason but that you have driving in common you're supposed to be some sort of fucking soulmates! What was he signalling for?

Pat, where are we going?

Eh well I thought we would just go into town, up Glasgow Cross way, the Trongate, that area. There's quite a few cafes there, near the Barrows, that open on a Sunday.

She tapped ash into the ashtray. She was nervous. It was him making her nervous. He was trying too hard and putting her off, getting her uncomfortable and so not able to assist the way she should, the way that was normal, when two people are alone together and attempting to communicate.

The driver who was signalling had just moved out into the opposite lane and was speeding past and giving an angry look. Well fuck him. A Sunday and you're supposed to break the world all-comers landspeed record. Patrick cleared his throat. He said, What time are your parents coming then? I mean this afternoon.

4 o'clock.

Aw.

Actually they're Drew's parents, not mine.

O I see.

I get on fine with them though — better than Drew does; he's always having rows with them.

What about?

Everything. It can be an ordeal at times, just being there in the same room. Ye never quite know what to do, what's expected of ye.

Patrick nodded. He looked at her and started to blush when he met her gaze and he turned his head immediately as if to see out his side window. He wound down the window a fraction.

It's too smoky, said Alison.

Uch naw it's okay it's just eh . . . He felt the blush now full on his face. It could only level out then decrease. He stared ahead. It was just that of their eyes meeting. It must have been the first such encounter since she had entered the motor. It was funny to think of somebody kissing her lips, touching her face, his fingertips maybe on her cheek just gently, it was funny to think that. There was a feeling in his chest or lungs, a rough sort of feeling — all that smoke from her fag right enough. Over the parapet of the bridge was the *Carrick*. Diving off into the Clyde. Catching a fish between your teeth. There was no rain in the sky. That dense white grey. They were going along to the Saltmarket. I dont even think the pubs are open yet, he said.

Alison made no answer.

Actually anyway I'm no even feeling like a pint, to be honest; are you?

No.

He grinned. Beer drinking's overrated. That was how I suggested the Art Gallery, just for a change and that, keeping away from pubs.

It's only that I have to watch the time Pat.

Of course, aye, I know — I just thought the surroundings, because they were different. I mean the Commodore Cafe! All these weans in for their Sunday brunch with the sherbet lollipops and coke etcetera, all giving us the eye!

Alison smiled.

The Commodore had offered security. Now she had none.

Dan d ran dan. What was the point. He shook his head. He noticed a cafe and signalled to park, and parked, putting the handbrake on and switching off the ignition – all of that, before looking at her.

Just to the side of the cafe entrance a man was standing, he was near enough a dosser as far as his clothes and general configuration could imply anything as to the nature of day-to-day existence and how a person makes progress, these small steps of advancement coincidental to the passage of the moon, the stars and sun, entire galazactic galazacticus. The actual cafe itself looked pathetic. I dont really fancy this place, he whispered as she prepared to get out of the car.

I dont either! she said.

Patrick laughed. But it wasnt a good laugh and the guy was watching them. He switched the ignition back on and as the motor moved out to the outer lane he said, He's actually the owner's nephew. His story's quite sad. A few years back he was the maître d'hôtel at the Albany and a disaster struck during a banquet he was preparing.

Alison was listening. Are you talking nonsense? she said.

No.

She was waiting.

I'll no say anything more but because I dont like gossiping.

She smiled, opened her handbag but closed it at once. I like to see you cheery Mister Doyle.

I'm always cheery Mirs Houston . . . Patrick swung the wheel, the motor passing through the lights and on up High Street. If only, and then they could have driven to some secluded niche near the Mediterranean seaside.

She looked at him. He smiled: Do you want to visit the oldest house in Glasgow?

No. She gazed out the window. I'd like to be able to sit down and drink a cup of coffee.

Pat frowned. What about just going to my place? having a coffee up there? Fancy it?

Okay. She nodded.

But why not; it was the ideal place. No worries about being seen by schoolweans or colleagues. It was one of the things that was bad, how it was so awkward just talking to members of the opposite sex, without the business being taken for something it wasnt. Especially awkward for someone like Alison, a married woman without weans, plus whose husband appeared to be not always living at home through no fault of either but just his job, its actual nature, leaving her the time and maybe even the mental state, to become involved with outsiders. And of course she was very much a woman who enjoyed the company of her colleagues, the company of other intellects, those with whom she could discuss freely the politics of the world. And no irony to govern that. Patrick said; I see Northamerica's being its usual fascist self. Did you see the papers? about the assassination?

It's disgusting.

Aye, and the rest of us just stand back and watch them do it.

Alison sighed but not passively. She was unsettled by the topic and no wonder either it was astonishing what was happening in the world these days and nobody seemed willing to even ponder on it in any even vaguely ethical manner such as usually fucking happened in the shitey west, amongst all these so-called powers who jumped to attention to offer a salute as soon as Washington so much as signalled an intention to fart. No point in talking. Sometimes you felt like making your own demonstration, like some of the monks in Asian countries, setting yourself on fire upon the steps of a public meeting house.

I'll tell ye something Alison, sometimes I think I'll just stop buying newspapers altogether, and just stop taking any interest in the news, in what's going on.

O!

Ye dont agree?

Of course I dont agree.

Pat grinned. He shook his head. So, you dont agree eh! He was still grinning; it became a chuckle.

Soon he was swinging the wheel for the turn into his own street. Tricky corner this, he said, I nearly crashed into the lamppost last night.

Alison glanced across and nodded. She was obviously miles away and thinking of something else. And she could also have been slightly irritated. About different things. Imperialistic interventionism, the usual hegemonic practices, and his not wanting to read about them or even properly discuss them. But he was wanting to. He had only been kidding on. Surely she knew that. In fact, it was highly probable she was thinking: Here I am outside his close and what's going to happen now. But really, it was out of order to think that about her because of the way it seemed to undercut the possibility of her total commitment to a political cause or stance, her own genuine perception of the world – a good perception of the world and very similar to his own i.e. she was opposed to hypocrisy and cant and fucking humbug. Patrick nodded. Actually Alison I dont really hide from things at all. I just said that there, about stopping buying papers and that. My fault is I take too much bloody damn interest and it gets me up to high doh worrying about it all, every last wee stupit bloody detail!

Alison smiled.

Good expression that! said Pat; up to high doh! DDooohh! My grannie used to say it.

Alison laughed.

Hey by the way, mind that pair of pipes I found at the back of the arts centre . . .? He had switched off the ignition and applied the handbrake while talking. And now he was reaching to open the door for her. He continued talking as he opened the door at his own side: I suppose ye know, he said, I suppose it's really I suppose because I need some kind of escape, to give my brains a rest, that's what I'm meaning! And he uttered the last bit simultaneously to his crashing of the door shut. And he strolled round to lock the passenger side. She was standing there gazing up at the roof of the building, perhaps allowing him to forget about the pipes for the sake of their common decency, their mutal face-saving, their unembarrassment, as if the pipes were an excruciatingly embarrassing subject and like a pair of bad-smelling underpants it was probably best to pap them straight out into the fucking midgy, instead of trying to get them clean.

Look at the weeds growing out of the gutter, said Alison, pointing upwards. The tall weeds could be seen way up there, their stems overshooting the edge of the roof.

Christ aye . . .

She had waited for him, and they entered the close together.

Is your close better than this yin? he asked.

Not much.

He gestured at the peeling paintwork as they ascended. He began whistling a tune, not pausing on any of the landings although he was aware she might be interested to see out into the backcourt – if only so she could gain time before having to enter his flat. In case he fucking grabbed her like one of these stupid Romeo and Juliet affairs of the silent screen. My darling, how I've longed for this moment! Smack smack smack. The sound of the kissing. And then too her somewhat sly wee insinuation of a comment to do with the state of the roof guttering which he was best to ignore – as if he was dutybound to start agitating over the probable build-up of rainwater or something.

There was a side to Alison, a sort of subdued sarcasm. It could be an attractive thing about her; there again though, othertimes – othertimes he could imagine being her husband and not liking it at all, not one wee bit. You would never be quite sure

On the top storey he had his back to her while unlocking the door and he stood aside to allow her entry. Inside he said, Monday tomorrow! as he closed the front door.

The weekends seem to get shorter dont they?

Yeh, aye. Patrick grinned. He breathed in deeply, smelling her great perfume so strongly. It was a good thing to have said, about the weekends. He hung his jacket on a hook, showing her into the kitchen. He walked past her to get to the electric fire switch. He shivered. It was bloody freezing of course and he should've kept the fucking jacket on till the place heated up. He frowned at Alison: You finding it cold?

A bit.

Yeh . . . he switched both bars on. Then he put on the gas oven, pulling wide its door to let the heat blast out. He rubbed his hands together, slapped them and blew into them quite fiercely. He chuckled at Alison. Her shoulders were hunched and she was making nervous kind of shivering noises. They didni have to be nervous of course they could simply have been natural responses to the cold. But no; of course they were nervous. Him as well, his actions, they were every bit as nervous. He turned and stepped to the sink, now with his hands in his trouser pockets, whistling once more. The kettle of course. He filled it with water, set it to boil. Alison had gone

[137]

immediately to the books, her attention quickly taken by one; she lifted it from its shelf, and moved that wee bit nearer to the fire in a beautiful, absent manner. She was beautiful. It was funny. There was just no getting away from it, as a fact, even if he had wanted to. And the breakfast stuff still lay on the tiles in front of the fire, plus the empty mugs on the mantelpiece and the *Observer* fucking sections on the rug christ. It just meant he hadnt envisaged her presence. It meant he had never for one real and genuine minute imagined she could ever arrive here in this place, his house. Who could have imagined that? No fucker. And too, quietly studying the book in hand, taking the weight of her body onto her left foot, the right leg bent at the knee. It was one of these poses, good kind of poses, classic; he could imagine being a sculptor and motioning her to the side a little, and back a little, and so on, capturing the shadows of the folds in her coat, these long spiral shapes – curved cuboidals. Curved cuboidals? He strolled to clear the crockery and stuff from where it was lying, stacked it on the side of the sink; he put away the newspapers. He had no milk. The powdered stuff would be okay but he should have had milk because it would be better. I forgot to buy milk, he said. He smiled and shook his head. Daft – I forgot all about it.

It's okay.

Are you sure? I've got powdered stuff; ye just mix it in; it's fine.

I dont take milk in coffee anyway, she said and she grinned.

Pat chuckled. He stopped it and nodded. Alison returned her attention to the book. The room would soon be warm now, and comfortable. In fact he was feeling comfortable now himself. He was feeling quite the thing. Quite the thing, that is how he was feeling. He was feeling able to handle things, in an okay fashion, without any sort of

A shouting and bawling down in the backcourt. A gang of primaryschool-aged weans clambering across a big half-demolished dyke and they'd have to be fucking careful or it would collapse on top of them and fucking crush them. Cops and robbers they were playing, the Greatbritish Army versus the Evilsocialists, polis versus pickets, something like that. It was the same with the third yearers he had, there was something bathetic about them, a terrible ineffable something. What the fuck was that now was it a peculiar form of sadness? Nothing peculiar about it. Just a sadness. And nowhere near ineffable. They were just like their parents, the crazy flagellants, just fucking doomed. He grasped the tap and turned it on, washed his hands and dried them. Getting warmer now, he said over his shoulder, making his face take the form of a smile, a swift smile. Alison didni reply. But that was fine. The water in the kettle was good and audible now, close to boiling point. He stuck the handtowel back into his place, and he said: I dont see my parents all that much myself, do you? do ye keep in touch?

Eh . . . Alison half shut the book. I suppose we do really. Drew's have the habit of dropping in. Mine dont, not unless they've been invited. Very formal!

Do you get on with them okay?

Well, yes and no I suppose, the same as everybody else. On the whole though I think I get on better with Drew's. I seem to be able to relax more with them.

Is that right?

My own just seem to go on and on about the loveable idiosyncrasies I showed as a child. It can be embarrassing.

I bet ye. What age are you Alison?

Twenty-six.

Mm.

Alison looked at him for a couple of moments, and she smiled. Why d'you ask?

Naw it's just I was wondering I mean I suppose really all parents are the same, when it comes down to it. Mine do it as well, with me and Gavin – my brother. Then too I think they're always secretly trying to figure out how come they wound up with me! How come they wound up with a boy who went in for his Highers and then went to uni and became a member of the polis. Patrick grinned.

Eventually Alison nodded. She made as if to speak but said nothing. Patrick rubbed his hands together and patted the kettle and it was close to boiling hot. He glanced at his watch: The pubs'll be open now right enough!

I'd prefer the coffee, said Alison.

Eh aye, of course.

She was smiling. She probably felt a bit sorry for him but not in a terrible way, just to do with his nervousness.

He snatched the kettle that instant prior to its full boiling point. If ye leave water to boil for too long you waste it . . . He raised his eyebrows and added, It's true. Ye burn out the oxygen. That's what all the bubbles are you're bursting, oxygen. It was actually a Greek problem, part of their physics.

Mm.

Aye. You'll actually notice though if ye boil your water for a long while and then ye pour it into a cup, you'll see how it goes a brown colour, and it tastes bloody horrible.

Mm.

Very interesting eh!

Mm, it is.

I'm full of interesting facts.

It is interesting though.

Uch fuck it's no really Alison. He snorted quietly, shaking his head. He spooned coffee granules into the two mugs; clean mugs he had taken from the cupboard and rinsed under the tap, to get rid of any dust inside they had been there that fucking long. They were nice china mugs but had been donated by his Auntie Helen and commemorated an affair of the monarchy which she assumed would fascinate him because he had become a member of the Greatbritish élite. Probably he should have smashed them at birth but he hadnt because he was mean. This was a signifier. It was

Do you take sugar?

No.

That's because you're a smoker. Your taste buds are almost out the game completely.

She frowned. He was handing her a mug and gesturing at the armchair. He said: Want to take off your coat now?

She took her coat off. He put his hand out and she gave it to him. His bed hadnt been made. He had been about to put the coat there and it would have lain on his sheets. I'll hang it in the lobby, he said and he went into the lobby to do so. She had her cigarettes out when he returned:

Do ye mind if I smoke Pat?

Of course no, christ! He grinned. There was an ashtray at the bottom of the cupboard. He passed it to her. I dont think I could afford to smoke, he said.

Alison didnt reply. No fucking wonder either because it was an absolute piece of infantile tollie. Absolutely stupid and fucking mad, it being a downright lie which was the most absolutely important fact about it. He sprinkled the milk powder on his own coffee; he sat down with it, facing her, making a smile for her. He breathed in. Christ. He smiled at her and scratched at his head.

So, said Alison, she exhaled smoke, are you worried about seeing Old Milne?

Naw.

I would be I think.

Would ye!

I think so Pat, yeh.

Hh. I dont think I would. I mean I'm no . . . he grinned. I just eh, I dont fucking take it seriously.

She sipped at her coffee. She tugged at the cuff of the sleeve of the jumper she was wearing; a fawn and lightish green colour. It probably isnt anything serious, she said.

He grinned.

She looked at him: Do ye think it is?

Eh . . .

Then she said: Do you know what it's about?

Pardon?

I was just wondering if you knew what it was he wanted to see you about. And you werent telling. Alison smiled.

Aw! You mean that I might be being a devious shite of the first order!

Yes.

Pat grinned at her. Then he sighed. Ach, I'm a bad teacher Alison, being honest about it. I get too worked up about everything. Then I get too fucking depressed. I just get too fucking depressed. And the classes all know. They can tell. Actually I might be a depressive, and I mean clinically, as an actual condition – not manic, but a depressive all the same.

[141]

Did ye know Balzac was a manic depressive? she said after a moment.

Balzac!

Alison nodded.

Christ! He's a great writer! I've no read a great deal by him but eh.

She smiled. Do you know what he did with his coffee, he was a big coffee drinker, he used to make his coffee a fortnight before he drank it. He let it sit and go cold for that fortnight. Alison smiled and inhaled on the cigarette. Then he would reheat it. Apparently it was thick as tar.

He must have got hell of a heartburn!

Yes . . .!

Pat laughed briefly.

You're right! Alison frowned.

Dont be so bloody damn surprised Houston! I'm no always wrong ye know!

No but . . . Alison grinned, It never occurred to me before. Sorry.

Do you actually read him in the French?

Well, I have done.

He nodded. He was waiting for her to continue but it seemed like she wasnt going to continue. On the side of the mug facing him this portrait of the head of the monarchy. He glanced at Alison and indicated the thing.

Mm. I must confess I didnt expect you to have anything like that, she said.

No.

It's a surprise. She smiled: You're a secret royalist!

. . .

A smile.

. . .

It was funny.

Alison was watching him.

. . .

Yet as well though

but as well, in her face, in her look this great mixture of worry, care, of also affection maybe for him; a feeling for him, it was just obvious – Pat smiled, he gazed at his kneecaps. If he really was cracking up maybe she would rush to his defence, in the future, whenever his name cropped up in staffroom discussions, nostalgic ones about long-gone colleagues

old Mr McGeechan, who had been there when Patrick first started back in Clydebank – a great auld guy whose attitude was spot on and P. Doyle would aye have emulated him if anybody, if ever he had wanted to emulate anybody, auld McGeechan was the one, he was fucking

Alison was watching him.

He said: I was thinking there about an old guy called McGeechan that I used to work beside. Great he was. A genuine socialist and not one of your fucking typical Fabian shites. Just like a Hollywood movie too, the way the weans related to him. Like fucking Clarence Darrow with Spencer Tracy, d'ye ever see that picture? Sentimental drivel right enough. I thought auld McGeechan was fucking great as well. He used to say, Doyle, you've got to tell more jokes in the classroom, you'll be fine if you tell more jokes, you dont tell enough jokes.

Alison was saying something about sentimentality. What was it she was saying it was about sentimentality. But she was wrong and so was he because the person that was right was fucking Desimondi, he of the cynical eye. The man called Desmond was correct and the man called Patrick was not correct and if you birl these two statements about and then say something about the birling process itself, why then you are on to a mystery that certain parties almost solved but no you arent because it isnt true and dont fucking believe it. Alison was there. She was there. The concept of the magic carpet, it being high time she was not here. That she became elsewhere. Because it was really time to ask her to leave. If facts were to be admitted. If he was to be an honest chap who told the truth for once in his life, he was never fucking cut out for it. No really. As a racket, the teaching game, he was never cut out for it.

I actually used to want to paint, he said. See for instance these guys – women as well, lassies I mean, painters, artists, who paint the gable ends of tenement buildings. Eh? Imagine it! Can you imagine it!

She smiled.

Can ye!

She smiled.

Patrick smiled back at her. And no doubt it was best not to continue the questioning, the entire conversation. She was now inhaling and she expelled the smoke into the fireplace while glancing o so briefly swiftly and fucking the next thing – terrible. He got up at once and shook his head – it was the wristwatch she had glanced at, in her surreptitious manner, her wristwatch, a nicely delicate effort in gold and fucking chintzy shite. Excuse me, he said and he walked out the kitchen and shut the door behind himself; he went to the bathroom.

He was sitting on the lavatory pan, aware that had he a couple of blankets to hand he would have stretched himself out in the bath and had a fucking kip. And by the time he woke up she might have vanished. That was type of stunt that happened in the *Arabian Nights*. Although there was much more of everyday reality in that work than people gave it credit for. If Pat had been a character in one of these yarns what would his characteristics be? and would

And afterwards he dried them thoroughly and cleared his throat while unsnibbing the lock on the door.

Alison was back standing by the bookshelves, her head craned. She said: I dont read as much as I should. I dont seem to get the time.

That's what my brother says and he's on the broo.

She smiled a moment, her head tilting to the other side now as she attempted to decipher the title of an elderly volume whose batters were torn and with this hopeless spine which he had sellotaped once but the sellotape did not stick properly down and simply hid the fucking title christ, stupid. You required a diabolic cunning to perform that sort of task in an adequate fashion.

No use talking. There is that stage. He was at it now. He had reached it. He felt, really not good, and no eh

Alison spoke to him. Of a mundanity so startlingly fucking – so banal, so actually banal. He sat down and sighed at the fire, staring at the fire, not too sure of whether it was all a ploy to get her attention, agghhhh agghhh, excrutiating excrutiating, it was

And that just also, laying, laying, the head, on the breast, the lap, onto her breastlap, breastlap

Alison was talking again. He smiled at her. She said, Did you ever consider trying to write?

Naw, no really, did you?

Well, I was actually wondering about you.

Pat shrugged. Just like I says to ye Alison I was aye more interested in painting.

She continued to look at him. She sat back down again.

I'll tell you what I did do, which I'd forgotten about, it was just after I graduated, I thought it'd be good to rework some of my essays and maybe have a bash at submitting them for publication in a magazine, a political quarterly or a monthly or something. But once I started I found I couldni do it properly. In fact, when I re-read the bloody things it was hard to believe I'd ever passed a fucking exam!

Alison laughed.

Naw no kidding ye it was really terrible. And trying to make them better I made them worse. It was I this and it was I that and the actual sentences kept getting longer and longer and would've ended up like that mad German who wrote a treatise with everything bar the verbs, he kept them for the second volume.

Alison grinned.

Naw but the I's were the worst. Everywhere you looked always this fucking I. I I I. I got really fucking sick of it I mean it was depressing, horrible. I mean that's exactly what you're trying to get rid of in the first damn bloody fucking place I mean christ sake, you know what I'm talking about.

She nodded.

What about you?

What about me?

In terms of writing?

O . . . no, not really. Although before I went to uni . . . I used to try writing short stories.

She smiled briefly, then dropped her gaze to the fireside. I love Flannery O'Connor.

Christ aye, that one about the murderer where the cat jumps on top of the guy's neck while he's driving! That's an amazing story.

She smiled, nodding, still gazing at the fire and smoking her cigarette. She looked – sad. Fuck! Doyle fucking depresses everybody. God.

Hey Alison, d'ye ever get sick of hearing your own name? I'm no kidding, see when the weans say Mister Doyle, I feel like kicking their arse for them!

She winced.

. . .

Her eyes had closed. Patrick leaned forwards as though to touch her hand and her eyes opened. He said, Are you okay?

Yes. She smiled.

I apologise.

No. Dont.

It was the word of course, arse, she didnt like it and hadni been able to cope when he had said it. It was an odd word right enough. Arse. There arent many odder words. Arse. I have an arse. I kicked you on the arse. This is a load of arse. Are-s. It was an odd word. But in this life there are many odd things, an infinite multitude of them. It is not as if this life. It is not as if this life.

He smiled at her; but the smile soon petered out and he was just looking at her while she was staring in a downcast way. Would you like another cup of coffee? he asked her.

No thanks.

Ye sure?

Yes.

Are you okay?

Yeh.

Fine then, if you are.

She smiled. I am Pat, really.

I believe you.

She raised her eyebrows, giving him a look that was mysterious.

He smiled, shaking his head. He said: Your trouble is you're too acute – too eh . . . christ I'm no sure what it is. You're to open to, to open to something. You're too . . . Sorry, I've lost it, whatever it was. O, by the way, just as a matter of interest, that bloke Norman, the temporary English teacher

What was he babbling about? What was this he was babbling about it was not a topic it was fucking hopeless, nothing, nothing at all. What was it

he was trying to say. Trying; to; say. He looked at her: she of course was looking back at him.

She was so totally in control.

She was staring straight at him. What a look! It was straight. It was a straight look she was giving him; it was dislike. She seemed maybe as if really she maybe just disliked him. It wasnt a surprise; ordinary dislike, she just didnt like him, Mary Busby didnt like him either, so it was nothing startling, she just didnt like him. What was he to do now? It was a difficult one. What was he to do. He smiled at her. It was the same with that poor bloke Norman. He should never ever have done it to him.

It was a habit but. It was something he did a lot. He could even be said to do it to his maw and his da, and to Gavin, he did it all the time to Gavin, his brother, and that was how that slight estrangement had happened, because of what Patrick had done and said and made known, he had this habit, of wounding. He wounded people. He actually wounded them. He was the one. It was him. He could fucking destroy people. It wasni Alison that did that it was him, he was the one – not Desmond and not fucking Old Milne or any other bastard, just him.

That was funny that. It made ye feel hopeless.

If Alison hadnt come of course. What would've happened then? He had been needing someone to talk to. He was just getting awful lonely these days, sometimes thinking he was the only person in the world who thought about things and worried about them. What he felt was as if everything was going to blow up. Even Alison, when she said that about Northamerica, that's how he felt. And then fucking the school, all the wee first yearers and the third as well. All of them.

Even the fucking sixth years. It was probably best if he wasnt here any longer. Altogether – just away altogether, right out of it. Maybe China, that district somewhere in the north-eastern provinces where they're supposed to be making incredible advances in the treatment of cancer-related diseases. Just go and fucking see for yourself, if it was all a communist plot or what the fuck, maybe it really was one up for socialism. And maybe get a job in the village itself, as an English-language tutor, or a lorry driver or something. There was a nice kind of life to be led in some of them, the villages, you could be happy in it, a self-containedness. Chiang Kai-Shek was the Greatbritish Hero. That, was the way of it, how things were in reality, the fact to be admitted. Greatbritain, the place to leave. Alison was looking inside a book. What was she looking into the book for. What was it she was to be doing by it, by that manoeuvre. Was

Was?

Was?

Was. It is not to be got beyond. It is not to be got beyond. Here is the moment and it is always out in the open, the palpability. Palpa palpae, a punch in the fucking mouth, feminine.

No. It is not anything; nothing.

The moment. It has lasted for seconds. Seconds. And her; her absorption in the book, not wholly a hundred percent; that fraction of awareness, a reflectiveness, and watching him out the corner of her eye. Yes. Fuck. Fucking terrible.

I know what we can do we can play the pipes.

!!

Alison was looking at her book. Patrick knew its cover. It was a fairy tale about a woman who comes to a sticky end through no fault of her own, but in effect is a victim of society i.e. a world of male manners. Fiona Grindlay, a mother in his sixth-year class. She told them all to fuck off, just like the woman in the story. Fiona Grindlay, a good wee lassie and real and strong and tough and ah christ strong and tough and ready to confront the dark forces, to stand there having said, okay, how far can a person retreat! I'm just going to stand here and brace myself, fair enough, let them do as they wish but they'll have to drag me off, they'll have to knock me down and drag me away.

Great.

Patrick was a teacher
Patrick was a fool
Patrick Patrick Patrick
da da da da school

Patrick sniffed: I think about their parents Alison. The way they just stand back and let their weans' heids get totally swollen with all that rightwing keech we've got to stuff into them so's we can sit back with the big wagepackets. It's us that keep the things from falling apart. It's us. Who else! We're responsible for it, the present polity.

Alison stared at him.

It is; us.

Is that what ye believe? Her eyes screwed up: genuine puzzlement.

Eh, yes.

Well I think it's nonsense. She shut the book and returned it up onto its shelf and leaned back on the chair.

Patrick said, Would ye take another coffee?

She nodded slightly. I really do think it's nonsense Pat and if you honestly believe it to be true then I think you should leave altogether.

Exactly.

Alison muttered, It's a ridiculous thing to say.

I dont think it is.

Well I do. Also I think it's damn silly . . . She shook her head and reached for another fag.

Pat nodded. It was best he wasnt here any longer although having said that of course it was his fucking house and if anybody was not to be here it was her, it was Alison; it was probably best she went away. Unless she started to talk. If she really started to talk. So he could find out what she actually did think about things – her herself, and not just received opinion and conventional bloody fucking wisdom.

There were water biscuits and cheese to go with the coffee if she fancied it, or bread, he could make a couple of sandwiches although he wasnt hungry at all, it wasnt that long since he had had his breakfast.

He stood at the sink with his back to her, the tap turned on and the water gushing, and he would turn to confront her in a moment, eye to eye. Here's your coffee Alison plus biscuits and cheese if you've a mind.

It was so.

The whole thing.

While the truth of the matter what was the truth of the matter was it sex? Is that what it was he was just wanting to have some sex with her yes of course he was he was wanting sex of course, of course he was, but not just that although what else of course he was wanting much else but the sex was so fucking important because of the way it would make him feel just wanted, just wanted by her as an ordinary bloke there in the ring like anybody else, a part of everything. Because he couldni even imagine it really, what like it would be the actual insertion and how she would be in the nude and that moment of insertion the tightening back it was just so disbelievable, the existence of it, the possibility; what would he be doing would he be holding her breasts. Holding her breasts.

Poor old Hölderlin. He was a poor unfortunate bastard. And Susette, poor auld fucking Susette, dying like that. It was a shame, it was such a shame, terrible, so pathetic, a downright fucking shame. He would be lying on her breasts.

How is the point arrived at it is arrived at by doing the things. He put a teaspoonful-and-a-half of coffee granules into his mug and exactly the same into hers. Then he worked off the lid of a tin he kept for biscuits although he knew fine well it was empty and the only biscuits were these stupit water efforts he kept in the cupboard and were only there for emergencies e.g. should he run out of bread and so on. And the dried milk sprinkled aboard, avast ye landlubbers, the crew of the jolly roger clambered aft the rigging. Fine, good. She didni take sugar of course. Why of course? Uch it was obvious. A woman like Alison. Far too fucking self-possessed for that sort of weakness. Yet she smoked like a fucking chimney! But that's different. He grinned. He lifted her mug. He paused a moment and looked out the window. He turned and walked to her, saying, There's water biscuits and cheese if you fancy it . . .?

No thanks Pat.

Because eh what I thought I would do and I dont want to embarrass you in any way at all but what I would like to do, or rather, what I thought I would do, only if you didnt mind right enough, obviously

She nodded.

It was just eh . . . He grinned and returned for his own coffee. He sat down with it on his chair. It's these two pipes Alison, I know it sounds daft, but what I've done is kind of rigged them up into instruments. And what I'm actually doing is blowing on them, getting sort of musical sounds out them, a bit like eh – I dont really know, the concept I suppose is to do with improvisation, the way people take and use what they see lying about and I dont know just bloody christ use them, make music, like these washboard waistcoats the old bluesmen wore to make music. They used to strap them round their middle and strum away. Absolutely brilliant and crazy, just absolutely brilliant and fucking crazy!

He chuckled, and added, It's a certain kind of nostalgia. A really valid kind of . . . nostalgia.

Alison had nodded.

Which was fair enough. Then when he didnt add anything further she made a quiet grunting noise that could have signified whatever was required. She stared at the fire. He could say something but he wouldnt. I just feel, he said and he stopped. She continued staring at the fire. It was as if she hadnt heard him or was just trying to ignore him. She gazed at the fire, the ash gone light grey at the tip of her fag, not bothering about the mug of coffee.

The silence continued. He was not going to breach it. If he did he would end up saying something daft and getting himself into knots. There were dangers in too much speechifying – that self-consciousness, and ultimate lack of faith in what you were up to. Silent folk aye gained the fucking advantage. Old Milne was an obvious example; he could stand for interminable periods, saying nothing in an attentive manner, as though you the speaker had only been halfway through your explanation when in actual fact you had finished the thing altogether. Which is how come the old dickie had wangled his way to praetorship. And this benign exterior he liked to assume: the wise old chap to whom one could march with the personal problems, no matter how unsavoury. Aside from that of course he was a rightwing fucking shite, a rightwing fucking shite, and it was best just to rise and in a swivel, in a swivel, of the palm of his hand on the arm of the chair, to be rising without having to raise his gaze to par, now on his feet and as though quite naturally, just staring ahead where ahead is ·the door into the lobby. Leave the coffee. Ignore it. Just fucking on ye go. He inclined his head a little to one side and muttered, Ben the parlour eh . . . that's where I keep them.

Out in the lobby the obvious temptation to enter the bathroom and lock himself in. Yet it was so out of the question as to merit nothing at all so far as thought or consideration was concerned. And was she rising to follow him. And yet presently of course she would still be wondering if this is what was asked of her. She would still just be sitting there. Well fucking let her. It was her decision. Whether to follow him ben or not. I mean after all, he had made his intentions known, he had told her and implied the palpable, the glaringly fucking obvious, a fact for christ sake, he had given her to know she should follow him. So then.

The way a seated jazz musician gets him or herself and the instrument prepared, these wee glimmers of a smile to the fellow musicians, the friends and the acquaintances in the audience, but also taking great care not to confront directly the stares from members of the ordinary people – otherwise enter irony: the kind that leads to a lack of overall control. But it was no bloody good without her being there. The whole thing was her to be there as audience, as a sort of ordinary person, so he could play with her there spectating. And she would not come unless invited. And had he invited her? Had he fuck! Of course he hadni. The lassie was sitting ben the kitchen and she did not know what the hell to do, was she to stay or come for christ sake for all she knew he was in the lavvy. Patrick laughed.

He cleared his throat loudly at the kitchen door, then opened it. She looked at him when he entered, a book in her hand. Eh . . . he smiled: Are you coming ben Alison?

She rose, tugging down the bottom bits of her jumper. She put the book back on the shelf. She looked so worried, yet without showing it. He left her to follow on her own, to close the door behind herself and to come into the parlour and close this door as well, him moving straight onto the wooden upright chair he used, trying to establish an immediate aura of concentration so that she would comprehend the seriousness of it, that he was in total earnest over what he was doing; and he quite envied the guitarist for being able to footer about in a very meaningful way with the keys and the strings.

He cleared his throat. He had almost forgotten her presence, he was lifting the larger of the pair to balance its bottom rim on the toe of his left shoe, positioning his left hand round the top, covering the gap between his mouth and the rim, and he breathed in through his nostrils – there was a reason for this method but it did not demand any exposition; and too his method of blowing without the slightest puff of the cheeks, it also had a good reason, the same reason, but later, later. He began the sound at the back of the throat, controlling his breath that the note might be sustained without any break, without even the slightest alteration in pitch, nor in audibility, just that one note, evenly and all, the whole thing of it; and too when shading off, retaining the note precisely, and no sign that his breath is almost gone. And the pause too, that same sense of it not being an actual pause strictly speaking, or perhaps it was, a pause just as that, pause as pause and nothing to do with a need to stock up on oxygen; and into the next sound, the same note precisely; everything about it was to be the same, it was what he was after, the key to what he was after. He wanted it to always be the same, in every way, to the ordinary listener; that was plenty, he wasnt after any extra-terrestrial point of com-munication. It was just a straightforward sort of evenness be needed, constancy. He had begun the sound at the back of the throat, his breath under control, the note.

It didnt have to be the same pitch all the time. But he sought the same sort of thing each occasion he sat down to play, and the only part he really wished to vary was the pause, it was all that was important, essentially. It was simple. There is not much to be said about it. There was just a certain easing of the spirit, an easing of the spirit. That was it really, an easing of the spirit. Nothing more, he said modestly, an easing of the spirit!! Alison looked a bit cold and shivery. He laid the pipe into the crook of his elbow and said, That'll do.

She nodded. She showed interest in them. He handed the thinner one to her and she felt its weight and looked along it and into its interior. Is it papier mâché? she asked.

I'm no really sure. I suppose it is. It's the kind of thing an electrician uses to rewire a house; they run them at the foot of the wall. Or for thick cables maybe, I'm no a hundred percent sure, to be honest.

You've just painted them?

Aye. But I've never been quite sure about that either, about whether I would've been best to just leave them in their natural state.

Though who's to say what their natural state really is, said Alison.

Aye christ, exactly.

Alison was still giving her attention to the pipe; he motioned with the thicker yin and she took it and returned the first.

It's amazing the variety of sound ye can get.

Mm.

Just by the way ye actually breathe, and where ye allow the sounds to come from, the parts of your mouth and throat.

Most instruments work on that principle though dont they — wind instruments I mean?

Eh aye, I suppose so.

She passed the pipe to him; he returned the pair to their places. She said, D'you listen to a lot of music Pat?

Eh sometimes. Sometimes I dont. What about you?

I'm a bit the same. If Drew's away I tend to listen more. I was borrowing from Desmond for a while, and taping.

Aye, he's got some collection! Mind you, he doesni usually like people borrowing. It's probably because he fancies you!

Alison smiled, but shook her head.

Ah well, either that or he's just bloody mellowing with old age!

O come on Pat he's no that auld!

Well he's fucking christ he must be near forty!

Mm.

No think so?

Alison shrugged. I dont know . . . She had her arms folded and now she shivered. It was cold in the parlour; he seldom ever put on the fire. It wasnt meanness, he just never used the place.

Fancy a cup of tea?

I'll have to be going soon actually.

Of course.

[154]

It's only because Drew's parents are coming.

Aye. Skip the tea!

I think I've still a coffee lying in your royal mugs!

It was my fucking Auntie Helen. I dont want to destroy her love by dumping the things in the fucking midgy! But I should, I should fucking dump them in the fucking midgy.

No ye shouldnt, she said.

Pat smiled at her and he touched her on the forearm, holding the parlour door open for her, and she entered the lobby, walking at a normal speed, her skirt swinging, maybe the way she still had her arms folded, having something to do with that. When he shut the kitchen door she was already at the fireside, rubbing her hands close in to the electric bars. She said: Do you have any dampness?

Eh I'm no sure.

It smells a wee bit like it. She shivered again.

Patrick nodded.

And that was that, that was to be it. That story of Joyce's where the wife thinks about the boy who died of the flu. There was nothing to be said about it really. It was best just accepting matters, the way matters were. And you could say as well that for fuck sake at least she listened with a straight face. She hadni burst out laughing. That was something. It was, yes, but still better if she left immediately; ignore the tea. Patrick sniffed. He said, I've got to go and visit my brother's family anyway, later on. He cleared his throat, turned to face the sink and filled the kettle after a few seconds' silence. He cleared his throat and continued to speak: My brother's kids are good; he's got two of them, a wee boy and a wee lassie. I quite like kids. He grinned: What about yourself Alison, did you ever think of raising a family?

Yeh . . . After a moment she said, Later, rather than sooner. It's not the best time.

Aw.

We're a bit unsettled the now, Drew and myself.

Is that right?

Her nose wrinkled. Touch wood, she said, this year's been a wee bit better but the last two were awful. The school I was at it was awful – really awful. She smiled: You've no idea. It was so good getting into here . . . She lighted another cigarette and sat on the armchair, sending a cloud of smoke into the fire, forgetfulness probably, thinking there was a chimney for smoke to go up. If you think Old Milne's bad, the headmaster where I was . . .! she said.

Simpson, I've heard of him.

The way he treats teachers! It was just a constant battle. He actually penalised us for things. If ye forgot to turn off the light when you were leaving the classroom. He had the janitors patrolling just to see. O! Too many things, it was just really as if he had gone insane.

Old Milne's insane.

No he's not.

Aye he is.

He isnt really Pat.

Well, your definition of insanity differs from mine.

That's as maybe.

Pat nodded. You're right. What I mean really is about the actual role itself, the function of headmaster, that's what's insane. It's an insane job. So that whoever has it has become insane, virtute officii – by virtue of the office. Even the way they aye prowl the corridors with their gowns on; you're expecting to see them swirl it the way Dracula does, so that they vanish in a puff of smoke.

Alison chuckled. She continued talking about the difference between the two schools. It was good hearing her in this animated state and yet when all's said and done she was usually like that, it was one of the great things about her, it was her usual self – whenever she was not in a state of extreme nervousness, like this afternoon. Because of worrying about him, about Patrick, about how he was and how the afternoon would turn out. Although it wasnt over yet, he could still turn nasty and do her a bad turn, kidnap her and set sail for the East Neuk of Anglia! Could she really have suspected him of something bad? It was awful to think that. She couldnt have. She must have been kidding him on. Which she does do. She had a good line in irony, a quiet kind, that fitted in entirely with her personality. It would be good just giving her a cuddle. Grabbing a hold of her and giving her a great big cuddle. Fuck penetration christ he just wanted to be close to her, to be holding her. Never mind her fucking body christ that's got nothing to do with it.

But.

But what?

But she would probably

because he'd probably fucking get an erection, if holding her in a cuddle for christ sake her body fitting into his, he would get an erection. And she would feel it, obviously. And it would fucking make things awkward. So she would have to push him away. Else things would just – move on. And from there; well it would have to be the possibility of bed, jumping into bed together.

So:

one thing he had learned this afternoon:

playing the pipes was not a substitute for sex! Eh, christ, and that in itself was worth all the hassle, that in itself would be worth giving her a cuddle for, just a cheery one and a friendly one, between two friends, one of whom has just helped the other through a bad time. Okay. I just canni cope sometimes, he said.

Alison was looking at him. She had said something requiring an answer. It was about school.

You're talking about your last school but I'm talking about this yin – in fact I'm no, I'm just trying to get away from the idea of making things particular, or even worse, specific.

Yeh but it's about individuals, said Alison, so it cant help but be specific. It's about individual teachers and it's about individual children.

Well okay but you're saying it in general plurals.

I dont know what ye mean.

Patrick nodded.

Could you explain it?

You're trying to insist on the individuals and yet you're doing it yourself with your pluralistic generalising.

After a moment she replied, I think you're nitpicking.

I'm no.

I think you are.

He nodded. She continued watching him because she was expecting him to proceed with an attempted explanation, but he wasnt going on. He had lost the thread anyway, of the argument. Or maybe the actual truth is that he just couldni fucking be bothered. Which is a terrible thing to say. He stroked the brow of his head and he sighed, turned to the sink once more. She didnt want coffee though or tea because she was about to be going. The window was steamed up. The tobacco fug wasnt helping matters.

He was not going to get into her head at all. That was that. It didni matter what he said it was as if something was missing and what it was it was just that basic interest in him, she did not have it. That was it. And did he have it in her? So far no, it was as if he was only interested in himself, just going over and over about himself all the time, about what he was doing and what he was wanting out of life. But never a word about her. Had he even asked her a question? A true question I'm talking about; one that concerns the other person, one to shed some real spark of light on the subject. It was doubtful if he had. Otherwise he wouldnt have forgotten about it already. Being so bloody damn taken fucking up with his own problems. And he was fucking sick of it, his own problems for christ sake you get sick fucking hearing about them. The trouble being of course that they do not go away. The closer you get to them the likelihood of their disappearance does not diminish. You get surrounded by them. Everywhere ye look you see the same things, like the shadow-lines down in the back close, they're always there no matter the time of day, the way the light hits, electric or otherwise, they are always there, like a greasy spot on the windscreen right in front of your fucking nose and everything you see is filtered through it, through the fucking grease, so there's a greasy tree and there's a greasy lorry and there's a greasy pedestrian and so on and so forth.

Three years is it you've been married? he asked.

Just going on to it.

It's a while.

Mm.

Patrick smiled. Tell me this, he said, seriously I mean: how come ye wanted to meet at that stupit bloody Commodore Cafe? Were ye actually I mean . . . suspicious?

You could say that.

Ah. Fine. Pat chuckled and collected his mug from the side of his chair. Mind you, okay, in your position, there's a lot of headcases going about — when you're a woman I mean. I dont fancy it myself.

I wasnt suspicious in that way Pat.

[158]

Aw. Glad to hear it! You just thought a place as public as that would be good?

I thought it might make things easier.

Do ye mean in general?

Yeh.

For talking?

She smiled.

Mirs Houston . . .?

What?

Nothing. Pat grinned. Thanks for coming.

Och!

Naw but it's appreciated, I was feeling a bit low. And then of course you've got the pipes.

There was a slight smile on her face.

The trouble is Alison I take the bloody things seriously.

In what way? how do ye mean?

Ach I dont know! He glanced at his wristwatch. Just sometimes I suppose, when I sit down and play them. When I sit down. And once I actually start playing. Ye forget things. That's what good about it.

Therapeutic?

Eh aye, I suppose . . . He cleared his throat. It was high time she went now, definitely; and he looked at his watch again. It wasnt good for her to remain much longer than this. He had objections to crying in company. He had objections to doing most things in company. Although there again, most of his decisions, they all seem to be arrived at in such circumstances. As if he had to force everything onto himself. He smiled, gesturing at the mugs. My Auntie bought me four of them; she thinks when you become a member of the teaching profession you become a member of the government. Mind you, she's no far wrong.

Alison shut her eyes. She didni like hearing such things. Too close to the fucking bone. An arse of a statement. He chuckled. But it probably sounded sexist. Affectionate, but sexist. You had to be on the look-out at all times. But what's wrong with that there's nothing wrong with that. It's good. And it's healthy. It means your world's continually shifting its base, the greasy bit becoming that bit wider.

I apologise Alison.

What for? She frowned: You dont have to apologise to me.
He nodded.

. . .

. . .

. . .

. . .

. . .

He shook his head.

He got up from the bed and pulled down the blind, he undressed, got beneath the covers, because he had to try and sleep, life being exactly too much, that precise amount. His nerves were jangling. They began to settle. He was lying on the bed; the light was out and he was thinking and trying not to, he was trying to block out his brains from their eternal imaginings and maunderings. Definitely this being alone, this is what it was. He was not thinking about her, the woman, he was not. What he was doing was getting himself aware of it, of things. He knew better now. He knew more than he had done.

A while since she had gone. Okay. And funny that he wasnt going to be seeing her again. He would not be seeing her again except by chance. Nor the school! which was even more incredible. He felt strange and almost happy. Happy. But no; it was too easy, too straightforwards. Just not going back to school. It made you want to laugh aloud.

He was obviously going back. He smiled and turned onto his side, still with his face outside the covers. Imagine not going back. What would he do? What would he not do. He would not worry about the headmaster because he would not be going to see him. He wouldnt do this and he wouldnt do that. It wasnt what he would do it is what he would not do. All these things that he would not be having to do, he would not be having to do this and he would not be having to do that.

He would play the pipes. There was a positive move if ever I saw one. He would do that. What else? He would forget the past. He would go up and see his brother. What would he go up and see him about. You dont do that with brothers, you just go and see them and that's enough, you just chat. What about politics, about politics and the nature of things in general – the Doyle family and revolution. How to negate the parents of the parents. The usual keech.

He would begin by staring the world firmly in the face. And with that to the fore he was now getting out of bed, and kicking his way into his shoes but he hasnt got his socks on so is kicking them off and getting back onto the bed to fucking look for them but there they were there just at the foot, at the fucking foot, of the bed. Because he was going to go out. He was going to go out for the night and that was that. High time he started enjoying life since here he was chucking it all in tomorrow morning. Christ that was a great holiday he had in West Yorkshire five years ago, on the coast at the seaside with the sun and the sand and having a laugh with the crowd. That was the Gillian Porter era. Ach Gillian was good. What had happened there? that was a pity. She was straightforwards as well, she wasni fussy about stupid things. Now here she was on the other side of Scotland. But christ almighty that was only sixty miles off. But she would be well away now, with other people. It was too late for him. As far as she was concerned. And why dwell on the past! But things did seem to be more straightforward then. People too. They seemed to be like that. But not now. Nowadays it was always as if everything was a big deal and you had to have or do something or something as if

It was just things had changed things had changed, it was years ago, the days of the teachers' trainers, when people were students together and life was sweet ya fucking idiot. There is no point dwelling on the past. It is a thing he was wont to do. But this is because he was a single chap and single chaps are single persons ergo they dwell on the past and there is nothing wrong in dwelling on the past. How can you dwell on the future? There is nothing to dwell on! It doesni fucking exist. It is a fucking blank. Everything has yet to take place. This is what the future is, the place where things have yet to occur. So how can you dwell on that. You're cheating. Okay but just think of it as an empty room. No. Well then think of 'place' as nothing. The future is the nothing. There is nothing to think about, so dont think about it. Do something else, something else altogether.

The time has gone.

The time has passed, is past.

There have been chances that Patrick has had. He has had his share of chances. He has simply failed, to take advantage of them. You take advantage of chances. Patrick didnt. He failed to.

Is there anything more to be said? And if so, why?

There is nought more one can say. Silensus. It would be nice not to think. Not to think and not to spoke. But he would have to spoke, because he was going out. That was the thing about going out, you had to spoke, you had to meet people and converse with them. He was putting on his good clothes. His going-out when going-out is not going-to-school clothes, that is what he was putting on.

What was he supposed to do. He was supposed to enter a shell and remain there moping, having an internal debate on the nature of the universe and specific feminine persona to wit the verb 'alison'. I shall alison this evening. I shall, with a bit of luck, be alisoning this evening.

Bastards.

He left the motor where it was and walked right beyond it. He turned and glanced at it. He continued walking. He was very hungry and the chip shop was shut. This was undoubtedly the fault of patronne the elder Rossi, his insistence that the entire family should observe the traditional Sunday of the Scottish Christians thus the solitaries of the district had to forego the daily fries. Then the odd thing:

he saw what looked like Gavin and Nicola and their kids. They were heading his way. Where were they going? was it really them? It was really them and here they were coming toward him and in that next instant would recognise him and he moved extremely fast, right into the mouth of the nearest close and down to the stairfoot, he stood in at a bit of the wall that sloped, where he would not be easily seen from outside. He kept in until they had passed, waiting a few moments before returning to the front, and he looked out after them, seeing their backs, the man and the woman and the wee boy and the wee girl. He was not sure whether he was playing a trick on them or no. He wasnt. He was letting them continue in ignorance. He was going to allow a terrible charade to take place. He was going to allow his brother and sister-in-law to walk on past, to continue on past, unchecked. They would be on their way up to his place, a quick hello before paying the weekly visit to Nicola's parents – maybe even to the maw and da, they could even be visiting them and maybe wanting to invite Patrick along; they wouldnt know he had been yesterday evening. He watched them turn the corner into his street. It was a very sad sight. His older brother whom he loved dearly. His sister-in-law whom he loved dearly. Then wee Elizabeth and wee John, both of whom he loved more than life itself. Because if it ever came to the choice between living and dying then christ almighty he would lay down his life, and glad to do it. They were great wee weans. Great wee weans. Even if they were horrible wee weans and selfish and spoiled brats, he would still have done it. And they werent, they were great.

And he was letting all of that go.

But it was his brother's fault it was not his it was not his it was his brother's, his brother's fault; it was not Patrick's fault. It wasnt. It wasnt his fault, it was his brother's.

But what about the pipes? Were they things? Were the pipes things? A man was crossing onto the pavement from the other side of the road and he gazed to the front of where he was walking as though deep in thought. Going up to him and saying: Are pipes really things? A serious question. Heh you, Mister, are pipes really things? Or are they not? Are they just a figment is that what they are a fucking stupit dream, a stupit dream. The man looked deep in thought. Could he be genuinely thinking of something? Often you get folk – especially pedestrians – who kid on they are thinking but they arent, they are just having a sort of internal gaze into space. And such space! Patrick could imagine gazing into that guy's space. Anaximenes – what's he got to do with this if anything? Does he have anything to do with that? with gazing into the space of other people. What would you see? All sorts of things. If you looked into the space of other people.

The man turned the corner into Pat's street which was funny.

[163]

You could picture him being Special Branch and trailing Gavin and Nicola because they were visiting Pat who was being kept under scrutiny at all times, a threat to the current rightwing government of the greatbritishers, a poisoner of the minds of the flagellants. Imagine having a bugle and blasting a gigantic tootoooootoooooot! For fuck sack. Christ! Well well well, god and Pythagoras, Señor Goya, the lot of yous.

Was poor auld 2^4: 2^2 metamorphosising into something else altogether! He seemed to be. It was highly likely. This sort of escapade happened all the time. Take Gregor Samsa as a for instance. He was a poor unfortunate bastard though having said that of course it would take a Giant to squash him. A Giant. A veritable Mammothian. And there were none of these lurking in this man's Glasgow, all of whose entities were so palpably impalpable.

Maybe he should get the motor. The motor could take him places. The motor could take him to the east neuk of England. There existed rowing boats tethered to small jetties. He could pilfer one and set sail for Scandinavia.

Set Sail For Scandinavia. Fuck sake.

And what about Mrs Houston. What about Mrs Houston? She was a thing of the past. No she wasni. Yes she was. She had proved it this afternoon. It was simply no longer here. And she was no longer it, whatever it was. It was not her.

It was himself from now on, that he was to think about and care about.

What.

Pat halted. This time of the evening on Sunday was aye peaceful. He was looking at himself in the window of a shop and seeing the face and the body and the rest of it. He was looking at a bloke who had difficulty in seeing himself. And he was wanting to see himself. He was looking at a bloke who was wanting to see himself and who was wanting to not be what he was because he could not be trusted to be doing it except by corruption of the hearts and the minds of the young. Fucking outlandishly sentimental, slavishly so, as if he's fucking another Socrates, that's what makes it so bad, so desperately bad and so desperately sad and perhaps evil, because of the ulteriority of the motivation, that he wishes to be King of the World.

Spring spring spring. Spring spring spring.

Spring is a time for change. Patrick has already changed. This was the year he had opted out, that he had, theretofore, said, No; I am not doing these things any longer, with specific reference to xmatic pantomimes. I am a happy man. Also sex. Patrick grinned. He chuckled and he shook his head, seeing his features creasing in this joviality, his eyes and his mouth smiling, and jesus christ it was good to see, himself smiling because for fuck sake it was simply not the done Doyle thing in life to smile, to laugh aloud my god for fuck sake on a public byway? almost a contradiction albeit that it is occurring in front of one's own reflection in the window of a shop thus in public and not in public, at one and the same time. Which is surely the manner life is to be led, that a fellow or fellowess, that s/he should be in harmony, one's figures in smooth control.

Children approach! Two males and a female. Second-year bracket. Smoking fags. One of the males is spitting through his teeth, making a tthhh noise.

At that age Patrick hadnt been a smoker. He had not been a smoker even then. That was it about the boy Doyle even then, him no being a smoker. A perverse wee bastard, let's face it. Pat grinned. He was proud of himself as a wee boy. He had been perverse, so fucking ha ha ha and he was not going to change now.

The launderette. The light was on inside. Nobody was in except the lady who ran the place. She was a Muslim. She spoke very little English, especially to men maybe but she gave good smiles and was often amused at the ways of the world. Here she was in Scotland after having fervently believed she would become a moviestar in Delhi. And it amused her because life itself she found amusing, knowing fine well that men were created from clots of blood so why bother if here you are in Glasgow on a cold and quiet and fairly dreichlike Sunday evening in March, you were best just to get on with things and soon you would be home in front of the fire with maybe a video out on hire to relax to later on, when you had locked up the launderette and fucked off down the road.

Patrick had his hands in his trouser pockets; he had been leaning against the window. He glanced along to the corner of the street to see if the coast was clear, then walked off quickly in the opposite direction, being careful not to collapse in a vertigonoreac heap.

Early morning was a time he enjoyed reading. His mind was alert, the attention span seemed to continue indefinitely, right until he remembered about having to go to school. It was a nice time, a peaceful time. There was something about giving your best to the things you liked the best. And he quite liked reading. He really did quite like reading. He quite liked the things you get in books. In this book it was China and the treatment of cancerous diseases. There was much to be said in favour of China. Pat could motor south, down the Bay of Biscay and dive across to Morocco and head straight left along the northcoast of Africa, bypassing the whole of fucking Europe because he was sick of it, the whole thing, its politics and its history. Even this kind of thinking was a malaise, a western malaise – a luxury. Far better to think about sitting in a desert without the energy to lift a beetle to your mouth. It was 5.47 a.m. And still dark. He could go down to the backcourt and sit right in the middle of that, next to the midgies and where the rats and mice and cats and dogs scrabble for the edible scraps. If nothing else it would affirm a general braveness of spirit and mental control. The animals would be quietly surprised by the human presence but would no doubt get used to it. How would it be to go spiralling at a furious rate upwards into the sky towards that ethereal spindle. Copernicus seems to have been a similar sort of personality to Schopenhauer but perhaps that's being unfair. Probably Patrick's largest error was the purchase of the petrol-powered automobile. He missed out on experiences because of it. The unexpected. His unexpected was just the occasional mechanical breakdown and that was hopeless, freezing cold and total boredom unless the breakdown chanced to take place near a pub. And then you ran the risk of being drunk when the mechanic arrived to right the wrong. Near to a brothel would be better. As long as you had the dough. This is another thing about being rich, how you take money for granted. So many of the predicaments of the Reverend Doyle MA (honS) are the effects of having no financial worries of any kind whatsoever. If he was skint for example he would never even consider a brothel, nor a pub for that matter. And all chatter on the subject of motor cars a mere bagatelle, a trumpery, a flumpery, a frumpery, fump. Arse is a better word than fuck. From now on Arse is Fuck. Fuck off. What does it mean. Hey you ya wee second-yearers! You're all snug in your wee kips! Little do yous know the trouble in store this morning! Heh heh heh he intoned evilly. In fact though it would be a fine thing to enter Old Milne's office with a trusty Dobermann Pinscher and a big fucking double-barrelled shotgun. I mean that really would be something. Good morning Mister Milne.

Good eh morning Mister eh eh ahh eh

D'you mean the beast?

Yes ah eh ehhh ah ah

The fucking double-barrelled shotgun?

Yes eh

Because ye see ya auld fucking conniving bastard ye I'm resigning my commission and then after my dog's fucking bit ye I'm gonni fucking shoot ye! Okay? So there! Stick that in your pipe and smoke it! But god, it would be nice to just leave the motor at home this morning, to just walk it the whole road there, and get the nut sorted out, a bit of mental equilibrium, get the fucking brains operating properly, some kind of fucking synchronicity. Because at the moment

At the moment! There was no at the moment. There was no at the moment. How could there be when it was so bloody damn difficult to gain any idea whatsoever of this coming fucking on-the-carpeting. If he could maybe work out a list of possible occurrences, a contingency list.

Patrick couldni find a pen. It is most odd indeed how objects disappear in rooms wherein the only moveable entity is oneself. Scary. And not at all the

On the sink next to the fucking dishes.

1) When your man enters the office the headmaster screams: Get out ya anarchist fucking bastard or I'll send for the MI5.

Which is where a knapsack comes in handy and Patrick just happens to have two of these efforts, one for long journeys and one for short yins. So he can fill the latter with a set of emergency goods and chattels. Renew the Youth Hostelling membership card, the passport and so forth, remember the driver's licence.

2) A posse of polis awaiting his arrival within the grounds of the school, the entire area having being cordoned off. And as soon as he drives into the carpark the barricades come down behind him.

So, he would drive round the back and park in a sidestreet, with a belaying pin and a massive rope coiled over his shoulder, and toss its looped end high round the topmost chimney of the main school building, and swing from an adjacent tenement roof, straight across all their heads, softly alighting in through an open window on the upper floor, surprising the awestruck staff and weans down in assembly as you sneaked ben the corridor and down into the office of the terrorstricken Old Milne. The image of a pair of frogman's flippers and a black SAS balaclava cum falseface, and crying to Old Milne: Your number's up auld yin! Say your prayers to the congregation and make your peace with the Christian God whom for the sake of common decency I'm begging the existence of this morning and just awarding the capital, 'G', as in 'God'. Okay okay get off your knees, I hate to see a guy humiliating himself in company.

3) Milne!! Yes you! I'm addressing you. You are an arse. You are a total arse. Aye, you heard alright – capital A R S E arse.

And what about going back to bed and staying there for the rest of the morning. Patrick had also considered that. Then he could sign off sick altogether, go and visit the doctor and maybe find out that his mental state, his nervous disposition, certainly warranted a six-month leave of absence the which he could fill by travel. It would not be difficult. He could make a phonecall to the secretary's office, at ten to nine, just to give her a fair chance at getting some other bastard to do his registration with poor auld 2e. 2e!! What a poor wee bunch of fucking bastards they were! Never mind. They would have to get along without him. Old Milne might actually be grateful if he went on the panel. Because it could render Friday's astonishing absence null and void. How can it be otherwise? Here you have a bloke being taken ill and having to sign off sick. So how the hell can you hold him morally responsible for an action, when that selfsame action was governed by the deterministic machinations of a bone-coffin? In other words sir he wasnt really being disrespectful to the forces of law and order in the classroom. He wasni really fucking doing something that was fucking quite upsetting in many ways that at first sight appear unimportant but in actuality, as you and I both are aware, is the very stuff of which the strongest citadel may ultimately crumble and fall into disrepute.

Now,

and after that, Tenerife. Tenerife! Does the sun shine in Tenerife on Marchday mornings! No doubt – these foreign bastards get all the luck, the sunny climes and belly dancers. And afterwards, afterwards

How come these afterwards aye rear their ugly mugs? What about Goya? go there, he lived in Saragossa and they've got no a bad football team. Christ it's great to have money, ye can just fuck off wherever you like and take a fancy to. What about Velasquez and auld fucking Rubens. Where did they dwell? Was the climate luscious. Did oranges fall off the fucking trees. Carlos Williams's grannie? Handgrenades? And of course El Greco who was a sixteenth-century chap from the isle of Crete.

There is no time that is not the present and if Master Doyle is to break out of his life then this early hour of a Marchday morning is ripe.

A boiled egg, a pot of tea, a couple of water biscuits. Picasso was a multimillionaire communist. So what. And then as well you've got Galileo.

Arse.

Patrick was having a bath; it was twice in three days and a new all-comers record. He had a selection of books in with him although he was actually wanting to have an uncluttered think. He knelt in the water. It was quite hot, thus he was not yet able to sit down. He uplifted a knee, it was redly pink. A book setting the limits of geography in a freemarket economy was lying on the floor. It was him responsible for having brought it in here. It was like a form of self-torment. Next to it was this novel he started last night which was

[169]

so horrendously boring that fuck it, he couldnt be expected to continue any further, not even on behalf of 5b, one of whose members had thrust the yarn upon him. Horrendous books are difficult. Patrick objects to being forced to complete them. There again but it isnt only horrendous fuckers he fails to complete. If facts are to be admitted even while one is bathing then let the following be admitted: that the latter chapters of books are often the more difficult to finish and upon the higher shelves of both the walls of the parlour and kitchen you will find a plethora of works that are yet terminated incompletely. This has nothing to do with existential psychology although, having said that, when he reaches the three score and ten mark perhaps he will bring them all down and get them terminated completely, read all these last chapters, get them all over and done with.

Now there you are about painting. You canni do that with a painting. You canni fucking

Or can ye? Maybe ye can. At some subconscious level. Imagine looking at that one of Goya's where the wee dog is staring out from the quicksand, and you fail to notice the dog. Or decide not to take it into consideration. But only later, suddenly, you make that decision: let me consider that dog now. Okay, I can see the whole thing in its entirety, the painting, all of it. I'm now in a fit state to actually consider it as a total entity.

Fuck it, he was even going to wear a tie this morning and an ordinary shirt. That would increase his advantage. Because something important about the forthcoming interview: Old Milne had no way of knowing it was set to take place. Patrick hadni been in touch with him. So how could he possibly know. He wasnt a fucking mind-reader. Old bastard, if he wanted to he could just forget all about it, or pretend to forget all about it. Nobody was breathing down his neck. Headmasters are fucking autonomous, just like police commissioners and admirals of the fleet and the foreign office and the fucking aristocracy and all the secret services, the Watchdogs of Greatbritain.

Everything depended upon the nature of the carpeting viz. what it was about. Being so freshly scrubbed and sweet-smelling, dressed in the fresh outfit, maybe a dab of after-shave perfume. It could put him at an enormous advantage. Or disadvantage – Old Milne's line of reasoning might run along the following track: Ah! So the chap appreciates the seriosity of the situation! Grand. It renders a tough task that wee bit easier.

And then he would proceed to dish out the punishment in man-to-man fashion i.e. you would do it to me if the roles were to be reversed and that sort of keech. The only fly in the ointment that Patrick would do no such thing if he was the headmaster. Not at all. If he was headmaster he would act very differently, very differently indeed. For a fucking kick-off he would abandon the entire practice. No more teaching. None. None whatsoever. Sorry but that's fucking that. No more okay wages for a bad day's work. That's you out on your fucking neck. It's finished, all over, no more teaching. You're all bad influences on these weans so good-night and thank you very much, buona sera ya bastards, you assumed the role of judge and warden on behalf of a sick society so fucking hell mend ye, away and read Cicero.

That's what P. Doyle would do if he was the fucking headmaster, so there, stick that in your pipebowl ya congregationalist person!

An alternative of course might be to go in for a government re-training scheme, and while engaged on that he could be

Fine.

Yes.

P. Doyle.

He also missed out on a couple of evening duties recently. The headmaster is sticky about evening duties. He likes them to be attended to. But it wouldnt be that. Surely not. Unless it was an amalgam of things, one of which was the evening duties while another was anything you like. The best advice in the world is just to be calm, be calm, take things easy, easy. Not to worry too much about events over which you exercise no control. Over which you have lost control is more like it. In fact that sums it up. Control has been had and eschewed so fuck it. Really.

And it is just as well in terms of sanity. Many years have come and gone since those far-off days of the sun-drenched uni. Surely high time to be getting ahead of things instead of just what just eh doing things, things that could be better, that could be much better, than what they are, because they could, they could be much better, they could really fucking be better than they are and it all lay in his power for fuck sake he really was in control and even if by some figment of the imagination Old Milne had honestly forgotten all about the stupit fucking interview then Patrick hadnt, and wouldnt, because he was just going to walk in quite the thing in his good clothes, okay, and that was that. Fuck. Okay. No danger at all. Shite. Shite and arse and fucking tollie, keech and so on. But he was doing it now and standing by it, he was standing by it.

Aye, and maybe things would have turned out differently if he had got himself involved in the Christmas Pantomime with the rest of the morons.

Exactly.

And maybe also if he did not procrastinate, if he did not procrastinate, if he went for a pish when he needed a pish, if he finished a book when he started a book, if he

O fuck. Terrible. Terrible terrible terrible. What was Gillian Porter doing just now! And did she ever recollect Patrick with affection! God, was it possible? A really good woman. It would be nice to talk to her. She liked a laugh. That was what was good about her as well, how she liked a laugh. And probably about the difficult things in life, she would laugh them all right up in the sky and away with the wind.

Even Mrs Bryson. It would be nice talking to her. But what would it be nice to talk to her about, anything, anything at all, anything she fancied. The trials and tribulations of being an old maid. She wasni, it was him, she was a married woman with grown-up weans while what was he he was a bachelor, an old maidenly chap, that's what he was. So what? Who's fucking bothered about such shite.

Also, he would have a flat tyre. Nothing surer. Auld fucking Zeus, that's what he would dish out. A flat tyre. So there he would be having to change this mawkit and clattily manky wheel, getting it all on the trousers and jacket and shirtsleeves; the shoes covered in it, plus the dog shit; and then kneeling in the gutter by mistake and having to dive back up the stair for another bath and a new set of clothes! In the name of the deity! Any fucking deity! Please assist a bloke in distress! The son of a pair of Aged P's. One with no expectations whatsoever. One with just this honest, god-fearing bunch of relatives and forefathers/mothers who have always done their duty by monarch, the rich and the church. Honest! So what's to be done? Well, an easy approach to the morning was number 1. And number 2: a well-ironed breakfast. Good. Number 3? A sharply brushed sandwich on toast. Okay.

In certain parts of the world licensed establishments open their doors at the back of four a.m. Four fucking a.m. In the fucking forenoon morning jesus christ and here you have a fellow who is not able to acquire a few jars prior to the nine o'clock showdown with a praetorissimo of the congregationalist protestant teacher class. So what is to be done what is to be done aside that is from suicide. Aside from suicide. Although there again, in terms of bon vivre, P for Patrick seldom recollects having felt so fine as at this exact moment. Talk about fucking high spirits! I'm no kidding ye this boy could do a wee jig, a wee jig. And I dont tell lies, no me, I'm straight-down-the-line

Straight-down-the-line must be a football expression, to do with running down the wing with the ball at one's feet, prior to crossing it to the far post where the striker is just moving in to Bump, that's another in the back of the net. One of the problems

One of the problems! There arent any problems. None whatsoever.

So what's to be done? Nothing. Nothing at all.

That temptation.

There is no temptation. None whatsoever.

None whatsoever. On the contrary:

To yield to occasion is the mark of the wise man. That's what Cicero says and Cicero doesni tell lies. What age was he when they extinguished his life's blood?

As soon as he stepped out onto the landing he knew it was cold, that it was back as winter once again. His chin always seemed to be the extremity most outreaching of all his parts, and caught the snell wind firstly. And as he battered his way down the stairs, the absolutely cauld dank dankness of these fucking outlandish efforts known as walls, floors and fucking bastarn ceilings of ice-frosted steam and he began shivering in an incredible, exaggerated fashion so that you had to ask is it genuine? is it the mark of a false consciousness? an indication of what's the fucking French for bad faith! If it had been Norwegian fine, fine, but French! O dear no. Maybe better if the silly fucker had returned upstairs for a more suitable item of apparel – mauvaise foi – the anorak for christ sake and a woolly scarf and a pair of gloves, the Vick Vapour Rub to dab beneath the nostrils and a couple of nice wee hot whisky toddies, with a large straw.

There was frost on the windows of the doors and all down the panels of the doors, and the windscreen of course fucking encrusted by it. The lock had iced up. He breathed hot breath on it, his hands cupped round his mouth and if successful he would needs move rapidly otherwise it would freeze up even worse when the cold got into it. And the windscreen. He used the side of his hand. Once upon a time he was a total idiot and threw hot water on everything and it was all fine for ten seconds until fuck ye and it was all ice again, and occasionally you saw folk still doing that. Okay, the very next time he did he would yell out and halt it, and be friendly for christ sake to his fellow human beings! That's all it took, just that note of warning, a friendly way of being in this evilish world wherein deities advance the net. And the glove-compartment too, its hinges rusted and cracking by the sound of it. Everything about this motor was absolutely fucking hopeless.

Yes, the ice-scraper was still inside the compartment! If he had tried for it in the first place the side of his hand wouldni fucking be bloody damn fucking numb. Och well, one cannot have everything. But by jesus it was fucking cold. Or was it all his nerves was it all his nerves and the cold was only compounding matters, was that all. He finished scraping the frost and was on the driver's seat and becoming comfortable and so on prior to testing the horrible starter and so on, trusting that it would connect with the battery and so on in

[174]

mechanical manner thereby the engine turning satisfactorily this not being a morning for dilly-dallying and push fucking starts please god.

And the Pythagoreans of course, not believing the fire should be stirred by iron. Exactly right as usual. Funny that so it is, how come these fucking ancient bastards hit the nail on the head plus of course peregrinations on the highways to which they were totally opposed, totally opposed, you can walk anywhere you like except the road, otherwise you'd get knocked down by a cart perhaps, or a chariot. Common sense, always common sense, steering clear of beans and the rest of it.

The motor car was moving. Patrick gripping onto the wheel and perched forwards on the very edge of the seat, the shoulders hunched rigid and making loud shivering noises, having to keep the demisters blowing cold air so the windscreen would stay clear. O it was good to be wearing a tie wearing a tie, athwart the adam's apple, giving this good sense of combating the elements and warding off the ill-omened bad-health inducers such as the flu.

Thoughts are no good. They are not a help, not an assistance; they do not come to the aid of a person in extremis, a person who suffers that others may indeed walk free – because that's what a fucking teacher is really I mean eh! she or he fucking spends his or her fucking life trying to fucking show people the ropes and the byways to a successful existence, a successful method of manoeuvering yourself through the twists and turns and nooks and crannies of the sinister universe, that's what they do. And then they get punched on the gub! Punchus punche on the fucking gubus.

Okay then, no more of it.

And Patrick, when he was parking the motor in the school parking area, saw some kids gazing at him and he winked, turned the key in the lock, strolled across the playground, skirting round the outsize slide some boys were sliding down. He hadnt been keen on slides as a boy, a couple of bad cracks on the rear of the skull because of them, which was where you aye seemed to land whenever you took the tumble, that terrible jarring crack. How does the cranium cope? And yet it does.

Mister Peters. Auld fucking greeting face the janny. The world was become bleak.

Patrick nodded. Morning.

Mm.

Any luck on Saturday? Patrick smiled. Nottingham Forest beat my da for a right few quid! The fixed odds coupon.

Whh. The janitor shook his head and gazed sideways, moving his chin as though his shirt collar was too tight and it was hampering his larynx. Patrick's own collar was feeling a bit tight as well and he inserted his index finger, tugging the collar out the way. Mister Peters said: I'm seeing your boss about it.

What?

I'm just bloody sick of it.

D'you mean about the upgrading?

Aye. I was talking to a guy from the Housing Department and he was telling me they've all got it. So if they've all got it how the hell have we no?

It's bad.

You're telling me it's bad, and if anything we've got a damn sight more responsibilities than they've got. And yet they give it to them and no to us. You tell me how they work it out.

Aye, bad.

It's bloody out of order. You look for logic and there isni any. Mister Peters's attention was distracted by a group of girls which was passing by and talking excitedly about something; and from them to a group of boys, one of them was bouncing a ball on the steps up to the doors at the entrance which was entirely against the laws of the school. The janitor's hand hovered as though to reach for his whistle. He said to Patrick. It's been on my mind non-stop, spoiled the whole bloody weekend.

Aye.

It's no that but if you're gonni stand by your staff then you stand by them, end of story. But that boss of yours . . .! Mister Peters glanced from right to left, clearing his throat, as if seeking a place to spit.

Patrick grinned. He's your boss as well as mine!

That's as maybe son but he doesni treat yous the way he treats us.

Eh . . . Patrick cocked his head to one side.

The janitor waited.

That depends.

Och. Dont give us it.

Well christ I wouldni say he was very good with us either.

Mister Peters shook his head and walked off along by the side of the building.

Pat stood there a few moments before entering the main school. He had enough time for a quick cup of tea in the staffroom. He smiled. He stopped it. But it was as if there was an odd feeling to the day, maybe the sensation of momentous deeds being already to the fore. He could imagine that. He could imagine momentous deeds appertaining to himself, that these deeds were set to occur. He walked along the corridor. He continued on up the stair. He walked along the corridor beneath the one that led to the staffroom. He walked to the offices of the clerks and the headmaster. When he reached the threshold he tugged at the cuffs of his shirtsleeves, smiled at Ms Thompson, the headmaster's secretary, a woman of some forty-five summers with black spectacles and a pleasant smile. She was wearing a maroon jersey this morning with a metal cross dangling from her neck. Is he in? asked Patrick.

Yes.

Ah.

Are you wanting to see him?

I think he might be expecting me.

She frowned.

I was actually supposed to be seeing him on Friday afternoon.

O yes of course . . .

I eh couldni make it.

Ms Thompson rose, she went ben the headmaster's office, leaving him alone, to gaze on the furniture, the electronic typewriter and computer and sheaves of paper and pens, and various calendars. A moment's reflection during this slight break in time. The presence of oneself. That age-old unity of thought and being, the cornerstone of a certain method of conducting your life in the face of the world. Is that correct? Perhaps not. Hegel is a devilishly hard fellow to comprehend. Some of what he has to say for himself is so positively disbelievably believable, disbelievably believable. Spell believable. Capital 'b'

Ms Thompson.

Old Milne looked surprised. There was the wrinkled forehead and the glasses slightly down on his nose. Patrick nodded. I have to apologise for Friday, he said.

Well ye know eh Mister Doyle I waited on until the half hour for you.

Sorry.

Old Milne continued gazing at him, scrutinising him, and Patrick said: It was really I just wasnt feeling very well. I had a sore stomach.

But you should have advised us of it; myself or Mrs Thompson.

I wasni really, to be honest, feeling capable.

Old Milne made no movement. He had one hand on his desk and the other on his lap; he was sitting in such a way that he may have been looking into one of the desk drawers prior to Patrick's entry. He was wearing his usual clobber, the gown and the brown chalk-striped suit and a tie of three shades of blue which was probably of a university or a club or something. And a brisk white shirt. Tinted fucking glasses. A dangerous man. He would have been at home with BOSS or the Tonton Macoute. Patrick would just have liked to be at home – with the fire and a pot of tea, the books and the radio. That's what he was cut out for, a life of academia, stuffed inside of an ivory tower, instead of being obliged to lead this life of revolutionary compromise all the time because he was fucking sick of it.

What would the maw and da be doing at this minute? And Gavin. And Alison, who would be in with her registration class and speaking quietly but with authority.

Fuck sake. Imagine being carpeted at the age of twenty-nine. He had only himself to blame. Old Milne was looking at him. Patrick looked back at him. Joseph K was thirty when the bad things started happening and Jesus of Nazareth was thirty when he started preaching. Who else? No one else, it's a load of nonsense. It is all a load of nonsense. How come he hadnt even been allowed to sit down.

Old Milne nodded. He said, Your transfer's come through.

Pardon.

Old Milne lifted a sheet of A4-size paper, he glanced at it then pushed it across the desk, twisting it around for Patrick to see. Could you just sign eh . . .

His name was on it right enough. It indicated the transfer was to take place at the Easter break. When he began the last term it would be at this other school – Barnskirk High. Barnskirk High was okay. It was out the south east side of the city and fair enough. But why was he to be going there. He couldnt mind asking for any fucking transfer. That was funny. He just couldni actually mind applying for it. He said: Is this how you wanted to see me?

Yes.

Pat nodded. He looked at the paper again. Eh Mister Milne, he said, I have to say this to ye: I dont mind ever having applied for any transfer. Are ye sure it's for me?

Old Milne looking at him.

Are ye sure it's mine?

. . .

I dont eh – to be honest I mean christ it's no the sort of thing I do. I usually stick things out.

. . .

I do. It's one of the traits I'm stuck with, my personality, its characteristics, I stick things out.

Old Milne smiled.

It's no anything I'm proud of, I'm just stuck with it.

He was still smiling.

Patrick shrugged and he frowned; he put his hand to his brow; it was like the beginning of a sore head maybe or something like that.

You must have applied for it.

Pardon?

I'm saying ye must have applied for it, the transfer, otherwise it wouldnt have come through. Maybe you put in and forgot.

Forgot.

It is possible.

Okay.

I forget things myself.

No putting in for a transfer but you dont forget that.

Well I havent put in for a transfer Mister Doyle.

Well I dont think I have either.

But you must have, otherwise it wouldnt have come through.

Patrick's armpits were aching and aching armpits are fucking

[179]

hopeless. He smiled at the headmaster: Do you actually want rid me?

Not at all.

Well I dont understand this then.

Mister Doyle . . . the headmaster smiled in quite a friendly manner . . . I dont understand this either.

Ye sure ye dont want rid of me?

Not at all. And Old Milne came sitting forwards on his leather chair, hands clasped and shoulders taut, the creased brow to indicate the worried but caring older person but do not trust it do not trust it because who could ever trust this devious old bastard, a sleakit auld fucking rascal.

And this is another thing, this Old Milne shite, let's have no more of it – so totally reeking in sentimentality – his name is Milne. His name is W. R. Milne. The W stands for Walter. His name is Walter R. Milne.

And he was glancing at the clock on the wall. Was Patrick supposed to dismiss himself? Ha ha ha.

How are your parents keeping?

My parents?

I recall your father wasnt too well.

He's recovered.

Ah. Good.

Patrick nodded.

Milne smiled.

Eh, how come ye asked me that?

. . .

As far as I can see it's quite an odd thing to ask.

In what sense Mister Doyle?

In what sense eh, in the sense that you dont know him, my old man, so how come you're asking after him?

If my memory serves he was quite seriously ill.

. . .

Wasnt he?

He was aye, but so what, what's that got to do with it I mean what gives ye the right to be asking after him, you dont even know him, no as a man, as an actual ordinary man. So what gives you the

[180]

right, this is what I dont know. I really dont – the presumption. What gives ye the right?

I'm sorry.

Aye but what gives ye the right to think ye can just ask me about him I mean do ye think ye fucking own him as well? cause ye dont, it's just me. It's just me ye own.

. . .

You think ye own me. Well ye do, but ye dont fucking own him.

I beg your pardon?

Ye dont own my da.

I dont know what you are talking about Mister Doyle.

Course ye do. Because I've been bought you think it applies to my whole family well it doesnt.

I am gibbering why am I gibbering, I am gibbering why am I gibbering. Poor old fucking Hölderlin. The headmaster is speaking what is he speaking about? Hush and let us hear hush and let us hear.

But my brains willni let me my brains willni let me. That's what happened to old Hölderlin. And what I want to know is, concerning your man, Georg Wilhelm Friedrich, his boyhood friend,

What is the headmaster talking about.

I cannot hear. My brains have been silenced. In silenso. Dear o dear, maybe I should give him a kiss. I shall give my headmaster a kiss. I shall plant a smacker on his greasy heid. My dear fellow, the trials and tribulations of being the praetor of praetors

a mistake it's yours or else you've forgotten about it.

What do you mean?

If the department had simply wanted to transfer you on their own account they would have gone ahead and done it.

I'm not eh . . . I dont know what you mean.

Milne sighed. He looked at the clock.

Look, it's just there's a certain hypocrisy going on here that I dont appreciate.

. . .

Being a teacher on behalf of a society like this yin, where the very last thing wanted is honesty or truth.

O! The headmaster shook his head and that was definitely that and it was best to just sign his name and leave now immediately because Patrick could never win here and there was something in the air told him that, that here he was and he was being humiliated right under his very nose, he was being humiliated for christ sake, right under his own very nose. And he signed his name because it was best to leave. He put his left hand into his trouser pocket, opening the door with his right, an attempted coolness; and he walked from the office without acknowledging Ms Thompson though it wasnt her fault and had nothing whatsoever to do with her.

And what to do what to do should he go to the registration class or just fuck off. More brave to go the registration. Or was it? It didni matter; he was walking towards the staircase, heading for his own corridor, to his own classroom. He didnt want to leave this school. He really didnt. He quite liked it. It was terrible that here he was having to leave. And not fair to the pupils either who were used to his particular style of teaching and were well on their way to a proper grounding in reality, the ways of the world, honesty and so on.

He had stopped walking. He smiled and leant against the wall at the alcove next to the staircase. What a fucking pong! The science labs. It was the smell he aye associated with the entire profession, rotten eggs. But that sounded ominous. Maybe he was on his way out altogether. But how could that ever happen unless he himself instigated it? And he wasnt about to do any such thing. Let it be done, okay. But not by his own hand. He would never allow them that kind of satisfaction. Suicide fine but not fucking resignation.

Down below in the assembly hall Margaret McNally the gym teacher was rigging up the stanchions for netball.

He was into his own corridor and he stopped again. He did not know why he felt as bad as he did. It was actually crossing his mind to vault the rail and leap to his fucking death! He probably wouldni get killed but for christ sake how come he should be feeling as bad as that anyway I mean it's daft. It's no as if he was gonni get his bollocks cut off. And here he was by the railing and pausing a few moments as if he was looking down at Maggie who was quite a nice woman but just didnt move in the same circle as he did thus they didnt really know each other although she was a single party and would maybe be interested in going out for a meal or just to the Citz Theatre for a night for christ sake without any strings and not at all pressurised, without any worries about the future, just a night out together for a bit of company. She moved well Margaret, she was wearing a dark blue short skirt and her pair of trainer shoes and a thingwi top, one of these whatdyoucallits that you wear if you're out training for fuck sake. Her whistle round the neck. It was always a nice sound, that harsh shrieking of rubber soles on the floor and the thumping of running feet, the whistle blowing and whatever christ. Gym teachers are divorced from the problems. Nonsense. They've got their own bloody problems, that's all; and they're every bit as fucking depressing in their own way.

But for christ sake, is it actually conceivable that he could have applied for a transfer and forgotten all about it? Just is it conceivable. That is all. That is all he would like to know. Nothing more than that. Christ! But it seemed so amazing. Are there any quotations to help? What can be said if not done to alleviate matters. Some great wee witty saying that can allow Pat to ease himself out from under. Jesus Christ for example, what happened to him? Or Empedocles, did he have any sort of aphorisms to help?

Patrick had continued walking. It would soon be time for 2e to depart the room. Ach well. Poor wee fuckers. He would be there in a second and that would be that. One solitary unique second. A momentous second. And the loud voices coming from the classroom. Patrick half expected to find MI6 lurking in the shadows, just to give due warning that he too was aware of the loud voices. O what a scandal. Loud voices in the classroom. O dear. A Monday as well for fuck sake when you're supposed to be stuffing theological musings in beside the registrationatus. He clasped the handle of the door. Nostalgia. He shook his head, smiling. The sense of it, the nostalgia, being so acute it was almost a strange déjà vu.

He stood in the doorway a moment, before shutting the door firmly behind himself.

Good morning Mister Doyle.

Good morning one and all. Okay, no time for denying the deities this morning. I've just been for an interview with Mister Big. So . . . Patrick clasped his hands together, then he unclasped them and clapped them twice . . . first question: What's this fucking load of drivel all about?

The hands of half a dozen.

Kenneth!

Eh is what this fucking load of drivel is all about is what this fucking load of drivel is all about?

Fine, no bad – but mind that 'eh' ye shoved in and then missed out for christ sake. But fair enough, this time of the morning and it being a Monday and all that, okay, a good start to the week getting something like that because it means you're on the road to under-standing a very crucial aspect of this existence insofar as this existence takes place in a country like ours I mean for instance it's something your parents'll no understand because on the whole they're a bunch of fucking idiots whose esteem of the ostrich is a byword in the corridors of high finance. Yous know what I'm talking about. Michelle!

Please Mister Doyle it's just Audrey's started her period.

Aw, okay.

Michelle had risen and she went to the wall cupboard where the pillow and blankets were kept. She and Caroline assisted Audrey to the back of the room. They helped her stretch out along the bench, hidden from the view of the others.

Is she gonni be sick? asked Patrick.

She doesni know, said Michelle.

What does she reckon?

She should go home to bed and get two hot water bottles.

Ah, fine, aye. Patrick glanced around the class; the pupils mainly stared to the front, apart from a couple of boys. Patrick nodded. The trouble with us, he said, we know almost nothing about bodies, especially female bodies. He focused his attention on the lassies generally: I mean we dont really know a damn thing about this pain yous all go through once a month, except that we can tell it's really really painful. I know it just by looking, just by using my eyes. And I dont need to know anything more. All I have to do is look. I just look truly and in doing that I see Audrey's in pain. Okay. You just fucking bear witness to things, that's how ye know what they are.

Patrick shook his head. He stepped back to the stool, sat up on it, the elbows on the edge of his desk. Anybody want to say any-thing?

James said: There was this guy on the TV last night and he said he was really pessimistic about the human race because they were all losing their faith in God.

Mm, what a load of shite. Patrick nodded. Of course he's telling lies. What like were his arguments?

They wereni actually arguments he was just blabbing away.

Did anybody else see this programme?

Bobby Dodds said: The interviewer let him off. He just let him talk and talk. It was like an advert.

Was it a programme for Christians or could anybody look in?

It was a programme for Christians but anybody could look in that it was a programme for Christians.

Aye. Pat grinned. That's a difficult yin but and my head isni up to it this morning.

A hangover? called a couple of others, and laughter.

Not at all if yous must know I've given up the bevy. It's just there to screw your brains down into pulp. It makes ye do things that are totally ludricous and stupit, stupit! I mean look at your parents, eh! Some of ye must've had horrendous experiences there. I just get sick of it myself sometimes; all that waste of time and effort; you can understand some of the auld socialists, the way they aye went on about temperance and the need to be at least a wee bit abstinent. Everything in moderation I suppose. From now on let that be the motto of 2E! Okay, anybody else?

Hazel Jones said: Is shaving sore?

Is shaving sore . . . Pat frowned.

Hazel pointed to a boy behind her: He always says men get it to make up for periods.

Fair enough aye but eh, naw, shaving isni really sore; it's actually just fucking boring to be honest. I'd grow a beard except that's even more boring and it makes ye want to scratch all the time. And I dont like having to scratch all the time. Patrick shook his head, he stared at the top of the desk. There was this uncomfortable feeling in bed as well when you're lying in bed sometimes, you're on your side and your legs are one on top of the other, except your fucking kneebones keep jarring each other and it's fucking awful, an awful feeling and you put your legs out and away from each other but it never seems to be satisfying and you end up the only escape is to fall asleep or lie on your

[185]

back. So these things arent fair either. But there's so many things that areni fair you've got to start inventing different words altogether. Patrick shut his eyes. His head was gone. The old nut, it was fucking away with it. He was just feeling awful. Guilt right enough. And the class. He opened his eyes and he said: Listen, what yous have to remember above all is that I dont care. I dont. Honest. It is a load of dross. DROSS. I mean ye shouldni even be here. If yous were my weans! Christ. Every last thing that goes on here in this classroom is utter and absolute dross. And I'm one of the ones that does it worst of all because yous all think I'm on your side and I'm no – even MI6's more on your side than I am! I'm no kidding ye weans I'm really fucking, not to be trusted. I'm actually gonni chuck it in and start doing something else altogether. And yous should do the same I mean there's no point hanging about here cause it's all a load of rightwing shite. Facta non verba, from now on. Why dont yous go and blow up the DHSS office?

That's no fair: called Lesley.

Wrong. Anybody else?

Nobody spoke. They were staring at him in different ways, none of which was good. Pat sniffed. But he really fucking hated the idea of letting them down. It was terrible, a terrible thing. What age were they again? Wee second-yearers. Fourteen, some were thirteen. In some countries they would be married with children; in other countries they would be tortured maybe to the point of death. So what. His eyes would water soon, but the bell had rung a few moments ago and the moment was past. Except nobody was making any effort to leave. Even Audrey at the rear of the room, her head could be seen above the desk there, propping herself up to see what was happening and she probably was having terrible cramp or something. It was enough to make ye burst right out greeting. The unspeakable sentimentality. Doyle's problem. A fact. At the root of everything, every last thing.

But it was because he was leaving. Surely people are entitled to get sentimental when they're leaving!

No.

A boy had his hand raised, Tony McKelvie.

Alright Tony, said Patrick.

It's just the registration Mister Doyle.

Patrick gazed at his watch, a twenty-first birthday present, the desk at where his wrist was resting, wrist was resting, not wanting to something, to eh, it being the kind of thing he couldnt cope with, this sort of perception, the way these weans saw straight through you, straight into your insides. He opened his eyes and he said to the girl who had told him off for not being fair: You've got to remember what I'm aye telling ye about questions, when people in positions of power ask ye questions.

She looked away from him.

Okay then yous better get away to your next class. Just say your names as you go. And if you say them in a certain manner the force of your identity will create an indentation in the fucking registration folder. He opened the folder and placed it on the desk and he took out a pen and flourished it and then stuck it into his top jacket pocket, clasped his hands on the desk.

The next class had been waiting outside the door. While they were trooping in he sidled out into the corridor, he stood beside a pillar overlooking the assembly hall where the netball game was about to take place. His life was finished. When the two teams entered from the changing rooms and the gym teacher blew her whistle he started walking, along to the stairs, and then leapfrogging the railing he fell twenty feet, his brains being dashed onto the floor. He went into the staff lavatory for a piss. He was actually needing a shit but he wasni sure how long it would take so he would have to leave it till the mid-morning interval. In the staffroom a couple of teachers were reading newspapers. He did not communicate with them. He washed his hands at the sink and drank a glass of water from the tap, rinsed the glass and upturned it on the draining board, returned to the classroom.

At dinnertime he remained at his desk until the place was deserted and he left the building by the rear basement exit to avoid passing the door of the staffroom. He couldnt face anybody at present. And of course Alison. And news would have spread. They would all know about the transfer he had applied for and been given. It didnt matter anyway. People could think what the fuck they wanted to think. Today was going to be his last for a long while. Yes, maybe forever.

But it was most odd how stupid he had been. This is what was niggling him. Although silly to let it get out of proportion, and he wouldnt let it get out of proportion. But it was definitely interesting. So many wee things he had done recently were just bloody of note. He wasni always like this for christ sake he could be a lot better. It was as if something was after him, a poltergeist for fuck sake or a Scottish leprechaun, a dybbuk for gentile atheists. He needed to get away out of things fast, but he wasnt able to. He could not escape. He was having to stay. It is this the sort of bloke he was. This sort of bloke.

The polis were looking the other way when he exited, crossing the street at once and walking quickly along the side of the long row of parked motor cars, on by the Commodore Cafe, not looking to the crowd of small smokers hanging about by the adjacent close and shop doorway. There was a pub he used to go to at the end of autumn last. That is where he was going now. It was a good pub because he didnt know any bastard that drank in it and what he could be was an absolute nonentity who was taking a drink of alcohol in an effort to just enjoy himself for a minute or two.

A big group of workies in from a tenement renovation site a few closes along from the pub. They chatted loudly, shouting comments to one another. Patrick stood at the end of the bar, borrowed a newspaper from the barwoman, read the sports and entertainments. He drank three whiskies and two and a half pints of beer. It was too much but on the road home he knew he was just befuddled enough to last the afternoon. Then he was starving. Absolutely fucking starving. Because he hadnt eaten. When was his last fucking meal christ almighty. A fish supper was what he felt like. A nice piece of haddock and a stack of freshly fried chips. But he didni have the time he would have to survive without. Three familiar figures ahead: Desimondo and Joe Cairns, and the temporary English teacher – old Norrimanno, a great wee fucking guy, and any resemblance to Bob Cratchit is an absolute misnomer, a disaster, something that is wrong and not the case at all, in fact, Norman is fine, fine. And deserves a fucking job the guy, he deserves a full-time start in the teaching racket. In fact the three of them were okay blokes. Pat liked them. As colleagues go he got on fine with them. It would be an idea to keep in touch with them once he had gone; they could go for a pint together, discuss the past and so on. He paused, staying where he was, he bent as if to examine his shoelaces, then unknotted and knotted them.

Weans went zooming by.

Two minutes to the bell the bell the be ell ell! Patrick chuckled. He watched the weans as they dodged in and out the pedestrians, making for the gates. They were funny the way they carried on. And so much better than their parents, so much more honest and lacking in hypocrisy. Even their self-interest was so much more fucking healthy. That is what he would miss, the weans, he would miss them. No really anything else. If he was being honest there never had been much of the camaraderie you might have expected, back from the teachers' trainers, what you might have been expecting from there, it never happened. Of course he had his own ideas on that, the whys and the wherefores, to do with – well, why even bother articulating such things. Although obviously bad faith does have to come into it.

Ah christ, Patrick was going to survive. His life might be finished but what did that matter, it didni mean he was totally dead and out of things altogether. All he had to do was play the pipes, if he could just concentrate on them, even just as a form of temporary measure. And temporary measures can be healthy. You dont have to look upon things as permanent all the time in order to judge their merit. A common error that.

A trio of bastards was waiting for him. They had spotted him and were waiting. It was fucking funny how the vultures start hanging about your deathbed. He set his face to a serious expression i.e. a frown, and said gruffly: Tell me this chaps, do yous think it a possibility one could apply for a transfer and then fucking forget all about it?

I know this sounds daft, began Joe Cairns quickly, and then he hesitated.

Naw it doesni, said Pat, come on, I need to hear somebody else talking. Tell me.

Joe nodded and glanced at Desmond.

Desmond continued: The thing is Pat we were actually talking about this a wee minute ago. And eh Joe was just saying about a similar sort of experience, from the dressing room.

Yeh, said Joe, it was a pal of mine.

And Joe Cairns went on to relate this banal yarn about

it wasnt so much banal as irrelevant: it concerned this quite good football player who was suddenly told he had been transferred for a five-figure sum, just like he had wanted – only he hadnt really wanted such a thing at all but seems to have been gabbing away about something in the communal bath one day and the manager had been eavesdropping or some such keech and then thought he would do the guy a favour and had secretly dropped a circular to a variety of clubs he thought might be interested, including Newport County, which is where the guy found himself on Monday afternoon. It had nothing whatsoever to do with Pat's case and it was almost like a strange form of sarcasm. Pat watched Joe and Desmond but could spot nothing suspicious, then he looked at Norman who smiled benevolently and remarked, Stories about professional football players, I could listen to them all day!

Pat nodded. He said to Joe: Is it genuine what you're telling me?

Yeh.

Honest?

What . . . Yeh.

Because it doesni sound it I mean it actually sounds eh, quite hard to swallow.

It's ridiculous the way athletes are treated, said Desmond to Norman.

Ah well football especially I suppose. Norman glanced at Joe Cairns: It's a bit of a cattle market Joe eh? Still and all but that's the way capitalism works in any field – football or whatever, it doesni matter.

Och come on, said Desmond.

Sure it is, the individual worker just doesnt have a say.

Desmond jerked his thumb at Norman, saying to Pat: He's a Marxist.

Pardon?

Norman's a Marxist, grinned Desmond.

So am I a fucking Marxist, so what?

Desmond smiled. I am not saying a word.

Norman said to Pat: You're a Marxist as well?

Pat looked at him.

Are ye?

What?

I'm just asking if you're a Marxist as well?

As well as what?

Seriously.

Seriously; you're just asking me seriously, if I'm a Marxist, in a school like this, in a society like this, at a moment in history like the present.

Norman grinned and Desmond laughed and shook his head. Joe Cairns had adopted the role of friend however and he was merely smiling politely while attempting to appear sympathetic to Patrick. Whereas it was poor old fucking Norman needed the sympathy.

I'm actually a fucking nothing, said Patrick, I used to be a something but now I'm a nothing. Being a nothing's preferable to being a something but no much.

I take the point, said Norman. I agree with ye as well. We were talking about this earlier on.

Amongst yourselves?

Norman grinned.

He's got a fine line in sarcasm, said Desmond in jocular tones.

Not as fine as you but Desmond.

Ah. I wouldnt underestimate yourself Mister Doyle.

Thanks, I'll bear that in mind. Pat glanced at Joe Cairns: Okay Joe?

How do ye mean Pat? Joe frowned.

Pat shrugged. I just thought there was something up with you.

No.

It's just the way he stands, grinned Desmond.

Norman had opened a small pack of tobacco and was rolling a cigarette and smiling at the same time. It would be good to wipe the smile off his face. But that wouldnt be easy to do because he was probably a better fighter than Pat. Pat glanced at Joe Cairns: This guy ye were talking about, him that got transferred to Newport through a misunderstanding.

Joe nodded: It *was* a misunderstanding. And we had quite a good team too; this kind of broke things up and we never managed to replace him. He's still around – Micky Jamieson.

Mansfield Town? said Norman.

That's right Norman, yeh. He played with us for three-quarters of a season. We were wondering if the board were just wanting to earn a few quid before it was too late. But it turned out it was the manager. He and Micky got on well together and he had honestly thought he was doing him a favour by shoving him on the transfer list. It wasnt too long after that that I went myself. Because like I say, the team had broken up, it was time to move on.

That was to Carlisle you went? said Norman.

Naw, I went to Carlisle later Norman.

Aw.

Pat said, So it's all gospel Joe? about this guy getting transferred and so on.

Of course.

The great skeptic! said Desmond.

Skeptic fuck all, said Pat. People just like to know what are facts and what areni facts. What is there something fucking wrong with that? christ sake I mean what, tell me?

Desmond made no reply.

Hey d'you want a couple of cloves? said Norman. He was already bringing out a wee paper bag of them from an inside pocket, and he handed a couple to Pat. Pat took them and stuck them both under his tongue:

I've only had the one pint, he said.

And Norman replied something or other while the other pair didnt say a word, but just were fucking who knows what, mounting another conspiracy probably.

Dring dring; dring dring.

It was the fucking stupit bell the bell the be el el. And Patrick was still standing there when the other three were not. The other three were going up the steps of the main entrance. Desmond paused and gestured at him to come on. But Pat stayed put. Then he strode after them, calling: So yous've heard then?

They nodded.

The so-called transfer request!

Pregnant pause.

Well Mister Doyle, said Desmond, as you are aware, nothing remains a secret within the education department of Glasgow. It's always open season on teachers, was and will be, always. Barnskirk's not the worst of all possible destinations by the way, a friend of mine heads things in matters historical across there.

What d'ye mean by 'matters historical'?

Desmond shook his head, chuckling.

O by the way, said Norman, Alison was looking for you.

Pardon?

Norman hesitated.

Are you talking about Alison?

I'm just saying she was looking for ye.

Patrick nodded. He glanced at Joe Cairns – the inscrutable. And Desmond seemed not to be hearing things.

If the world truly was a magical place.

Norman and Desmond were now off along toward the staircase and Joe Cairns had turned the corner in the direction of the science laboratories where shortly he would be leading a class in the dissection of a frog. This frog would be prostrate and its legs would be fucking chopped off the poor wee bastard. It would never again manage a jump but would have to waddle about on its elbows. But it's no fucking got elbows. Or has it? This is the problem with inferior educations, one fails to

He actually felt like going to sleep. If only he was the type of guy who could resign from things unofficially. That was the type of guy he would wish to be, if ever he managed to come this way again, if transmigratory souls proved more than a wayward explanation of the possibility of déjà vu. He felt like going to sleep. He was tired. He hadni slept last night. Nor the night before, not properly. And nor the night before that for christ sake so no wonder he was tired now. Mrs Bryson at the end of the corridor. She didnt see him. Then he fell, tripped; he tripped, a sort of stumble, banging his right shin on the edge of the step and it was a bloody crack okay it was painful. Mrs Bryson still hadni seen him and had gone from view now. Nobody else had seen it either. Unless they were keeping quiet. Pat walked on at once. He would only have to last it out this one period because the one after it was spare and then the interval. His chest was sore when he breathed; and where were the fucking cloves because they wereni in his fucking mouth. Unless he had swallowed them, maybe he had swallowed them. It could have been worse he could have cracked his chin or his nose, or his jaw, and broke his teeth; that would have been terrible.

The quietness! The classes having all begun by now. That Hollywood movie where people wished they had never been born. His chest was actually sore in this sharply painful way, sharply painful. Christ. It was cheery but. Good old pain.

Patrick sat on the stool and became alert. Fourth year. World weary. Raymond Smith was staring at him. He was a boy who worried. It was his parents' fault. Hey Raymond, what does your da do for a living?

He's on the broo just now Mister Doyle.

Aw aye. What was it he worked at last?

Eh he worked in a factory.

What doing?

Eh I dont know.

You dont know. Quite right. Well done. Patrick nodded; he looked at the rest then back to Raymond: My da's been working in a factory for the past twenty-two year – that's when he's no having fucking heart attacks. He's a real yin so he is, a right fucking numbskull. He's got a wee baldy heid and sometimes I feel like giving it a brush with a brillo pad.

LOUD LAUGHING.

In the name of christ. Pat clapped his hands very loudly; then he had to do it once again. They all stopped their laughing as soon as they could.

Okay, he said, there's no need for that carry on just because I told you something of the way I feel about my auld man – especially because we were talking about somebody else's auld man. Eh Raymond?

Raymond nodded, his face reddening into a large blush. What age was he? fifteen. Mind you, the truth of the matter is that Doyle P. is also a blusher; he too has a face that reddens. There is nothing you can do about it except forgive yourself.

[194]

Raymond Smith, said P. Doyle, you've got to forgive yourself. Look at me: I forgive myself. And I'm okay.

Muffled giggles. Which was not good at this late stage.

Sardar Ali had his hand aloft: Is it true you're leaving Mister Doyle?

Aye.

How come?

The fucking powers-that-art have decreed it. And being absolutely honest and truthful about the subject, I really wish not to discuss it, if yous dont mind.

It's your obligation to tell us, said Sardar Ali.

Pat gazed at him, then generally: I want a girl to state the same question.

You've been bevying, said Peter MacFadzean.

I've aye been bevying.

No you've no.

Aye I have.

Have ye?

Aye but look for christ sake if we go on like this it'll become sentimental maudlinity of the first order. What I want to know is if the lassies arent talking as an affirmation of something. Eh? Will one of yous tell me?

Silence. Then Debby Munro looked away when their gazes met. Patrick continued to gaze at her and she started to blush immediately. She had a more purplish colouring than Raymond Smith. Pat's blush was akin to his rather than Debby's. All in all he probably had a lot in common with the boy.

Most bachelors have an awkward existence, he said. I'm talking strictly about those bachelors who are single men. But I think it may be true for most single women as well.

A head could be seen passing along the corridor: and slowly, going slowly, as though in an attempt to overhear the slightest piece of untowardity. Patrick indicated the head and the class turned to see it. Notice that head! he called. You're probably all thinking it's a spy from Mister Big's office. And fucking right ye are cause that's exactly the case, the way of things, how matters are standing, at the present, the extant moment. Arse.

Arse; o jesus christ; and he was about to blush. Arse. Imagine saying it out loud at this exact moment. What could he do now, to get beyond it, to get beyond it, everything. The magic carpet, if the world was indeed

I apologise: he said, his eyelids shut now and he placed his palms on the edge of the desk for support.

. . .

. . .

There was nothing that was happening.

But now he was to do something else all would be lost.

Are you leaving school altogether Mister Doyle? Are you stopping being a teacher? William Moreland.

Are you stopping being a teacher altogether? Sardar Ali.

Muffled giggling.

Patrick glanced at the gigglers at once. Well well well. Muffled giggles and here yous are in fourth year! I mean fuck sake, surely it's high time ye threw the heid back and bellowed a big horselaugh – whatever that might be! Did anybody ever see a certain Marx Brothers' picture where the auld Groucho fellow played this doctor of horses?

Several hands aloft immediately, including a few girls'. When I am dead. What happens when I am dead.

You're no being fair, said Julie Stewart. It was a name he always loved. Women have better names than men. Patrick nodded:

Listen Julie Stewart, who is it gives names to women or do ye truly believe they give them to themselves and each other because you know full well what I've been telling yous all about the naming process and imperialism, colonisation of the subject, obliteration of the subject, you as object, even in your own eyes. What've ye got to say about that!

She waited a moment. Then she answered: It maybe used to be imperialism but I dont think it is now. I'm answering a question. But I want to say something else to you, to Mister Patrick Doyle, to you, I really dont think you're being fair because what ye do ye start all these things and then ye dont finish them or even just in a way follow them through properly.

Properly.

She stared at him.

Aye okay but I've got to do that. It's the teacher's real job. It's up to yous to get the things finished, or followed through properly. Think of Plato.

Yeh I know . . .

Patrick smiled.

What're ye smiling for? Joan Murphy.

He frowned.

She was frowning.

Joan Murphy. To have come out and said such a thing to him.

I think it's patronising, she said.

It is. It is patronising. Aye. Yeh; you're right. But I'm no ashamed. Nor do I think it has to be essentially bad. I'm not ashamed.

About patronising people?

Fair enough. But in the case in question no. As far as I recall it was a true and straightforward smile to do with young people and older people. I think there are honest patrons of the young and these honest patrons can be those who are not young themselves, at least relatively. I will agree though that I'm fucking stretching a point. But points are there to be stretched. That's what a point is, something that is not finite. Look what happened to motion when Zeno got that yin sorted out! Absolutely fuck all says you, but is that true? Ye might actually just say he was being a friend to auld Parmenides and it was a joint venture to capture the Pythagoreans. So what says you. Okay says me. But Plato came along as well and he went into the attack. His attack was a good yin. But I've got to wait a minute here . . . Patrick smiled falsely.

He was not giving them a chance. He couldnt do anything else. Could he do anything else. He couldnt, he couldnt do anything else. He turned from them, swivelling on the stool, he faced the black-board though blackboard is stupid, the thing being a green canvas. They needed time to reflect, to get to his falsity. What was interesting was the hostility, almost an anger. Of course he was letting them down. Quite right. But he was only a man. What could he do? And it was not possible to withdraw the request. He certainly did not want to leave them. Not to put too fine a point on the matter, they were saving his very fucking existence, his life. Without them he was dead, a dead man. The pipes.

O the pipes.

He didni want to go to another school. I actually dont want to go to another school.

But you put in for the transfer, says William Moreland.

I did not put in for the transfer, says Patrick Doyle, at least as far as I can remember. I'm being honest. I dont fucking remember putting in for this fucking transfer. Maybe I did and I was mentally deranged at the time. Maybe I was drunk! But I honestly dont remember putting in for it.

Is it possible to do something like that and forget? Jaqueline Boal.

I dont know. I think it has to be otherwise here I am not. But: either I did it and then totally forgot; or else I didnt, and some folk are not telling the truth.

Pause.

What d'you mean by that? Sardar Ali.

I dont know. It probably sounds like a weird kind of paranoia. Maybe they just prefer me to get shifted from school to school!

But you've been here for three years.

I know. There again but and I'm being honest, putting in for a transfer and then going away and managing to forget about it: I can imagine myself doing that. It's the kind of mischief I get up to. There are all sorts of flagellation. Mind these paintings by Goya I was telling yous to take a look at?

Hands aloft.

Great, said Patrick. He sniffed vigorously to clear the upper membranes, strolling out from behind the desk, hands in his trouser pockets. As the class of ye are very aware I'm not exactly a firm believer in the religious teachings of the great religious teachers; nor am I a believer in forms of tomorrow – nor any other fucking thing that manages to snatch folk away from the moment that is actually actual and right there under their very nostrils at this very next very this very gone a minute moment, yous know what I'm saying, the usual argument against the different ways of nullifying a person's actions. Mind you, this past couple of days I would be a liar if I was to let yous all imagine things have not been more odd than is usually the case. The things that have been happening, to some extent I'm left with no option but to regard them as more odd than is usually the case. Patrick frowned and turned his head sideways, then sideways in the other direction. Ye see if I dont regard them like that then I'm gonni be forced into seeing myself as odd, distinctly odd in fact. But is that true? Probably no. Probably it's a load of keech.

And by the way, pass all this on to whomsoever you want to pass it on to, I dont care, I dont care; because as well yous know there are people the same age as yourselves getting beaten up and tortured and killed in countries not all that far from here and I wont name them because if ye dont know what I'm talking about ye dont deserve to. People of twelve, thirteen, fourteen; they're getting tortured and murdered. Okay, so yous've got to do something. There isni any fucking point looking at me. I'm a fucking no-user, because that is what teachers are, no-users. If I wasni a fucking no-user I wouldni be a fucking teacher in this stench of a society. It's up to yous yourself. And now, is the best time to call a halt. Fine.

I've said before I'm away to play the pipes. Aye well I'm no kidding! Patrick grinned.

The class half smiled, half frowned. He felt very sweaty, very clammy. It was clammy in the room. He had his tie unloosened. He unknotted it and folded it away into his side jacket pocket.

Which wasnt at all symbolic; he only wore the tie to please himself anyway.

And here's another odd thing it's best no to lose sight of: I've been feeling happy. And I'll tell ye something, I've no been feeling happy for years. I mean genuinely. I'm no talking about the false stuff. I tell lies to myself in the same way yous do. But I've just been catching myself out now and again and christ what I'm realising is right at this moment I'm feeling as happy as ever I've done since the student days. Patrick laughed. It was an abrupt kind of laugh. He closed his eyes. But when he opened them he started laughing again.

There was a head at the window.

Patrick cleared his throat. He winked and grinned, but the grin would not be noticeable to anyone beyond the four walls of the classroom. That's the head back at the window, he said. There again but how do we know it's the same head? Is it something we can verify ourselves, that that there is a head and it might be the same one, the same head.

Well fuck sake of course he says. Heads cannot float. Heads can float. There are heads that do not float and heads that cannot be said to not float. That over there behind the window is a head that is not floating.

How come you're gonni go away and play the pipes if ye think the world's in as bad a state as all that?

Pardon?

Joan Murphy: If ye think the world's as bad as all that then how come you're just gonni go away and play the pipes instead of doing something more useful?

Patrick nodded. Mind you, a brief summary would be better: for example, Mister Doyle, you are a shite. Pat smiled at the girl but she did not return him a smile, she looked away.

I just want a rest, he said.

Do you think ye deserve one? Neil Rankine speaking. A big quiet boy who doesnt like Pat Doyle very much.

Your question is a good yin Mister Rankine.

Are ye gonni answer it Mister Doyle?

Pat smiled at him.

There was some movement going on. People were fidgeting. Maybe Neil Rankine speaking had signalled something. If his question was a signal. If maybe he was a ringleader

Debby Munro had risen from her seat. She had shoved her stuff into her bag. She was about to leave the room. She was going to go, to go from it. The others would follow. What was wrong with that. Nothing. It was fine. If they all went. If they were all to go. Yous may all go, he said, and go quick, quick. Come on, away ye go, the lot of yous, hurry up.

He sat sideways on the stool. He was facing away from the door, leaning his left elbow on the edge of the desk, his chin now onto the palm of the left hand. More shuffling noises. Another class! He turned his head slightly. It was only ghosts. A whole crowd of them. A whole crowd of ghosts had entered his classroom. And yet this period was supposed to have been spare.

What was their identity. Do ghosts need an identity. Need an identity always be a prerequisite. What does that mean. Is such a question the sort of thing one should be faced by, one should face up to. Here is a list of questions whose answers are not easily to be taken. There are moments to have gone, to have passed. Before arrival at one's destination one requires to have travelled halfway, and halfway of that, and halfway of that, and halfway of that.

The smiling faces.

I am cracking up.

The smiling faces.

P Λ -P.

. . .

. . .

Patrick Doyle's stomach erupted and what came out was a mixture of heavy beer and blended whisky, the stuff sold to ordinary folk. No doubt if it had been the single malt stuff they sold to rich folk he would still have spewed it. Okay. On the floor the mixture. Fucking grooooiy grooooiy grooo ercchhh ercchhh ercchhh o dear, fucking awful, but there you have it. All of it there. Nothing more. It was all out. O dear. He closed his eyes. He wasnt actually sure if there was more to come, there wasnt, it was all out. His head was cold and damp but it was fine.

It had splashed over his shoes and all around the bottoms of his trousers, slabbery stuff there as well. What he could do was just leave it so it would dry and then he could brush it off but people wouldnt be coping with that, the sight and the niff, so best to just actually

Wiping it was not easy. He had torn off several sheets of paper from jotters and was using these but they werent fucking proper for the job, not being built with wee holes, the paper, to take in waterish substances the way tissues and sponges did, it just being the ordinary type of paper which

was not fucking porous!!!!!!

Patrick yelled a laugh. But christ it was everywhere and you had to be careful how you stepped otherwise you would slide, ending arse over elbow on the bastarn fucking floor!!!! And there were snotters down from his nostrils for fuck sake with the laughter and snifflings that were going on. In the name of god right enough what a fucking state to get into, looking really christ whatstheword disfuckinggusting.

Zoom   Zoom

The patter of tiny feet. The corridor. The weans. The drama. What a situation for our hero!

Eh yous canni come in here the now.

Why not sir?

Because I fucking say so that's why not.

He turned out the lights and shut fast the door wishing he could lock it but teachers never being given actual keys to doors in case they fucking – done something or other that was who knows what the fuck, unwholesome maybe. He walked along and down the stairs, moving fast though appearing casual. A lot of pupils were about but they were paying no heed to the bottom sections of his trousers.

And farther down, into the basement area, along by the boilers for the trusty brush and shovel and the bunker of sawdust. He grabbed the sawdust in handfuls and rubbed it into his trousers. The sickness rolling off in wee lumps. He rubbed in more of the sawdust, making the things as presentable as possible. Then he was back up the stairs and into his room in moments, with brush, shovel and fire-bucket, clearing the mess as best he could in the time, the door now being pushed ajar and the nosy wee faces would be poking in, and making their decisions

and in walked the first batch – girls, talking to each other and looking at him quite the thing, just to see what he was up to. He said nothing. He kept on doing what he was doing with shovels of sawdust and brushings and shovels, the sawdust, into the fire-bucket, and that dampness left on the shovel and the fucking smell all too recognisable. It wasnt the best of jobs okay but it was reasonable and it was okay, okay. The youthful parties were all watching him work but without a great deal of interest. He finished. He was to return the implements immediately.

None of the maintenance folk was about in the basement. That was good. No reports. He didnt especially want people to know. I'll blame it on the cloves anyway, he said, reassuringly to himself in a loud whisper.

A game of five-a-side football had started in the assembly hall. He watched a couple of minutes. It was funny how come he had missed the only goal of the game at Yoker on Saturday. Then he shivered, a sudden spasm; and the volts went right up the backbone to the base of his skull. The idea of laying oneself down for a sleep. What was he doing here, in this den of iniquity, when he could be elsewhere. While in a room not too far away dwelt the woman Houston. He was shivering; he yawned. That was the good thing about flinging yourself over the banister to go crashing to your doom, how you might waken up in a cosily warm hospital bed. It could have been worse of course, he could have eaten a big curry. That wasni even funny. And the time? Not long. Not long. While in a room not too far. What did she think. What did she think about things, in general; the generality, of things. Did she think of him with kindness. These are the sorts of questionings the Doyle fellow must encounter if ever he is to survive as a person. MI6.

Patrick continued to lean his elbows on the railing. Then he smiled at him. MI6 smiled back at him.

And seemed about to say something to Patrick but Patrick had stepped roundabout him and walked on, without the slightest hesitation. My life is just an ordinary life. I am just a person from the depths of the universality, who is leading his/her life as best s/he can, never asking for much except just an avoidance of the nooks and the crannies the twists and the turns. There is nought that is unusual about it either. One drinks and one spews in an almost public manner. But this is aye the way of it for the ordinary fellow or fellowess. It is not something that doesni happen. It happened to me as a schoolboy during the earlier periods of experimentation and now when I am an adult and attuned to the highways and byways lo, it is happening still, when I am a schoolboy no longer, it can still be happening. I walk into the room and confront the class, the pupils. I continue

heads or no fucking heads windows or no fucking windows
I continue

heads. There are heads at the window. Is that two heads or is it one head?

Pupils! Here you have a chap. This is a chap here. Look at that fucking head there, that is the head of the second head, the master of headsis assistant. Let us open our jotters and discuss the following: time. Time. Matters that be temporal. Time is the healer. Time is a thing, that

One has time and one's time is not, the time that belongs to one, it is not, it has existed. But not now, not longer. I am formerly one of yous and am always one with yous. That is religious.

Yous are all fidgeting because yous are not liking what I'm fucking talking about in this manner that I'm doing it

Yous dont actually like this. This is that yous dont, yous dont actually like. So be careful. Yous'll have to fucking be careful. Exercise caution. Be honest and truthful and fucking courageous for christ sake dont be cowardly because that's what they want, what they demand, they demand cowardice, and when they've got that off yous then they might deign to drop ye a wee gratuity. Bastards. My life is just an ordinary life. I drink sometimes too much in the wrong way, my belly not being attuned properly or something maybe to do with a lack of an item, food or milk or what. But time recovers itself time recovers itself, when allowed to get on with it, to march unhindered.

People are fidgeting. I just stand here ye see, rocking back and forth on the balls of the heels of my feet which lurk uncovered beneath the socks and the shoes. I continue, even if some of yous are laughing — what at? at fucking stupit puns — but I continue, I continue. I face my fellows and I face my fellowesses, the lassies and the lassieds. All yous wee bastards, deceivers in embryo.

One has drunk and one has spewed, okay, it might have been a bad pint — it happens, especially at dinnertime when some bar owners get their staff to throw last night's dregs in along with the good stuff, okay. And the floor has dried the floor has dried. I just continue. I see your faces, your faces are smiling now and again. Yous are good wee weans, to some extent. I dont worry. I dont worry. Time recovers itself. I shall be asleep. I shall be without consciousness. I can rock back and forth and back and forth, back and forth and back and forth, and that will be that, and I am healed, the healing having been taking place. It happened to me as a schoolboy and here it is happening to me as a man who is fully grown and is twenty-nine years of age. I have walked into the classroom and looked upon ye. I am healed. There is a dringing, a dringing. This is the period ended. So what happens now. Dismissal.

The exits are soon to be open and the ways lie ahead, ahead.

Patrick was going to go home because going home is best. To be alone and without gods is death says Hölderlin but Hölderlin was wrong and is a poor bastard. Patrick is not a poor bastard. He strolls. He is lost in thought. He is deep in the province of inner psychomachinations. Weans are puzzled. They do not zoom. They are quietly there, they are awkwardly there, their feet shuffle, but not for long not for long, this being ten minutes to four and liberation is upon them thus their interest wanes. But there are teachers who are looking, whom I am not seeing, being lost in thought etcetera etcetera and I stroll on in fast time, a straight line, down the steps and outside, across the carpark, wherein the motor. But not to get in not to get in not to get in not to get in and the faces all fucking looking and the two polis as well over by the gates and fucking looking what are they fucking looking at the bastards the fucking bastards because the key get the key get the key in the fucking lock and come on now calm down just fucking calm down and insert the long bit in there, and turn it clockwise, click, click click. Doors aye open. That's what doors are for, to open. Come on now, just take it fucking easy else you'll bang into the gatepost for christ sake. But his hand was shaking he was so cold, his body having lost so much of its heat and also the actual temperature seeming to have dropped to something approaching zero once more. It was as if Glasgow had become a form of antichthon. Hot water bottles. He was looping the belt and plugging it in to the bit where it goes, the seatbelt lock, shivering but gaining control, getting his arms to stiffen, his hands affixed to the wheel. He would not crash into any fucking gatepost. He switched on the ignition and the engine started first time. He revved it, seeing the clouds of exhaust in the rearview mirror, some elderly weans scowling at it, and there too was Alison. There she was. That was her there, and walking;

on her tod and walking, along the driveway, handbag swinging, looking so fine, so fine. She was there. He let down the handbrake, clutch up and the motor was moving, steadily it would have appeared but his hands were clinging onto the steering wheel for dear life. He would be into bed soon. He would be into bed so quickly that maybe even he would be wearing his clothes, maybe not even bothering to get them off, being so tired and not having to worry about what folk might think since there he was alone and not answerable to a soul, to no bastard, he could just get into the house and bang shut the door and throw himself under the blankets. Ah, bliss. His mind shutting, his mind just shutting, his memory, all of it going, a formalised system, a theorem of sleep. A loud screech. A taxi, it nearly crashed right into him. The driver was sticking his middle finger in the air, angry and sarcastic at the same time. Patrick had swerved without warning. The taxi had had to brake, the anchors flung on, an emergency stop. Its nearside wing only about nine inches from him. Patrick waved an apology because he was definitely in the wrong but the taxi driver just glowered at him because of course you're not allowed to make a silly mistake in this man's Glasgow. I willni apologise twice!!! thundered Patrick to himself reassuringly. He wound down the side window, getting some icy air in on his face. He was going to give up driving. Driving went with teaching. The idea of stopping it there and then. Just getting out and grabbing the chattels chattelus and running like fuck,.or no, just sidling off round the corner, avoiding the curious stares from the passersby passersbeelzebub. And no fucking wonder either for christ sake when you come to think about it because here you have a car that's fuckt, a vehicle that is no longer sound insofaras motor vehicles are thought to be articles of motion or the term motor vehicle is scarcely to be regarded as valid, as true, as something one can verify by simply walking roundabout its outer bloody damn bastarn fucking perimeter, that's if you can crawl out the bloody damn door without its fucking metal hinges grinding your eardrums to death, to death, literal death, the head and shoulders stiffly in the coffin as the church shutters close and the fingers of fire come swooping down to clutch you ever inwards, into its all-cleansing flame.

You must continue. You must see it through. You have got to

pull oneself together and fight like fuck to arse your way clear of trouble.

Okay?

Yes. Aye. I'm just breathing deeply in an attempt to clear the head. I'm aware that by increasing the intake of oxygen into my skull, my brain – the way it works, the way it carries on without cracking – that the intake of oxygen, the prerequisite

A mammoth queue. at the entrance to a shoe shop. There was a SALE!! BIG REDUCTIONS!! And your man needed a pair of dancers you're darned tooting. He settled the car at the kerb opposite. He strolled across the road. The last man in the queue looked at him as if to say something. He was dressed in a fawn trenchcoat and a tweedy bunnet or kep as they used to say here in The Land of Heather probably around the time Grandfather Doyle's old man was toiling at whatever the fuck he was toiling at. And then again, this guy in the trenchcoat with a really thin face, a really thin face. But what the fuck's up with a thin face!

Thin faces. What do we say about them. Is there something to be said about them, thin faces.

No, there's eff all to say about them, because maybe I've got one myself and if so I'll report ye ya racist fascist bastirt. Let me see:

the display shoes in the large doorway contained lefts only to thwart the would-be shoe thief. He smiled at those queuing here in case they thought he was trying to skip in past them.

The shoes were cheap efforts. You could ascertain this just by peering at them and bearing witness to the nature of the plastic uppers, also the narrow foot entrance which means your feet just at the ankles would end up constricted and rubbing against the rims, thus sore feet, the big watery blisters and so on, hacked and raw-red skin. No good. No good at all. He pursed his lips, indicating his dissatisfaction with the quality to the rest of the queue but they appeared not to be bothering about his opinions. They had their own opinions. Okay. He frowned but gazed to the floor. How come they were all going to buy such shite. Because they were skint. Because they had no fucking dough. People would buy anything if it was cheap. It would be great to have something to sell. If he had something to sell he could take it out and sell it. He returned to the opposite side of the road but continued on past the motor to a nearby newsagent; the truth of the matter, that he needed to buy something; it didni matter what, just something that could be anything, preferably an item of luxury but, an article sweated over by all the weans of Thailand for the wage of a lollipop, some article whose function they would only be vaguely aware of

> da da, da da, da da
> da da, da da, da da
> da da, da da, da da, da da
> you're in the army now
>
> you're in the army now
> you're in the army now
> you'll never get rich digging a ditch
> you're in the army now

Cockadoodledoo. Christ was denied three times. This was the sort of stupid conundrum the famous Mirs Houston had left him with. What had she meant by it, calling him that, saying that to him, Judas Iscariot. It was actually Peter who did the denials. Just as well he was a nonbeliever. He smiled, then chuckled. A woman was awaiting his every pleasure behind the counter. She wore a dark brown overall and checkered blouse and in her smile at him, that perfunctory smile which in this case was no such thing but a thing of warmth and great beauty, which in all such cases

I dont want to buy the *Guardian* because it's a load of rightwing shite and there's nothing else.

Yes there is, there's a whole rack of radical stuff you can go and dig out if ye really want to look except you canni do your looking in here because we dont sell any of it.

I wouldnt want to anyway.

Why not?

Because I find I cannot read such stuff on a regular basis, that I become too quickly scunnered, feelings of nausea in the belly and so forth.

Aw.

Aye eh they dont fucking seem to fit into my everyday existence. I dont know how to explain it. I blame my parents and society, how they bare their arse to The Powers That Be.

The woman nodded. The crest of the newsagent chain on her left breast, her own name in a wee brooch down by her throat.

I blame my parents and society.

The woman nodded.

I'll take a bag of sweeties. I'll take these ones there with the marzipancoatedchocolatus-a-um. And do ye have any Andrews Liver Salts?

No. You'll have to go to the chemist shop along the road.

O well, I'll just have to drive it to save time.

That's entirely up to yourself but see if it was me, what I'd do I'd just hoof it and kid on it wasnt mine, that it didni fucking belong to me, that no-longer-good vehicle, that I didnt know it from Adam, these fucking doors rusting to fuck with the grating bastarn hinges, to be honest about it, I dont understand how

You're right, thanks.

Yet it has to be said there exists something about it, about this motor car, a certain indefatigability, the way the bonnet slopes so chirpily upwards from the rusted wings, the manner in which the lack of adequate mudguarding

No, just leave it. Dump it! Grab the tax disc and run for your life – except it's fucking out-of-date anyway and if ye dont buy a new yin that big polis'll come back and get ye done for breaking the law.

Funny how come so many officers-of-the-law crop up these days. Patrick appears to be surrounded by them. Everywhere he looks. Even if they are all jovial big chaps, it doesnt matter. And how come they're all seven-foot-high I mean I dont want to get paranoiac about it christ though there again the big yin that gave the warning on the tax disc was okay, he was cheery and seemed good-natured for christ sake you could see it in his eyes, the way he was giving Master Doyle the telling-off. It was never a true telling-off, more of a jocular comment, the sort that occurs between good neighbourishly acquaintances. Ergo: not all polismen are bad chaps; not all poliswomen are bad chappesses. Only those who work for the government in such and such a way and do not perform in this that and the other fashion, know what I mean, tap the nose and say nothing, there's too many clicks on my telephone these days.

Patrick has nothing to worry about. Honest. He's a fucking okay bloke. The Magisterial forces are not out to nab him. Patrick Doyle your honour. MA (HONS). I got my 'honours'. My (Honours)! My !!!honours!!! I became a registered civilian on behalf of forces that corrupt. I am the messenger. I have to convey the tidings. I am the means to their end. I perform in public. I am the fellow with the likeable personality who is to influence the weans of the lower orders so that they willni do anything that might upset the people with wealth, power and privilege.

So dont fuck off.

Okay?

Yes.

Aye.

Back you come.

Fine, hullo. I am pleased to meet ye. I truly am. I am a likeable personality. If you are not an unlikeable personality why then, we may converse. Hullo back. I am your alter ego. Alter alteris masculine. When your personality splits I am the back end. I am the ugly bit, the counterforce. In order to release me as a pleasantly docile manifestation you have to resort to instruments of wind – pipes can suffice. What they do they release me, and I am another likeable personality. Thus we have us two and the ugly one. Then as well as you get this other yin, me; I creep in, I creep in while yous all sit about gabbing in that friendly getting-to-know-ye type of way; I creep in and edge closer and closer till I'm so much a part of the company you didnt notice my absence earlier, that a gap had existed, that it has now been filled.

But that motor car! God! Imagine being abandoned at the side of the road! Imagine it, early to mid March, a time of year when wintry chills can flood the eternal watervapourish canopy. I mean to say and all that your man here, P for Patrick Doyle, a good protestant atheist, a good glaswegian protestant of the nonbelieving class, not only a virtual atheist but a literal one, a total and literal one since a wee boy of some twelve summers. Imagine it but, getting abandoned at a pavement towards the latter part of a dismal winter, enlivened only by the absence of Xmatic Pantomimes. I am the Piper Doyle. I pipe. Up piped Doyle to enliven the proceedings. That story of Kafka's about the nice wee woman who is a vain mouse and who pipes a song of astonishing, of astonishing

Astonishing what for fuck sake I've fucking forgotten.

I hate all these arsish fucking banalities I mean they're so fucking stupit, daft; I prefer to march ever onwards getting bumped by folk rushing to the SALE!! BIG REDUCTIONS!!

That wee lassie Audrey. She's a wee beauty. She is such a beautiful wee lassie it makes ye want to greet for the rest of your life.

So P. Doyle enters a pub.

P. Doyle enters a pub. Well well well. He strolls to the bar. The smell of wines and spirits and diverse beers, also carbolic soap and incense. The bartender. Your new found resolution Mister Doyle. Could I have a tomato juice please?

A tomato juice?

Yeh, and a half-pint of heavy

(ya fucking coward ye)

As the bartender got the order Patrick yawned and leaned his right elbow on the counter. He yawned once more. He carried his drinks to a side table. The place was almost empty. A middle-aged couple at a table farther along. Two guys about Pat's age standing at the bar, with the bartender a part of their company. The television set was on, but its volume had been turned completely down.

He unrolled his *Evening Times* at the football page.

For fuck sake, the two guys and the bartender were looking at him. They were looking at him. Imagine that, for christ sake, what to do, he turned a page; he turned the page and flattened it down on the table. Because he had bought the tomato juice and the half-pint of heavy. They would have thought it an unlikely combination therefore worthy of comment, of pointing it out to one another. Glasgow drinker buys tomato juice, you could picture the headlines. What the fuck else could it be was his fucking fly open or something! Maybe he should just bloody go and ask. Excuse me ya trio of fucking halfwits why the fuck are yous staring at me?

Ignore them. Ignore them.

The sickness!! Aaarrgghh!! The slabbery fucking sawdust!!

Errcchh errcchh!! Aaarrgghh!! The fucking bottom sections of the boy's trousers, they're fucking minging with this green and tan and yellow ochre substance!

It's no his fault though. He tried to clean them as best he could in the time he had, which wasnt much, he had a class of weans awaiting, and these weans are all perceiving little bastards, persons who are never to doubt, nor to be doubted.

Hang on a minute. It is certainly true the guy's wearing sick-stained trousers but this should hardly produce such inferences as: the fellow himself is responsible for it, the manner of it, these bottom sections, their current condition. He could easily have been strolling along the fucking road when up pops a sick dog, a drunken vagabond on all-fours. Anything. Anything's a possibility in this man's Glasgow. And he's leaving. He's left. He's gone, this very man, he's away, never to return. He has left school forever. Now that he is a fully developed male adult he has left the halls of education forever.

RANGERS SIGN EIRE WINGER!

Rangers sign Eire winger. Sammy O'Flaherty, a naturally gifted winger. In fact he was a good player. Pat had seen him on the box a couple of times and he showed a lot of neat touches.

But enough of football.

How come these bastards are looking, that's what I want to know. Probably shites from Special Branch, parties who disagree with truthtelling. Truthtelling is the one word. Truthtelling is a verb. It is a doing thing or a not doing thing. I truthtell, do you.

Rangers sign Eire winger. Sammy O'Flaherty, a naturally gifted winger, will today sign the dotted line at the home of the famous Glasgow club. A crowd of fans was waiting on the Ibrox doorstep for a glimpse of the new boy.

So drink up and leave.

Come on, time to leave.

Patrick was tired so it was time he left. He was not leaving. How come he was not leaving? Was there something wrong with the dickie? Let us examine the circumstances:

Patrick, how come you're no leaving?

Because I'm fukt. I'm knackered. I've been leading a dog's life. I've been braying like a donkey.

How do you mean?

Pardon?

You were speaking nonsense there. Garble. Something about donkeys – braying like a donkey or something.

O. Sorry. I shouldni do that in case it upsets ye. There are guys looking at me but I dont want to upset ye so I wont show worry, I wont show discomfort, in case you get upset.

Mm.

I mean sorry, dont let my plight interrupt your life. At least they're no torturing me, it isni Pakistan or Ulster.

Shut up, you're garbling, people'll start worrying.

I know fuck sake, exactly.

So hold onto the table.

I'm trying to.

If it's magic it might rise up and carry ye home. That's what happens in certain tales from the Orient. Always allowing for the fact that the Arabian Nights arent Oriental. They're from the Middle East. Yes. Who gives it capital letters. The naming process and Imperialism. Arse is a typical form. Poor old Mirs Houston. Her problem

her problem.

Seriously but, she doesni have a problem. Especially not Patrick Doyle.

Patrick Doyle

is holding onto the table and is now letting go and lifting a glass of tomato juice. What gives them the right. That is what he wants to know. Okay they've fucking bought him but no his da. Why not? Of course they have. Bastards. Thales of Miletus. How come he's so fucking important. My nut. It is aching. It is just a sore head, that's all, a case of water on the brain. This day has been extremely difficult. It has taken the form of an anti-climax. The weekend had built towards it and now it has come and is past, passed. And Patrick is, and no wonder, absolutely fucking shattered. He should just be collapsing somewhere. Into his bed with a hot water bottle and a strong milky bastarn drink, Ovaltine or somefuckingthing.

He farted.

Not too loudly but loudly enough. Farts and arses. How vulgar.

How dashed fucking uncivil of the dem bounder. The two guys looked like they might have heard. They were still chatting with the dem bartender. And now they were gazing across at him, all fucking three of them what was wrong. What could they do? Pat is neither big nor small nor thin nor fat and he would fight back and with luck could snatch a bottle or glass or anyfuckingthing that came to hand. But maybe not. Maybe he would just go hysterical and start screaming and yelling and kicking his feet like a baby who doesnt want to go to bed. And it is full of wind. Which is how come the fart. When you spew the way he did in the classroom the lungs gasp in oxygen and it all gets mixed up with your belly and intestines, thus expel boarders, out it has to come, or tries to come albeit in company one attempts to restrain it; unfortunately, as in the present case, it can catch you unawares. I mean what is he supposed to fucking do? go and apologise because he farted! That would be so typical of this life. You must forgive me, the belly and intestines

Salvador Dali: better to fart in company than die in a corner.

What about vegetarians? Do they fart as much as meat-eaters? With all these anti-Pythagorean bean mixtures! So much for the luscious Houston.

The lack of food. When did Doyle last eat. He hasnt eaten for fucking months! He could purchase a poke of potato crisps, and he could dunk these potato crisps into his tomato juice. Which would appear the perfect way of applying this liquid, of using this liquid, this juice.

There are two guys staring at Patrick, that's what I want to know. He got up off his seat and he walked to them. He said: Is there something up?

They glanced at each other.

Naw it's just eh, the way I keep catching your eye and all that, I'm wondering how come I mean if we know each other or some-bloodything.

What ye talking about?

Patrick nodded. He gazed at the two of them.

What's up?

Nothing's up with me, said Pat. I thought there might be something up with yous. The way yous were looking at me.

Who was looking at ye? said one of the guys. Ye kidding? He shook his head and he said to the bartender: He thinks we were fucking looking at him!

Hh! The bartender frowned.

Patrick nodded. And he added, Give us a bag of crisps.

What did ye say?

Patrick stared at him: A packet of crisps.

What kind?

Any kind. He laid the exact cost in coins on the counter, looking at the bartender as he reached to the side of the gantry, to where about twelve cardboard boxes were stacked, each one offering a different flavour of potato crisps. Cheese & onion.

One of the two guys glanced at him. Pat stared to the front as he returned to the table. He sipped at his beer when seated. And now they would definitely be looking at him; they would make it plain; it would have to be seen as a challenge. But he had made his point. It was become best to leave. Now. He finished the beer, stuck the crisps into his pocket, got onto his feet again and, taking care not to face the bar, he walked steadily to the exit, the hand grabbing him and birling him roundabout and getting battered by a fist on the jaw – but no, and he stepped somewhat jerkily outside, the door closing behind. He felt like laughing, he had to stop himself from laughing, and he succeeded easily, it not being funny, it being no funny thing, no funny incident. It was deadly serious. Pat glanced back over his shoulder then continued along the road quickly.

Scott was unlucky. He got pipped at the post by The Foreigner Amundsen and received a posthumous knighthood, arise Sir Robert. While plucky old The Foreigner Amundsen kept going until being lost at sea some score of years later, out looking for a missing frigate the *Nobile*. Imagine being aboard the *Nobile*, one of its hands, and getting lost. What like would that have been! And was it even a frigate. It could have been a yacht. Out there drifting noiselessly midst the freezing, ice-laden fogs of Kilimanjaro.

What the fuck are ye blethering about ya fucking donkey!
Poor old donkeys.

If prostitutes' feet are not warm should the client accede to the moral imperative vis-à-vis the bearing of hot water bottles as the universal male obligation? And the corollary:
what is the nature of a contract?
And:
was Kant a frosty auld shite?
Who knows. Who cares. Nowadays people dont even consider such idle controversy.

The serving of steak pie suppers in chip shops, with salt and sauce and vinegar.

An effervescent ending to his life, a sparkling effect – something to fire him straight upwards and outwards, out from the mire. He laughed at the tin of Andrews Liver Salts. He could swallow the whole fucking lot, the entire contents, followed by a bottle of disinfectant. Or maybe the other way about. All he sought was death. Death: purely and simple: simply and pure.
How come he was not able to just be dead like everybody else. Everybody else was dead. They were dead. How come he was not like them, and not able to just be dead. How come he was not able to just be dead and buried and out the road of trouble and strife and all things rotten and putrified and shitey.

Was it his fault? Was he the bloke to blame? The chap at whose feet etcetera.

Without other parties the house is cold. The house is not warm. The house is a cold place to be. To live in such a state in such a house, to not be with parties, to be cold and to be there, a party in such a state, of cold, a numbness, that lack of warmth, all-embracing, that cold clutch

a cold clutch, of something. There is a cold clutch of something. There in the house; a house of coldness, where nobody lives except this solitary, this one, when he has returned.

There can be spectres. Ghosts. Apparitiones. Nightly death-shades. An ethereal shade. Hosts of gloomy spectres.

One is dutybound. One is bound by one's duty. One has made the contract towards life, the essentiality. Okay? Aye. Fine. So I can fuck off now? Aye, go ahead, I'm fine, fine, everything's fucking okay.

So how do you do it. Well, you pick them up; but one at a time, obviously. The thinner one. It doesni actually seem as friendly as heretofore, but so what, it is just an instrument and not really anything, until being called into action. He blew the sound, his eyelids shut; then he was looking at the carpet, there was a threadbare patch; he laid down the pipe and knelt to examine it – it was almost a hole it was so thin. His maw had donated this carpet. But back to business. He picked up the pipe, the thinner one again. It was no use going to the other one, that would be wrong and silly, as though it was the pipe's fault rather than his, for not attending to it properly. And concentration was just fucking there was not anything else; he closed his eyelids, back seated once again, and blew this note, not big enough then big enough and straightforwards, a note that was straightforwards, the sound. He paused for air, keeping his eyelids closed. But he opened them. Okay, it was still fine and he closed them once more and breathed in through his nostrils in a move and started then, there, at the back of the throat, the air expelled by the roof of the mouth fuck it was fine, right, and good also, exact and precise and the thing, just correct, correctly stated. A drone: not exactly, not exactly; no, not

It was rubbish. He dropped it to the floor and left the chair and went to the window. A crassness about it all. And there was that lassie across the way, the tenement across the street facing, the window looking out.

Perhaps he should not have painted the bloody things, that stupid enamel paint. Had he turned them into objects that were just fucking garish? Was he responsible for a quality of garishness? Until he had tampered with them they could not be said to be impure. Now they could be, they could be so designated. The lassie across the street used to stand by the window quite a lot but Pat hadni seen her for several weeks – a good couple of months – maybe back about December. One could construct a fantasy about her but that would be unclean. She could even have been one of his pupils. What age were folk?

What age were folk.

Patrick lifted the thicker pipe and settled himself on the floor, his rear to the settee. But before anything happened the settee shifted back the way on its castors and he needed things to be solid, if things were not solid how could he be expected to play things. This was the worst of it. But it was true. Things had to be solid. If they were not solid, christ.

He sat on the armchair. He very rarely used this armchair for any purpose yet here it was now becoming functional at long last. What did that imply. It implied that a teleological

And when the armchair was pushed back against the cupboard he could sit down on the carpet with his back placed firmly, solidly. That threadbare patch was quite large all things considered so why the fuck had he never noticed it before. How come his mother had never said anything about it. I mean that was distinctly odd. Most not like the Mistress Doyle who was rapidly becoming older than she used to be, the da's last heart attack probably. She was getting quite absent-minded. She was only in her mid-fifties as well and scarcely to be described as 'old'; you dont describe somebody in their mid-fifties as 'old'. Having the wealthy schoolteacher for a son, who fails to remember her birthday till the very last moment, when it is over and in the past, this is the sort of son she has, a son

But that was fine that was fine.

How come him and Sheila Monaghan had never slept together? It was so good getting her bra off and there was that time as well when she let her hand lie on his bollocks and maybe you were thinking she knew more than she was letting on, maybe that was it and just Doyle being too inexperienced to see what was what. But surely if they had truly, if they had truly, if

fuck off

He blew a sound, deep, long; a good sound. He blew another one, the same sounding. He did another one and extended it. These sounds were good sounds. He was pleased with them. He had wanted to prove he could do it and he had been successful. He had achieved it, he had blown them – he was blowing them. He blew another, shortened, a shortened version. He laid down the pipe and got up onto his feet. The lassie had gone from the window.

Sex.

Pat was at the mantelpiece, elbows up on its edge and his chin on the backs of his clasped fingers, staring into the wall. If he stared hard enough he could see this wee toty hole in the wallpaper, it being porous. He

What was wrong with him there was something wrong with him, with he. Had Alison

What had she

What was the question, the form of questioning.

The transfer was a strange thing except for the most stupit of all explanations, just that he had done it in a fit of pique, maybe while under the influence, but not drunk, just having had a couple, maybe after a Friday's lunch with the colleagues, and he had got truly browned off, more than usual, and then he had just gone ahead and fucking done it, anything's fucking possible, for christ sake, probability, that's all we know about, fucking probability. And these bloody strange damn stupit events. This was a problem with being Doyle pee for Patrick, one was inclined to perform the less weightier feats, the slightly more absurd actions, the grosser deeds. What was wrong with him. What was actually wrong with him! What was actually fucking wrong with him christ you felt like asking such questions with a blanket over your head they were so shameful, so fucking shameful. What he should do is get out the house. He had to get out the house. He had to get

out

the house. Why was he not out the house? Why was this him here? Why was for christ sake and not partaking of the glorious riches of this postindustrialised western capitalisticobliquesocialisticexploitative

How come he wasnt blowing it up? Yessir, that was the first fucking out-in-the-open question he had posed for quite some certain length of the present.

So sentimental but that was the problem.

A motor car arriving down in the street. A man without a hat, on the pavement opposite, entering the close next to the one where the lassie lived. With a blunderbuss etcetera etctera, one could have blown him apart if perhaps he had been a member of the baddies. Pat's shins burnt: the material of the trousers touching against them, and burning, from where he had been in front of the fire at the mantelpiece; and what a sharp pain when he rubbed the right one! really fucking sore – he raised the trouser leg, the skin being ripped asunder, there on the shin, the skin was torn. Some blood too although dried and hardened. It was from when he had tripped and cracked it on the stairs earlier at school. The image of a splintered shinbone; hopping to the hospital, queuing there with all your health insurance certificates, seeking a good firm glue and the aid of a strong pair of hands. The nurse telling ye to stop behaving like a spoiled brat and to cut out that sobbing. But please miss I've got a splintered shinbone! Stop your fucking nonsense and away home at once ya naughty boy. But I'm twenty-nine! I'll twenty-nine ye!

Imagine finding a nurse like that. And probably she would want to take you home and insist on you hiring an ambulance so ten minutes later there you are home with this nurse, would you care for a coffee while we're waiting for the glue to set; well okay, if you would; well I actually would so will I just pour you one, or what; aye, just fucking pour it; and her tits soft and supple, in the name of the holies.

When I am dead.

When I am dead I shall be thingwi and there shall be no more problems insofaras the world ceases to exist when I shut the fucking eyelids. Okay! I'm going to fucking wipe yous out ya bastards. One quick blink.

Sex though.

Sex. Erections and fantasies.

Here you have women and men
This is a man
Doyle needs a woman.

What a fucking syllogism that is! A fucking beauty! No wonder the dark ages were so fucking absolutely unregenerative.

Right.

Okay. One could actually make a sign at the window to the lassie. What would be the nature of the sign. In what sense could it be true for her while being true for myself. And if this sign managed to be true for us both what would happen next.

It wouldnt work that way. She would just see me and know straight off what was happening and when I flickered my eyelid a fraction that would be that and ten minutes later she would meet me at the foot of her stairs and off we'd go for a night on the town, and on to a cosy wee restaurant maybe followed by a quiet disco for a wee dance, then home, her head on my shoulder as I drive slowly in that direction:

I had been standing by the window for the past six months awaiting just such a sign Patrick.

For god sake woman how did you no tell me!

I was too bashful.

Too bashful! Aw . . . I see . . . But you could just have maybe I dont know, waved or something. But her father of course. The lassie didni want to take any chances in case he spotted her. What a jealous auld guy her da is! Never lets her out his sight. So she has to just stare out the fucking window all the time. Some fucking social life! Almost as bad as Doyle P. MA (Hons). That's how come the pair of them are so suited. That's how come

The phrase 'hollowness of tone'; what did it mean. Why was it in his head. Hollowness of tone. It was a fine and smashing phrase. There is something of it in the work of old Goya. It is a thing that what is it. What is it. I wonder what the fuck it is. An ineffability about such abstractions, these affairs that arent tangible, the slippery yins, and only their names remain, arcana celestiae

Back to the drawing-board! Yet the lassie: still standing there, not too close to the window, so that she can remain unseen from outside. She will have a body. Yes. Legs and torso and arms and all the rest of it. She will have them, she herself. And maybe she isnt a lassie, maybe she just looks young from a distance. She might be a lady of some seventy summers.

The pipes.

This thinner one was the first Patrick encountered and usually it is the first he lifts whenever he begins

it all falls to ashes

he lifted the thicker, raising the top to his mouth, closed the eyes to help compress the lips, inhaling through his nostrils; and then the blow, and he controlled it; the sound from the back of the throat and by the roof of the mouth, the air deriving from the pits of his lungs. He was producing it. It was strange but true, that such a thing could be produced by him. He kept his eyes shut, there was a shiver from his shoulders. What the hell was this act and aye that bloody shiver. Was it actually conceivable what was being produced was a genuine musical art? No. There wasni any point in going as far as that. What was important was just — that here was an act that had an essential quietness about it, a breathing space, it was more like a sort of breathing space, that he was producing.

Jesus christ.

It actually made sense too. Through whatever it was he was doing he was managing to produce this effect of space, a thing that was spatial. That is what it was. That was fucking how it called up such phrases as 'hollowness of tone'. And these associations with Goya's wee dog. Fuck. Jesus christ. A calming! He was on his feet. He looked at the pipe. He sat back down on the settee. He was doing it wrong he had to do it right, the playing, before anything else the conceptualising especially especially the fucking conceptualising the bastards, the fusty fucking webs; he blew a note and it was not correct, he blew a note that was not correct; he was not blowing a note that was correct. He laid down the pipe. He had spoiled it, for now. He had had it and he had lost it. He was to see Alison immediately.

But he was to phone firstly. He had to give her warning. He could not simply fucking arrive. The husband and perhaps all her bloody in-laws all sitting having their tea and there he is chapping the door and seeking an interview with her, your woman there the em for mirs. He was just to phone. Torture torture torture. He was just to phone. You lift the receiver, inserting the fingertip, dragging out the opening digit; and the second. And the third! The next and the next

Hullo?

Hullo? 3836.

Eh hullo eh is that eh can I speak to Alison Houston please?

Ah, who shall I say?

Eh is that Mister Houston?

Yes.

O hullo eh it's Pat Doyle, from school – we've actually met twice eh, at the Halloween Party and eh, I was wondering if I could just have a word with Alison a minute

(ya fucking bastard ye because my heart's fucking exploding)

Right.

. . .

Pat?

Hullo Alison I need to see you a minute if ye dont mind, just for a quick word, if that's alright.

Alison didni reply. She didni say anything. She was thinking things over. Mulling. Alison, mulling.

Pat?

Aye?

I see ye about nine o'clock?

Nine o'clock?

Will that be okay?

Aye.

Nine o'clock.

Aye. Alison, were you looking for me today?

It was nothing really. Alright then, nine o'clock.

Okay eh . . .

Miller's.

Miller's aye; fine.

Bye.

Bye.

But he had to be careful he had to be careful; otherwise the very worst could befall. Of course there were temptations there were always temptations, these tempting things always exist, will-o-the-wisp affairs, you've got to be careful from, wary, you have to be wary, of.

And Alison could not help him. She would want to help him but she couldnt. He didnt want her help anyway. If he wanted to do things like perform on the pipes then he had to do them alone. And not tell folk either. He was to carry on alone. He was not to think; thinking was death. And that was odd, how thought became death. That's probably why the rationalists need other worlds all the time.

There is the basic fact that he has produced sound and space that are precise. He has achieved it on different occasions. He has had to push hard, hard. Above the mantelpiece was a print with a glazed frame and in this he could see his reflection, his face being reflected, his eyes gazing at him, his eyes gazing at him.

What is the point of certain stuff.

He stared out the window, keeping to the side, in by the curtain. The lassie had gone of course. The night. The North Star. The North Star in a mirror. An ocean.

Down in the street the tar and the flagstone paving and the concrete and the bonnet of a no-longer-good vehicle if ever the fuck it was, the kids playing and the teenagers yapping, and the adults getting by getting by.

Suicide is never that good a solution. Suicide is a great temptation but it is not that good a solution because it is only two-dimensional. It should go three deep and then have a lassoo thrown round that. Beg pardon? Sorry, it should be three, and then have a fourth as a sort of lassoo. Aw, I see. Fuck off. Nah, only kidding, back ye come. What about me, can I come back? Okay, you as well. And me? The fucking lot of yous, I dont care, yous can all do what yous fucking like.

As long as ye keep quiet. I like the pipes because they induce peace. The few times I ever smoked dope I was told I would get peace but I never ever got peace I just got fucking trouble in one way or another. One time it was at this party when the brother and the sister-in-law were present and what happens but trouble, trouble trouble trouble. We've aye had these problems: I have never been able to understand him and he has never been able to understand me. We fight about this and we fight about that. Fraternal battles, they're the worst kind. Then there is the poor auld fucking maw and da. Mind you, I dont have that much sympathy for the pair of them. So I canni be bothered either, with them I mean, on their behalf. But fuck it, there is a sadness about this existence, these existences. Patrick always, he feels, there is a sympathy, there is a sensation, there

there must be more than that. That cannot be enough. There must be something more. Well there isnt. There must be. There isnt. Yes there is. What. Plenty. Plenty. If there wasnt something more than that

Aye?

If there was not something more than that

More than what?

. . .

. . .

One must retain the grip on one's lugs.

What about the crazy flagellants?

What about them, they're just particular Christians and Muslims and whatever, the same as all the rest, the Jews and the Hindus, they're all the same. I dont know other worlds. I just know my numbers and my figures. What do you mean by that? Is this you returning to some sort of nonexistent creed of the ancients that you've just fucking invented, some bastardized offshoot from the school of post-Pythagoreans. Yes. Of course. Fine. It's true. Fine, I was just asking, just making certain. Making certain – does that mean you had some inkling before the statement.

A blast of music.

Patrick strolled to the radio, switched it on, turned up the volume, just loud enough to be loud, without overwhelming the neighbours. Pianos. Pianos are okay.

The lavatory. He needed a shite, a tollie. And then he needed to see to the toilette; he had to prepare, what he was to don for the evening, a pair of trousers and a fucking shirt and jersey and jacket. Another bath and he would evaporate.

So:

so grasp the lugs and get the head battened down. And maybe she will sleep with you. Maybe she will return here, home, maybe. Maybe she will quite the thing go to bed with ye, exorcising the demons, ridding the place of its cold, its lack of human something or other – worth, value, bodily and mental togetherandatoneness for fuck sake god give the boy a break he is in fucking dreadful danger, his only recourse to a pair of electrician's pipes which he is truly thankful for amen; he is, and it truly is a blessing because most folk dont even have that, he is well aware of this and truly thankful amen lord please look down on your son and spare him, spare him, allow him to be a fellow amongst fellows and a father amongst fathers, a lover amongst lovers poor auld fucking Hölderlin I mean look at him, your man there, poor old for fuck sake and then he goes off his head, succumbs to that insanity the bastards maintain he was only just always managing to survive from, and what about Hegel, did he help? of course he must have helped, Hegel was fucking good, good, a good ordinary man amongst men who enjoyed a bevy and a screw and a good laugh and carousing singsong with all his cronies, and at 1770 look at the fucking cronies! Beethoven for christ sake! So okay, fine, right. Fine, smashing, quite the thing. A cup of strong coffee. Patrick should have bought the fucking steak pie supper, instead of just scoring another goal against himself. He at least should have eaten something. And he did not eat that something. He should have eaten it. He did not.

But he does have a packet of potato crisps which he can stuff between two slices of margarined bread. A piece on crisps. Aye beautiful. Crunchy and munchy. And a cup of good strong coffee.

The best thing was to close the eyes. Patrick laid his elbows on the mantelpiece, cradled his head. The possibility of relaxing was so acutely great that he withdrew at once and sank back down onto the settee, the only problem being sleep, sweet soporifimus, which he better not go to, sleep, sopor, aahh, life somehow sleep, sleep, its actuality, sleep, how it could always render the world a better place, just the idea of it, sleep, its soothing nature; what the hell is its origin? renewal; the time for renewal; how come such a thing could exist? the vales of strife vales of strife, what he could do was just get the alarm clock and set it for half-eight, so's he could sleep.

He did that and he snoozed as planned, so that was good. He wakened on the first peal and got ready, drank a coffee and ate the potato-crisp sandwich. He would have to shave again but that was okay that was okay. He felt good. He smiled, aware of the nature of it, of how it was he was feeling: he was truly relaxed and he felt as if he hadnt been truly relaxed for years – years! away before he ever fucking got lumbered with teachers' fucking training colleges and all the rest of the carry on, fucking university and all the shit. Fifteen minutes until nine o'clock and here he was so relaxed he was sipping a coffee. He reached to switch off the fire. Being here in the parlour had been a comforting experience. He tended to use the kitchen 99% of the time and it was a mistake. Perhaps he should shift the bed back into here again, and maybe begin work on erecting the platform. Gavin had once offered to assist on the project: so let him do so, let him help, the way big brothers are supposed to.

Fuck the trousers and the shirt and the tie, he was wearing jeans and a fucking casual jacket. That was another thing about this life, how come you even started looking like a fucking teacher never mind fucking have to be one of the bastards. High time he started to dress differently although fair enough just now was not the time because the one thing about now was the need for a healthy attitude and a healthy attitude meant a relaxed attitude, it meant being comfortable, nothing out of the ordinary, fuck the jeans and the casual jacket in other words. No, not precisely. Wear the jeans. Just dont fucking go overboard on it. Dont fucking

ach shut up.

He was getting into the motor at a couple of minutes past nine o'clock and into Miller's Bar shortly before 9.15. Alison was sitting in the lounge. It was busy, other people were at her table. She didnt notice him. She didnt seem to be looking at anything in particular. He walked to her fairly quickly. I'm really sorry I'm late, he said, his voice lowered, I'm really sorry.

It's alright. She smiled.

I was actually asleep, I fell asleep on the chair. Would you like something to drink?

She wanted a gin & tonic. She was already sipping one. She wanted another. He was going to get himself a tomato juice and plenty of ice cubes and no beer or whisky. He wanted to touch her hand. Her face had been looking up at him, he wanted to put his hand onto her chin. He was going to get an erection. At the bar he stared at the bottles on the gantry. It was busy. He was to wait his turn and hope nobody went before him because such a thing was always an irritant and here in this lounge there seemed to be a policy that waitresses were given preference over standing customers but what was wrong with that there was nothing wrong with that, it was perfectly reasonable and brooked no argument, certainly not from him anyway. He waited. He glimpsed Alison; she was observing the company at the table next to hers. It was interesting. It signified things about her. He had noticed it before, how she could seem to enjoy just watching people. It was something to smile about. Patrick smiled. She was human after all!! There again though it could just signify things about him, things in reference to himself, in relation to her, that there she was observing other people while there he was, standing at the bar. And now she was lighting a fag. Patrick grinned. He shook his head and closed his eyes a moment. The girl behind the bar was really attractive. The uniform she was wearing: white skirt and red satin blouse. She smiled at Patrick. He smiled at her. Probably she smiled because she knew he was with another woman ergo not a threat in the usual male to female fashion. He smiled again. When she handed him his change he said, Quite busy the night eh!

She smiled. He lifted the drinks across to the table. Alison smiled at him and shifted on her seat so that he could sit in beside her. The seat was an upholstered bench and he had to squeeze in there because there wasnt very much room. The bloke who was sitting at the edge of the company at the next table had to squeeze along a bit to help create space. Patrick apologised. A bit of a squeeze, he said, eh!

Aye, said the bloke.

Pat winked at Alison. Busy in here the night eh!

Yeh. She indicated the tomato juice in such a strange, peaceful way, that his heart sank to the furthest depth of his belly. He could not speak.

It was also her thigh solid jammed against his and they were jammed together, it was silly. He put his hand towards her but stopped it in the act and got it onto the glass of tomato juice. Things were running away from him, they were coming to a head. She was so kindly too, her intentions were with being gentle and if he could get touching her hand. If he could get touching her hand. What like would that be. And he was going to actually get hard, he was getting these twinges from the tip of his prick right to beneath the bollocks and if he relaxed his knees even a moment that would be that for christ sake. He tried a smile but it would not have been appearing right it would be too strained, what a strain, his forehead was strained, into something or other, something else, altogether, he was touching her hand, her hand was obviously soft, he was holding it, it was softer than his, or was it, was it really, was it not just like his and therefore okay different but the softer-than-his business just being stereotypical because she was female and he was male. He studied it. Her fingers. They were soft as well. She wore rings. He had to be intent on it, what he was doing, not to notice it, what he was doing, to give that impression to her. Sorry, he said, withdrawing his hand.

Alison didnt smile. On her face there was a rueful look.

I'm sorry, he said.

She stared at her gin & tonic, and the bottle of what was left of the tonic alone; her cigarette lay smouldering in the ashtray.

Sorry, he whispered.

She continued to stare. Eventually she muttered, O Pat.

. . .

I dont want to have a relationship with ye.

No.

It would just make things so complicated. It would make things so complicated. Her head was bowed. She lifted the cigarette in her left hand, inhaled on it, her head moving to the side, so that the smoke wouldnt interfere with other people. She blew the smoke down the way, to beneath the table. She kept her head bowed. Pat looked at the bar. It was busy. It was busy at the bar. This was a Monday evening. She raised her head. They glanced briefly at each other. Do you understand? she said.

It sounds like a Hollywood picture o my darling! he said, smiling.

Alison didnt smile in reply.

Aye, he said, I know what you're saying.

She didnt respond. She looked at the table. The bloke squeezed in on the side of Patrick seemed to be jumping about or something and Patrick felt like digging him one in the fucking ribs but he restrained himself because maybe it was just to do with scapegoats.

So:

that was that. He gulped. Saliva at the throat and a feeling across his shoulders. He lifted the glass of tomato juice. It was all up now it was all over. But it was good to have it in the open, to have had it in the open.

But just getting things out, aired.

Some sort of song was playing on the stupid muzak jukebox as if this was the fucking stupid piece of goods he would always remember in association — I remember the night etcetera etcetera. Would he fuck. He stared at the tomato juice. He felt like flinging it at the wall. What had he bought it for? He would never fucking buy it again, that was for fucking definite. He looked at the waitress: a waitress had come to gather the empty glasses and give things a tidy up. An older woman; methodical in what she was doing. Alison said very quietly, I wish ye hadnt done it Pat.

He nodded.

She was gazing at the table.

She touched his hand.

She smiled and said something. He missed what it was. She said something but he couldnt make out what it was. He laughed a moment. He shook his head to clear or settle his brains. She smiled and said something, he missed it. Their hands were not touching now. He said, I appreciate what ye did there. He smiled at her. He raised his hand to cover his eyes, but he just smoothed his forehead instead and he smiled and shook his head.

After yesterday, she was saying.

I appreciate it, he said.

Alison touched him on the hand again, but just this touch and she had stopped it. He looked at her hand and then he put his onto it and she didnt withdraw it. He said: I've just been I dont know, I've just been wanting to talk to ye properly because things areni fucking just really christ they're no really going well at all, just now. And I've been needing to get things clear with ye, with you . . . He turned his head to look at her more directly; she didnt avoid the look. Then she leaned to stub out the cigarette.

I heard about the transfer, she said.

It's terrible. I dont know how it's happened. I dont know how the hell. It's terrible, really terrible.

Did you apply for it?

If I did I canni remember.

2E was telling me.

2E, christ. Mind you, better to hear it from there than the staffroom.

O they were talking about it there as well, said Alison; she smiled. But they werent as surprised, more especially after your Friday morning announcement.

Aye . . . He nodded. It's embarrassing.

Och away ye go.

It is but, it's bloody embarrassing. It's embarrassing because

. . . I dont want to go. I dont want to bloody go. Patrick shifted slightly and he put his right hand around, taking hers in both of his, cupping it there, and she put her left hand on top, so that the four hands were now bound together. Neither spoke. Then he said, It's so unusual to get talking to ye like this, just with the two of us and no having any of them in the company.

Alison said nothing. Then she withdrew her hand from the top, but her other was still in between his. She whispered, You're speaking a bit too loudly Pat.

O.

She smiled, but it wasnt the best of smiles.

In extremis, he said, one's voice is allowed to rise.

Her gaze dropped. She stared at the hands and Patrick opened his so that hers just lay on the left one and was free to do what it wanted. He smiled after a moment. He took each one of her fingers in turn, pinching them very gently between his thumb and first two fingers. She smiled. Pat.

Daft.

It's no daft. Then she glanced at him and took her hand from his, glanced round the lounge. I dont want a relationship with ye, she muttered. And she was looking so sad and worried that Patrick wanted to give her a cuddle and say, Look everything's okay for fuck sake dont bloody worry.

Dont worry, he said.

I just cant have a relationship with ye Pat.

It's okay.

Is it?

Yeh.

I just cant.

It's alright.

She gazed at him.

Honest.

I cant.

Fine.

She smiled. He took her hand and studied it, he grinned at her for a moment. I have never held this hand before tonight, and it'll probably be the last chance I ever get.

Alison shook her head and withdrew it.

. . .

Things are always so complicated, she was saying while opening her cigarette packet.

Pat nodded. When she glanced at him he said, I'm no going back to school. I'm just gonni chuck it as from this afternoon. That includes Barnskirk after Easter, I'm no going, I'm just chucking it all the gether.

It's supposed to be quite a good school.

He shrugged.

It is.

There's no such thing.

I hate ye when ye say that.

I've never said it before.

Yes you have.

I havent.

Ye have.

He nodded. His hand moved towards her and stopped.

Sometimes your cynicism makes me feel physically sick.

Jesus christ Alison I'm no cynical I'm the very fucking opposite. Pat sighed, he looked away from her. She exhaled smoke and snapped shut the handbag. He had spoken too loudly again. He knew it by her manner. I'm sorry, he said quietly. His hand moved towards hers and stopped.

I dont mind, she said.

He grasped it and replied: I just feel better touching ye, at the moment.

She nodded and he grinned:

It's giving me strength.

Pat . . .

D'you think I'm daft?

Of course no.

Ye sure?

She nodded.

Not too convinced but eh!

Dont be silly.

I'm no being silly, just daft!

[233]

Ssh.

Do you love your husband?

Alison dropped his hand and glanced roundabout. She was silent for a time. She didnt smoke the cigarette; she looked down at it.

Patrick said: Sorry. Sorry Alison.

Immediately she answered. Come on we'll go.

He gestured at her gin & tonic, then squeezed his way out when she didni respond, waiting for her by the side of the table. She walked past him, restricting her gaze to the path ahead. She walked to the exit, he following and attempting to reach the door first, but she was opening it and going along the lobby, staying in front of him.

She didnt speak until outside on the pavement, and along and into the doorway of a shop. It was a small general grocer and it was open. A young couple with a toddler came from inside, the man carrying the toddler while the woman had the plastic carrier bag of messages. When they had gone Alison said, That was not fair. It was not fair. You put me into a position.

I'm sorry.

It was just not fair. Alison stared into the road.

I really am sorry . . . Patrick pushed his hands into his trouser pockets. The young couple had crossed to the pavement opposite; they turned the corner of the street there.

The people behind the bar know us, said Alison; they've seen us together before.

Aye but christ Alison they never heard what I said. I wasnt shouting. I just said it aloud, I wasnt shouting, I said it quiet.

The people at the table would've heard ye.

No they wouldnt.

They would, they would've heard.

They were involved with themselves, said Pat, they wereni listening to us, they were away enjoying themselves, they were talking about funny things that happened to them, they wereni interested in us, what we were talking about.

Alison didnt respond. Then she shivered. She said, O God . . . and her right hand went to the side of her eyebrow.

Okay? he said, he touched the cuff of her coat-sleeve.

She shook her head.

Alison, I didni recognise one single face in that pub, apart from that lassie behind the bar.

It's not the point.

He nodded.

She looked at him. It's not the point.

Patrick stared at her. He kept his eyes open. He pushed his hands into his trouser pockets and pulled them out again. He smiled for a moment, she was looking at him. He raised his hands, placed them on the sides of each of her upper arms and moved a half-step closer to her, craning his head to her so that her hair was onto his face and he smelled it, his eyelids shut and he got a fit of trembling and it was down below in his knees it was worst and he pressed his feet more solidly on the ground and smiled, shivering. Christ, he said. Alison was standing in the same position, as if she hadnt moved. He took care not to increase the pressure in the way he was holding her. He sighed. It was a straight relief and he was aware of himself relaxed all over. He sighed again. His eyes were shut and he drifted into a sleep.

Alison was smiling when she said very seriously, I'm not going to have a relationship with ye.

No. He breathed in her hair and his lips touched her on the forehead in a kiss. There was a fierce draught in the doorway, blowing around his legs.

Are you cold? she asked. Her hands were to the sides of his waist.

It was just a shiver. What about you?

It's cold in here . . . Alison glanced sideways as though she would be able to see it – the cold. But she would be able to see the draught. Her hair smelled of perfume. A shampoo maybe. Patrick breathed in it. His hands held her at the elbows.

Am I allowed to kiss ye? he asked.

Dont.

He nodded. His mouth was only a couple of inches from her forehead and he could kiss her again if he wanted. He put his lips against her forehead then away. He felt an increase of pressure on his waist. He had an erection. He had had an erection for a long time. He had been holding her for a long time. Her hair was dark dark brown and her eyes were dark brown as well. There was a warmth too, it came from just holding her, and he moved that wee bit in closer, and her

[235]

chest was to his chest, he put his right arm round her back and she lifted it off by the wrist; he returned his hand to the side of her elbow. He felt like making plans for the future. He felt like saying something to her. What could he say to her he didnt know. He smelled her hair, the shampoo smell, it was so much better than his, he didnt have any shampoo like that, that smelled as good as this. He grinned. She was so beautiful. And he was not! He grinned, shook his head.

What is it? she asked.

Nothing, just daft.

You keep saying you're daft.

He smiled.

She stepped away from him, looking at him. It's time to go home, she said. And she was out from the doorway glancing at him, continuing along in the direction away from Miller's Bar. The motor's back there, he called.

I'll get a taxi Pat.

He sniffed and walked after her, strolling, keeping a couple of paces behind her. And she kept going although the direction she would be travelling lay in the direction opposite. A taxi appeared quite soon. She signalled it immediately. He stood to the side as she tugged open the door. Dont phone me, she said.

He nodded.

Okay? I would prefer ye not to.

Aye.

Thanks . . . She slammed shut the door; he couldnt see whether she was looking back when the driver drove off.

So that was that. That was her gone. The tail-lights in the distance. She was sitting there getting whisked home. Lighting her fag. The idea of jumping into the motor and racing after the taxi, catching it up at the next set of traffic lights.

At the interval next morning he went quickly to the staffroom and got his mug and his tea and was sitting on his chair across by the window, the computing magazine on his lap, before she entered. She was with Mrs Bryson and Diana. Pat gazed at the magazine and sipped his tea. Others came in, there was a queue at the urn. A middle-aged bloke called Martin Russell, who was attached to the Crafts and Arts department, leaned over and asked if he had read the *Herald* this morning. No, Patrick hadnt read the *Herald* this morning. The *Herald* was a thing he had not read any fucking morning. Martin said, On the Centralamerican assassination . . .

I dont know fuck all about it, replied Patrick. He raised the magazine nearer his face. Martin Russell sat back on his chair. Patrick had offended him. He had offended him and he shouldnt have. They had been sitting on these selfsame chairs for the past couple of years and he was not a bad bloke. Pat lowered the magazine a little, and he said, I'm trying to avoid the news at the moment.

Martin nodded but he was obviously a bit hurt. It would be horrible to arrive at middle age and still be capable of that kind of emotion as an effect of that kind of trivia. Patrick glanced at him. He was no longer reading his *Herald*, just smoking his cigarette and staring at a spot on the carpet by his shoes. Patrick could ask him about his family; he was lately become a grandpa and liked to talk about families generally. Martin was okay – very quick and skilful with modelling clay and plasticine and he had produced some nice sculpture work for different school festivals and functions. Patrick could say something about that. Plus there was this habit he had of allowing his tea to cool without drinking any of it, then when the bell rang he would swallow the lot in a couple of long gulps. Probably it had to do with the wish to prolong the moment, that time which was his time, his time alone.

Desmond had arrived and so had Norman the temporary English teacher. They were in their chairs along with Alison and the others who belonged to the main group of talkers; at present the topic centred on a television comic adventure programme about undercover military detectives in Australia. Out the top of the window you could see quite an okay morning indeed, bright and sunny. It would soon be April. Maybe head down to Eric's for the Easter break. The two of them could set sail for Scandinavia. If Eric's wife came along she could maybe bring a pal to make up the foursome; nothing too forceful, just the break for Easter, a wee holiday away from the problems of everyday living in this time of technological, desanitized

Patrick had laid the magazine on the coffee table and stood up. He stepped to the window which was frosted but for the upper pane. Outside and across the playground lay the Renfrew Hills and beyond them the sea. If you dived in and swam due west you would end up probably in Greenland or northern Labrador. If you got that far. Probably you would drown first. In parts of Labrador and Greenland you can travel for days and not see a soul, a living soul. What like would that be. Not seeing a living soul, travelling across the icy wastes of Antarctica. Desmond was watching him. Patrick acknowledged him with a nod of the head. No doubt he had read Patrick's mind and was scoffing at his daydream. Ach no he wasnt for christ sake. He had just looked away from the company for a moment towards the window, at which Patrick happened to be standing, and that was that. And he was now back listening in to the group's conversation once more. Plunging through the glass window as in a highdive, landing feet first on the playground and making a dash for it through the gates, surprising the two polis who would probably be having a sneaky smoke while nobody was looking. But of course if he did want to leave he only had to walk out the door, because no one was stopping him, no one was stopping him.

Alison's back was to him.

He sat down. He was actually quite tired. He hadnt slept too well. He had gone to bed as usual and went to sleep as usual but woke up at half-past two and from there on just dozed and woke up, dozed and woke up and gradually he lost all sense of reviviscence. When it was time to get up he felt in desperate need of a real and genuine sleep. So there you are and this explains the current lethargy of spirit. Unlike Alison who seemed to be fine. She seemed to be okay. She wasnt doing much of the talking but she had her rightful place in the group and was no doubt making a great contribution simply by the differing expressions on her face. Her face had differing expressions. You could cup her face in your hands and stare into her eyes. You didnt know what she was thinking though. In company with her she would be watching all that was happening but saying little and what was she thinking, you couldnt fucking tell. Alison, I desire to know precisely

[238]

what you are thinking, at this very damn moment. Pat grinned, he chuckled, but stopped it. He frowned at the magazine and turned a page, and smiled, as if having found a thing there to be smiled at.

Martin Russell was still lost somewhere in the nethermost regions, perched on the edge of the chair and staring down at the floor, the carpet. Miles off. Probably on a different planet. That here he was thirty years on from the teachers' trainers and what the fuck was it all about and why the fuck had he not just committed suicide with a straight good will all those years ago. And the skin having formed on his cup of lukewarm tea. Pat closed the magazine and dropped it onto the table, and he turned to him: Hey Martin, how was the weekend?

O – nothing startling Pat, what about yourself?

Eh, quite hectic I suppose. Up seeing the parents and the rest of it!

Martin nodded.

They're great television watchers as well. If you dont like to watch the telly then dont go and visit them.

I know what ye mean. Mind you, sometimes there's nothing better than putting the feet up and lying back there, letting it all wash right over ye.

True.

Switching off from everything.

Aye. I've no got a telly these days, I used to have one but I've no got it now. You think you're watching it but you're no, they're actually watching you!

What?

Pat smiled, I'm saying when you watch the telly, ye aye think it's you that's doing the bloody watching but it's no, it's you that's actually getting watched – the government's got the fucking security forces all taking notes!

Martin nodded. He smiled briefly. Then he frowned for a moment and lowered his voice: You are leaving then Pat?

Aye.

Ah.

Ye heard?

Well, I was here when ye made the announcement last week.

Aw aye christ! Patrick nodded. He glanced at Martin, who was obviously awaiting further information. The cheeky auld bastard. He was expecting the all-important clarification: would Patrick be severing his links with the halls of education forever, or would he just be transferring to Barnskirk High which though of interest was scarcely earth-shattering.

And there too was MI6, right on cue. The door had opened unnoticed by anyone, and there he was, this jolly faced second headmaster coming to see if the troops were enjoying life and was anybody saying anything they shouldnt be saying. And he called: Morning gentlemen, ladies!

Some of the teachers returned the greeting. Such a fucking charade, when everybody hated the dickie. Good morning, called Patrick with a large smile.

Morning, said MI6, also with a large smile the bastard.

Patrick smiled once more; he was about to say something further but what was that something to be because he couldnt think of it. And he didnt want to say something stupit, something daft and silly. What was Alison smiling at? The side of her face was visible and she was smiling at something, which Desmond had probably said. And MI6 was still gazing across at Patrick, and he came a couple of steps closer, and he said: Exam Paper Study Group this evening Mister Doyle?

Eh aye, yes, I'm remembering.

Good. Fine.

Alison was saying something within the group at the fireside god, what could it be, she couldnt be saying something about him, she couldnt be making a fool of him, saying something that would make a fool of him, in front of them, Desmond and all them. You could actually imagine them all in league with the government security forces − like that Hollywood picture where the aliens take over one by one. Patrick had stopped reading science fiction at the age of fourteen, maybe it was time to start again. Maybe there were things of value to be learnt about foreign planets and the prevailing wisdom.

Martin was just sitting there on the edge of his chair, puffing very slowly on his fag and not taking the remotest interest in anything. He was a survivor. There was that skin as well. From now on Patrick would never drink another cup of tea until it had gone cold. Fine ya fucking bastards. He lowered his voice . . . Hey Martin, you know that German poet Hölderlin?

Who?

Hölderlin: he was a pal of Hegel's; they were students the gether.

I cant say I do Pat, no.

Pat nodded, he sniffed slightly.

Was he good?

Uch aye, he was, I must say.

A pal of Hegel's?

Aye. They were both born in the same year as a matter of fact: 1770 – the same as Beethoven.

Ah! 1770! Wordsworth was born then too.

. . .

You dont like him I take it?

Well, I fucking hate him, to be honest, but it's probably just prejudice. I've never really read him all that much.

Did ye not have to study him?

I got round it.

Ah.

Do you like him?

Well eh I dont think he's easily dismissed Pat.

Mm.

James Hogg was born in 1770 as well ye know.

Christ!

He and Wordsworth were the same age. Walter Scott was their junior by one year. Martin grinned. Ye didnt know that?

Fuck sake naw! Pat laughed.

Martin also laughed: There must've been something in the air eh!

I bet ye, aye. If ye track down the records you'll probably find some strange data to do with temperatures and rainfall.

That's right; plus the price of ruddy corn! The political situation in general! Martin flicked open his packet of cigarettes and got another cigarette alight . . . one wonders what was happening in 1769 eh? the million-dollar question!

The American War of Independence?

[241]

No, that was eh . . . When was Thomas Muir on the go? The '90s. Hey, do you know that when Walter Scott was a boy of fifteen he actually met and was introduced to Burns?

Christ.

Yeh, fifteen years of age.

Patrick chuckled.

Mind you, said Martin, I wouldnt fancy having a classful of Walter Scotts!

For fuck sake, said Pat, can ye imagine them all sitting there! What would they be doing! It doesni bear thinking about.

Martin laughed quite loudly. A classful of Walter Scotts!

Add 1 7 7 0, said Patrick immediately, 15. 1 and 7 is 8 plus 7 equals 15.

Martin looked at him, then grinned. No it isnt, it's one thousand seven hundred and seventy. Take your thousand and add your seven hundred then your seventy, and that's what ye get, 1770, seventeen hundred and seventy.

Spoilsport!

The two of them chuckled. And Martin added: Change of subject Pat, were you not down for that Disciplinary Scheduling last night?

Not at all.

Ye sure?

Definitely. Otherwise MI6 would have made some sort of bloody comment.

Mm.

How?

O I was just wondering.

Patrick frowned.

It's not important.

What did ye ask for then?

I was just wondering.

Pat shook his head. Christ sake Martin I mean ye wanting to get me really paranoiac!

I was just curious.

Pat gazed at him. Then he saw Alison by the door, holding it open for Diana and Mrs Bryson and Patrick stood up at once and looked at her and she looked away and followed Diana out, leaving

Mrs Bryson to come behind. The door was shut now and nobody else was there. Desmond and the others were still sitting by the fireside.

Patrick stretched his arms aloft and he yawned in as genuine a manner as he could. But he didnt succeed and it sounded totally false and horrible and he walked to the window immediately and he stared out the top pane at the sky and the white clouds flying past at quite a fast clip, it had to be blowy outside, windy; sharp breezes. He would count to thirty and then leave the room. And south lay the hills. He turned. Martin was exhaling smoke and glancing at his wristwatch. Pat said, I wonder how far it is to Labrador from here?

Be about 3 to 3500 miles I would think.

Patrick nodded. Ten minutes in the sea and you'd be dead: hypothermia.

Is that right?

Aye, terrible eh – imagine being a fisherman that canni swim! Every day you were out working would be a form of hellish torment. Ye heard of these miners in South Africa? According to their religion hell is in the nether regions of the earth. So what that means is that these guys, when they go to their work every day, believe that they're actually going to fucking hell – literally. Eh? That kind of thing's beyond comprehension. Poor bastards.

Martin shook his head. Unbelievable!

Aye, said Patrick, except that it's true.

God!

Yeh, terrible eh.

Wwhho!

Patrick collected his empty cup from the coffee table and carried it to the sink, rinsing it out and leaving it upturned in its place on the draining board. She would be well away by now. She would be in her classroom. She would be at her desk, browsing over the forthcoming lesson. The temporary English teacher was looking at him. Patrick gave him a brief wave.

Hiya Pat.

Hullo Norman, how's the missis?

Fine.

Good. Patrick glanced at Desmond: Alright Desmond!

Morning Mister Doyle.

Yous going a walk at dinnertime?

Probably.

Pat nodded. See yous later then eh!

1769: in this year Napoleon Bonaparte was born. The information came via the sixth year and the sixth year is never wrong.

Fiona Grindlay was talking. Her da was still giving her a hard time because she wouldnt reveal the name of the father of her baby. Fiona was relating it to a short story she had read where there was this romance between young lass and young lad plus the dreaded mixture of horrendous parents and relatives, ending in death for the young couple. Fair enough; slightly sentimental but so what, you're entitled to be slightly sentimental about something like that. Fiona went on to develop her own position in reference to the media. It was a good piece of reasoning. When she finished none spoke for several moments. But you could never be certain that these silences werent simply in deference to her motherhood. Patrick nodded. I think your reasoning's fine Mirs Grindlay but when you're talking about parents I wonder if maybe there's space for Camus and his killing of these fuckers the kings.

Yes.

I dont think so at all, called Evelyn Reilly.

So what, said Pat.

She glared at him. She was a lassie who took her fags out. Her packet lay on the desk and she was twiddling a box of matches in her hands.

So what's too simple, replied Paul Moore.

Wrong.

Paul stared at Patrick, then shook his head.

Good . . . Patrick glanced at Evelyn Reilly: Not you Mirs Reilly.

Fuck off, she said.

If ye want to smoke smoke.

If I want to smoke I'm smoking.

What about Fiona Grindlay?

There's nothing about Fiona Grindlay plus that and the baby.

Brian Nixon stood up. He put his hands into his jerkin pockets and shut his eyes, laughing; he shook his head and sat down again. And the bloke behind slapped him on the shoulder then stood up. The others looked to be waiting for him to speak. Danny Persse was his name.

Patrick said, Okay; if there's nothing more on the referent it's time, it's that moment. And you're the guy Mister Persse.

Evelyn Reilly struck a match suddenly, lighted her fag.

Fiona Grindlay called to her: That's unfair!

Pat grinned. Your first tautology for a fortnight Mirs Grindlay. Well done.

Fiona smiled.

Patrick! said Evelyn Reilly.

Sir!

Wait till ye hear this! She pointed at Danny Persse who took a book from his inside jacket pocket and turned to a page he had marked:

I'll read from the front, he said, strolling out and down to stand by the blackboard: It's from a poem by Okot p'Bitek; okay:

> Ten beautiful girls
> Are walking in single file,
> Along the pathway,
> They carry axes
> They are going to the bush
> To split firewood,
> In the grass lurks
> The black mamba,
> Its throat burning with venom.
>
> The first three girls walk past,
> Then the fourth and fifth,
> And all nine girls go by,

And your daughter
Who is at the tail of the line
Is struck!

She stands there,
The reptile refuses to unhook its fangs,
She drinks a whole cup of death,
She gives a brief shriek
And mumbles some farewell
To her loving mother!
Then she drops
Dead!

Danny Persse shut the book immediately and added, I'll just finish there. He glanced at Patrick and laughed, then he laughed to the class and particularly Evelyn Reilly who was chuckling away quietly, smoking her cigarette and blowing the smoke towards the window. When he returned to his desk he and Brian Nixon slapped their right hands together.

Well done, said Patrick.

And Danny Persse called: And all nine girls go by, except your daughter alone, who is fucking poisoned to death! Danny laughed again and shook his head.

Males! said Patrick Doyle MA (Hons), what about life?

It's worth having: Danny Persse.

It's better than nothing: Brian Nixon.

It doesnt belong to the bastards: Francis Connolly.

Sentimental tollie, said Evelyn Reilly.

Okay females . . . Pat said: A mate of my da's who used to work in a carfactory down in Linwood before they got done in by the capitalists, he worked on the assemblyline and his job was to grease the insides of the doorpanels. And the poor fucker had this recurring nightmarish fantasy, that he would get wedged inside one of them – one of the doorpanels, and then he would get sealed in and flattened by the heavyduty punchgun process with his mouth twisted so unnaturally and badly awry that he wouldni be able to shout for help. Okay.

Then one day he fucking disappeared. It was teabreak. The guys didni know where he had got to. He was never fucking seen again.

Silence.

Patrick said: But him and his missis had been having some difficult quarrels at the time so when he didni reappear she just put it down to that, the quarrels, and that he had just fucked off to start a new life in England or something. Instead of which he had got squashed.

That's sickening, said Sheila Ramsay.

If it was the capitalists who done them in it was the capitalists who started them, said Ingrid Jones.

Wrong, replied Patrick. Males?

Ergo bibamus: Brian Nixon.

Laughter.

It's a load of shite: Paul Moore.

Fiona Grindlay: What do you mean by 'squashed'?

Sheila Ramsay: What is 'a new life'?

Well done, said Patrick. Negation!

What is not a new life what is a new death not what is an old death, an old life, not the old life, not a rebirth, the same old renewal, that other way of not being, that unabsence . . . Sheila Ramsay raised her eyebrows, turned to Evelyn Reilly who handed her her cigarette; she grabbed a couple of long drags before continuing. She said: I just dont accept 'new lives'. To me it's a sign of floundering around. I think it's not something to ever be proud of. I canni conceive of a person who can think of it.

Would it usually always be a man? said Ingrid Jones.

A male to answer! called Sheila; she returned the fag to Evelyn Reilly.

Silence.

Patrick! called Sheila.

He cleared his throat before replying: I would never think of 'a new life'.

Booo! Francis Connolly.

Honest. I'm no kidding ye.

Paul Moore: How often do you consider suicide?

Daily.

[247]

Wrong.

Patrick nodded.

What about a synthesis! said Ingrid Jones.

Paul Moore smiled. Anybody that agrees with me and therefore nobody that can agree with me that agrees with me if nobody is agreeing with me, especially not our great teacher, Mister Patrick Doyle: and so forth.

You're letting me down, said Patrick.

Pardon?

. . .

Paul Moore stared at Patrick and Patrick eventually looked away from the wee bastard who had gazed right into his heart and seen something rotten. Patrick could crawl into a corner. He could crawl under his desk. He could crawl into the wastepaper basket. He strolled to where Danny Persse had read from the poem and he said: I want some advice to do with my immediate plans. What I feel is I'm not enjoying being the person who teaches and if I canni do it here I dont want to do it anywhere. I'm saying to ye that there is a bit of a crisis in my life. I'm sick of being alone and being a teacher in a society that I say I detest all the time, to the extent that the term 'detest' isni really appropriate christ because it's a form of obscenity.

Gary McGregor speaking for the first time since last week: You dont want to get transferred I take it?

That's correct Mister McGregor.

And you dont want to leave either.

Yes.

But you canni stay?

Aye, that's it.

Suicide?

Yep ya bastard ye, well done.

Laughter. And Gary McGregor was so pleased with himself and he grinned along at Fiona Grindlay. He was in love with her. He had been in love with her for quite a while. Patrick was now noticing this. Now that Patrick was noticing it he saw that he had been noticing this for ages without having registered the fact. Gary McGregor was in love with Fiona Grindlay. These things were aye happening right under your nose and you never ever bloody saw it, you never ever bloody saw them. Because of your total preoccupation with self. I think therefore I am: and the thing that I am is all of that which everything else isni.

Patrick said: Thanks for laughing one and all. You as well Fiona because you're a hard nut to crack.

Thanks.

No sarcasm intended. Okay. I first considered suicide at the age of twelve, the same year I gave up believing in deities. It's a good age for it. I suppose all my teachings are based on that. I regard the wee first-yearers as imminent suicides and if they areni they fucking should be, and I try to convey that to them. Did any of yous want to commit suicide at twelve years of age? Apart from Brian Nixon I mean.

Laughter.

Brian Nixon stood up and saluted; then he sat down again.

Francis Connolly said, When Tolstoy was eleven years of age he met this boy who told him God didni exist. Him and his brothers thought it was a very interesting piece of news but Tolstoy kept on believing for another five years.

I think he was telling lies, said Patrick.

Honest?

Yeh, but I might be wrong.

Ye dont think of Tolstoy telling lies, said Francis Connolly.

That's because you're a man, said Ingrid Jones.

Patrick grinned, he glanced at his wristwatch. He looked at the class; most of them were still smiling. Look, he said, I wouldni mind just calling it quits the now. Does anybody mind?

He stared at them all.

He lifted his good fountain pen before leaving.

Down in the assembly hall a crowd of weans was running team races, tossing beanbags at each other and making a hell of a racket, shrieks and yells and the PE teacher shouting at them to be quiet. There was still a few minutes to the bell. After a moment Patrick returned along the corridor, to Alison's room; at the window he tried to peer in but he could see very little, except that she was engaged with a large class, third year possibly. To just open the door and call her out for one second, to see how she was. But what did it matter.

O christ but he felt very happy. He started swaggering. He had his hands in his trouser pockets and he began moving his shoulders from side to side, Al Capone's Guns Dont Argue. A last word to Old Milne. He could go in and tell him something or other – what. Just a last word. Cheerio. Fuck off ya tollie. Amen. Death. Arse. Aeroplanes. Buttons. Fish-fingers. Toast. Fish-fingers on toast. Fish-fingers and chips. A fucking while since your man ate any fucking grub. What he could do right now is go for a fucking meal; a nice threecourse businesslunch in an Indian restaurant for christ sake a beautiful chicken tikka with all the trimmings. And what could he do he could linger, he could linger; he could buy a nice big pint of draught heavy beer and just fucking sip it quietly and peacefully, sitting there on his tod and no worries about anything and that includes o tempor tempore; a huge plateful of fucking pakora and samosa and fucking onion salad and just peacefully nibbling, quiet music and the poor auld exotic fish swimming about in their tank.

He would not draw attention to himself. He would stand and wait in by the door until the bell. Only then would he cross the playground to the carpark. The weans would camouflage his exit. They were always out to the street before the dring had died. The dring had died. It sounded so final.

At the door he stood in by the shadows in case the polis were looking from the outside gates. He closed his eyes. There was a continuous buzzing in his left ear. It was not the blood roaring through his veins. It was not being caused by mental activity. He kept his eyes shut and concentrated. It was quite a high-pitched sound. A drone. No – drone signifies something fairly low and this was definitely high. Buzz probably described it best. Empedocles was Hölderlin's favourite philosopher. The story goes he was kicked out by the Pythagoreans. There is a continuous buzzing.

The polis appeared at the gates, chatting to each other. Ten, nine, eight, seven. Old Milne could be at his study window! Patrick smiled and stepped out the door and walked smartly across towards the carpark, and the bell rang.

He was gone beyond the point. There was a point to be gone beyond and he had managed it. There was no further movement. But which way to travel! It was okay saying the point had been reached, that it was past. But which way! Okay, fuck. But which way?

He could bear left.

But this would take him in the direction of Maryhill Road thence Cadder: up where the dreaded big brother dwelt. And he would be at home, thus unavoidable. He would be watching television or reading a book or maybe listening to radio or the music centre or keeping an eye on the weans or doing a husbandly chore round the house.

But he had to see somebody. He really had to see somebody. And if ye couldni fucking see your family who the fuck could ye see, that's what I regard as the type of questioning

Christ sake.

Okay. This is a fellow needing human intercourse. Let him visit his big brother. And his sister-in-law because she's good as well.

But what about the motor, the motor willni go, the poor auld fucking motor car!

Of course it will go. It will go if you fucking drive it. But I cannot. I am unable to. I must just sit here and let it have its head. Nonsense. You've to take it where you require, where you desire. If you desire to take it to see your family then take it to there, to see your family. You can do it; come on. No. Yes. No. Aye ya fucking bastard ye come on; and get the boot down on this fucking accelerator pedal.

Okay.

Patrick simply shifted his hands while the steering wheel was being held by them and the entire motor car executed a perfect turn at the next junction, and on into Maryhill Road, driving up and swinging right, along by Lochburn Park, home of Maryhill Juniors, not a bad wee footballing side but no chance against the Yoker. And on under the canal bridge, up the hill and down by the cemetery.

He parked the car. He shut fast the door and locked it, glancing up to see if anybody was out on the veranda. The flats all had these verandas which were ideal for parties to dive from. Excellent for the district's twelve-year-olds. He patted the car bonnet en route to the pavement where he proceeded to traverse the flagstones up the stairs and into the closemouth. Traversed the flagstones up the stairs and into the bloody closemouth. Is this fucking Mars! Traversed the fucking bastarn flagstones onto the planet fucking Vulcan for christ sake

except that it no longer exists. That poor old nonentity Vulcan, being once thought to exist, and then being discovered not to. Imagine being discovered not to exist! That's even worse than being declared fucking redundant, irrelevant, which was the fate of ether upon the advent of Einstein. Whether it existed or not it had become irrelevant to the issue. Fuck sake. Ether. After all these centuries. Who was responsible for it originally? One of the Anaxes – imenes or imander. What would Hölderlin have to say about that! Fuck Hölderlin he's deid and buried. You're no. And neither's your big brother. So chap the door and ring the bell:

Gavin answered. He was holding a pint-glass of beer. He didnt smile but squinted, puzzled. What's to do! he said, by way of a greeting.

Patrick shrugged, smiling. Just passing. Just saying hullo.

Aw. Gavin gestured with the glass, returning inside; leaving Patrick to enter and shut the door. Fiddle music was playing. The smell of this house. Weans. Nappies and milk and stuff. And a wave of heat and cigarette smoke. Gavin was holding the living-room door ajar for him. Inside were two of his neighbours, sitting on the settee while on top of the dining table were about a dozen assorted bottles of homebrew beer. Davie Jordan, and big Arthur who lived in the flat up through the ceiling from Gavin. Gavin called to them: The young brother . . . And he waved at the table: Bottle of beer for ye brother.

Like the fiddle Paddy? asked Davie.

Aye, I do.

Davie pursed his lips and jerked his thumb at the record playing: This guy's spot on – Shetland-style but I forgive him!

Arthur winked at Pat; Davie's a Highlands & Islands man,

whereas your brother, he likes the Shetlanders. Me . . . he tapped himself on the chest: I prefer Rock & Roll! He winked again and proceeded to make a cigarette. It's all ye get in this house with these two cunts, he said, the fiddle and fucking whatever – the bagpipes!

Davie glared at him. Dont denigrate the national instrument! Then he laughed and slapped his hands together and called to Gavin: What about that bowl of soup Mister Doyle!

I'll Mister Doyle ye ya cunt if you want a bowl of soup away and fucking pour it!

Was he always like this? said Davie to Pat.

Pat grinned.

Heh you still at the teaching? asked Arthur.

Eh more or less, aye. I've just took the afternoon off. My head was birling. He sighed and poured the remainder of the homebrew into his glass and he drank a large mouthful. He sat on a dining chair to the rear of the settee and not too far from the door, and he called to Gavin: What time did yous start this . . .? And he raised the glass of homebrew.

Two months ago.

Naw I mean the actual bevying?

Two months ago! Gavin laughed and so too did Davie Jordan and Arthur, and Pat felt excluded immediately but he had decided to fight off any such feelings and he conquered it for the time being by simply getting himself relaxed upon the chair while the beer itself was pleasant, a light-tasting flavour and quite mellow and very enjoyable, like the company itself fuck which was good anyway and not at all difficult to enjoy and feel relaxed in. Davie Jordan was really into the music and keeping time with both hands flapping at his kneecaps, his head rocking and occasionally looking back the way to wink at Pat.

Do you smoke dope? said Arthur.

We were talking about it before ye came in, said Gavin.

I dont actually smoke at all, said Pat. I wish I did!

Strange statement, replied Arthur.

Gavin laughed.

It is but, said Arthur.

Davie said: I used to smoke dope. Before I discovered sex! He laughed and flourished both hands at the start of another air and he cried: The Deil's Awa Wi The Exciseman!

As the music played Pat called to Gavin: I saw maw and da at the weekend. Saturday, I was up on Saturday.

Aye.

Da was looking fine.

Aye . . . Gavin nodded and his eyelids closed and he leaned back on the chair, his head resting on the back of the frame.

Patrick understood that he was not wanting to speak of family matters, not at present. Not in company. Fine. Quite right. He was probably a bit intoxicated anyway and not in the right mood. This homebrew was strong. Everybody got intoxicated these days. Even the poor wee first-yearers were drinking too much. Mind you it was better than heroin. Or was it; at least with heroin they got an early death whereas with alcohol they were left to traverse the flagstones for a further couple of score years.

Heh Gavin how's the kids? he called.

The kids are fine the kids are fine, fine. Gavin smiled falsely and added, We went up for you on Sunday and you werent in.

Aw . . .

Gavin's eyelids were closed again, his head back on the frame of the chair: Nicola was worried about you. Gavin opened his eyes and said to his mates: The wife worries about him but no about me. She worries about her brother-in-law but no about her husband, she doesni give a fuck about him, her man.

Typical female, muttered Arthur.

Davie shrugged. I've no seen the wife for a month. She went away and hasni returned – sounds like the line from a song eh! Naw but Gavin what d'you expect; women have got this thing about young brothers. It's a fact, every woman likes a young brother. They're no bloody interested in husbands. That right Arthur?

Dont fucking ask me.

Davie glanced round to Patrick.

Gavin cried: No point looking at him ya daft cunt he is the young brother, he's fucking biased! Gavin shook his head, sitting forwards on the chair; he swallowed a mouthful of homebrew and said, Plus he's a fucking teacher, a brainbox. That correct brother!

It's true aye, I'm a brainbox; I passed my exams at uni and so on right to the very top and now here ye are this is me the man ye see in front of ye. Here's fucking looking at you brother! Patrick smiled falsely and raised the glass to his lips, pausing before finishing what was left in it. Mind you, he continued, I could go to sleep here if you've got no objections, I'm beginning to feel a wee bit sleepy.

Gavin gazed at him; then he replied, No objections at all, do what ye like.

It's a comfy carpet, said Davie. I'll vouch for it. Top marks.

Ten out of ten, grinned Arthur.

Patrick smiled then stopped the smile, he counted the bottles on the table. The levels of irony were become slippery. The problem was this: should I remain in the company and surmount all? Or should I give up, make my excuses and leave? The fact that here in the living room of his big brother's home was exceedingly comfortable played a large role in the final decision which was this: let us remain and surmount all. My head was birling this morning, he said directly to Davie and to Arthur, so I fuckt off at dinner time. I just says to hell with it I'm going home, I'm going home. So I went home. Well, I came here instead.

Quite right too, frowned Arthur.

Aye, said Davie.

I disagree . . . Gavin had lighted a cigarette and he blew a puff of smoke at the ceiling. I disagree, he said, I think you're both talking shite. He's got a job and he should look after it. We've no got a job. More than half of Scotland's no got a job. So you dont start treating it with impunity if you're lucky enough to have one.

Silence.

Patrick chuckled.

You dont, said Gavin.

Patrick nodded, smiled.

Gavin glanced at Arthur: No think so Arthur?

Eh . . .

Davie grinned and winked at Arthur. Brothers, he said, you're better to keep out of it. I had a brother once. Know what I did? Eh Paddy? Know what I did? I fucking killed him. So I did. I done him in. I grabs a hold him by the neck: heh you I says I dont like you – and

I had this blade on me so I stuck it into him. Just like that! Davie laughed.

Patrick laughed a moment later. Gavin didnt; but he did smile. Then Arthur muttered, You're going to end up in a fucking institution ya mad bastard.

Davie slapped himself on the kneecap and laughed loudly, then gestured at the bottles of beer: Seize us one Paddy eh?

Pat handed him one, then he hesitated and got to his feet. He said, Eh . . . I think I better add something to the cargo.

No need, replied Gavin.

There isni, said Arthur. Honest, I've got loads up the stair – even if I say so myself.

He has, said Gavin.

Davie chuckled. His kitchen's chokablok with it. Everywhere ye look, bottles and bottles, all shapes and sizes; milk bottles and ginger bottles, bloody medicine bottles and bleach bottles; jamjars as well!

The others laughed, including Gavin.

Patrick added, Nevertheless chaps, a wee halfbottle would come in handy.

Well, said Gavin, put like that . . .

A man after my own heart, said Arthur.

Rain was drizzling down. He waited at the closemouth but it wasnt about to cease for him so he upturned the jacket collar and stepped out and down the steps to the pavement and hurried along to the main road. The man serving behind the chicken-net in the licensed grocer looked so unlikely he could have been the owner, dressed in such a clatty manner; clatty shirt and clatty trousers and a clatty cardigan of immense nondescription. A man of fifty-nine years and four months by the looks of it. A man of slackish jawbone, of scraggy neck tissue, dropped adam's apple and large hairs hanging from his nostrils and ears. If this man was an invalid and very close relation of Patrick's, not to say father, and had Patrick been obliged, as dutiful son or nephew perhaps, to shave this man's neck and face – then in the name of God and Immanuel Kant he could never ever manage to perform such a fucking obligation even be it fucking filial for christ sake never mind morall and this sort of morall demands the extra 'l' at all times, being the noumenal essentiality.

A bottle of Grouse and a dozen cans of superlager please.

The guy that helped Hölderlin was a Scotsman by the name of Von Sinclair. He was one of the mainstays of the wee coterie of folk who intellectualised around the taverns and cafes; he wrote a bit of poetry himself – it was maybe him that got Hölderlin set up as a tutor to Susette's kid.

Behind the counter and well away from the possibility of sneaky little fingers lay a fair selection of chocolate bars and sweeties and Patrick added a variety of them in on the order for wee Elizabeth and John. There was a strangeish kind of smell breaking through that of the diverse spirits and wines. A sweetly kind of smell which didnt seem to have much connection with chocolate bars. It was maybe the guy serving, wearing a strong after-shave to disguise the pong from his socks. Or maybe he smoked a pipe with that funny Dutch tobacco that smelled of myrrh and frankincense.

Or was it carbolic soap and incense?

Death was close at hand!

It cost him an extra five pee for a plastic carrier bag. The man stared craftily at him while asking for the dough, then he looked away. Patrick had already signed his cheque for the sum and had to dig into the pockets for the coin. But he brought his hands out his pockets, even though there was money there, and he said: Look this is out of order, charging me for a carrier bag after I've spent so much on the actual drink itself I mean let's face it, you should be quite happy to give me one for nothing.

I dont make the rules son, it's the boss.

Son? I'm actually thirty-three years of age.

The man gazed at Pat.

So I mean what're you calling me son for?

I call everybody son, it's just an expression. I'm no meaning anything by it.

Patrick shook his head but he laid the five-pence coin on the counter and pushed it beneath the grille to him. Well you better tell your boss it's out of order charging folk for a daft carrier bag when they've spent a fortune on buying his drink.

I've telt him before.

Aye well you better tell him again then.

The man frowned as he packed the cans into the bag. He sniffed, pushed the bag through the space in the grille; then he passed out the bottle of Grouse and the packets of chocolate and sweeties which Pat stuffed into his pockets. It was ridiculous. The idea of charging for carrier bags was just so absolutely fucking ridiculous. And obviously the auld bastard pocketed the five pences for himself. What chance could there ever be for the world when dirty skunks like the latter were in positions of power! Durty skinks like the latter, having arrived via the flagstones of Vulcan, armed with a bunch of fish suppers à la the good Rossi, whose pathway through the hordes of hysterical flagellants

Goya. Goya said that. O did he. Yes, he fucking did. I never knew he was noted for his witty sayings. Well he was, take my word for it; I'm an authority on Goya who was three years older than Johann Wolfgang von Goethe whose love affair with the beautiful Kathchen Schonkopf

fuck off. That includes Werther.

Here we are up a close. The close as an article of faith. A nice-sounding guitar was coming from somewhere – Gavin's place obviously. Patrick climbed the stairs two at a time, but took care not to stumble with such booty in his arms. The front door was ajar. He must have done it himself. Does the world fit together or is that purely sentimental.

Davie Jordan was yapping. Patrick deposited the bevy and stuff on the dining table. He was being watched by big brother who said nothing and pretended a full interest in the yappings of Davie. Pat sat down and listened also. Davie was speaking of his relations. They lived up around the Kyle of Lochalsh area and were well known for their surprising movements here on Earth. Patrick opened a can of superlager and concentrated. This guy who was an astonishing bevymerchant and practical joker who earned his living on the ferry to Kyleakin which without any question had to be regarded as the finest job in all possible universes

Patrick smiled. But it definitely was. Imagine working on the ferry that sailed across the sea to Skye!

Gavin was watching him once more. Patrick grinned: I'll tell you something but and I'm being serious – Davie, that cousin of yours, that job he's got on the Skye ferry – it must be about one of the best jobs in the entire universe.

Good when the tourists are about Paddy, but no so hot in the winter.

No so hot in the winter! Arthur shook his head.

Davie smiled. It was unintentional.

Skye isni cauld in the winter, muttered Gavin, wet aye, but no cold.

That's what you think, said Davie. He swallowed homebrew beer; swallowed more of it, and smiled and nodded at the record player. Hear that guitar!

Skye's wet, said Gavin, but dont turn round and tell me it's cold.

Everywhere's cold in winter, said Davie.

The islands areni, they're wet. They dont get any fucking snow either. Did ye know that?

Davie looked at Gavin without saying anything.

They dont, said Gavin to Arthur, and he glanced at Patrick.

And Patrick said suddenly: See that auld shite in the licensed grocer! he charged me five pee for a stupit carrier bag! I mean christ almighty I thought he was kidding.

It's bad in there, muttered Arthur. They dont even let the weans get a cash return on their bottle deposits; they've got to buy something for the amount.

That's against the law, said Davie.

Ah well you go and get the polis! Arthur laughed, and he shook his head; he started to roll another cigarette. He nodded at the drink on the table. We're gonni be here for the duration by the looks of it!

Just a carry-out, muttered Patrick, getting to his feet. He unscrewed the whisky bottle and asked his brother if there were any wee tumblers. Of course there were wee tumblers. There were wee tumblers in the kitchenette, as he knew fine well. He got them himself, filled a big jug with water.

Nicola's no gonni be your pal, said Gavin, too much drink.

Bit of truth in that, said Arthur.

Davie chuckled: Tell the boy to take it away then! Never mind Paddy, at least I appreciate it.

Ach I'm wanting to drown my sorrows. Pat said, I've chucked my fucking job.

You've what? cried his brother.

Naw, just kidding.

Gavin stared at him then said to his mates: He's no fucking kidding at all. That makes me really angry, so it does. He's a bloody teacher and he earns a bomb, a single man, he can do anyfuckingthing he likes. Anything; anything at all. So what does he do he wraps it! It makes me sick so it does. I mean . . . Gavin gazed at Patrick and when Patrick said nothing he continued: That's the daftest thing you've ever done, and you've done some fucking daft things in your time.

After a moment Patrick said, Will you listen a minute?

It's the fucking limit, said Gavin.

He'll no listen, Pat told the others.

Aye you're fucking right I'll no listen . . . Gavin shook his head and he leant back in the armchair and inhaled deeply on his fag and blew the smoke at the ceiling. Patrick had poured four whiskies and he handed them about and also gave out the jug of water. Gavin accepted his drink without reply. And Patrick said, It's my life.

Dont say that to me.

Cause it's the truth?

I dont want to hear that, it's rubbish.

Patrick nodded, returning to the chair at the rear of the settee. Gavin was sitting forwards, sipping at his whisky and looking at the blank television screen – the set was to his right, standing on the appropriate section of a piece of tall wooden furniture. Patrick drank from his can of superlager. It wasnt so much that it was better than the homebrew – and it wasnt at all – it was just that it tasted so much thicker and sweeter; in fact it was quite sickly; the homebrew was better, tastier.

Davie Jordan was saying, The last job I had was when . . . when was the last job I had?

How the fuck do I know, muttered Gavin.

Arthur said, You had that wee driving job.

Och I dont count that that was murder so it was.

It was a job, Arthur said.

Och I dont count it I mean for God sake the money was rubbish; ye gave them their whack and you took what was left it was rubbish. Private hire, he said to Patrick.

Some guys do okay on the private hire, said Gavin.

Freddie Sweeney from Gilshie Hill, said Arthur, he's working out Duntocher way and he's making a fortune. Ye want to see inside the cunt's house! Me and Maureen were up visiting a couple of months back; it's a fucking palace. Videos and hi-fi and all new furniture, ye want to see it!

Gavin was nodding.

Ah but ye aye hear these stories, answered Davie with a look over his shoulder at Patrick. Eh Pat?

Some guys are doing well, said Arthur. That's just a fact.

The trouble is getting the wheels, said Gavin.

That was my trouble. Davie continued speaking to Pat: See I was in partners with this fellow, but it was his motor and he took all the best times I mean he had bloody Friday and Saturday nights and all that whereas I was getting left having to rely on it raining on Sunday morning so the cunts would want a lift to the bloody church or the chapel.

Pat laughed loudly.

Know what I mean Paddy! Davie grinned.

If it was your own transport but, ye wouldni have had that problem, Gavin said.

Aw I know, that's what I'm saying. But I'm saying as well that it's no a goldmine.

Who's saying that! Nobody's saying that! Gavin frowned. Arthur was indicating to him that the music had stopped. Anything you like, said Gavin.

A change of mood?

Gavin shrugged.

No want to just flip sides? asked Davie.

A wee change of mood eh? Arthur winked at Patrick: Just trying to get this pair away from fiddles and bagpipes.

It's your national heritage, replied Davie. Dont tell me you're wanting to stick on rock music!

What's wrong with that? cried Arthur.

Nothing at all, said Gavin.

Davie said, Ah well I just feel as if I'm getting too auld for it sometimes.

Rubbish, cried Arthur, you're never too auld to rock and roll. Bo Diddley! On ye go the Bo, you're a dancer!

Davie winked to Pat, jerking his thumb at Arthur.

Stick him on if you like, said Gavin.

Gonni climb up the stair and get me my records then? Arthur laughed, he stubbed his roll-up out at the side of the tiled fireplace.

Gavin stared at him. Arthur, for fuck sake, there's an ashtray at your fucking feet!

Aw aye Gavin sorry . . . Arthur sat back on the armchair. It's yous putting down rock, it's getting to me!

I used to quite like Elvis, said Davie to Pat, but I'm talking about when I was a snapper I mean fuck ten or eleven year auld I was at the time, I grew out of it . . . Davie tugged at the corner of his moustache. The King of rock and roll but you've got to admit it.

What? frowned Arthur.

I mind when he died, the wife was upset but I canni say I was particularly bothered except in a kind of sympathetic way.

What d'you mean? Pat asked.

For Elvis. I felt sorry for him. A big fat bastard as well remember? But still and all, ye had to feel sorry for him. He was the greatest right enough.

Elvis was fucking rubbish, muttered Arthur and he stood to his feet. I'm going up to get auld Bo – let Pat hear what it's really like. Fuck yous and your highland music!

I know Bo Diddley, said Pat, he's good.

Aye well just to let ye hear it, replied Arthur and he placed his glass of homebrew and whisky tumbler on the window-ledge as he made his way from the room.

Gavin raised his eyebrows at Davie: That's you upsetting the big yin again Jordan!

Well I'm no meaning to, said Davie. I dont think he should call Elvis rubbish but do you? I mean a lot of folk liked Elvis.

Gavin said to Pat: The big yin's a purist. He likes the blues and all that; he thinks Elvis stole a lot of songs.

Pat nodded. How can ye steal a song.

Aw quite easy, replied Gavin, and then ye make a fortune off your records and dont pay the poor cunt that wrote it.

Aye, true, I was actually more thinking of the traditional stuff.

It's probably just because I said the word 'fat', said Davie – know what I mean, the way he's putting the beef on himself! Mind you, if somebody did steal the songs it wouldni have been Elvis, it would've been one of his entourage – that Colonel Parker maybe! Who says he stole songs anyway, apart from the big yin?

Gavin shrugged. The record business is as corrupt as fuck, who knows.

When Gavin finished the last of his homebrew Pat gave him across a can of superlager then he gave one to Davie and put one on the arm of Arthur's chair. He should have contacted the secretary's office to tell them he was going home at dinnertime. It wasnt so good of him not to. The boats were definitely being burnt to a cinder. He just hadni been up to it. He needed to get away: and so he got away. End of story. Pat shivered. He was staring at the carpet and he closed his eyes because of something almost like its echo, the echo of the shiver, passing across the top of his spine and neck christ was somebody thinking about him at this moment in time? Alison? Was Alison god the very thought that she could actually be thinking about him. In any way whatsoever. Imagine her even thinking about him. In any way whatsoever. And yet, after last night.

He wasnt going to say anything at all to Nicola about it. Maybe that had been at the back of his mind in coming here, a quiet word with her about it, about the situation. Nicola was good.

Davie Jordan was speaking to him: Is this the first time you'll be without a job Paddy?

Eh I suppose so.

You'll learn, answered Gavin.

What will I learn?

You'll learn it's no funny, for a start.

I dont expect it to be funny.

Davie said, Heh Paddy how long ye been at the teaching?

More than five years now, nearly six.

Your first job?

More or less – I had a labouring job for a few weeks.

Gavin shook his head: A very few! They gave him the bullet. It was me got him in as well! Then he started giving cheek to the siteclerk.

It was him that gave me the cheek.

Ye fucking got me into bother so ye did ya wee cunt! Gavin grinned, The Doyle family was bad news!

Pat laughed, but only for a moment, and he sighed and his head bent, he stared at the floor then shut his eyes.

Davie was speaking to Gavin about something. Pat felt like crying. He kept his eyes shut and his head lowered. The outside door closed. Big Arthur came in carrying one LP record and he said to Gavin: No chance of a bowl of that soup you were boasting about?

I was just waiting for you! Gavin got up and walked to the door, he paused and said quietly, Okay brother?

Aye.

Sure?

Aye. Just no feeling that good.

Ye want a lie down?

Naw.

I'll give you a bowl of soup.

I'm no really that hungry.

Gavin's soup's a legend! called Davie.

He makes it with flank mutton, said Arthur, then he shovels it onto a couple of slices of bread and we get tore in!

It's a family trade-mark; I learnt it from my maw . . . Gavin was smiling as he opened the door. Then he wagged his finger at Pat, indicating the bevy on the table: Nicola isni gonni be too pleased with you brother!

Uch well.

It's him she loves, said Gavin to the others.

Young brothers, said Davie, what can ye do except lie down and die! It's cause they're no a threat.

Gavin had left the room.

And Davie said: It's true, that's how women like them.

I wish women liked me, muttered Arthur. He looked at Pat and he seemed to be speaking seriously, so Pat nodded and he continued. They never ever fell for me, know what I mean? and I'm talking about when I was a boy. I was quite a good dancer as well – no that that makes any difference – jiving and that, I was good at it, even if I say so myself.

You better, said Davie, cause no other cunt will!

I'm talking about before I got married Pat . . . Arthur shrugged and swallowed whisky.

A sob story, grinned Davie.

Is it fuck.

Davie winked at Pat.

It's the truth. Whenever I was interested in any woman she was never interested in me.

Aye but was there no ones that were interested in you and you wereni interested in them? Patrick asked.

What?

I'm saying was there no women that were interested in you, but you wereni interested in them?

Naw, no really. Arthur paused a few moments and when he stopped frowning his forehead became a mass of wrinkles. He unzipped his pouch of tobacco.

Sob story, said Davie.

I'm just telling ye the fucking truth Davie.

Pat nodded. I've never been that lucky with them either. I dont know what it is, maybe being there in the right place at the right time or something. I never seem to really knock it off. That's me turning thirty as well.

Ach you're still a boy, said Davie, I'm bloody forty-two. Forty-two!

When did you get married?

[265]

Bloody twenty! Stupid. Better being like yourself, single man and all that, playing the field. Eh Arthur?

Depends. I was twenty-eight when I got married so I know what Pat's talking about. Sometimes ye felt as if ye were getting stuck. It sounds fucking stupid but there ye go. Arthur glanced at Pat: Is that what you feel?

Sometimes aye.

Do ye no go up the dancing or that? said Davie.

I canni be bothered. I mean there is this woman I fancy, but things areni working out at all at all. But who cares! Slàinte! Pat chuckled. He studied the whisky in his tumbler before drinking most of it.

Slàinte, said Davie and he also drank.

So I'm thinking of maybe heading south.

London?

Naw.

Birmingham?

Maybe no England at all.

You talking about emigrating? said Arthur.

Naw eh, just, I might go to Europe. Spain.

Spain? Arthur was surprised.

I quite fancy it.

Ah well, said Davie, you're single; so you're as well enjoying yourself while ye can. If it was me but I think I'd shoot off to Canada or Australia. If you're there it's so bloody big ye can just fuck off to wherever ye like, whenever ye like. Eh Arthur?

Aye. When I was a boy I was going to join the Hudson Bay Company of Canada. Ever heard of it Pat?

Aye, it's a famous name.

True but nowadays a lot of folk wouldni know what ye were talking about if ye fucking said it to them.

Davie said, You never telt me ye were going to join them before.

Aye, fuck sake, nineteen I was; I sent away and filled in the forms and all the rest of it. I was all set to go but I changed my mind.

What kind of a deal was it? Pat asked.

Well ye see it was a big trading company and they went right across the north part of Canada, trading with the Indians and the

Eskimoes and white men as well, fur trappers . . . Arthur puffed on his roll-up, then had to give himself another light to get it smoking. Ye bought furs and pelts. Ye could be twenty-one years of age and get charge of your own trading post. And I think at that time you were on your fucking thirty quid a week. But I'm talking twenty year ago so it was good dough. See as well Paddy what I was thinking was because ye were stuck away up in the fucking wilderness and all that, the ice and snow, that you'd have fuck all to spend the wages on. So you could save a fortune. Then move down to the city if you wanted. Maybe four or five – even six – year working for them and then you move down to the city with a right few bob in the tail. Okay it would've been fucking lonely but you would've stuck it out. It would've been fucking worth it.

D'you regret no going?

Aye; sometimes.

The door opened and Gavin pushed in carrying a tray with bowls and spoons and slices of bread that were already margarined. He returned to the kitchenette and came back with the pot of soup, he laid it on top of two place-mats on the table. What happened to the music? he said, carrying his own bowl of soup to the armchair.

We were yapping, Davie replied.

I was telling them about the Hudson Bay Company in Canada. I was going to join them when I was a boy. I fancied the life. Plus being able to make a few quid . . . Arthur had risen to get himself a bowl of soup.

Davie and Pat also began helping themselves.

It was good soup. It was thick with vegetables and there were bits of flank mutton floating about which they ladled out and put between two slices of bread. Pat ate his without paying attention to the others and when he finished he refilled his bowl immediately.

Gavin called: Help yourself!

Pat grinned. He hadnt bothered eating at dinnertime and was starving and this soup was probably the best grub he had had for a fortnight. He would definitely have to acquire better eating habits. Learning to cook vegetables would be a good place to start. It was more of developing the habit than anything else, if he could just get into the habit of it, of buying carrots and turnips and cabbage etcetera. He could buy it all at the weekend and then work out what he was going to eat on a daily basis, and then pin the menus on the wall. Making a big pot of soup was something to consider. He could make a really big stack of it on the Sunday evening and it would last him through the week, and then when he came home from work he could just heat a bowl of it up for himself. It would be ideal.

He got another slice of bread, gave himself another ladleful of soup.

Remember and help yourself to the soup! called Gavin.

Pat grinned. I'll remember!

He telt me he wasnt hungry, said Gavin to the others.

Arthur was putting the Bo Diddley album on and Davie was getting more soup. The company was relaxing. It was good.

They were friends, this trio of neighbours; they shared their grub and they shared their drink. They got on fine together. They were friends. And they were not all making him feel excluded; that was one thing, they were not making him feel awkward. That's two things.

So, two things is not bad for one afternoon. Plus here is a third: that Doyle P for Pat Paddy or Patrick is actually here in this abode when parties of the teaching profession are dutybound not to be, when they should be at their fucking desk and giving the weans what-for. If he had known they were into the homebrew earlier he would have left school at the morning interval. No he wouldnt have. And there was no point trying to lasso the moon. None of it mattered except that here he was at this present moment. And eventually, should he so desire, he could just lie down on the carpet and go to sleep. A bit of something hard caught in between his two front teeth; he picked it out. A wee stone. A wee stone in his teeth. The hazards of being a soup-eater.

Some family photographs were on the glass sideboard near where he was sitting. They looked fine. Pat could see himself in a small group study that had been taken on the wedding day. He hadnt been Gavin's best man but there was nothing sinister about it. They had been friends at the time, just with Pat being in his early days at uni he was not always around the place. And Gavin always had a lot of friends; he was a popular type of bloke.

[268]

These family photographs could render a person jealous of somebody else's existence!

Gavin and Nicola and wee Elizabeth and John. God. He just hadni been feeling well recently, mentally, these past few days and weeks – otherwise he would never have dodged up that close to avoid seeing them. That was a fucking awful thing to have done. As awful as anything he has done for a long while. But he wouldni have done it if he had been okay. Imagine if they ever found out! Imagine how it would be! Heh Gavin, Patrick said, I actually saw yous the other night. I'm talking about Sunday. Yous were coming along the road but I kept out your way.

What?

I kept out your way. It's a long story . . . Pat smiled. Actually I was a bit halfcut and I didni want to gibber in front of the weans!

Is this gen?

Aye. I hid up a close.

Gavin didni say anything. He had placed his empty bowl on the mantelpiece and lighted a cigarette. Patrick dunked the bread he was holding into the soup. Gavin pursed his lips, then said, We were only wanting to see if you fancied coming with us up to maw and da's. We had been in at the Barrows and we were going straight. I says we'd be better phoning first but Nicola says naw because you would've made excuses. Gavin sniffed. He said to the other two: She worries about him. Cause he's on his tod and that, she thinks he doesni look after himself properly. She thinks you're in a rut Paddy my boy.

We're all in a bloody rut! said Davie.

Gavin continued, If ye just phoned maw and da occasionally. Ye know what like they are. They worry. In other words they're normal parents.

Pat nodded.

They're getting on Pat know what I mean.

What age are they? Arthur asked.

Eh . . . Gavin frowned at him for a moment, before answering. The auld man's fifty-seven; my maw's a couple of year younger.

Fifty-seven's nothing, said Arthur. My auld man's seventy-eight.

My auld man's deid and buried, said Davie, I killed him myself, with my own two hands.

Arthur muttered, Your head's wasted ya cunt.

The da's had eh three strokes . . . Gavin dragged on his cigarette and he didnt look at Davie. It's no a joke.

I saw them on Saturday, said Pat.

Aye I know you did but we never knew it at the time, otherwise we wouldni have bothered, obviously. It was just with ye phoning on the Friday and that.

Sorry.

It doesnt matter.

Patrick gazed at his brother. Gavin sipped the superlager, dragged on the cigarette and blew smoke into the fireplace. It's because I was halfcut, said Patrick, I didni want the weans to see me in case I started gibbering.

Gavin nodded.

I didnt.

Fine.

Davie said to Arthur: Does Maureen make a good pot of soup?

No bad. Her maw's better. No great, but better.

Davie nodded; he turned as though to speak to Gavin but Gavin held his gaze for a few moments and he said: I didni like your remark there Davie. That rubbish about your feyther, it's stupid patter.

Davie looked at him.

Stupid patter Davie know what I mean.

Davie smoothed the right side of his moustache. He lifted his whisky and drank what was left of it.

It was unjust. Patrick had annoyed Gavin but now here it was Davie getting the row. He uncapped the whisky and gave an exaggerated sigh of appreciation, poured himself a small one and then topped up Arthur's and poured Davie a fresh one; he handed them the jug of water and lifted away their empty bowls. He offered the whisky to Gavin but Gavin declined. I'll have one in a minute, he said.

Okay brother! Pat grinned although he didnt of course feel like grinning. In circumstances roughly similar to this one, in certain tribes of chimpanzees, individuals bare their arses to each other, a method of pacifying the aggressor. But this wasnt the place to display arses. This was family. Grimly and sternly. They set their faces grimly and looked sternly at one another. It was funny the way folk acted. Patrick laughed suddenly and he said: There's this boy in one of my classes who's in love with one of the lassies, and she's got a wean already – no to him. They're both about sixteen, seventeen. True love.

Nobody spoke.

Och! Tch! Pat laughed again. He put his hand to his forehead and shut his eyelids. Fuck it. It's funny but, he said, you watch them for maybe a couple of years; you see things. How open they are. Kids. They're so fucking open, the way they trust you. They think you can do anything when you're a teacher. They think you're the heavyweight champion of the fucking world. No kidding ye! They think everything you say has to be right and true.

What like is your class? said Arthur.

I've got a lot of different ones.

Ragamuffins?

Pardon?

Are they ragamuffins?

I dont understand your question. Could you define ragamuffins for me?

Gavin said quickly: Dont. He's trapping ye.

Pat glanced at Gavin: You referring to me?

Naw, I'm referring to him over there! Gavin gestured vaguely at the door and Patrick couldni stop himself from looking, and he replied:

I think you're trying to tell me something. Because in fact he was getting told to leave. His big brother was asking him to kindly vacate the premises. Which was really a bit much when you considered their relationship was blood-based, consanguineous. It's not as if he was a stranger in off the street. Pat grinned and raised his tumbler of whisky. Am I allowed to finish my drink first?

What?

You obviously want me to vacate the premises?

What you talking about?

Do you want me to leave o brother?

Do what you fucking like o brother.

In other words I can finish my drink?

You can do what you like. Gavin smiled briefly.

Patrick raised the tumbler: Prosit brüder!

Prosit brüder to you too.

Patrick smiled. He swallowed the whisky and sipped beer. His brother was now saying something to Arthur and was maybe deliberately excluding Davie. Things were not alright. They were alright. Before I came. Before I came things were alright. Things were alright before I came. Now that I am here things are not alright. I should not have come and then things would still be fine; yous three neighbours would be fine. Instead of that in came myself and fucked up the proceedings, the atmosphere, clouded things over, making things go awry. Gavin was watching him. Gav was okay. Gav. That was from way back when. Heh Gav going to take me with you.

The whole world is there. Where. In a family. The family grouping. Hegel was not wholly right about things. There again mind you

but here is a truth that is axiomatic: the existence of $2^4 \, 2^2$. Och this fucking self-congratulatory pity it's a load of fucking out the window with it away, away away away. Away where. Just away. Get to fuck. Into the nether regions with you of whom it must be said that Dante alone could have placed you. Dante alone. What is to be said of that. Is something to be said of that. Before something can be said about something, before anything can truly be said, we are dutybound to find a – sorry, we are dutybound

this is the gibbers

these are the gibbers

Gavin is watching me

And poor auld Davie Jordan who has a wee black moustache and is of this planet forty-two winters, having just had a row from one's brother on behalf of one, a father of four weans, two boys and two girls: Davie is looking.

When I get pissed I start gibbering, said Patrick. The gibbers descend upon me. No kidding ye Davie, the gibbers.

Davie nodded. I was thinking there about this uncle of mine's, a snobby bastard, he's retired now, used to work for the Forestry. He's a Wee Free. His best mate's a big bloody polis sergeant. There's this place they go fishing up by the Kyle, out near Plockton. And it's poaching. They'll no tell anybody where it is either. I was up there once and I was with my auld man and he wouldni take us with them. Eh! Christ. Hell of a cunt that sergeant, he was supposed to be shagging the manageress of the hotel and she gave him free bevy. The word was too that her man knew it was happening . . . Davie reached for his can of superlager.

Maybe he was shagging somebody else, said Arthur.

Davie shrugged. I dont know. He was a snobby bastard the uncle, didnt like our side of the family. Him and my da hated each other.

After a moment Gavin said, He was a snob *and* a poacher. Unusual. Then as well the polis sergeant.

How do ye mean? Davie asked.

I dont know; it just sounds unusual.

He thought my maw had married beneath her, the uncle. Davie lifted a half-smoked cigarette out of an ashtray and he set it alight via flame ignition. He struck a match and the flame appeared, the flame appears; he places the end of the fag into the centre of the flame and then breaks the match into two pieces, the flame going out. He sits back on the settee and then sits forwards again, balancing on the very edge of the seat, staring at the floor.

Hegel, the German philosopher who influenced Marx a lot, Pat said; he had things in common with Heraclitus, the auld Greek philosopher who was a frosty auld bastard funnily enough whereas when Hegel was a student he really enjoyed life. But the both of them believed the individual has to succumb to reason in a sense – but Heraclitus, what I'm saying about him, he believed fire was at the root of life, that everything was composed of fire – everything comes from fire, or rather is *of* fire. Unlike Thales for instance, the old Milesian, he thought everything comes from water, everything is water.

Water-based? asked Davie.

Aye, more or less, and he wasni far wrong when you come to think about it.

Ninety percent of the body's water.

Is it? asked Pat.

You're the teacher!

Hahaha. That's right! But what I'm really on about is fucking eh see when a match goes out, when the flame vanishes, leaving the smoke . . . It's like your life. It's like your existence. The spirit departing from your body – you could even think of it as the soul if ye were into theology and worshipping deities. Plus think of the Arabian Nights for instance, the genie of the lamp, the smoke issues from the spout and then whoof! the genie appears, called into existence, I'm here to do your bidding o master.

Sounds like the bloody working-class, said Arthur to Gavin.

Aye you're fucking right, replied Gavin.

Aye but where's there's smoke there's fire! said Davie.

The eternal optimist, said Gavin.

You've got to be. Eh Pat?

I dont know.

What do you think of Marx? asked Arthur.

Fucking great.

Aye. Arthur smiled.

Some things ye just cannot take away from him. No matter how hard they fucking try!

Gavin said, I'll always agree with ye there brother. He was for the workers and that's that, end of story.

I'm drinking to that, said Arthur and raised his whisky.

The others followed. Afterwards Davie said, There was this auld guy used to hang about with my feyther; he was a good auld cunt, a bit crabbit I mind – course I was a boy just, a snapper. Him and the feyther used to go for long walks; they'd meet up with their cronies down at Partick Cross subway station and then they'd all set off.

Where to? asked Pat.

I'm no sure. I dont think it was anywhere special but. Sometimes they just walked it to Whiteinch Park to watch the boys playing football . . . Davie nodded, he looked at the carpet.

After a brief silence Arthur said, What you telling us this for Davie?

I dont know, it's got bloody lost somewhere. Davie chuckled: It must be the homebrew!

Dont fucking blame the homebrew! Arthur laughed and called to Gavin: Hear him! Blaming the homebrew because he's getting fucking doty!

I am getting doty, Davie said, it's that house of mine it's like living in a bloody mental asylum. No kidding ye Paddy four teenagers I've got fuck sometimes ye wait an hour and a half to get to the bloody toilet!

Four teenagers! Horrendous.

Fucking worries! Ho! Davie shook his head, swallowed a mouthful of superlager.

After a moment Gavin said: What game did you go to on Saturday?

The Yoker, they were playing Perthshire. It was alright; no outstanding but alright. Heh what do ye make of this, there was only one goal scored and I missed it!

Gavin replied, Were ye gabbing?

Gabbing. Naw.

That makes a change!

Ha ha, said Pat.

Gavin laughed. He signalled for the whisky bottle and Pat got up to hand it across to him. But when Gavin made to take it Patrick snatched it away and laughed: Too slow brother, the reflexes are definitely going!

Aw aye? Anytime you want to prove it son. The table-tennis table is aye available down the road.

I'll maybe take you up on that.

Last time he challenged me I thrashed him, said Gavin to the others. He thought he would beat me as well! What was it the first game again? Was it 21–6?

For fuck sake, cried Pat, imagine minding the score from a game of table-tennis ye played a fucking year ago!

It wasni a year ago.

Near enough.

Six fucking month ya lying bastard.

Imagine calling your brother a bastard!

Strange statement! said Arthur.

It is indeed.

Pat grinned, returning to his chair. And Arthur said to him: Tell me this, you being a teacher and all that I mean, do kids the day still get homework? The reason I ask, as far as I can make out my two never do anything, I mean fuck all Paddy, nothing. Where's your home-work I say to them. They just look at me as if I'm a fucking eejit.

The days of homework have gone forever, said Pat.

How come?

Times have changed.

Aye well it's the weans that're suffering.

So what?

Arthur continued to gaze at him, then he frowned, puzzled; uncertain as to the nature of fighting talk apparently because if one thing was sure it was the following: a glove had just smacked him on the gub. Maybe Pat should have flung a glass of beer over him instead, then he would have twigged what was what. But there's only so much one person can do and that includes that great arbiter in the sky the teacher, s/he can teach the weans but no the fucking parents.

Patrick said: Do you know what I tell parents Arthur? I tell them to go and fuck themselves. Patrick held both hands up in a gesture of peace, he smiled for a moment; I'm no trying to get at you personally but I just fucking feel that you cant expect the teacher to be the everything, the heavyweight boxing champion of the world.

Arthur stared at him.

Know what I mean, I'm just being honest with ye. I dont think ye should expect the teacher to do everything. If you want your weans to get homework then give it to them your fucking self.

Gavin said: That actually sounds quite right-wing ye know.

Well it's meant to be the fucking opposite and it is the fucking opposite.

Gavin nodded.

I'm just sick of folk getting at teachers all the time, said Pat to Arthur directly.

I wasnt getting at you.

I thought you were, sorry.

Well I wasnt. Arthur looked from him to Gavin, then he frowned, he started rolling another fag.

No think some of them deserve to get criticised? said Davie.

Aye but that's the same in any job.

Some of them dont fucking teach at all, said Arthur. Let's face it. They just sit at their desk and read a fucking book!

Pat didnt answer.

And then they expect these long holidays all the time!

Aye, I agree with ye there! Gavin glanced at Pat: Ye canni deny that.

Of course I can.

Ye mean ye do deny it?

Of course.

Gavin gazed at him, then laughed briefly. He looked at Pat but Pat looked away. Nor was Pat going to say anything further because he was fucking off home as soon as he swallowed what he had lying. There was no point sitting here yapping to a bunch of fucking prejudiced rightwing bastards. And Gavin turned on him once more: What d'you mean ye deny ye get long holidays?

I deny I get long holidays, that's what I mean.

Back it up.

What d'you mean back it up?

Show me what you're talking about?

Naw. You show me what you're talking about.

I think I know what Paddy means, said Davie.

Good, tell me, replied Gavin.

I think I know what you mean Paddy.

Pat nodded.

Ye dont think ye get long holidays because when you're off from the school you're still doing other things connected with it, making up timetables and all that.

Patrick nodded.

I still say it's the weans that suffer, muttered Arthur.

Patrick cleared his throat; he glanced at Gavin then sat forwards, hands on his knees, gazing at the carpet. He turned and lifted his whisky, sipped at it. He also had a bottle of homebrew lying now which Arthur had opened for him. It was too much. He was going to screw the head as far as this all was concerned. And the last thing was to get into fights, especially with guys that were twice your size. Arthur could just fucking sit on him and be able to carry on rolling one of his fags while Pat would be floundering beneath him trying to wriggle free. Although most of the weight he was carrying consisted of lard, lard. Gavin was speaking. Nicola's name had cropped up and

[277]

he was saying he had forgotten to go and pay an outstanding electricity bill. He called to Pat: She'll no be too pleased brother!

Pat gazed at the carpet another couple of moments before raising his head. What did ye say?

Nicola, she'll no be too pleased with me.

Cause of all the bevy?

Naw I dont mean that it's because I had the electricity to pay this morning, and I never made it into town.

Aw aye . . . Patrick added: I'm no wanting to drink that much anyway cause of the driving and all that.

The driving and all that! Gavin grinned briefly, then he frowned: You're no driving.

Naw I suppose I better no.

Drunk driving's fucking mental, muttered Arthur.

A very bad habit, said Pat.

A very bad habit? It's fucking death, Gavin said, I thought you had chucked that.

I have.

Well you fucking better.

I've been hitting the tomato juice. I have a couple of pints and then I stop. In fact I might fucking stop it all the gether, never mind the driving. It is a fucking rut. The bevy; it makes ye do things that are so totally absurd you feel as if fuck like you're enclosed in a wad of plastic sheeting. That's the only thing to describe it, plastic sheeting. Patrick chuckled.

Sounds more like dope, replied Arthur.

What I mean is if you're really guttered and looking out at the world but without being actually crawling on all fours.

That *is* more like dope! Arthur smiled.

Davie said, That's what we were talking about before you came in.

Gavin laughed and he drank a quick mouthful of homebrew . . . Christ I mind fine the first time I smoked a joint . . . I was just a boy at the time, about seventeen.

You never telt me, said Patrick.

What would I tell you for?

I'm your fucking brother.

Gavin laughed again.

Tell us the yarn, said Davie.

Naw it was just . . . Gavin grinned: I mind I was walking down the street and it was like I had discovered myself there, I just came to my senses. It was the big tree on Argyle Street. And this big fire was raging up a close. And the fire-brigade was there. Two or three of them. Lights flashing and all the noise. Big crowds of folk. And the polis as well, everywhere ye looked, polis. So then, for some fucking stupid reason, I started going up and asking them all sorts of questions, daft yins; how much of a wage they got, what like was the O.T.; that kind of stuff.

To the polis? asked Pat.

Aye. They were fucking looking at me too, they didni know if I was taking the piss or what. Do ye like shift work; what age is it you retire.

The others laughed. Arthur said, You're lucky you never got huckled!

They didni know what to do with me! Gavin chuckled. They were fucking baffled!

It's a wonder they never smelled it off your clothes, said Davie.

Christ aye, I never thought of that!

Whereabouts was the actual close where the fire started?

And Gavin went on to explain. It was a good type of straightforward question Davie had asked: one which Patrick would aye be incapable of making. Why? Because it was fucking boring. Was that particular close near to the such-and-such pub or was it along a bit farther. Naw, it was nearer to that wee post office. Aw aye, and what was the name of that wee post office again. It was the so-and-so. Aw the so-and-so! God sake, I had a mate used to work there. O did ye! That's fucking really interesting. His wife's feyther was a pal of my greatgrandpa's auld man. Was he! Aye christ, they used to play football the gether whenever they werent drawing their fucking supplementary benefit or dying of hypothermia. Yet these questions were so germane to the issue. There were no other questions to be asked. All these other questions and queries derived from another world altogether. Vulcan. Which is the derivation of 2^4; 2^2. In fact his questions were abysmal. Bloody abysmal. They werent actual questions at all. They were statements. These statements had been given a going over, until they began to resemble genuine questions of everyday inquiry, such as: How much of a fucking wage do ye earn? Are you getting exploited badly or just ordinarily so? Is your rate for the job fixed by person or persons unknown? Is your union as corrupt as mine? Did your leaders sell ye out that last time as usual? If so at what fucking point in the manoeuvre, before or after being bribed and were they offered promotion and a permanent seat in the front stalls at Scottish fucking Opera with the managing director of the regional planning department for financial dealings, prior to being offered the possibility of a fulltime paid-up job as a labour consultant for the rulers of this wonderful land of the free. In fact, I've hated being a teacher. No kidding ye. It fucking stinks. It stinks. A genuine stench, of corruption, everywhere, rotten decomposing flesh being nibbled by a few fat vultures, everywhere you look a genuine stench. Just name a place and ye can be sure of one thing and this one thing is that it fucking stinks. Patrick shook his head.

Immediately Gavin said: What d'you mean?

I mean it fucking stinks, it's rotten, from the outside in and the inside fucking out. Every last fucking thing about it, it stinks. And what goes on in the classroom, it's a load of dross. This is how I'm fucking chucking it. And all these wee weans christ they think ye know everything, every last thing in the fucking universe – especially about how to change for the good. I'll tell ye something else, bastards, people think lies are true and even when they know they're no true they'll say fuck all because the shitey fucking arse who's telling the lie holds the position of power. It's a load of keech Gavin and I'm fucking sick of it. That's how I'm chucking it.

Gavin nodded. Right then.

Okay?

Aye – fuck all to do with me.

Pardon?

Gavin shrugged.

What d'you mean it's fuck all to do with you!

What I mean is it's up to you what ye fucking do brother.

If that's true then how come ye dont allow me the fucking freedom to just pack it in?

After a moment Gavin replied, Because it doesni fucking matter what I say, you'll just go and fucking do what ye like anyway!

Aye but it's your blessing I'm after, you never give me your blessing!

What do ye think I'm the fucking Pope!

Naw but you dont. You never fucking give me your blessing! Pat glanced at Arthur and Davie who were both laughing at the Pope comment, and he said to them: Honest, no kidding ye; see trying to please him that's sitting in that fucking chair there! You'd be as well fucking . . . I dont know.

Gavin jerked his thumb at Pat, saying to the others: He doesni really hate being a teacher at all. If you fucking believe that you'll believe anything. He fucking loves the bloody job! He loves it! It's all he ever fucking talks about! Fucking teaching! It does your nut in listening to the cunt! It's fucking murder! What's he fucking talked about since he came here! Teaching. That's all. Nothing else. He doesni talk about nothing else except it.

Pat stared at him.

Gavin raised his right hand and started flapping it open and shut while calling: Rabbit rabbit rabbit rabbit; rabbit rabbit rabbit rabbit. All your teachers and all your fucking students and pupils and all your fucking headmasters and your cronies from the fucking staffroom. Fucking middle-class bunch of wankers ya cunt! Gavin sat back on the chair and drew his feet up onto it, sitting on his heels, and he swallowed the whisky in a gulp and put the tumbler up onto the mantelpiece. He got his packet of fags open and stuck one in his mouth, then threw the packet to Davie a moment later. He glanced at Patrick briefly: I'll be glad to see you finished with it, dont worry about that.

What do you mean middle-class wankers? said Pat.

Gavin shook his head. He replied, I didni mean them all.

You fucking said it.

I know I fucking said it.

Well ye fucking must've meant something.

Aye, I meant something, I meant middle-class wankers; middle-class wankers, that's what I meant. Okay? Middle-class wankers.

Who exactly?

Whoever you fucking like brother.

Do you mean me? Are you fucking calling me a middle-class wanker?

Gavin laughed and snapped the spent match into two pieces, dumped them in the ashtray. He stopped laughing, but continued to look at Patrick until Patrick felt he wouldnt be able to stop himself laughing he was going to burst out laughing, right in Gavin's face, but he fought it without any problem because what was happening was not funny and his own face was become set and grim, set and grim, because here you had a big brother just staring at him now and not saying a word. And Patrick said, Dont come it Gavin.

Come what? Then Gavin grinned and shook his head, reached for the superlager. After drinking from it he picked the cigarette out of the ashtray and dragged on that. Arthur and Davie were both doing their best not to be involved in the shit. They were just aw christ fuck all, they werent doing fuck all except sitting and drinking and smoking and being alive and doing their best and fucking stupit, Paddy's glass nearly dropping out his hand. But was he playing for sympathy? is that how come he nearly dropped it? Maybe he was hoping they would step into the fray and fix things so that all would be okay again and they could all be muckers and just sit back and I dont know christ anything, tell stories or something, wee yarns about going over the sea to Skye and Heraclitus and genies. The whisky was finished in the tumbler so he put the tumbler down and lifted the superlager and sipped that, lifted the homebrew and had a wee go on it. The bottle of whisky stood there obviously but he let it stand there, he was not going to drink from it as of this moment, life being too risky.

I dont want to argue with ye Gavin.

I dont want to argue with you either Pat.

Pat looked at him for a moment; Gavin was looking back at him; he lifted the superlager. Gavin lifted his superlager; and he raised it and toasted with it. Slàinte, said Pat.

Good luck, said Gavin.

Pat shook his head and spoke to Arthur and Davie: He wisni always a good soup maker ye know. See when he was a boy he was fucking rubbish. Honest, he couldni boil a fucking kettle. It was always me made the supper in our house, just ask my maw. He never fucking done a thing except eat whatever ye laid down in front of him. No shame either!

Gavin smiled.

Big brothers, said Davie; what do ye expect! They aye get away with it as well. That's because mothers always give in to them. They're notorious for that. All down through the years, it's ancient history.

That's garbage, said Gavin.

Naw it's no. You just watch, mothers always bloody let the eldest boy get away with murder. But see the young yin! He aye catches it. I've seen it with my own two. Everybody knows that Gavin it's bloody common knowledge!

Ah I wouldni say that was quite true, said Arthur. In our house okay the eldest boy doesni get belted as much as the young yin but that's because he doesni get up to as much fucking mischief. I mean that young yin's a fucking ragamuffin I dont know where he gets it from! Her side of the house probably, they're a bunch of fucking gaolbait. No kidding ye Paddy a bunch of fucking outlaws. That's my wife, Maureen, her folk. They come from the Garngad. The Simpsons. You heard of them?

Naw.

Aye well ye dont want to! Especially with a name like Paddy! Bluenoses. Bitter as fuck.

Tell him that one about your cousin, at the wedding . . . Davie said.

Aw you mean the eh, the auld feyther?

Aye christ. Davie laughed and glanced at Gavin who nodded and laughed quietly.

Ah well see . . . Arthur gazed at Pat, and while he spoke he glanced at the other two from time to time. It was a wedding, one of the cousins, the wife's team I'm talking about; it's a big big family there's fucking stacks of them. And as I say Paddy they're all fucking Orangemen bitter as fuck. Wouldni let a tim in the house. Aye shouting about how they're filling the country with their weans — no contraception and all that.

Well they have got some contraception, said Gavin.

I'm talking about the pill but Gavin or the coil, how the tims areni allowed to use anything except will-power.

Free will and contraception, said Patrick.

The rhythm method, said Davie, me and the wife used to try it. That's how we've got four bloody weans! He chuckled and tugged at the corners of his moustache.

Pat got the bottle of Grouse and refilled tumblers. Gavin asked for another homebrew to be passed across but Pat gave him another superlager instead: Save your homebrew for later, he said.

There's no gonni be a later! Gavin smiled.

What d'you mean?

What do I mean . . . Gavin gestured at the drinks on the table and at the drinks each individual had lying beside him. Patrick gazed at it all and nodded but he didnt quite understand precisely what Gavin was intending. And Davie said:

Know what I feel like doing, getting the women.

Getting the women? replied Arthur.

Aye. Davie put his drink down and took a half-smoked cigarette from behind his ear and got a light from Arthur's box of matches. I dont mean a party, he said to Gavin.

Nicola wouldni go for it Davie.

Naw I mean I'm no talking about that fuck I'm just meaning bring them into it, for a wee night, we could make a wee night of it – just what we're doing the now, having a crack and that, hearing the music.

Sounds good to me, said Arthur.

It sounds good to me and all, said Gavin, obviously. But it's whether the women'll go for it I mean christ Nicola'll walk in that door and she'll be knacked . . . Gavin glanced sideways, lifted the can of lager and pulled off the stopper. The electricity I mean that's gonni annoy her. Being honest about it, I would probably feel like keeping out her road all the gether. See as well there's the weans to feed and all that, they've got to get their tea.

So's mine, replied Arthur.

Well so's mine too, if it comes to that, Davie said.

But yours are all fucking grown-up; they can feed themselves man!

[284]

That's what you bloody think!

I wouldni have a woman to bring, said Pat suddenly getting up from his chair, requiring a piss desperately; his first since arrival. He paused by the door to say to the effect that there was this woman he was seeing but she wouldni be able to make it if they did have a wee night, but he changed his mind and said nothing. Plus he really did have to get to the bathroom. This very very astonishingly bad habit of waiting and waiting before getting off the arse to go to lavatories was symptomatic of his life. There had to be a connection between it and things of mammoth import. Well of course there was. But maybe he was entering into states of hallucinatory imaginings brought about by urinary dysfunctioning. That would explain the fucking pipes. If he was waiting too long to piss. That was definitely a habit to cultivate, proper bladder emptying because this was stupid, he would just end up with a damaged kidney which demands constant cleansing via the regular drinking of fresh water. Especially those who consume more than sufficient alcohol they require to give their poor auld kidneys every assistance because they are having a difficult enough time without that for christ sake. Gavin was actually very out of order in what he had said I mean you dont call your fucking young brother a middle-class wanker I mean fuck sake. A middle-class wanker! Aye, it's nice to know who your friends are; and if you dont have friends amongst your relatives then etcetera etcetera, who the fuck are you and so on, supposed to have friends among.

Patrick waited till the cistern had refilled before leaving the bathroom.

The other three were laughing at something which did not include Patrick obviously since he had been elsewhere at the yarn's commencement. He sat on the chair and coughed slightly, looked for his glass of homebrew but couldnt find it, it was not there; he took a swig of the superlager. Then Arthur called, Heh Paddy, wait till I finish what I was telling ye there before ye went to the cludge. It was just eh . . . he glanced at Gavin and Davie and it was enough to set the pair of them into further laughter, and he smiled and said to Patrick: Naw, it was just there was a wee bit of a contretemps during the reception. Mind it was a wedding I was saying?

Pat nodded.

So – actually I never saw it, to be honest, the incident itself but what happened was there was this fucking commotion man, a big fucking rammy; it started ben the main dining room; it was a function suite where it was being held. Me and Maureen were in this lounge room with some other folk, a couple of her auld aunties – when in comes this cunt, fucking shouting and bawling, and we're all looking at him wondering what the score is with all the noise and that because we'd heard it, the fucking rammy, before he came fucking in shouting and bawling and panicking away; and he screams out to his missis: Hey Sheila your auld's man's done a disappearing trick out the window! Arthur laughed. Gavin and Davie also laughed. And Arthur said: Naw Paddy what it was ye see this woman Sheila, her auld man, her feyther, he'd got into an argument with this team – Maureen's fucking cousins I dont have to tell ye – and what happens but they fucking grabbed the auld cunt and chipped him out the window. Thank fuck it was only one up. It could've been a bad yin that if he had landed the wrong way! Arthur grinned, shaking his head. A disappearing trick out the window!

There was a noise from the lobby. Gavin glanced swiftly to the door.

Nicola and the kids were home. Arthur turned the volume of the music down and he lifted the cover of the Bo Diddley album, sat back on his chair and started reading the sleeve notes. Davie half turned on the settee; he began talking to Pat about school and how it had changed since he was a boy but Pat didnt pay much attention. He glanced at the door when it opened. Nicola gave a mock look of surprise: My God! I thought I heard voices! And you too Patrick Doyle!

I was just passing, going home from school.

Just passing! She grinned. So Gavin Doyle, as soon as I leave the house you invite folk round for a drinking session!

Not at all!

Mammy . . . called John, Pat's nephew who was coming up for seven years of age. Wee Elizabeth, followed; she was four-and-a-half years of age. Patrick patted them both on the head. The two of them stared at the company. John said, Hullo Uncle Pat?

Hullo John, said Pat in an exaggerated baritone of a voice, and couldni stop himself from adding: How's school? Are you getting on with your lessons?

Aye.

What about you Elizabeth?

She doesnt get lessons, said Nicola, dont you no hen?

Just drawing, said Elizabeth.

She could be getting reading at that age. Pat said, If they had the right attitude to nursery education. No kidding ye Elizabeth I'd have them on mathematics.

Slave driver! chuckled Davie.

Naw but they'd enjoy it. Sure you would Elizabeth?

Elizabeth smiled from Pat to Nicola and she said to Pat: Did you and daddy fight when you were wee?

Everybody laughed. Patrick replied: Aye, he used to give me doings all the bloody time!

Was it clean fighting? said John.

Naw.

Was it dirty?

Aye.

John grinned.

Patrick noticed Nicola and Gavin exchanging looks, and it was to do with the alcohol lying on the table; and he spoke at once. It was me responsible for the bevy Nicola, entirely. I bought it.

She grimaced. It's an awful lot.

Aye, eh . . . he stopped, he was not going to make any daft excuses. He lifted the pile of chocolate and sweetie packets from the sideboard and gave them to the children and while they were holding them and looking at them and grinning at each other, Nicola had stepped nearer to Gavin and she quietly asked him something about the electricity; instead of answering her Gavin rose from his armchair and he said, I was wanting to eh . . . He sniffed, touching her on the elbow and walking ahead of her to the door. Nicola's face. Pat glanced away and he winked at John who was asking him about a packet of sweeties, were they the ones with nuts in the middle? Gavin and Nicola left the room.

I dont know, said Pat, bite into one and see!

Can I open it? John asked.

Aye, of course.

Maybe they've to get their tea first? said Davie, winking at Pat.

Aye, said Arthur and he gave an exaggerated sniff.

Have you to get your tea? Davie asked John. Does your mammy say you've to get your tea?

We can get it after, said Elizabeth.

No flies on her, grinned Arthur.

Ach it'll be alright, said Pat. Okay kids yous can eat your sweeties. But no them all! Save some for later on.

Heh by the way, said Davie to Arthur, did I tell ye that lassie of mine's got the job she was after? It's in a wee restaurant, he told Patrick, waitressing and that – good tips supposed to be.

Great.

She was never one for lessons. The boys were better. Mind you she was fine at the primary school; it was after she moved up.

Ah that's common, said Pat. Lassies generally start chucking it when they hit adolescence; they just give up, they stop trying.

Is that right? asked Arthur.

They tend to, aye. Lessons come second-best to everything, especially boys!

Is that no the same the other way round but? said Davie.

Eh, no really; it's to do with sexuality and the competitive nature of society; how males are aye supposed to win and lassies are aye supposed to come secondbest, and the way the education system colludes entirely. Patrick grinned at Elizabeth and he patted her head: Sure that's no gonni happen to you my fine young lassie? Sure you're gonni do all your lessons and beat these lassieds hollow!

Elizabeth was smiling and looking from Patrick to Davie and to Arthur. And John said, I got the best mark for spelling yesterday.

Great, said Pat, well done my fine young fellow. What did ye do with that best mark?

John smiled.

I dont have any lassies, said Arthur, but I'll tell you something for nothing, if boys are the ones that do do their lessons, I wouldni like to see the ones that dont! No if my pair are anything to go by! Lazy pair of swines so they are.

I thought Billy was quite good? said Davie.

Nah christ. He's like yours, he *was* good. Now? Now he's a lazy
. . . Arthur sniffed without finishing the statement. He winked at
Pat and indicating the kids he said quietly, The problem is, with my
pair anyway, it's trying to warn them away from the . . . junkies . . .
Arthur mouthed the word.

Davie said to him: You dont want to talk about certain things
with the weans and all that.

Naw I know, replied Arthur, I'm just saying to Paddy, it's a
worry.

Aye you're right it's a worry.

So you've got to talk about it.

I know that Arthur, I'm no meaning nothing. It's just because of
the . . . he winked at John and Elizabeth who were both looking at
him and at Arthur, both standing beside Patrick.

Ah but some things are good to talk about in front of weans, said
Pat.

True. But some things areni Paddy, you with me?

Pat nodded. I know what you're saying.

Some things are best left till later on.

Well . . . Pat shrugged.

I dont think you agree with me . . . Davie smiled and added to
Arthur. What do you say on that one Arthur?

Ach it all depends.

Aw aye, I know.

Pat grinned at John and Elizabeth and he said: What do yous two
young folks have to say about all this?

Davie called: Maybe you'd change your mind if you had a couple
of your own!

I hope no, said Pat, but you're probably right Davie. Notice but,
how when we as adults are discussing what's to happen to weans, the
only ones we dont ask are the weans themselves! It's the same with all
exploited groups; they never get asked a question if the question's to
do with them. It's always the bosses that have the dialogue and then
arrive at the decisions for them – well in fact it's for themselves really
but they kid on it's for the slaves they're doing it.

Good point, said Arthur.

Pat laughed: And when we do ask weans a question it's aye the most stupidest question in the world. I'll give you an example: a boy flings a stone at one of his pals and it goes through a window by mistake; out comes the man of the house and gets a grip of the boy. What did you do that for! And if you dont tell me I'm gonni give ye a belt on the jaw! And the poor wee boy canni say a word because the question just doesni have an answer. Do ye know how? Cause it's no an actual question, it just sounds like one. But it isni.

Davie chuckled. I'll give ye a better one . . . but he paused when he saw that Arthur was signalling him and the clock. And Arthur glanced at Pat.

Uncle Pat . . . John said: We went up to your house and you wereni in.

I know.

We went to grannie's.

Was she in?

Yes.

And granpa was in?

Yes. We got our tea.

Elizabeth opened the packet of sweeties she had and offered it to Arthur and Davie who both took one.

Davie sniffed. Heh Paddy I take it we're abandoning the idea of a continuation? getting the women up I mean, later on?

Arthur was shaking his head. I doubt if it's really on, no the night.

Pat shrugged.

Should we ask G. D.? said Davie.

If ye like.

I'm no so sure, said Arthur.

I tend to agree with you Arthur; Patrick continued, I dont think a certain lady would be too keen, and I'm just reading between the lines, about the reaction when the certain lady came in and saw the alcoholic beverages.

And to be honest, said Arthur, I dont think Maureen would be too keen on the idea either.

Right then; right then . . . Davie held his two hands aloft. Another time another place eh!

Aye, said Pat; he grinned at the weans: Yous two dont know

what we've been talking about because yous werent supposed to. It was a code that grown-up people have so yous mob of children canni hear.

Davie gestured at the table: Should we tidy it up?

Don: bother, said Pat, I'll do it.

I'll take my empties though, Arthur said, already gathering the empties together and putting them into a plastic shopping bag he picked up from the other side of the armchair he had been sitting on.

Gavin came in. He said: Yous going?

Aye.

Wise move.

It looks the best, said Davie, another time another place eh!

Another time but no necessarily another place. You're aye welcome here as well ye know Davie.

Aw aye, I wasni meaning nothing.

Gavin nodded. Mind your Bo Diddley! he said to Arthur while strolling to his chair and reaching for his cigarettes. Elizabeth came to sit beside him immediately. She squeezed in on the edge and he put his arm round her shoulder.

John said: Can I switch on the telly dad?

On ye go, but no too loud.

We'll leave yous to it then, said Arthur.

Pat gestured at the bottle of whisky but Arthur and Davie shook their heads and he nodded.

So, said Davie, nice seeing ye again Paddy. Dont make it so long the next time eh!

Naw, said Pat and they shook hands. Then Pat and Arthur shook hands.

Nice seeing ye, said Arthur.

Aye Arthur.

Okay Gavin . . . said Arthur.

Maybe see ye on Friday, said Davie, down by I mean, Box D and all that.

Aye, said Gavin.

Arthur held the door for Davie and nodded at Pat, and said to Gavin: Maybe give ye a bell the morrow night.

Gavin nodded. The door closed. The two men could be heard saying cheerio to Nicola and it was a further couple of minutes before the front door finally shut. And Arthur's footsteps were audible on his way up to the flat above. And that door opened and slammed shut. Gavin and the two kids gazed at the television screen. Pat turned the whisky bottle about on the table, he started reading the label. Then he glanced at his wristwatch.

It was best they went away, Gavin said suddenly. Otherwise we'd have wound up getting guttered. It was a hell of a big carry-out ye got.

Pat made no response since it might have been construed as a criticism. In fact what else could it have been. I just thought a halfbottle would go too quickly, with four of us all getting into it I mean . . . Patrick gazed at his brother. His brother gazed at the television; when he spoke he spoke calmly and quite quietly:

Davie! he'll always just sit and guzzle what ye put down in front of him. And he'll never think of putting his hand in his pocket. That homebrew was all mine and Arthur's. Arthur's mainly but some of it was mine. I've started making it myself and he gives me a hand. Davie's really tight. It's the exact same with the fags. You might no think so but he is. You've got to watch him, take my word for it.

Patrick nodded.

He's a nice enough fellow and that, but . . . Gavin shrugged. All I'm saying is he'll sit and guzzle everything ye put out and never think of chipping in with something to help.

I wasni looking for him to chip in.

I'm no saying that. What I'm saying is he can catch ye out. I'm no meaning you personally, I mean everybody. Gavin glanced at the drink on the table: Was that a dozen superlager ye bought?

It was, aye.

Bloody fortune that must have cost.

It did, aye, it was a lot. If I had thought about it I wouldni have done it but I never thought about it I just actually done it, it was spur of the moment. I was gonni get a halfbottle like I said but I changed my mind, there and then, when I was getting served by Ebenezer Scrooge. And I just bought the bottle.

[292]

Neither John nor Elizabeth seemed to be listening to anything being said. But weans are devious specimens and nothing could be taken for granted with them. Patrick and Gavin had been using the most matter-of-fact voices but John could have been making sense of it. It was a children's cartoon show about a Northamerican white hero who was defeating socialist forces of evil who were of alien extraction.

The weans were engrossed, or seemed to be so. Probably they were in a world of their own.

Arthur as a nineteen-year-old and all set to travel to the Northern Territories of Canada as a trader in furs and pelts! Yet given that he was so fucking brawny and big insofar as physical individuals were a desirable commodity in relation to the hostile environment and one here thinks of the grizzly bear or fierce snow wolf as opposed to the rascally badman.

But the fundamental fact of the matter is: that he should have made contact with the secretary's office to advise them of the leave-taking. Ms Thompson would have been genuinely inconvenienced. And that is not just. You have to be just. If you cannot be just then that is that. And the idea of her getting into bother with the authorities because of one of his daft actions! A simple conversational phonecall to redress matters. He could explain he had been feeling upset both psychologically and physically. And he wasni at all feeling as bad as that now, at this point in time. And what time was that?

Eh Gavin . . . okay if I make a phonecall?

Sure.

Pat was already onto his feet: I want to phone the school.

On ye go.

When he began speaking to Ms Thompson he assumed what he was saying was more or less untrue but then he realised it was the truth: he *had* not been feeling well; he *had* been aware that it would prove impossible to make it through the afternoon without having some sort of something or other, a thing that would be not good.

Her position was simple; if he had advised her at the dinner-hour then she could have made provision. Since he had not advised her she had been unable to make that provision. Apparently the janitor overheard a couple of kids talking during the changeover from first to second period and this had alerted him to the situation. Then as he was heading to the classroom itself to check he had been approached by Mrs Houston who had informed him that Mr Doyle had the beginnings of what looked to her like the flu but whatever it was he had gone home in physical discomfort.

It's true, said Patrick, I felt really bad . . . And while he was speaking he started smiling at the receiver. He was thinking of Alison. That was really sharp of her. He would have to phone to apologise. Plus auld fucking girny gub the janitor, he would have to say sorry to him as well. Fucking auld bastard. Some janitors were good but he was not good. But what was he? He was just a guy with a job he didni like and he couldni help showing it, he just couldni act as if he was enjoying himself. So what. That was no reason to call him an auld bastard. Poor auld bastards, what had they done to deserve such universal acrimony. And what was a bastard anyway but a guy or guyess whose parents had not been married in a socially sanctioned manner? What a load of fucking hegemonic shite.

Was he going into school tomorrow was the question. No he was yes he was. He was. He would be fine tomorrow. After a good night's rest. If by any chance he wasnt although that was very unlikely, he would phone, and phone early; but in terms of how he was feeling at this moment in time yes, he would make it tomorrow, so that was that. I apologise for the inconvenience Mirs Thompson.

It's not me Mister Doyle it's only the fact that if we had known we could have made due provision. And with your evening duty this evening on the under-thirteens' Exam Paper Study Group . . .

I'm sorry.

Which just makes it that wee bit more difficult to rearrange matters you know; it was the same three weeks ago when you missed the Talk on the new Dental Programme.

Yeh I know, I'm sorry about that.

It's just that someone else has to do it for you Mister Doyle.

After a moment Patrick said, I just as I say felt I needed to get home to my bed as soon as possible. It was that feeling where you start wanting to lie down on pavements. It was just good I had the motor car as well otherwise it would've been terrible having to wait for a bus. I would've been able to take a taxi right enough. Patrick frowned at the receiver, which was not Mirs Thompson. When he replaced it his nephew was standing next to him. Pat winked at him.

Uncle Pat . . .

Aye John?

Can I show you a picture I did in school?

Aye, course . . . He took John's hand and they went into the living room. The television volume was still down fairly low and wee Elizabeth looked as though she was falling asleep, still squeezed in beside Gavin. The whole house was warm and cosy. If he liked he could just sit down and remain for as long as he wanted, except not forever.

The smell of food now wafted ben from the kitchenette. Nicola was finishing off the meal which Gavin had prepared earlier on. Patrick was staying to eat. He enjoyed eating with them; they were good at doing food and while he was sitting pretending to be watching a television programme for adults about English country villages he was sniffing away at this aroma of casseroled ox liver. Mirs Houston might be a vegetarian but that was her problem, she probably only did it in a silly attempt to offset the dangers of lung cancer. Henceforth, whenever he was to see that woman in the staffroom he would just march up in the most straightfoward of manners and say

what would he say though? He could think of nothing at all. His mind was devoid of thought; there was nothing that he was thinking of that there was nothing that he was thinking of; nothing that his mind was in control of but that nothing that his mind was in control of — the country upper-class english squire is chatting to this upper-class english woman about the impending show of

but his mind is never in control. No one's mind is in control; that is not necessarily a function of the mind, to be in control, not necessarily.

Patrick did not want children of his own, not necessarily. He loved John and Elizabeth. But that did not give him the desire to have some of his own. Okay if he happened to be involved with a woman who was desperate to have a couple then he would obviously have to consider the matter very seriously indeed, but if left to his own devices no, no. And tie that in with the lurking wish to become vegetarian. How does it get tied in but. Fair enough; just perhaps that there are incredibly fucking massive feeding problems in the world at this actual moment in the movement of things insofar as toty wee weans are dying of starvation so that if meat-eaters of the wealthy West all stopped and cut out such obscene extravaganzas like feeding herds of animals on stuff that would stop these weans, that would halt

No more meat.

Horrendous.

And yet it was not possible to say such a thing to Gavin and Nicola – maybe Nicola but not Gavin. Gavin would just tell you to fuck off. Quite right and all. No it's not. But you could speak to Nicola. Whereas you couldnt speak to him. Nicola would listen. She had some respect for Patrick's viewpoint whereas his brother didni, not really. But fuck sake did he have any respect for Gavin's viewpoint!

Is that the problem. No. That is not the problem. Whither it is nobler in the mind to suffer the slings and the arrows. Shakespeare. What can we say of him. Well, here you have a chap who is an actor turned playwright. Okay? Fine. Cheerio.

One sits and one says nothing. The brother and the niece and the nephew, whose attention seems concentrated on the televised happenings in the land of fantasy. An old pal and former colleague of his believed the television was a device for people being watched instead of people watching; in other words while the poor old flagellants were gazing upon the magical events from the world of stage and screen there was an army of security folk taking notes on what was what in the world of the British living room. Patrick unscrewed the bottle and poured himself a minuscule whisky. That was why he wanted into computers before it was too late. He glanced at Gavin but Gavin was already shaking his head in anticipation of the offer. Patrick nodded. The whisky had a slightly sickening quality about it which could mean only one thing; that he had drunk a fair amount of the stuff yet remained totally sober, a sobersides, an old sobersides of a chap. If intoxicated the whisky would have tasted fine but in this condition it tasted only of a retchingness. A quick sip of super to drown it out. And that would do it. He pushed the drinks away. Nothing further. And maybe after the good and plentiful meal he would be fine for driving home; to be on the safe side he could sit on for an extra hour or so, just yapping maybe.

Who with.

Nicola.

It is fucking distinctly funny peculiar and most odd how come one's brother can sit with you and say fuck all. I mean it is absolutely fucking the dregs. What can be said about it. Fuck all. What did Wittgenstein have to say on the subject. Who wants to know. Me. Him and these brothers of his. In the name of the holies. One thing was for fucking definite: he couldni remain here forever. He needed his own wee house. He needed his own wee house and his own wee pair of pipes. Ye joking! Without these pipes his fucking life has yet to begin, it has yet to even begin.

Without his pair of pipes.

Patrick rose from the dining chair he had been sitting on throughout the afternoon and he stepped across to the armchair opposite Gavin, and he plonked himself down on it and he gave a mammoth grin at the kids, whose visual space he now occupied to about 15° or so. He had thought of something to say. He stuck each forefinger into either corner of his mouth and pulled apart his lips in an eye-catching manner. He grinned. Heh yous two kids, he said, I want to tell ye a story. It's about a pair of magical pipes. I was out walking about a week ago exactly from today and guess what I found, a pair of magical pipes.

A slight irritation from both, which they dutifully attempted to conceal; they were wanting to watch television

naw listen a minute, honest, it's quite interesting

while Gavin's face fixed stonily in that same direction.

So what actually happened was this: I was round the back of this building, down a very dark and shadowy lane, an eerie and dank-smelling lane with high moss-covered dykes that kept out the light, where owls were hooting and cats miaowing in a very controlled but semi-scary manner; you should've heard these damn owls and cats my fine friends!

naw, no kidding ye, it was quite scary; I mind at one minute I happened to look up, I just happened to look up, and there I saw this lithe grey cat stalking along the very top of the highest wall, its round eyes glistening because it was getting the glare of the moon high up there with its old pockmarked face going back thousands and thousands of years, and this cat, its hairs all bristling like thin wee jaggy spikes

and for one quiet, very very quiet and drawn-out, long, long, solitary solitary majestic moment in time, I thought like running, running fast, running away fast, getting away quick, quick quick quick, quick quick quick, quick quick quick quick quick quick quick!

Then the physically active bit here of the sudden leap off the armchair onto the settee and tickling the two of them in the bellies and they were roaring in laughter. Their gazes returned to the television screen immediately after that but only for a moment:

so, just along a bit down the lane I found these pipes; one was long and thin and the other yin wasni so long and it wasni so thin either, it was more like I dont know, just sort of a wee bit shorter and a wee bit thicker. Okay now what I did I just bent down a wee minute to see them the better, and looked this way and then looked that way, just in case people were watching maybe, a big bad security man from the government that would want to take ye away and put ye into prison!

but nobody was there

so what I did, I just bent down and lifted one up, because do you know this weans, I had a sudden wee think to myself that I wanted to play a tune! Patrick laughed aloud. He looked at the kids and shook his head, then laughed aloud again, but stopped it quickly in case it lasted forever.

Gavin was now gazing over, smiling, not falsely.

Naw kids I'm no kidding, it was an urge, like a magic spell had befallen me. It was as if these two pipes themselves were calling out to me to come on and play me come on and play me, so I lifted one up and what I did I just, okay, blew into it, and out came this long and deep sound that made me think of scores and scores of years, and generations and generations and generations of people all down through the ages, and this tune – not exactly a tune, more of a sound, the one kind of long sound that you could occasionally just pause from doing, then start again as if ye hadni stopped at all except when you came to the very end of it you would know about the pauses you did, they would all be a part of it. It was really really beautiful weans and it made me think of magic. I'm no kidding ye on. Magic. These pipes had something special about them and it was a magical something. So do ye know what I did next?

wide eyes. Elizabeth with her thumb in her mouth and John with his hands holding his chin. And Gavin smiling, watching them both.

Naw I'm no kidding ye, what I did I actually lifted them both up off the ground and after I played them I smuggled them away home with me. And that's where they're lying right at this very minute in time, this very second in the universe, in my parlour, that selfsame old parlour where yous pair of weans always sit whenever yous come up to visit your stupit auld uncle Patrick MacDoyle.

Elizabeth and John smiled.

Naw but I'm being serious. The two pipes are in my parlour. And I've painted them colours. Says you what colours! Well I'll tell ye so just be quiet. Bright silver and red and black. All shiny. And whenever I get down in the dumps I just sit back and play these pipes and I get cheered up. I dont always get the tunes right but sometimes I do and it sounds great. Well it sounds great to me; I dont know if it sounds great to anybody else – or is that just being stupit and sentimacbloodymental!

What like is the pipes? asked John.

They're just ordinary. They're round and they're made out of a kind of thick cardboard stuff. And what I do ye see I cover one end up with my hand and and then when I'm blowing into the other end I just let my hand off at the bottom end a wee minute and so the air comes out.

Is it real magic but? John asked.

Just listen to this: I let my hand off the bottom end for one wee minute and the air comes out making a sound. And I've got to really concentrate; I've got to really concentrate really really hard; I just

[299]

close my eyes and I switch off my ears and then what I do I just put the brakes onto my brains so they seize up and lie still for a wee minute, and then everything's fine, all fine, and I start – and I dont know when I've started, it's just as if it's magic. Honest, I'm no kidding ye.

The weans continued to watch him and he smiled, he winked; then he leant back on the armchair; they smiled. When they knew he had definitely finished they gave their attention back to the television screen. But it had been well worth it and Patrick felt very happy; he would like to have shut his eyes and dozed off but this was not his place and it would not have been a good thing to do and also something at the back of his mind saying: fucking watch yourself Doyle or the game's a bogey! What did that mean? It meant he better fucking watch himself or the game was a fucking bogey. Okay.

Gavin had looked at him.

No signs of a job? said Pat.

Eh naw, no really.

Nothing doing then?

Naw eh no that I know of. Gavin lifted down the cigarette packet, extracted one and got it alight. No that ye have to bother looking anyway, he said, the way things are in this place if there *is* anything going there's aye somebody tells ye. Rumours are on the go all the time.

And nothing in the papers?

Ye kidding! Gavin smiled; he was gazing at the screen, dragging slowly on the cigarette. Plus the fact when you do get the paper you know every other able body in Glasgow's looking at the same time. Be better in the summer once the building game starts proper. Then I'll really start worrying if I canni find something.

You think it'll pick up then?

Bound to.

Pat nodded.

Gavin glanced at him: You dont agree?

Ah well ye never know right enough.

So you dont think it will?

Eh . . . do you?

Gavin frowned; and grinned: I asked you first.

Aye but I'm biased as ye know; I hate Greatbritain. It was fine before all these selfish and greedy aristocratic capitalist mankindhating landowners started dividing things up between them and saying where ye could walk and where ye couldni walk – it was fine up till then, before these effing boundaries roped you in, when it was just a big chunk of stuff you could just set out and do what you liked on.

Such as?

Such as – such as build yourself a mud hut and feed your effing chickens! Patrick smiled. Course I'm talking about thirty thousand years BC. Seriously but, maybe; maybe things will improve. I dont know. You'll have a better idea than me. Do you think things'll improve?

Gavin shrugged.

I'm just no over-confident. I think jobs are a thing of the past in this country, even in the building game.

So what're you chucking yours in for? Gavin coughed slightly, and he coughed again, then he put his arm back round Elizabeth's shoulders. She looked as if she was about to close her eyes.

Eh . . . I dont like being forced into things. Plus them transferring me to a different school just when I feel in some ways as if I'm getting used to things. If they would leave me to get on with things myself! You know me brother, I dont like being told what to do!

Gavin nodded.

I dont like being forced to live my life a certain way.

. . .

I dont.

. . .

I prefer to make up my own mind.

Mm.

Life's too short to let people push you about all the time.

Gavin nodded. He inhaled on the cigarette and exhaled the smoke towards the television screen, away from Elizabeth.

That's what I think anyway.

Aye . . . Gavin tapped ash onto the ashtray and Patrick squinted at the television screen. Gavin said, So you're getting pushed about?

[301]

Aye.

Mm.

I am.

I believe ye. Gavin nodded and his tongue flicked out his mouth and licked his lips; he took one more drag on the cigarette and nipped the burning ash into the ashtray, laid the good piece down on the tiled fireplace. He said to John. Away and see when tea'll be ready!

John did so at once, leaving the door wide open, then the thump thump thump as he raced back . . . Mummy says she shouted a wee minute ago! Dinner's on the table waiting! He laughed and rushed back to the kitchenette.

After a moment Gavin said, I never heard her did you? He got to his feet with Elizabeth clinging onto him and he hoisted her up so that she was leaning her head against his neck with her arms roundabout him. She gazed at Patrick as he followed them out of the living room and across to the kitchenette.

Nicola was eating. She was sitting at the small three-sided table that was affixed to the wall. The two places beside her had been set for the children. She said to Gavin: I thought you and Pat would prefer to eat in the room.

We could've set the table for everybody, he replied.

Nicola nodded. He had seated Elizabeth on her stool and John was up seated on his and already digging in with his knife and fork. Gavin passed a plate of food to Pat.

Thanks for the eh . . . Patrick said to Nicola.

Dont be daft, she said.

The two men returned to the room without speaking. Then Gavin returned to the kitchenette. He was gone almost five minutes. Patrick cleared the cans and remaining bottles from the dining table, stacking them on the floor. Gavin came back. He lifted his plate, balanced it on his lap and ate while watching the television. It was the news showing and Patrick glanced at it too. A couple of items were of interest and the subject of the Centralamerican assassination recurred. At one stage he was set to comment but changed his mind. Gavin was obviously not in the mood for conversation. And politics was the last subject on Earth; especially if it called for a dialogue with the brother on a basis of equality. Gavin didnt wish to speak to his young brother, especially on a basis of equality. His young brother had a good sort of middle-class job and a good sort of middle-classish wage whereas he had fuck all. His young brother could make all the comments and criticisms he had a mind to, then walk along to the licensed grocer and buy a bottle of whisky and a dozen cans of superlager – just about the most expensive lager in the entire premises. So what was the point in talking to him, to somebody like him.

And that was precisely the case. Patrick was somebody like himself. It didni actually matter a fuck that he was Pat Doyle a young brother. He was not an individual. So what right did he have to be treated as such. None. He had no rights at all. He had sold his rights for a wheen of pennies, a large wheen of pennies. Alison was correct after all with that Judas Iscariot patter, it was just that Patrick had misunderstood her context. And Gavin was correct to think as he did. Good teacher or bad teacher it made no difference. He was an article that was corrupt. He was representative of corruption, representative of a corrupt and repressive society which operated nicely and efficiently as an effect of the liberal machinations of such as himself, corruptio optimi pessima, not that he was approaching the best but just a person who had certain tools of the higher-educational processes at his command yet persisted in representing a social order that was not good and was not beneficent to those who have nothing. What right did he have to be treated differently to any member of the fucking government or polis or the fucking law courts in general who sentence you to prison. Doyle had sold his rights.

There was not an answer. It was most depressing. Gavin had never asked him the question of course. But only because he loved Pat. Only because he felt pity for him. He knew there was not any answer that the young brother could make. Look at the food on the plate. He did not have an answer to give. Most depressing. Most depressing. Tasty food as well it was nice ox liver and mashed potatoes and carrots and cabbage. Very very tasty indeed, just the occasional splash of gravy onto his trousers if a bit of something fell off his fork. It was most depressing. He did not know what to do. Not any longer, he just didni know. He didni know what was right and what was not right, what was wrong and what was not wrong that being not wrong, that being right

[303]

He did not know what to do. An answer could be to walk out on it all, to get away completely and get the tonsils straightened out. Get the tonsils straightened out. The idea of heading across the channel to France and driving on down south via the Basque country and Spain, maybe stopping off to see Eric in Anglia. There was a screech of brakes outside and Pat was up on his feet and over to the window immediately but much of his vision was obscured because of the fucking veranda. But his motor was okay whatever it was. He could just see the rear bumper of a van in the middle of the street, not all that far from his but absolutely nothing to do with it. Possibly a dog or cat had dashed out and forced the guy or woman to slam on the emergency brakes. The van moved off. Patrick stared but could see nothing. That bad habit cats have of hiding up the insides of a mudguard and then dashing out for no apparent reason.

Gavin was looking across.

Nothing – no that I can see anyway.

A wee boy got knocked down last week, did you hear? He's still in intensive care. It was a paki that was driving.

Pardon?

A wee boy got knocked down, it was a paki that was driving the car.

The car that knocked down the wee boy?

Aye. Gavin had stopped eating. He placed the plate in beneath his chair, reached for a cigarette.

Patrick had stopped eating as well because his stomach had dropped out and what he had taken already was close to being on the carpet because this was just so bad it was barely possible to say a word but that it had to be said and faced up to. He stared at his big brother. His big brother was staring at the screen and he was fucking poised there what a challenge, knowing fine well what he had done, fucking bastard. Patrick breathed out and shut his eyelids but not to screw them up, seeing the redness of the interior lids, the blood no doubt. He was not going to carry on with any of this sort of shite. His stomach, the insides, were just fucking it's amazing, amazing

where's the whisky. But I dont want a whisky with that evil bastard because this is evil this is the existence of pure evil, a putrefication, a putrefaction of the spirit, the spirit of life but I dont feel like crying I feel like fucking battering but who the fuck to batter, who do I batter,

who do I kill

I dont know whom to kill. I dont want to kill my brother not only because he's my brother but because he's a person and not only that but he is a person who is in ignorance. He is my brother who is in ignorance. I dont want to kill him. And I dont want to cry. I dont want to kill myself, I dont want that. I may want to be dead but that's another question; a different form of questioning, a logic from another world.

Is it fuck a logic from another world it's a logic from the same fucking world and you've just got to find that method which lassos the bastard.

So okay; let us not depart. Let us all be together. Let us all be at one where to be at one is to be at peace, beyond conflict, a reconciliation of opposing forces.

What is the connection between being a man who is a Pakistani who has knocked down the wee boy who is now in intensive care o brother that the relationship includes you and me and your kids plus Nicola and the existence of maw and da and the ancestors, erupting their way out of the sewage system, when some form of fucking enlightenment, some form of fucking enlightenment

Let us just for fuck sake go up and visit the wee boy in intensive care and then go and visit the guy that was driving the car that knocked him down: let us just do that as a beginning. Me and you o brother ya bastard except that we cannot talk, as a beginning. Let us talk. Even just as a beginning. What is that. There isni a beginning. There is no beginning. You cannot discover a beginning. No beginning exists. There arent any at all. There are two blokes in quicksand with cudgels belaying each other. There are two blokes one of whom is the ignorant Gavin Doyle from Cadder man and the other the ignorant or not ignorant man who may or may not be from Pakistan.

Meanwhile the wee boy is in intensive care.

He is the beginning. And after that there isnt anything. I dont matter and you dont matter. Nobody else matters. Not even the wee boy's parents. None of us matters at all. Fucking ignorance and warped brains and diverse corrupting forces in the name of fucking shit and fucking swamping keech, keech and fucking shite and soiled semen and blood that is congealed.

Fine. Fine. I dont have any doubts. My doubts ceased a long while ago. I am fine. I am in instrument of all that is fine and far-sighted. I receive almost twice as much of the provender of survival as do my brother and sister-in-law and nephew and niece all rolled up into one neat bundle. And we are all to be at one, yes, at peace, reconciled, fully. Says who? Says me. I say it. I say to my big brother, dont for fuck sake do what you are doing but listen to me as an equal and let us talk to each other, and in that talking we shall be finding the way ahead.

What a pile of fucking shite! What a pile of absolute gibbers! The very idea that such forms of conflict can be so resolved! This is a straight bourgeois intellectual wank. These liberal fucking excesses taken to the very limits of fucking hyping hypocritical tollie.

Now we know the truth. There is only one way to go

home; home to one's own house and draw the curtains and set yourself down and out with the pipes

What would Hölderlin do under such circumstances? Would he re-read one of Diotima's letters?

What in the name of fuck does Hölderlin

Does Hölderlin. Does Hölderlin what. The poor guy. He's simply a dead fellow who was involved with this married woman who 'belonged' in the arms of another, viz. her man, the husband. So what? So fucking what. He was a good bloke and he went mad, supposedly. Only supposedly? Well let us say yes for the time being I mean to all extents and purposes he did go mad, not so much mad as suffering a prolonged mental breakdown, being no longer able to exist as a tutor or whatever, and this bloke called Sinclair helped him, and then a home was found for him in with this carpenter and his family, and he stayed there for the next thirty odd years.

It matters. That's all. It fucking matters. In relation to what? In juxtaposition to which? Go and fuck yourself. Go and have a fucking wank in the bathroom. Go and have a fucking wank in your single man's bed. Go and spill your fucking oneness ya fucking idiot.

No.

No no.

No no no.

What's up, are you not okay?

Aye you're fucking right I'm not okay. What could fucking be more not okay than this. Fucking big brother there in the corner like a fucking overgrown ham sandwich. An overgrown ham sandwich, what does that mean. He's actually quite skinny. Blame his feyther, our auld man who is on his third stroke and still smokes like a chimney behind the back of his wife the good maw, he smokes behind her back as though she was the sheriff of Dodge City. Why is Nicola ben the kitchenette? Why is Gavin married to Nicola when Patrick is not. If Patrick had met her first he would have married her. He would have got on well with her. They get on together. They can have good conversations. What is Alison doing just now. Where was she at dinnertime? Did she go for a bloody walk with Desmond and Joe and that other guy? Is it possible to phone and ask her if she could come out and they could have a quiet shandy in a peaceful pub. Is it possible she would wish to hear from him. Is it best that he does fuck all. Is it best he just does as she asked in other words fuck all, she asked him to do fuck all, is that what he is best to do, fuck all, like she asked, just fuck all, that is what she asked him to do. Is it best, is it best, that he does fuck all and relaxes and acts like an adult male of the human species and just does what he is supposed to i.e. fuck all.

I just cant relate to you when ye say something like that; to me it's just racist.

What? Gavin's frown.

What you said there, a wee minute ago, about a paki knocking that wee boy down I mean I dont understand at all what bloody fucking difference it makes if it was a paki or it wasnt a paki. Even using that word, paki, I mean it isnt a word it's just a bloody derogatory racist bloody term. If ye mean a guy that was from fucking Pakistan ye should say so.

I'm no wanting to have a fight with you.

I dont want to have a fight with you either.

Then dont act it.

I'm no acting it.

Just let's leave it.

. . .

. . .

I think it's best I go.

You can suit yourself what ye do.

I think you're actually trying to tell me something.

. . .

. . .

. . .

I think you're actually trying to tell me you want me to leave.

That's right.

You're wanting me to leave?

Aye.

Okay. Fine. Patrick laid down his knife and his fork.

Nicola and the kids were in the kitchenette. Patrick waited a short while before opening the door. That's me away home now, he said, see you all soon!

Cheerio Uncle Pat, said John and Elizabeth.

Nicola just looked at him.

So I'll see ye a week on Saturday is that right? that wee party or whatever it was.

You'll definitely come?

Of course.

Well for a start get the date properly fixed in that skull of yours! it's *this* Saturday night coming.

Is it?

Yes. Half-past eight.

Just as well I mentioned it then eh!

You wont come.

Aye I will.

Bring somebody with ye.

Could I?

Of course.

Patrick nodded. He winked at Elizabeth who was watching him and making funny faces. I could just take you Elizabeth, eh! You could be my girlfriend!

I'm serious Pat; bring that lassie you mentioned.

He didnt reply.

Och I know you, she said, you'll no come; you'll find some excuse!

I wont. Honest. And by the way eh, that carry-out Nicola, it was me that bought it; the lot, the bottle of whisky and all the cans. Naw I mean just in case you might be thinking Gavin was responsible or something; it was definitely just me myself.

I know it was. But the point wasni to do with that it was to do with getting the bloody electricity cut off. Nicola gazed at John, and she said, We're well past the final notice now and they've threatened us, and we canni take the risk by sending it by the post or even paying it in a post office. We've got to go right in and do it at one of their showrooms.

What if I paid it the morrow at dinnertime I mean if you give me the bill and the money and that, I could get away at dinnertime and pay it.

Thanks but . . .

Thanks but no thanks.

No, it's just that Gavin's going to do it. How's school these days?

That's usually what you say to a wean and I am not a wean, there again but, coelebs quid agam which is latin for something like here I am a single man, what else am I to do. Which isni really relevant at all. In answer to your question Nicola; school is lousy. They're transferring me to a new yin without even so much as a by-your-leave – which isni quite true. But that's the way of things, that's how things are; things are like that these days, ever since they hanged James Wilson, Andrew Hardie and John Baird back in 1820; that's when the Greatbritish Ruling Class perfected their policing system, the finest the world has ever known. They've been refining it ever since. I'm one of their less subtle weapons.

Heavy stuff.

Patrick smiled.

Are ye no waiting for a cup of tea?

Ah for god sake come on, a cup of tea wont kill me.

Nicola waved her hand at John: Give Uncle Pat your stool.

I'm just feeling a bit jittery just now . . . He lifted the stool and examined it before sitting down – in case there was spilled food.

Is it all big children in your school? asked John.

Aye. They're actually all young adults in the school I go to. Their ages go from maybe eleven up to eighteen. They can legally get married and have weans of their own and still be there. One of the lassies in my class has got a wee baby; it's a wee girl and it's called Deborah. Are you listening Elizabeth?

Elizabeth was still footering with her liver and vegetables. Nicola was at the oven now and pouring tea. She was slightly smaller than Alison, around 5′4″ and it was maybe a cliché to talk about her strength but fuck it she had it, a strength. Patrick would love to have been married to her fucking beautiful besides anything else, fucking beautiful beautiful woman, her whole self.

Do the boys play football in your school as well?

Yeh they do, aye. The teacher that takes them used to be a football player and he played for Stirling Albion and also an English team called Carlisle. You heard of them?

John nodded. Nicola gave him a biscuit, offered Pat one which he accepted. John said, Sure daddy was a good football player?

Will you take him his tea ben and give Uncle Pat a bit of peace, said Nicola.

Aye but sure he was? John said.

I canni answer your question. It's the kind of one I dont like ya wee pest ye; that's because it doesni leave me anything to say! Pat winked at Elizabeth who was watching him instead of eating, or maybe using watching him as an excuse for not eating. He said to John: But these questions are the best questions; if ye keep asking them you'll be fine.

When the boy left the kitchenette Patrick drank his tea swiftly. I better hit the road Nicola . . .

Are you sure?

Me and Gavin had a wee bit of a eh contretemps.

No again.

Uch it wasni bad I mean it was just . . . he shrugged.

So we wont see you on Saturday then?

Aw naw, not necessarily.

Nicola continued to look at him. Then she said, I found somebody to take that puppy. Mind me telling you about it?

Aye christ of course I do.

A woman at the nursery knows an old woman she thinks might want it; and if she doesni she's just going to take it herself, to add to her collection! She's already got three cats.

Good god.

She's a real animal lover. She's wanting a shift to a ground floor so's she can get a garden. Nicola chuckled: She says she's gonni start keeping hens.

Hens in Cadder; great. Amazing. You forget there's folk like that, dont ye. The way some of them love animals, it's really terrific, smashing, you feel like giving them a kiss.

The animals or the people?

Both.

Nicola laughed abruptly. Her head craned forwards, chin touching the top of her chest; she closed her eyes. Patrick was wanting to place his hand on the back of her neck because he looked upon her as a sister and not just a sister-in-law. He loved her and he wanted to comfort her because she didni look all that fine at the moment, now that he had come to actually look at her, she wasnt looking that fine.

It was a good meal, he said.

Gavin made it.

Aw. He says you did it, he just prepared the ingredients.

It's no true.

It was some pot of soup he gave us earlier.

He's a good cook, he's better than me – when he can be bothered, but he canni always be bothered. Pat . . . Nicola sat upright; she had her hands now clasped in her lap . . . I know you're sick of hearing this but you should keep in contact more with people. I wish you'd make a regular date to come here for your tea. Also your parents, your mum and dad – they worry about ye.

Och they're parents. That's what parents are by definition, those who worry. They're never done going in to see the headmaster about

[311]

the stupidest things. Draughty corridors. Somebody was up complaining about that recently!

Elizabeth was watching him. He had been looking in her direction while talking although he had not been aware of it until now. And she said to Nicola: Mummy, can I go and watch telly?

She nodded. She said to Pat: And if ye came here once a week for your tea? Why dont you do that? Just one night a week. Even once a fortnight.

Thanks, it's appreciated.

But you're not committing yourself.

Pardon?

Some commitments are good ye know. They can be good.

In what way?

Because they're commitments. They can be good for folk.

I just dont understand how, I mean how they're good.

Dont be silly Pat.

I'm no being silly. I have got commitments already: that's the bloody problem. What do you think teaching is, it's a commitment. Unless ye just think of it as a job, okay, fair enough. What about you, your own commitments, your family and all that, do you keep in touch with them all the time?

Pat, I'm a married woman, a mother; my life's full of commitments – I dont have anything else but commitments.

That's like routines the way you're talking.

Of course.

Is that what you mean by commitments; routines?

Nicola didnt answer.

If that's what ye mean by commitments . . . Pat shrugged.

It's no what I mean at all. But routines do come into it. Although they're no the same.

Glad to hear it! He smiled.

She looked at him.

There's nothing worse than routines; commitments are something else.

I know what commitments are Pat.

He nodded. When Nicola looked away from him he said, Naw Nicola sorry, I was just meaning the way so many folk mix the two things up, they think they're committed to something and they areni at all, it's just a bloody routine. I know you know the difference Nicola, I'm sorry.

I'm no one of your pupils.

Patrick smiled. Are you and Gavin fighting the now as well?

How did ye guess. We're just too much in each other's company. It's always better if one of us is away and then comes back. A month ago he got a couple of days work at his trade through a pal he used to work beside and it was good, it was nice when he came home. It's just he can be a huffy so-and-so at times. He is. You dont get a word out him for days at a stretch.

It runs in the family, except me and him are different in the sense that you canni stop me talking. I just talk all the time. The weans in the class canni get a word in edgeways. Hey Nicola your two are looking good. They're growing. John's bloody sprouting! How is he in school?

Cheeky.

Pat laughed. Cheeky's good. And the wee yin, how's she? ach she's astute – even at four years auld ye can see she's got it, and she gets it from you.

What're you talking about!

Naw I just mean christ Nicola ye *know* what I'm talking about, really, it's to do with the quiet way she has but ye know she's taking heed of every precise detail, every precise detail. Maybe it has to do with an essential difference between the sexes.

Well we're no as cheeky.

Patrick nodded, but he was not sure if she was being sarcastic. He stared at his cup.

There's more in the pot.

Aye . . . he got up and refilled his cup and he topped up Nicola's when she held the cup to him. I think I've had four whiskies, two superlagers and two bottles of big Arthur's homebrew; two-and-a-half bowls of soup and a couple of slices of bread, a plateful of liver and potatoes and now two cups of tea, and a biscuit. He frowned: How in the name of the holies can the belly stand such carnage!

Nicola chuckled, covering her face with her hand for a moment.

Naw, when you think about it! Hey have ye ever heard of the

Pythagoreans at all? I mean you know auld bloody Pythagoras and his theorem?

The Pythagoras Theorem. Yeh.

Aye but he was more than that – if he was a he, the whole thing's so dense he might've been a she; almost nothing's known about him at all, a genuine legendary figure – he had a lot of followers and amongst other things they put together a list of dos and donts, many of which concerned the eating of grub. For example, they wouldnt eat beans. They also abstained from the flesh of dead animals.

Vegetarians.

Vegetarians. Patrick frowned. You're dead right. I had forgotten that. The Pythagoreans were vegefuckingtarians. That's me finished with them and their harmony. And they can shove their transmigration up their bums! Cause that as well was something about them that was quite interesting, they believed in the transmigration of souls. Interesting in terms of after-lives. I was wanting to get these second-yearers of mine onto that as a wee bit of detection work. What was I going to say anyway? In fact I think it was to do with farting and beans and common sense, being full of wind. Just like me! But eh there's another interesting link as well and that's the Manicheans who used to actually stuff their kids so full of vegetables that many of them died . . . Pat smiled at Nicola. I'm actually bloody gibbering. A bag of wind. All teachers are bags of wind. They should stick us all into these black plastic bags and tie up the ends and then wait for a strong gale force wind to be blowing and fling us all off the top storey of the Red Road flats. Have you ever been at the top of the Red Road flats, beautiful, looking right down the Clyde Valley and seeing Goat Fell across in Arran?

The Red Road flats is a terrible place to live.

Aw I know.

Are you going to be driving home?

Pardon?

She smiled. She studied the cup she was holding.

Pat waited for a few seconds before speaking. What I meant there about Elizabeth is she's got a sense of peace. John has it as well right enough but I think she has it more. It's a real sense of peace.

Pat. Women have to listen more than men, that's why they've

got a sense of peace as you call it; they're used to listening – that's what they have to do all the time, listen to men talking. Yet to hear them you'd think it was us did it. And not only listen to them, women have to watch them all the time as well, they've got to study their moods, they've got to see it's alright to speak if this is the bloody time you can ask the question or no, is it the wrong time and you'll have to wait, because half the time men just areni willing to listen to something if they dont want to hear it, it gets ye down. I canni be annoyed with it. I'm not criticising you Pat but I think you've got a glamourised view of women which is wrong, it really is wrong. The Red Road flats is an awful place to live. When I was at school in Balornock I had a friend and she had a cousin living there and her mother killed herself.

Pat was about to say something but he stopped.

Nicola said, It was an awful place to live; it still is.

I know.

Well okay Pat but how're you no saying that instead of talking about the bloody view ye get down the Firth of Clyde! It's the same as driving. Gavin told me you were thinking of driving home, but you're no fit. You'll take your car out there and you'll kill somebody, or you'll get killed yourself.

I'm actually okay Nicola.

You're not okay at all. Take the bus.

I'm totally sober.

Totally sober. How can ye be with what you've had to drink?

Aye but Nicola I took it over a period of time and plus I've had the grub.

You've slurred your words.

. . .

You have.

Naw I've no.

Yes you have Pat. Since we've been talking the gether.

I've slurred my words?

Yes, you've slurred your words.

He nodded.

Nicola glanced about her, and got her black handbag from the floor; she brought out her cigarettes and lighter and when she inhaled

smoke she coughed a very internalised sort of cough. Pat said:
Tobacco's a drug as well.

You dont kill people by doing it.

Eh . . .

I hate drink.

I'm no gonni drive home.

It just destroys things.

What I'm saying I'll just leave the motor car. I'll take a bus . . .
Patrick smiled . . . This new guy in school, he was telling me he had
to make the decision about drinking and driving, an either/or case –
guess what he chose?

The car?

He sold the bloody car!

Nicola laughed.

Honest, I'm no kidding ye, he selt the bloody motor. That's
what I call free will and determination!

Nicola was smiling. You'll definitely take the bus?

Aye.

Gavin was actually worried ye know.

Was he?

Yeh. He was.

Ach! Pat shook his head. He glanced at Nicola: That lassie I've
told you about, she's married.

Married!

Aye.

Mm. That's no so good. I didni know she was married.

Patrick nodded. That's because I didni tell ye. The other thing is
as well, really, I've got to say: we're no . . . going the gether. If ever
we are gonni reach that stage then we definitely havent reached it at
the minute, just now, at this present moment. Although last night
was eh good in the sense that eh I suppose I really actually managed to
tell her, to actually let her know what was what, with me I mean.

Och Pat.

What? Och Pat what! Dont be sorry for me. Christ that's all I
bloody need – pity!

It's no pity.

It's just taken me a while. It's taken me a while, to work things out. I've had to work things out, that's all. I've just wanted to make sure things were right. Otherwise it wouldni have been fair.

Nicola nodded.

It just wouldni have been fair. I had to try and make sure. So that I knew, and I wasni gonni sort of upset everything, if I just kind of maybe I dont know, rushed in or something. It wouldni have been fair.

In what way Pat?

Aw just to do with her I mean. I dont actually care if eh well I do care – ah christ I'm no sure, I've got to work things out.

But then you're saying ye have worked things out! Nicola was smiling.

Aye. I'm just no sure. I'm just no sure. But I'm resigned. I'm resigned. Christ, I think that's what it is, I'm resigned. This is me realising it for the very first time. There ye are. That's one thing. That's the one thing. Patrick smiled: Did ye hear I was chucking the job?

I didni know it was decided.

Well aye, more or less, I'm gonni pack it in all the gether. Uch Nicola I'm just bloody sick of working for the government, I'm sick of doing my bit to suppress the weans, not unless the headmaster starts letting me wear a polis uniform – if I can wear one of them that's a different story. He grinned.

Nicola was not replying.

Okay? he said.

She dragged on her cigarette. Then she shrugged. I dont know Pat, ye just seem to make life difficult for yourself – but it runs in the family. And look at your dad! okay, I'm speaking as a smoker who's been trying to stop it for ages, but I mean he's actually smoking more now than ever he did. And it's so awful, so selfish. Your mum's going about in a daze and it's awful to see it, and it's because of him I mean she doesni know what time it is. It's because of him.

Aw Nicola.

No aw Nicola Pat ye dont go beyond three strokes. What the hell's he playing at? The next yin's the last.

Pat rubbed his eyes. He closed them.

Ye canni talk to Gavin about it either. As soon as I begin I know

I've to shut up. I know that he doesni want me to speak. He makes it quite plain. So it's up to him, and you, what yous do; yous're his sons. If ye want to tell him then ye can tell him.

Tell him what Nicola?

To stop killing himself, to take it easy, to give himself a chance. We've all got to go.

Och dont say that it's so bloody stupid and selfish, it's no worthy of you.

Sorry.

I'm so sick of men and their problems . . . She placed her cigarette down on the ashtray and folded her arms, her elbows on the edge of the table; she stared at the cigarette burning, the smoke rising. Even the idea of you giving up your job . . . But it's not my business.

Aye it is.

It's not. It's your business. It's nobody else's.

But Nicola it's the family's business that's the bloody problem. I mean I think I actually only became a teacher to suit the family. Do ye know that? I definitely only went to university to suit them. Sometimes I think I'm only actually alive to suit them!

. . .

He smiled.

That's a rotten thing to say.

He nodded. I think I'll go away for an extended period; leave Glasgow. I sometimes feel as if I'm no longer capable of doing things that are good, things that are not bad. He smiled. That's what I feel like. That's why I think I better get away.

She shook her head. I dont know what you're meaning.

No.

I dont Pat, I dont know what you're meaning.

I only mean . . . he covered his eyes then uncovered them and clasped his hands together. I only mean, he said, that I canni be sure of my influence. What time is it? He glanced at his wristwatch.

Your influence! Your influence is great! Look at John and Elizabeth! And that wee story ye told them! Gavin says it was really amazing! It was really amazing, that was what he says to me.

. . .

Pat, honest.

I canni handle it.

Pat, for goodness sake.

I dont know what to do – but I do know what to do, get a bus home.

Pat, you've just got to get things worked out for yourself. And stop acting like a wee boy! Nicola smiled.

I dont know what ye mean.

The way you're going on just now. Maybe all men are the same but. I get so sick of it, your moods, having to watch all the time not knowing when's the right moment to ask something. Even listening to you just now . . . all you're doing, complaining – if ye listen to yourself – complaining, that's all you're doing. Nicola smiled briefly and shook her head; she sighed and puffed on her cigarette. I dont understand ye. You're clever and you've got a good well-paid job. You've only got yourself to look after. You can do whatever ye want. If ye dont like something ye can just get up and leave. You're free. And yet you're still no satisfied. That's what I think's wrong. But that's always how things are: the ones that want something never get it and the ones that get it areni satisfied, they just want something else. She flicked ash at the ashtray.

After a moment Pat said, Aye but Nicola what you're asking, you're asking me no to think. That's what you're asking. And I dont think ye can do that. There's too much at stake. I'm clear about that I mean christ that's one thing, that's one thing I'm clear about. Because I've got a job doesni mean I have to stick it because people dont have a job I mean that's exactly what the system wants off ye; the last thing it wants is folk making their own decisions about working or not working and taking matters into their own hands, cause then the next thing ye know they'll be acting as if they're masters of their own fate and the next step on from there's making social change, structural change. Revolutions dont come, you've got to make them happen yourself. And once people start making their own decisions, well, that's when things might start to happen. At long last – because they dont feel: O I've got a job and they haveni so I better look after it. I mean that's crazy, it's mental, as a way of thinking, a stupit logic, totally mad.

Nicola sighed. I dont accept what you're saying.

Look at my da then right, it's no just because he smokes and likes a drink he's ended up with three bloody heart attacks christ Nicola he's been working in that crazy job for fucking donkeys' years and worrying himself sick about it. Bloody job! It's a joke too! It's a joke-job. Most working-class jobs are the same, they're jokes. Joke-jobs. Just a fucking joke! Patrick laughed briefly. He closed his eyes.

Are you as bitter as ye sound?

What do ye mean?

Ye sound so awful bitter Pat.

O aye well I am, I am bitter, awful bitter. Are you no?

Me?

Are you no awful bitter? I mean I canni understand people who arent awful bitter. I aye think there's something up with them, that there must be something up with them; as if maybe they've never thought things out, otherwise they'd bound to be bitter. It's like being black in Northamerica, if ye meet another black person who isni bitter. I think if it was me I'd be amazed and I'd just think well here's another silly bastard who's never sat down and thought about slavery and the way people are still getting totally fucked across there and even so much worse in places like fucking South Africa or whatever. That's the way I feel here. I feel christ almighty look at the way my family's been treated for the past few hundred years and my fucking belly drops out and I get so fucking angry just at the thought ye think ye might end up collapsing. I wish da had got his strokes because he was in an apoplectic rage . . . Patrick grinned. He glanced at the door and at the clear-faced clock on the wall. Nicola not saying a word.

What I try and do, he said, in the classroom I mean, is just make the weans angry. And other folk as well; I try and make them angry. That includes relations!

Nicola was still saying nothing.

Because making them angry's a start. That's something. Even just making them angry. I was trying to make big Arthur angry earlier on. I didni really succeed. I was trying to make him angry, I didni succeed. I have a lot of failures. My failure rate is quite high. I get reminders about it at school. I get subtle tellings off. But I dont care, ha ha ha. Naw but seriously, I dont. I really do not care one way or the other. Ach.

Pat covered his face with his hands and he sighed, feeling the muscles at the back of his neck. All I seem to do is talk. He rubbed his hands together, the slight stickiness, dampness. Funny thing is too, he said, this past wee while back I've been starting to feel quite okay again. And I feel as I haveni been feeling quite okay for bloody years. If I have I dont bloody remember. Maybe I was and just wasni aware of it. Maybe ye can be happy without knowing it. Maybe as soon as ye start knowing it that's you stopped being it. Straight existential psychology I suppose. It's hopeless if ye reflect too much on yourself.

The door clicked open.

Gavin.

The position Pat was sitting he couldnt see him properly. But he could see Nicola glance at him and in the glance were a mixture of smile and question and the question was clearly a challenge.

The kitchenette was a narrow wee space; both Nicola and Patrick had to lean over the edge of table to allow him past to the sink, where he emptied the dregs from the teapot down the drain. He rinsed the pot out under the cold tap. I'm making a fresh lot, he said, anybody interested?

Aye! Patrick smiled.

Gavin said: I never heard the front door go so I figured ye still had to be here!

Ye figured right brother.

But, I thought ye had maybe crept into the weans' room for a kip.

Thanks mucker!

Well, I seem to mind ye performing such a trick in the past.

That Hogmanay! replied Nicola. We thought he had wandered off, then somebody saw a pair of feet sticking out under all the coats!

A downright lie! Imagine saying that about your poor auld brother-in-law who canni even fight back, because he's a bad bloody fighter! Pat grinned. Heh Gavin, did ye ever tell this wife of yours about that experience ye had as a boy? when ye smoked your first joint?

Eh . . .

What one's that? asked Nicola.

Ach it wasni really anything, just the usual kind of experiment ye do.

Come on, said Pat, what about the big bloody fire! That was like something out of I dont know what. Plus these stupit bloody questions ye started asking the cops! Crazy.

Gavin smiled to Nicola. It was the time we had just moved away from the Vernon Street house we used to live in.

The Vernon Street house. That was your favourite.

Gavin nodded. Aye, he said; and he said to Pat: Did you like the Vernon Street house?

Well I did, but it was different for me I think, being that bit younger. I dont think my memories of the place are as pleasant as yours obviously are.

It was the neighbours you liked though . . . said Nicola to Gavin.

Eh well aye although mainly it was just I think the general atmosphere. He grinned suddenly and said to Pat: Mind auld Tony Ferguson? Gavin laughed. Him and the auld man went mental on the drink sometimes but we usually wound up getting good parties cause of it. Mind Pat?

Aye, said Pat. But what about Charlie Murray! That 'disgusting wee man'!

Charlie Murray!

He was a disgusting wee man, replied Nicola: Your mother's quite right.

Ach! Gavin grinned.

Aye it's okay for yous but I wouldni have left the kids in the same room as him.

Ach come on Nicola!

I'm serious Gavin.

Gavin looked at her. Then he smiled. The time I mind best was the one they all broke into the betting shop. Crazy. I mean christ they must've been expecting to find all the takings lying in the till! Eh? as if the bookie was gonni just leave his dough lying! Gavin laughed and shook his head. But they were all pished. I mind it well, me and a couple of mates were standing there at the corner of Bilsland Drive and we saw this wee team heading out from the boozer. It was the way they were walking, we thought there was gonni be a battle. The Caber Feidh it was, that was where they drank. Auld Tony was leading the way. He used to go to town in a fight. Some reputation he had. So that just made us the more sure it was a battle. So we followed, and then they all skipped down a close so we crossed the road and skipped down the next yin along and then we crossed the backcourt after them. It was dark, after ten o'clock . . . Gavin chuckled. They were all banging into each other and then telling each other to shut up. Sshhh they were going! Ssshhhhh! It was comical! What age was I I must've been about fifteen or something.

Pat laughed. What night was it?

I dont know. Friday I think but maybe no, maybe it was through the week – if they were all skint I mean.

Where was I at the time I wonder . . . Pat smiled. If it was a Friday I must've been at the bloody BB! You wereni there because you'd got flung out! Did he ever tell ye that Nicola, your man there, how he got flung out the bloody BB!

Nicola nodded. Often.

Often, said Pat, grinning.

No that often, replied Gavin.

On with the yarn, said Pat, and he rubbed his hands together with a smack.

Naw, said Gavin, but ye could hear them a mile away . . . Gavin chuckled. Them all telling each other to be quiet. And they would've heard them down at Gairbraid Polis Office if they had been paying attention! Ssshh they were going, sshhhh!! Wee Charlie Murray was bloody moroculous – blitzed! I think they were bloody having to carry him. And he was singing away! Mind that voice he had! A bloody coalman! Anyhow but I mean ye know the crack, they had it planned to go in through the floor of the first storey flat, it was lying empty at the time. They actually got as far as lifting the floorboards at one corner but christ, they were so amateurish. That is what I remember feeling most of all. I couldni bloody believe it! They didni even bother keeping a lookout down at the foot of the close! They just bloody battered on regardless.

The drink talking, said Pat.

[323]

The drink talking, said Gavin. But it did look like it was the first time they had ever tried to screw anywhere in their life.

Probably was, said Pat.

Probably was, aye. But it was embarrassing. In front of Jackie and Dunky. It was embarrassing. I mean their das werent there, just mine, and all his daft mates! Gavin shook his head and laughed briefly.

But it shouldnt be embarrassing, said Nicola.

Well it was.

It would be, said Pat, I can understand that.

Up to a point, replied Nicola, alright.

Gavin shrugged. Then he said, You're talking about your da remember, no knowing how to go about screwing a bookie shop; what I mean, no even knowing there's gonni be nothing there!

Uch the bevy was talking, said Pat.

Aye. Ah it was funny but! Gavin smiled. Hilarious! They still talk about it down at the Drive.

Pat said, I find stories like that really sad. No depressing – sad.

Aye, said Gavin.

Nicola said, How come?

Uch I dont know . . . just maybe to do with a world that's past, over and done with, gone and never to return. I'm no saying there was anything good about it especially, I just think it's a bit sad, to think of it all.

Jackie MacDonald was with me that night. He got killed. Mind? Fell off a pylon.

Aye, that's right. Who else was there?

Just wee Dunky – Ian Duncan.

Christ that's a name from the past. What's he doing these days?

Dont know. No seen him for years.

How did the boy fall off the pylon Gavin? said Nicola.

He just climbed up it; I've told ye before. He had got through the barbed-wire bit at the bottom. Then what it was I think he just felt the tingling, or heard it maybe – that was what happened on pylons, that kind of tingling noise. He had got quite high up at the time and it was like he might've thought he was gonni get electro-cuted . . . Gavin had put his left hand up to his mouth, and he continued: It was bloody terrible so it was it was really bloody terrible. I had to go up and tell his mammy god man fifteen we were Dunky was in a fucking hell of a state and then for months after it we were bloody blaming ourselves, blaming ourselves, bloody stupid. We thought we should've been able to rush over and maybe grab him or something, or even as if we could've managed to catch him. Jesus christ it was terrible. That fucking barbed wire as well man christ.

Did you climb through it as well? said Nicola.

Aye but no as far as him. See we were trying to find out how far up we could go, to see who could get nearest the terminals. Gavin folded his arms. Then he unfolded them, he lifted Nicola's cigarette packet.

Pat said, Did Jackie have an alsatian dog at any time?

Nah.

Mm.

Gavin struck a match, dragged in the smoke. He chuckled. Jackie was forever falling into the bloody nolly! That was his game. We used to wander for miles along the bank, as far as bloody Kirkintilloch we went. And if there was any locks we could get onto then we would get onto them and see if we could see any fish. There was a lot of perch and roach in the canal – and some big pike as far as I know. D'you mind Jackie Pat?

Eh . . .

Uch I'm sure ye do. He came up the house a lot. A boy with ginger hair, a wee bit bigger than myself. His maw worked in the eh City Bakeries shop down Clarendon Street, the second-day shop. Remember how Jackie used to hand us in a couple of loaves now and again?

To be honest Gavin I dont really.

Ye sure?

Eh . . . my memories of the Vernon Street house just areni as clear as yours. I'm four years younger than you!

Aye.

Three-and-a-half, said Nicola.

Three years and seven months, said Pat.

Still but I thought you'd have minded Jackie, said Gavin while handing cups of tea to the other two. He sipped his own standing with his back leaning against the sink. Me and him and Dunky hung about the gether most of the time. He winked at Pat, indicating Nicola: We used to go on big knocking expeditions up the town every Saturday morning, plus any time we dogged school – in fact we used to dog school just for that bloody reason!

Gavin! said Nicola.

We used to specialise, pens and pencils and rubbers and bloody whatdyoucallthem pencil sharpeners, and stamps as well, these yins ye stick into books when you're a wean.

Pat laughed.

It's a wonder ye never get caught! said Nicola.

Too much savvy!

Pure luck! said Pat.

Savvy!

Luck!

Gavin chuckled.

Nicola said, Never ever tell John about that.

Of course no.

No even as a bit of fun Gavin.

Okay.

Nicola glanced at Pat: You as well Pat.

Aye.

Please.

Never, of course.

Because it would be terrible if he started thinking it was something good.

I'll no say a word.

Boys glamourise that sort of stuff.

I wont say a word, nothing.

She nodded.

Is it just boys that glamourise it? asked Patrick after a brief pause. I would've thought it was both.

Possibly, said Nicola.

Patrick nodded, after another brief pause.

It was close to a downpour. He peered out at it before darting from the close, upturning his jacket collar and hunching his shoulders and although he had fastened up the buttons he gripped the edges of the jacket as if he hadnt. Then he had walked past the motor. He continued. He was definitely not going to drive it. He continued, doing his best not to look back but eventually came the lapse: he gazed at the old thing, how it was looking quite sturdy, with that air of bravura about it, even allowing for the heavy rain drops pattering off its roof and bonnet. But fuck sake, a person had to do what he or she set out to do in this world else where would we be and where would it all end. And it was strange to leave it behind, especially in this weather. He felt totally sober. He was totally sober. But if the polis breathalysed him he wouldnt be. So he was not totally sober at all. But he was close to it. If he hadnt been close to it then this sort of rational decision would have been out the window. Maybe it was bloody daft to leave it.

Why was he leaving it!

Fuck sake!

The trouble was walking concerns elemental factors. Patrick was dressed for driving motor cars or journeying by taxis, he was not dressed for this, for getting fucking soaked to the skin. He did have an overcoat but he never wore the fucking thing because he didnt usually fucking need to. Now here he was a pedestrian and getting bla bla bla drenched. He had passed a bus stop before the end of the street but no point waiting there according to Gavin. People died of exposure waiting there. It was one of these bus stops you find in outer-city housing schemes all over Glasgow, only there for the benefit of the fucking canine population and a few desperate drunks because no buses ever went there. What a shame; the poor old flagellants, having to suffer such iniquities; ach well they've got fucking feet havent they so hell mend them, let them fucking use them and them that havent, well, let them climb on some dickie's shoulders. Patrick for example. If anybody wishes to climb onto his shoulders why, he will let them. Where's the fucking bus stop but, that's what I want to know. It was on the main road. It was beyond the pub and across the way from a wee post office and there was a shelter, at which nobody was inside. Bad news. Bad news indeed. Probably a bus had passed very recently and there was going to be a big long wait till the next. Who knew when that would be for christ sake it could be tomorrow fucking morning because you never know with public fucking transport this is the problem that it is so fucking inconsistent unlike your own, your own transport, because you always know when it's coming I mean cause you're fucking driving it yourfuckingself for christ sake poor auld Pat's gonni have to wait till 1999. Shut up and relax for fuck sake.

Okay.

Right.

But the whole notion of standing at bus stops! Awful. The whole notion of a bus even! Because he required the exact sum of money for the fare. If he didni have this exact sum the driver would refuse to give him change, he would just take the entire £1 or £5 or whatever it was and keep it on behalf of the transport company that employed him.

A situation fraught with awkwardidity.

But he was definitely not about to take a taxi. No sirree. None of that sort of nonsense. But not one single fucking taxi had passed anyway.

There was a solid smell of urine in the shelter. A multitude of pishes down through the years — the main problem of erecting a shelter across the road from a pub. Patrick unbuttoned his jacket and gave himself a good shaking, flapping the trousers. His bloody leg was still sore from yesterday. He should have borrowed a raincoat from Gavin. If a taxi came he was fucking grabbing it. Okay! If ye want a fight you're fucking on. Nor did he have sufficient coins in his pocket to purchase a bus ticket. But that was no excuse because there was a chip shop fifty yards up the road. He could get change from there.

It was brightly lit inside. In comparison to the Rossi's place it appeared friendly. The Rossi's place was not so much unfriendly as dull, the actual walls were yellowing and always the semblance of a bluish fug because of the inferior animals whose fats they used for frying. Plus they continued to use the fat long after it should have been tossed overboard. It is bad how folk continue to use old fat to fry people's food. But this place, this place appeared to be fine. There was a healthy array of goldenly battered fish and haggis, hamburgers, black pudding and sausage both smoked and unsmoked, lying in neat rows in the warming compartment above the ovens.

He bought a poke of chips. He wasnt hungry but it was either that or chocolate bars or something.

Still nobody at the bus stop. The rain didnt seem so heavy. He had started eating the chips but instead of returning to the bus shelter he walked on towards the next stop. Better to walk than stand still. Nor was the idea of eating chips in the middle of that urine stench very appealing: it was so bloody overpowering and thick it would probably solidify and cling onto the chips. And who wants to eat urine-flavoured chips I mean in the name of fuck right enough. He should have bought shoes. He should have bought shoes. The ones he had on were useless. His feet felt as if they were slipping around. Maybe it was blood. What was that story about the guy who is marching for months and thinks his feet are wet and then discovers they're saturated with blood. Was it a story at all. Maybe it was to do with Scott and the Foreigner Amundsen? Maybe it wasnt anything at all and he had just fucking invented it. There was this chap who was marching for months, and his feet were wet, and then when he took off his boots he discovers his feet are fucking bleeding. He should have bought shoes. It was to do with a defect in the wee eyes where the laces go, plus right enough it was because they were cheap, they were cheap cheap cheap – cheap fucking efforts, and that was how come he never bought at the sale either because they were all fucking cheap efforts as well. And the poor auld flagellants the silly bastards there they all were waiting to buy them. Ach well, it was their own fault, they only had themselves to blame I mean why didnt they crash in the fucking window and just lift what they wanted. That's what P for Patrick would have done. Well why didnt he. Because he didni fucking want to, so ha ha ha.

Round the bend and on to the traffic lights. Another pub over the road. The temptation to enter was quite strong, if only to find a telephone that worked, so he could make contact with a taxi firm. He kept on walking, on past the next stop. The bus situation was truly deplorable though; there was just no getting away from it I mean it really was out the fucking question. Thank christ he was a rich bourgeoisie because it meant you could travel privately and secretively,

avoiding all the terrors of being witnessed by the random popu-
lace. No doubt he would have to walk it the whole way home, a
distance of let us see probably about six miles. Six miles! In the name
of the fucking holies right enough. Heh you, less of that fucking
whatdyemacallit blasphemy. But does blasphemy exist if the holies
dont. These are the types of questioning

Nor was there any other method of getting home. Neither train
nor underground rail lay within a good couple of miles of where he
now was striding, having recently dumped the remaining chips in a
rubbish bin opposite what looks to have been a former railway station,
irony of ironies. And another bus stop, at which precisely none of
Glasgow's denizens was standing so Doyle would also be giving it the
go-by. Fuck that for a game, being the only dickie shivering at the
fucking stop when you're trying to get home in the fucking rain and
all that when for all ye know there's a strike on but no bastard's
remembered to tell you. Murder polis. Out the question. A situation
fraught with unreal awkwardidity, awkward unreality.

But there a bus on the other side of the road.

Patrick stopped and stared at it, hoping the person driving
might infer his plight, but no, the rascally evildoer maintained
pressure on the accelerator pedal. So there ye are all you believers in
telepathy and the diverse forms of telaesthesia, none of it fucking
exists. And how come all these tales are Greek and no Roman! Fuck
off.

A wee cafe and another chip shop down by the bingo hall, plus
Chinese-style food carry-outs. No pubs. Patrick could buy another
load of chips. He had finished with the last lot, and the rain was
become a mere trickle. So he could buy another lot and maybe it
would cease falling altogether, because here you had a case where there
seemed a necessary connection, a contingency, between the purchase
of potatoes chipped and fried in the fats of dead animals and the
rainfall of a nation albeit a nation who knuckles under to another, and
ships them all its freshest fish. But he just wasnt hungry. Not even for
the sake of comparing notes for a very large oil painting he was
thinking of doing on the whole damn racket, a sort of survey, entitled
Chip Shops of Auld Glesgi Toon. With poster sales it would
transform him into a dollar billionaire overnight and he could give up

the teaching game totally. Northamerican sales and our kith and kin in the colonies would go daft for such a product. He could get old Martin of the Crafts and Arts department to model some examples and really give them their money's worth: here is a piece of chipped spud, there is a lump of lard. A crowd of teenagers stood laughing and shouting at each other. They could have appeared threatening. Patrick was used to it but and didnt find it especially awful. Although if they discovered he was a teacher they would no doubt murder him. The soaked clothes were a fair disguise. Part of Patrick's problem and let us face it he does have a problem, is, that he actually looks like a teacher and he dresses like a teacher and he even speaks like a fucking teacher as well for christ sake there is no denying it, there is simply no denying it, and remaining an honest man. And at least he is honest, at least he is an honest man, a man who is honest, at least he

But would it be classified as murder? bringing about the death of a schoolteacher by violent means, by the actions of young folk of school age. Had Patrick been the judge he would not have found such a case clear-cut. They were also soaked, the teenagers. They didnt care. They didnt give a hoot. His mob was exactly the same. If it was thunderstorming outside in the playground that selfsame playground is the only place where you would find them all standing. And then in they'd stroll, dripping, saturated, soaked through and sitting there at their desks without catching pneumonia – not even a fucking cold! they didni even catch a fucking cold. Thus rendering all of his comments on that probability absolutely fucking ludicrous, the ravings of an aged schoolteacher.

Remember how auld Doyle used to tell us we'd all die of fucking pneumonia if we werent more careful! And then we fucking didni! Ha ha ha.

Why in the name of christ had he neglected to buy a new pair of shoes. It was just crazy. There was no other word for it, it was insane – he was insane. He was fucking outsane never mind fucking insane for christ sake this stupit rain as well now getting worse, plastering the cranium craniamus a unt. One requires to bear up stoically. Socrates was a Stoic Socrates was all Stoics therefore exeunt Socrates Socratetus masculine, one who is or was a stoical member of the male sex singular, the woman he fancies being married to a millionaire seller of double-glazed windows who drives a cadillac car with an incredible extravaganza of in-car entertainment. Okay then, fine. Okay then. Fine. No ravings of a lunatic here. An ice-cool rationality. Just a straight fucking perception of the fact.

The lights had changed. Two women passed him crossing the road. They were chatting about something. Imagine saying to them: Excuse me; what is the nature of the chat? what are yous chatting about? Yous must be chatting about something, so what is it, if ye dont mind me asking.

Of course we mind ye asking ya fucking sexist prick ye.

But it was just a simple question.

Go to fuck ya dickie.

Which is not fair. If you can no longer get asking members of the sex opposite your own a straight and ordinary question. Because if we canni get doing that where are we! Fucking nowhere! Some of the girls in Pat's classes refuse to talk to him too – and not just the wee Muslim lassies, other yins as well, they just refuse to talk. But there again some fucking boys refuse to talk so where does that fucking leave ye? nowhere – the fucking usual. How come they dont talk! If these two women had just stopped and tried to guess at the extraordinary neural activity within the skull of that male they just passed – why then, my god! revelation! henceforth they would renounce their lives of dutiful support to their husbands and come to devote themselves to being the bedmates and domestic servants of P for Patrick Doyle MA (Hons). Okay? 10 out of 10. Tick. √.

And here was another bloody damn chip shop at the Cross Of All The Saracens. Youths in doorways. What would happen if shop doorways were declared redundant. If Pat Doyle was to be transformed into a teenage person he would go and sit in a gutter, at a stank, and wait for something to float past on its way to the sewers – preferably a large dod of shite, and he could climb aboard and set sail for pastures new. At the bus stop round from the corner an elderly man was standing in at the mouth of an adjacent close. He was quite grumpy looking, dressed in yellow oilskins, coat and leggings/ trousers – going up to him and saying: Excuse me; is it leggings or trousers you've actually got on sir?

He gave Pat a grumpy look when he stepped in alongside him. But Pat replied with a benign smile, not about to get involved in any behavioural power game with him, while wanting at the same time to give the guy the benefit of the doubt, just in case his face was always like this. And he said: Bloody rain eh!

It was forecast on the wireless this morning.

Was it, I never heard . . . Patrick was shaking himself. The fronts of his trousers were completely soaked now. But the backs seemed to be as dry as a bone. Is there a bus due soon? he asked.

I couldni tell ye son, I'm no actually waiting for one. It's my missis, she's in seeing somebody up the stair.

Aw aye.

It's an auld biddy. I just tag along to keep her company. But I dont go in, I just wait outside. Some of them areni too keen on a strange face, the auld yins, they dont like folk coming into their houses. Quite right and all eh?

Aye christ. Pat peered out the close. Ye didni notice any buses going past?

Naw son.

Pat nodded.

She's a volunteer worker the wife. The man slapped his hands together and frowned in the direction of the black close which looked to be needing a new lightbulb, it kept blinking.

Could do with a new bulb eh?

Aye. Bloody draughty! Ye working?

Nah . . . I used to be involved in making shoes − the shoe industry − but then they shut down the factory and transferred all the stuff out to Taiwan or maybe Thailand I'm no sure but I think it was Tai-something, one of these places where they get the same job done by six-year-old weans with the added bonus of only having to pay them a flat rate of three lollipops every second century.

The man nodded. I took early retiral myself. I'm sixty-two.

Are ye okay?

What?

I was just wondering if you were okay − you and the wife I mean. Yous getting on alright?

[333]

D'you mean like the money and all that?

Aye.

Aye okay, I wouldni grumble about it. She does this volunteer work. I tag along and that. Keeps ye away from the telly.

I've no got a telly.

Have ye no?

Naw. This doctor I know, he says we areni the actual folk who're watching: we're actually being watched; they've reversed the process on us.

Is that right! The man grinned.

It's true, aye.

The man nodded. Then he glanced out at the street. Naw, he said, there's no been any buses since I've been here. That's about quarter of an hour.

Ah well, I better get walking. Patrick smiled: No point just waiting, he said, and he stepped out, still smiling and then chuckling and trying not to guffaw and maybe it was this awareness, that he was about to actually guffaw, that stopped him in his tracks for a couple of seconds. Because it was bad. It was fine and it was okay and proper that he should give himself rows and lectures and sarcastic adjuncts, but no other folk, and especially not to good auld guys like that. He didnt have the right. If things continued like this the bitterness would engulf him completely. It was getting to the point where he could envisage himself lashing out and fucking belting somebody on the mouth.

When does rain cease, or does it carry on forever. Yes. And that is what led old Thales into deciding upon water as the primary element because at that time ancient Greece had been waterlogged for hundreds of years and their islands were only just managing to surface and no more, because of that shift in temperature towards the latter part of that cold and dismal Third Millennium B.C.

The Glaswegian male doesnt ask much in this man's army, just an umbrella and the occasional fish supper, a nice looking woman and a big win on the fucking football pools. Then one could fuck off to a pleasant and cosy wee hotel in the Inner Hebrides, there to partake of single-malt goldies in the company of one's partner, thence off upstairs to a large double bed with views of the boisterous Atlantic, waves thrashing the shore but inside your room no, no noise at all apart from the ticking of an antique clock above the peat fireside and then that very slight rustle while she is carelessly undressing sitting on the edge of the eiderdown quilt, one leg drawn up so that the heel of her foot is on the bed near to her curved bottom, as she proceeds to unpeel a tight – unpeel a tight. But the rain was not so heavy as it had been. If neither bus nor taxi appeared he would simply walk it the whole way to Cowcaddens subway station. He stopped walking. He began again. The motor. It was not too late to return for the motor. What in the name of god was all this in aid of? Here he was totally sober and walking it home it was a fucking joke. No it wasnt. Aye it fucking was a fucking joke he was totally fucking stone-cold sober. No he wasnt. Yes he fucking was. A huge meal and then the chips and this bloody forty-five minute walking in a fucking torrential downpour. He was stone-cold sober. He was just needing a pish desperately. How come it was desperately? It just was. Cosy hotel rooms with Alison in soft eiderdowns for christ sake, resulting in minor stirrings, around the fucking groin area, having led to the condition of attendant bladderial flickerings. So damn, that's him finished with erotica if a pish is all he gets out of it.

To return to Gavin's or not. Whether it is nobler. He didnt even have to return to the house, he could just sneak back and drive away without telling them. And phone them once he got home so they wouldni have to report it as a theft.

No.

And that is that.

Along at the corner of the street he approached was this national bank from whose topmost windows beamed a nightlight and this was the window Patrick's brick would smash. If he was about to become seriously engaged in the world then this was the time and this was the place. And as he progressed towards Cowcaddens he could be smashing in the windows of each and every bank he chanced upon. And also those of building societies and insurance offices – anything at all connected with the financial institutions of the Greatbritish Rulers. He should have taken the car. He would've been fine. He would've been home by now. Where could he pee for christ sake! It was quiet, it was quiet. The weather was keeping everybody indoors, apart from elderly volunteers and teenagers. It was time to put a brick through a window. Come on. Let us be honest and truthful about this, a brick through the window. But he couldnt be bothered doing it. He just couldnt be bothered. He would have to hide up a close after the event and it would be damp and draughty and if he got captured christ it would be so horrendously awful and pathetic: disaffected teacher puts brick through window, embarks on property rampage down the streets of Possil except everybody knows there's no property in Possil anyhow because they've no got fuck all, the rich having stolen it from them. So, the banks of the city and big bricks. At least it would be a bloody start. There was a pair of polis across the street who needless to report were observing him openly and frankly and not giving a fuck about who was noticing. But now they watched him watching them. And he stopped walking to call: You've no seen a bus by any chance! And he smiled a big smile, proferring the arse to the aggressors as usual.

No response. They half-turned from him. They had appeared at the very thought of insurrection, the very thought, and there they were. These fucking odd things. Why were there no bloody damn taxis either. Just when a body needed one. Most odd. Most odd indeed. But there again, oddidity was the name of the present. The things that were happening, they were all of that quality. Here he was with a pair of pipes and the woman he thought well of had touched his hand, had taken him by the hand, and applied the pressure of one whose sympathy for the other is overcoming whatever else she may be feeling, may be feeling. Why were there no bloody damn taxis. No bloody damn fucking taxis just when you fucking needed one quite desperately, when you just needed one, and there wasnt one, just like they said about the polis as well, when you wanted one you couldni get one, just like with a bus, when you wanted one of them you couldnt bloody get one, there werent any because they just bla bla bla and he was fucking running, steadily, and not too fast, his right hand gripping the edges of his jacket where it buttoned, shoulders hunched and head bowed. A large and wide expanse of water, huge puddle, ahead, and he splashed straight through the bloody centre rather than attempting to either jump it or skirt roundabout it in case of skidding or something and falling. The polis watching him now in a serious and suspicious manner. About to give chase. Catch the bastard, there he goes. He had started running now instead of later once they were gone and that was daft and really stupid because they would worry as to his veracity or something after that silly fucking comment about the bus, probably calling in on their walkitalki and getting ordered to pick him up on suspicion – daft, fucking daft, but too late, if he was to pause to see what they were doing because them taking that as the sign of guilt, of criminality, of his being suspicious, a suspicious being, that sign of guilt, that assumption of, silly, absolutely fucking silly, and dangerous, these acts he commits on a daily basis, acts of stupidity, stupidity, a daily basis of it. Yes Doyle is dangerous, dangerous to himself. He is dangerous to himself and thus to the weans he teaches on that daily basis. If he skids he will fall and crack his skull and the wheel of a vehicle will run over his neck and kill him. That temptation. What is that temptation. That temptation is aye the same temptation and it is suicide, it is actually suicide. What is that story in the bible about a guy who commits suicide. Is there a story in the bible about a guy who commits suicide. Who is that guy who commits suicide, as a thing to be committed. And there they were is that them there, the polis, the flying rugby-tackle to bring him down, in mid-flight, and him no being able to know because he wouldni be able to hear that heavy pitapat of their boots because of the rain a-falling. That was them there, shouting; they were shouting at him from the other side of the road and just there waiting for the traffic to slow. They must have come running after him, to be shouting. What are they shouting. They're just shouting they hate him they hate ye we fucking hate ye, that's what they're shouting. It was dark and it was wet but not cold; if it had not been so dark you would have seen the sky. Ah fuck off, fuck off.